Only Now We Are

A Novel

Nathan Kato-Wallace

Paperback ISBN: 979-8-9998320-0-9
eBook ISBN: 979-8-9998320-1-6

For my mom and dad who taught me a love of books.

Prologue

My reeducation began shortly after his funeral.

    I could barely see through the thick morning fog, and the sky above was heavy and gray as if it still cradled smoke from the world we set alight. As the Mouth enumerated the accolades of the dearly departed, I thought we couldn't have asked for a better day to mourn. And yet, for a funeral, there was very little sorrow. They went through the motions because it felt like the thing to do, but they had lost the ability to be pained by the past. The followers yawned. The Circle sat pompous. The Mouth glowed with consolidated power.

    But *my* walls were down. I felt everything, and I barely contained the urge to collapse into a puddle of tears before all of Isidora. I was broken, and I suspected it had something to do with killing the poor bastard.

    There was no need to dig, there being no body left to inter, no ashes not already scattered by the updrafts that consumed the theater, consumed her apartment block, consumed the Anglican church and the warehouse and the vagabond city at the heart of the capital. Fire was our ally now, and even in this small way the holocaust served our needs. We stood in front of a cairn—rocks delicately balanced one atop another—but he was not there, and I knew he would never be there again.

The Mouth spoke, and the followers pretended to wail, and the Wooden Boys shot their rifles in the air—seven times one, times two, times three. And then we raised our glasses to the first founder to have ever been martyred for Isidoran TRUTH and toasted the Pyrrhic victory he had led over the figment world that surrounded us.

After draining the vats of All-Weather, we left the Green and climbed the slope up to the machine shed that sat at the end of the train yard. The faces of the followers that trailed behind me were lost in the cloud such that it was not individuals who made up Isidora—not anymore—but a mass, hundreds strong. The wind in my sails, perhaps. Or the anchor holding me back. I no longer knew what the followers thought of me, no longer had enough context to venture a guess. I didn't exist anymore. There was only the Omicron. My heavy robes dragged through the mud as the others sloshed along, struggling to keep up.

When we reached the doorway to what was his sanctum, someone from the crowd stepped forward to hand the Mouth a wreath tied with a black bow. He then gave it to me and said, "As an evergreen holds onto life in the coldest winter, so shall you preserve him in your memory, and he shall live forever more." I hung it on a spike driven into the door and wished only to forget.

"Friends," I said, looking out over their heads. Their voices hushed. "I have left Isidora, and Isidora has left me. And maybe I'm sorry for that. But there is no future here. There is no past."

The Mouth jumped up beside me. "Yes, Omicron. The Isidora we have known is dead. The new Isidora is constantly reborn."

"We talked of TRUTH, but where is TRUTH in a world full of ignorance and lies?"

"It is in your sight, oh great Omicron." Slowly, discretely, the Mouth slid his foot over to rest upon mine. "As you see it, so it is true."

"We have lost everything," I continued. "We foolishly thought we could attack the shades and win. We thought we could burn our problems to the ground. But the figment world is eternal, as everlasting as a bad idea."

The Mouth shifted his weight to his heel and ground it into my foot. "There can be no light without shadow. It will always be so. But we are those who have chosen the light. May Isidora burn ever brighter!"

I tried to slide my foot out from under his but could not. The weight of the man was a familiar kind of pain. "It's time for a new direction. It's time I left. What more can I say than 'good luck'?"

"We salute you, Omicron, and are grateful for your benediction."

With that the followers raised their hands to their faces and covered their eyes, and I did the same, blinding myself to them and to Isidora.

The Mouth pulled my arm down and shot me an intense glare. "Dismissed!" he shouted as he grabbed me by the shoulder and dragged me back to the Ark.

Part One

Chapter One

Four years ago, I was let go, and I've been gone ever since.

> — But maybe I should go all the way back. Maybe
> I should start with childhood. Isn't that what you pay
> a psychiatrist for? To relive those arbitrary early
> traumas that explain why you're such a broken adult?
>
> —*That and the opportunity to lie flat in the middle
> of the afternoon. But I'm no psychiatrist.*
>
> —And I'm certainly not paying you.

I was never comfortable at home, never allowed to just be. I spent eighteen years in that claustrophobic ranch, dropped down in the depression of a midwestern cornfield, squat and inadequate in the face of its neighbors, overwhelmed by the mass of its own sloping roof, and for as long as I can remember I dreamed of getting out.

The air of the place was a constant battlefield contested by Heath's discarded jock straps, Missy's drugstore body spray, Little Chris's dirty undies, and dad's ever-present aura of Skin Bracer and Winston Blue. And yet somehow it felt like I was the only one ever struggling to breathe. It wasn't enough to just open a window. For what? To suck on the exhaust of Hawke's new riding mower? To smell the jettisoned fat fumes from the latest strip mall burger, washed down with a glass of bubbling river water and red dye number 5? The smell of that ambitionless nowhere. I craved more rarified air.

So, every night I'd climb the AC unit out back, hop onto the roof, and sit there at the pinnacle of our abode reading Kafka and chain smoking pilfered cigarettes until the light gave out like the disconsolate lordling of all suburbia.

—*It wasn't Hawke. Not yet.*

—Who said anything about Hawke?

—*You . . . Never mind.*

—You said you weren't going to interrupt.

—*Yes, I did.*

—Because I don't need your commentary. I don't need your words. Not anymore. This time I'm going to find Isidora on my own.

—*Then let's fast-forward a bit. Let's start with the capital and the way the fat cats squatting in that city of broken marble kicked you to the curb.*

Like I said, four years ago I was let go, and I've been gone ever since.

The going itself was unremarkable. In fact—in TRUTH, I should say—I barely remember it. It was a Friday in mid-June, a couple of weeks after the buyout was finalized, when Todd tapped me on the shoulder and walked me down to her basement office. She was waiting for me there in that corporate waystation for the newly-arrived and soon-to-be-departed, a utilitarian fixture of limited-liability incorporation, as necessary as the single-serve coffee machine or the waterless urinals clogged with piss.

"Sit," she said, and I did.

She fluffed the cup of pens on her desk and straightened a letter opener that gleamed like a wakizashi. Then she turned to her monitor.

"O, O, O . . ." she hummed to herself as if she were back in her garden, pulling weeds with nothing to bother her but the occasional buzzing of a curious fly. My leg bounced furiously below her desk.

"Oakley, Olivier, Ouattara . . ." She squinted, then raised the bifocals up from the beaded chain that hung about her neck.

"Ah, here we are. Omicron."

A glacial double-click.

"You've been with us for a little over a year in the operations unit, yes?"

I nodded.

"Right. Well, as you may already know, since its acquisition of the company, Demeter has asked all units to analyze their staffing patterns to find greater efficiencies. Operations identified various positions of redundancy, and unfortunately yours is one of them."

"Excuse me?"

"You are being made redundant. I'm very sorry."

I was familiar with the euphemisms of corporate bloodletting, and I had already seen many colleagues take that one-way trip to her office in the weeks following the buyout. It wasn't for lack of comprehension. But still, I felt if I was to be so casually kicked to the curb to goose the P/E ratio, the least they could do was tell it to me straight.

"Redundant? You mean like the compensation plans of Demeter executives?"

—You didn't.

I did. But it didn't faze her. She wrapped herself in the flaps of her cardigan and folded her arms across her chest. I tried to explain to her that I was already redundant when they hired me, that as the median of five children, I had been redundant my whole life. And maybe she started to see me differently. Perhaps sitting before her, a mere boy, I reminded her of her own—a mess of floppy hair above a face drowned in aftershave, a wrinkled shirt and matching tie bought together at a department store from the executive collection of some gameshow host, the only masculine refinement he had ever known. She said this pantomime was for my benefit, but if I insisted on being mouthy, she wasn't opposed to spelling it out.

"Parting ways, then?"

"Like worn-out lovers? What would your husband think?"

"Fired?"

"Like clay in a high school kiln, tempered against the vicissitudes of the world beyond? If only."

"Terminated?"

"Please."

She said the words were irrelevant, but still her arsenal was vast. Would I prefer to be sacked or canned? Dismissed like a schoolboy or discharged like a vengeful firearm? Should we settle it now, or would I prefer a discrete pink slip be left at my workstation? So long as I didn't ask for a month's notice, didn't ask for severance, didn't ask for health insurance, or a pension, or any other durable commitment that would outlive our conversation, I could have it any way I wanted.

In the end, we agreed I was being let go—like a carp—returned to my natural state of un-work with no hard feelings despite the hole in my lip and the memory of asphyxiation in their care. To be released smacked of freedom, and when I considered the alternative—flailing around at the end of their line for the rest of my short, miserable life, being hauled up into the world above, my scaled skin scraped aside, the rawness of me dropped into an ice box next to a dozen identical others—I decided the modern corporate fondness for catch and release was not so bad.

No, I didn't hate her for it. I pitied her. I could tell from the mini-fridge of Diet Coke, from the ergonomic peripherals, from the tendonitis band clinging to her forearm that she was as much a victim of late-stage capitalism as I was. And she was planted there—permanently—in a basement office bereft of natural light, counting the weeks to administrative professionals' day. She had liberated me. I was free. Only then was I free.

When it was all agreed, her disposition softened. I signed the papers for my release, and she offered me a box for my personal effects. Her envious eyes followed me as I rose and walked out her office door, never to clock in again. I grabbed my backpack from my cube, swung by the executive conference room to snatch a few redundant cookies from the morning meeting. And then I was gone.

I emerged from that downtown office building into a monochromatic midday, the sun piercing and the streets filled with well-ordered commotion. The hands of a sepia clock spun past Roman numerals. Steam rose out of a covered manhole as big-bodied Buicks sauntered down the avenues. Women in wide skirts teetered on heels, their handbags swinging from the crooks of their elbows. Men in white collars skipped in and out of taxis, doffing and donning panamas and clutching pebbled briefcases. Blue-collar men wiped sweat off their brows with grease-stained hands and swallowed sandwiches whole before returning to their odd jobs.

—*Oh, really?*

Of course not. It was nothing like that, not even for my parents. The realms of man and woman had long ago collided, their boundaries written on yellowing cadasters now useful only to debate. Hats were out, the Buicks were Mexican, and we all piled into subway cars like subterranean cattle. No one wore collars, no one tolerated gluten, and the jobs, if we could keep them, were always odd. Everything I was taught as a child about the world of adults, the taxonomy I was to navigate to become one in my own right, was broken and betrayed—the phyla, orders, genera, species now a meaningless mess. I didn't know what to do, so I did nothing, changed nothing, continued to live a life of posturing and puffery, a self-importance sustainable so long as my checking account held.

—I don't think this is helping. The past already

refuses to die. It sits with me when I sip my morning coffee. It lays with me each night.

—*This will help.*

—It's been weeks since the pyres were lit, but my lungs still burn, and I cough, and the cough wakes me in the night. And there it is, the past, relaxing in my armchair, sprawled out on the chaise. Even in sleep, it's there. In dreams, in hallucinations, in visions of yesterday.

—*You drifted too far from Isidora. It's only natural you feel lost.*

—Idisora is dead.

—*Then where are you right now?*

—Even the temporary reprieve of a night of blank sleep would suffice.

If only the memories of the last few years could shrink themselves down to the size of a childhood trauma and tuck themselves away in some dark recess of my mind, waiting to reveal themselves in a flood of tears when a melody from yesteryear comes floating through the room. But they won't. If anything, the past is growing. Every day it seems to swell.

—*That's why you must let it go. If you hold onto it any longer, the burden will overwhelm you. Give voice to the past. When it's spoken, when it's laid bare, you will see it for what it really is—an illusion, a mirage, a falsehood—and you will be free to return to the true Isidoran present.*

—When I was a boy, I remember stumbling on a coin from a foreign country and thinking I had, by chance, become fabulously wealthy. One thousand shillings. Ten thousand pesos. For a kid who rarely saw a zero on his own country's money, that hunk of golden metal and its ostentatious display of digits was beyond comprehension. I was sure I only needed to sail across an ocean or fly to another land to live like a king. When I got a little older, I learned that to the right of a decimal point lives an infinite number of zeros, and central bankers can flip them over to the left whenever it suits them. The traders and merchants adjust, and markets churn until the true value is revealed. But a ratty little kid in his parents' basement? He can be deceived. Perhaps, it was a lesson we should have taken to heart.

—*Yes. Perhaps.*

—When you're done with me, maybe the history of this place can be like that coin—a token from a foreign land, useless in every way but with all the trappings of limitless value.

—*Shall we continue?*

****

Being let go was both banal and devastating. The job itself meant nothing to me. It was a nondescript admin position, the kind you get as a twenty-something with a BA and a lot of white space on your resumé. The kind of job you fall into and, when the time comes, fall out of just as easily. For an astronomy and philosophy double major, it was exceedingly well matched to my qualifications, but it was never going to be a career. While it lasted, it subsidized a lifestyle that, to me, felt like adulthood.

If necessity is the mother of invention, conformity is its hard-knock father. When I first arrived in the capital, I obediently invented myself the same way everyone around me did and called it self-actualization. We rolled into downtown offices sometime around 9:30 and promptly left at 5:00. We patronized the bars at happy hour, flooded the metro in matching adult kick-ball jerseys, and propped up the capital's home values by splitting rent on rowhouses a dozen ways. On the weekends, we raged in the clubs like beasts unleashed and then plopped ourselves down at brunch the next morning like well-heeled sophisticates.

After a month of unemployment, it was increasingly difficult to keep up with the pantomime. But still, the night I met the Mouth was the same as any other.

—The Mouth? Oh, I see.

It was at a house party up where the streets have three syllables. The bar was a modern case study on the tragedy of the commons, perfect for a broke freeloader like me. There was dancing on the hardwood, flirting on the thrift-store couches, and smoking on the patio. My girlfriend had already dissolved into the festivities, and a girl whose face was vaguely familiar was telling me about her internship on the business development team of a development contractor. Over her shoulder, a game of beer pong was being set up, and I was desperately trying to make eye contact with the guy in charge, hoping to be recruited to a side before her monologue ran out of steam, and she thought to ask me what *I* did. But the teams were already formed, and the question came and went, leaving behind an awkward silence.

Soon our conversation merged with another, and then another, and soon we were many, standing in a circle with our feet crossed, listening to a dude in a color-block polo pontificate about the regrettable effects of gentrification. As obliging guests, not wanting to devalue the social currency that is liberal guilt, we summoned in equal measure that same wistful dejection and cursed the progress that brought us to the capital in the first place and sustained us still.

In that city of intersections, we lived like mockingbirds isolated in a forest all our own. We sang the elegant song of our neighbor, trying as best we could to mimic his intonation, hoping it would please him. And when we finished, he would sing it back—the same elegant song, mimicking our mimicry, hoping it would please us. But the melody was never ours. It was something ancient, repeated over and over again by generations, its originator lost to time.

Then one day a stranger arrives, a crow with waxy black feathers, beady eyes, and a hooked beak. He lands on a branch at the edge of our forest and lets out a horrid caw. It is grotesque and profane, but also genuine and true. The next day the forest rings with caws. The ancient song is forgotten.

"So, when are you moving out?" The Mouth yelled from his recumbent position on the couch.

"Excuse me?"

He stood and marched across the room, as fearless as an apothecary in a beaked mask surveying a village of plague victims.

"As a recently-arrived white guy concerned with the influx of recently arrived white guys, when will you be self-deporting? That is the solution you're recommending, right? Or are you just full of shit?"

As we recoiled from the collective gut punch of candor, the Mouth mercifully turned and left.

"Can you believe that guy?" the speaker said after the Mouth was out of earshot.

"No," we all replied. "What an asshole."

But, yes. Of course I believed him. As soon as he spoke, I knew he was the only one in the room I *could* believe.

I pointed to my cup and bowed out of the circle to find the Mouth in the kitchen, a bottle of Jack in his hand. He gave me a nod and offered to make me a drink.

"Whatever you're having."

"Man, I get so tired of these blowhards. Three months in the capital and they become its savior. As if they have any clue what life is like for people here."

"Yeah," I said. "It's insufferable."

"That's a word for it. Insufferable. And yet here we are, suffering it. So, what's your deal, chief? You know Kara?"

"No, my girlfriend heard about the party. I think from Kara's friend Joe."

"Your girlfriend, which one is she?"

"Brunette. Black dress. Unnaturally long eyelashes."

"The girl who's been puppy-dogging that silver-spooned dilettante all night long?"

"That would not surprise me." I grabbed the red plastic cup from his hand.

"Shit. Have a double on me, buddy."

He splashed a layer of whiskey on top of the drink he had already mixed. At that point I believe he told me his name, but given what followed it's a miracle I can remember anything. No one ever buys enough mixers for a party like this, and over the course of a night a Jack and Coke becomes a Jack and ice, then a Jack in a cup, then a Jack straight from the bottle. Before long you're thoroughly ripped and rooting through the pantry of a stranger for stale Doritos like a vagabond raccoon. I assume we talked about the capital—that city that would transform us into respectable men; that city that sat on top of the world and would, if we were lucky, share with us a bit of its elevation. We were both after her, my courtship something quite recent, his toxic obsession a lifelong pursuit.

—I wouldn't say it was my "toxic obsession."

—Sure it was.

The Mouth grew up among Protestant churches and VFW halls in a riskless hamlet in the Commonwealth. Before the organic food stores, before the chain restaurants, before the charmless apartment buildings with focus-group-approved names like "The Flats" and "Equinox," the Mouth spun his Huffy down placid streets lined with split-levels and ranches in a sterile boredom, seeking out any opportunity he could find to be unclean.

—*That sounds about right.*

He would steal cigarettes from the corner store while his buddy created a diversion. Reuniting in the parking lot of a taco joint, they would split the haul, their hearts bursting in their throats. With each new pack pilfered he would turn one cigarette upside down and call it his lucky, vowing he'd always smoke it last. They never got caught. On the weekends, he would venture across the river to hear some go-go, and if his friends had the weed, he would get high in a darkened alley between sets. Now, when he looked at the city and what it had become, he held for it the intimate contempt one can only feel for home.

We played presidents and assholes and flip-cup until the well ran dry, at which point I ditched my girlfriend, and the Mouth and I grabbed jumbo slice in AdMo. We pointed our feet south and stumbled past lines of heavily perfumed college kids, taking bites of four cheese directly from the box. It was a balmy night in late August, and the girls stretched themselves tall with high heels and short skirts. The boys panted behind them in pressed collared shirts, Rorschach blots of sweat pooling on their backs. The sky was a sleepless orange.

"You know, it's for the best," he said, folding the pizza and taking a bite.

"What is?"

"Your unceremonious sacking. Your forced ejection out the airlock of Starship Capitalism."

"I guess," I said with a half-hearted nod.

"Did you even like the job? Spending all day in a cube, strangling yourself with a paisley necktie, bowing down before some un-fuckable middle-manager type?"

"I liked not being broke." I laughed. "No, it wasn't that great. Most days I just went for the free coffee."

My head was swimming, and I struggled to resist the urge to lie down on the sidewalk and fall asleep. We came upon a bench in front of a tennis court, vacant but still illuminated, and I dropped onto it. He sat next to me, and for a moment we said nothing, listening to EDM spill from the open windows of 18th Street.

"You know, if I'm truly honest..."

The Mouth shook his head. "I wouldn't recommend that."

"...if I'm truly honest, the worst part will be telling my dad."

"He's not the forgiving kind?"

"Hardly. My father bottles disappointment in Mason jars and stores them in the cellar of his soul, each one labeled by year and protagonist, ready to be brandished at a moment's notice. Krissy, '05: the year she broke it off with the buzzcut Marine and ran off to the mountains with Chet in his rusted-out Honda. Little Chris, '98: the year he flubbed his clarinet solo and cried in front of the entire school, my dad in the bleachers seething while the parents around him tittered and cringed. Mom '92: the last jar she ever filled. And now me, the prodigal son who ran off to the capital to do big things, to be a big man, who came running back with his tail between his legs like he knew I would. Nothing is forgotten. Nothing is let go."

"And what? He's got it all figured out? If he's anything like my old man, he's filled most of those jars himself."

"Oh, sure. Dad was a geology teacher in a plains state locked in a futile struggle to interest the sons and daughters of farmers in something more profound than topsoil. Every year was a bumper crop of disappointment." I felt the bubbling of a geyser at the back of my throat when I considered returning penniless to his house, his rules, his air. "No, he has nothing figured out. He's a failure."

"They're all failures," the Mouth said with the confidence of something long known. "Every last one of them. The greatest generation laid down and died to give them peace and prosperity, and what are they giving us?

Unadulterated capitalism, the decline of Western democracy, and a planet that's one stray spark away from combusting. They had careers, we get gigs; they had a cold war, we get desert invasions; they had social security, we get the debt ceiling."

"And yet they think they know," I interrupted. "They think they can lecture us about how it's supposed to be. 'Do what I did, son. Follow my path.' But your path's not there anymore, is it? You've trampled it down to a muddy quagmire and jumped on a plane to Palm Beach."

The Mouth roared with laughter.

"I'm done with it," I continued, nearly yelling. "The miseducation, the misdirection, the lies. Nothing they gave us is real. It's all a mess."

"Fuck it all!" The Mouth was vibrating with giddy agreement. "Burn it all down."

"Fuck it all," I sighed. My heart was racing, spinning the alcohol in my blood around like a uranium-enriching centrifuge. I pulled a pack of cigarettes out of my breast pocket, only to find it empty. The Mouth opened his. He had one left, flipped upside down, and he handed it to me.

I lit it and took a deep inhale, the smoke filling my emptiness. "I don't want any of it. I don't want to live with their lies. I don't want the life their lies represent. It's time we made our own way. It's time to create our own reality."

The words were exhaled in a thick stream, rising into the night air.

>—*You see? It's all right there. The spirit of Isidora was with you even then.*

>—But that was just the beginning. You never end up where you began.

>—*You do if you begin with TRUTH.*

****

The next afternoon, I awoke feeling grim.

My eyes opened to a young woman standing over me, cradling a glass of orange juice. The curve of her breast hid in the shadows of her open bathrobe. When my eyes eventually found her face, she looked down on me and smiled.

"We've got a live one!" she called over her shoulder. "And this one's new."

"So he is." A bearded man in sweatpants stepped forward, his faded Badgers T-shirt stretched by his ample belly. "Cleaner than most but smells the same. When will that freeloader bring us something useful?" He shook a coffee mug toward the loveseat where I saw the Mouth facedown in the cushions.

"I'm so sorry," I said rubbing sleep from my eyes. "I thought this was his place. I just followed him up. Really, I don't even remember coming in."

She put a hand on the bearded man's shoulder and smiled. "Well, here you are, flat on your back in the middle of our foyer. So, how do you like your eggs?"

"No, I should go. What time is it? I'm really sorry for crashing."

The bearded man shrugged. "Please. You're not the first. This place is practically a hostel." He set his mug on the counter and reached down to offer me a hand. "Easy does it now."

He pulled me to my feet where I teetered before finding my balance. My stomach, awakened by the smell of popping bacon, was one part nauseated, one part famished. I slinked across the room and fell onto a barstool at the kitchen's edge. As I walked, I introduced myself and explained in an unprovoked monologue everything I could recall from the night before.

"It's nice to meet you too. My name is James, but everyone calls me Squire. This is my apartment, at least contractually."

"And I'm Regina," she said. "And how about those eggs?"

"Scrambled is fine. But really, it's not necessary. I should probably get out of your hair."

"He'll take them scrambled." Regina handed him a spatula and cinched her robe.

Squire gave her a playful bow, then busied himself in the kitchen. The stainless-steel appliances and marble countertops gave the room an air of luxury, but on every surface pots and pans, dishes and glassware were carelessly stacked, some still encrusted with old food. Regina walked to the bedroom, and my eyes followed her to the adjoining room where ragged furniture obscured beveled chair rails and a pair of fixed-gear bicycles leaned against walls painted in delicate egg-shell. It was not a cheap apartment, but it was used cheaply by decidedly unrefined tenants.

The door behind me opened.

"Back so soon?" Squire said as he continued whisking eggs.

"That bitch at the front desk kicked me out again. *Residents only. Residents only.*" The man's hands, clad in weight-lifting gloves, unscrewed the cap on a plastic gallon jug. The muscles of his bare arms articulated as he lifted the water to his lips.

"In fact, the policy states the workout facility is for *rent-paying, non-loitering, announces-their-presence-in-advance* residents only. I'm sorry, Hawke. You don't meet the qualifications."

His eyes were a rich hazel, deep set against his almond skin, and for a second they caught mine, but he said nothing.

"If the one who's paying rent never goes, why shouldn't I be allowed? Shit, Squire, they're just free weights. I'm not even burning electricity." Hawke dropped the jug by the door, kicked off his shoes, and went into the living room. He flipped the coffee table onto the couch, its legs vertical like an upturned beetle, and began doing push-ups on the space below. He exhaled at the top of every rep with the regular respiration of a steam engine. *Tst. Tst. Tst.* A crown of soft yellow spirals rose and fell like a dandelion seed in the breeze. The floorboards creaked.

"Are you . . . *Tst.* Just going to sit there . . . *Tst.* And watch? *Tst.* There's room for . . . *Tst.* One more . . . *Tst.*"

My stomach soured at the thought of even minor physical activity.

"Nah, I'm good."

"You say that . . . *Tst.* But are you really? *Tst.* "He held himself in a plank and pointed at the loveseat. "Don't let that guy fool you. You won't *think* the world into shape."

As if summoned by Hawke's words, the Mouth stirred and moaned. Then he rose, ambled across the floor, and fell onto the barstool beside me, letting momentum carry him in a slow, dreamy revolution.

"Woof. What a night, huh?"

Regina came back into the room dressed in flannel and blue jeans. She had an angular, projecting nose, a soft chin, and swept-back cheeks, and her frowning countenance could best be described as marmish. But her hair was a silken sandy brown and fell in obedient, obliging waves. She carried a green, long-necked watering can and began nourishing the ficus in the corner. Plants, I now realized, were everywhere, and she visited each one in turn, pouring approximations known by heart.

"Dean, how many times do we need to tell you to call ahead?" she snapped over her shoulder at the Mouth. "Squire's place is always open, but how about a heads-up before you come back blitzed?"

The Mouth spun around on his barstool, reaching for her with a flourish. "Regina, my queen, why do you close your castle doors to me? Why leave me stranded on the far side of your moat? Must I always swim to you?"

"Regina's right. God forbid I'm allowed a semblance of ownership over this place." Squire wagged a spatula in the Mouth's face and landed a piece of undercooked egg on his forehead. "There. Breakfast is served."

"Squibs, this has become the unofficial HQ for our little movement, has it not? Don't hate on my abundance of loyalty to our cause." The Mouth picked the egg off his face and ate it. "A touch more salt, deary." Squire groaned. The Mouth grinned. "And look, I've recruited another supplicant to our new faith. I should get a fucking medal or something, not a scolding."

Squire looked at me like Mr. Bennett discovering another daughter he needed to marry off. He slid a plate of eggs my way and turned to rummage through drawers for a fork.

"What faith did I join, exactly?"

"Oh, Dean's just full of it," Regina said as she poured herself tea. "We're not a religion. We're not even a *we* exactly. A group of us come here to talk about social justice and think about ways to get active. That's all."

"Oh, don't undersell it, Reg." The Mouth turned to me. "We're a movement. Well, we're the seed of a movement, which is the same thing, really, because doesn't a seed contain within it all that comes after—leaves, branches, and bark? We see the world for what it is and, more importantly, what it is not, and we're ready to fight for change. We're actually just about to get kinetic, so you're joining at a great time."

"I'm not sure I'm joining you, am I? I mean, I don't really have time to get kinetic."

"Whatever, man. Like we discussed last night, you're gone. You've got nothing but time and plenty of reason for grievance. Don't stand in your own way."

I rubbed my face and looked at Squire but found no refuge there. A smile emerged on his bushy lips as he passed the Mouth a plate.

"Hell, you don't even have a girlfriend anymore," the Mouth said, taking a bite of toast. "What have you got to lose?"

"A girlfriend?" I hadn't thought of her since waking up, and I was instantly gripped by panic. I left her. Without saying goodbye. Without reminding her that her purse was on the bed in the upstairs room. Without texting her to see if she got home OK. It wasn't the first time we left a party separately, but normally, I was the left and not the leaver, and I felt uncomfortable with our roles reversed.

I raised the plate to my mouth and shoveled in the rest of the eggs. "I need to go," I said between painful swallows. "So sorry to eat and run. James, thanks for the breaky. Buddy, I'll give you a call. Regina, enchanté. Hawke ..."

I pushed off the barstool and had her number up on my phone before I reached the door. It rang twelve times on the elevator ride down and once more in the lobby. It would be three more days before she called me back.

Chapter Two

—You don't need to go over this. She means nothing.

—No. I don't think that's true.

—Whatever. I'm gonna grab a J. Don't hurt yourself.

We met at the Walnut Grove Community Pool the summer after senior year. It was my first job and they stuck me in the concession stand while she, a lifeguard in her second season, sauntered about the pool deck in a tight one-piece and aviators. Once when she came to me for her daily white cherry slushie, I found the courage to tell her she was doing more to endanger the lives of the boys in the pool than save them, that it was impossible to keep water out of their lungs with their mouths permanently agape. She scoffed and spun away from me, leaving behind a cloud of coconut and shea butter, but I caught her looking down on me from her tower all afternoon, and by the end of the week we were making out on the picnic tables during our lunch break. For the rest of that soap-bubble summer we were inseparable, in love with the clumsy intensity of youth.

It ended as quickly as it began. By September, the pool was shuttered, and I was a freshman again, washing dishes in the college mess hall between classes. She was at an all-girls school the next state over, but despite our proximity, neither of us made the effort to stay in touch. There was too much coming at us from the front to give the past a second thought. For the first time ever, I got drunk. I got high. I learned a little about a lot and formed unshakable opinions about everything in between. When it was all over, four years and several failed romances later, our unfinished relationship remained something of a touchstone—an exemplar of love—a loss of innocence indelibly written, more myth than memory. It's only natural, then, that when I caught a glimpse of her across the dance floor in a deafening club in the capital, I thought I'd seen a ghost.

In many ways we picked back up where we left off, the flames of passion fanned by our newfound freedom and a cursory understanding of sex. It felt like a reclamation, a redemption of a sensation lost to time. But something about her had changed. No longer the sun-kissed Venus perched on her clamshell, she existed now almost entirely in twilight, and to be with her was to chase the night. Her jet-black hair, her pale skin, the mascara inked in circles around her opal eyes. In the heavy velvet shadows of dance clubs or the dank hallways of bars, she was radiant, the only star in my evening sky. But she was never mine to possess. In the frenetic mixing of bodies, we would tumble in and out of each other's orbit. She would flirt with friends, accept drinks from strangers, dance on stage all by herself. Sometimes she would disappear entirely. I endured it all, hoping at the end of the night she might drop her heels at my door and fall into my bed like a top, its energy expended.

Most nights she would. Most nights.

My unemployment changed all that, though for a time I tried to pretend otherwise. I went to the clubs, but they demanded a week's worth of groceries to get in and filled the highball glasses with liquid rent. I tried to freeload at house parties, but when the group moved on to something more exciting, I had to fake exhaustion and slink home before the night had even begun.

We played phone tag for two miserable weeks, a penance I was forced to pay for my impertinent departure with the Mouth. When it felt like the ice was finally thawing, I asked her to come with me to the National Gallery.

"Hhy do you 'ant to go to an ar' ooseum?" I could tell from her unenunciated consonants she was applying eyeliner, her face contorted before the mirror like the man from Munch's *Scream*.

"Why not? It's a beautiful building full of beautiful art." *It's free.* "Let's grab coffee and spend the day there. Besides, what else do you have to do on a Sunday morning?"

"Sleep."

"Just come with me once. There are some great spots for pictures, and you haven't posted anything new in a while."

"Fine," she said. "But only because you're so adorable."

The next morning I pushed through the doors of the atrium entrance a few minutes before we agreed to meet. The docent handed me a map, and as I stood in the tiled foyer pondering the arrangement of numbered squares, a group of kids burst into the hall and with them the din of a dozen conversations reverberating off the domed roof and green marble columns. The glint of a nickel from the central fountain caught their attention, and soon a handful of boys were elbow deep in that unnaturally blue water, fishing out Jeffersons and Lincolns only to launch them at the face of the cherub rising from the highest level.

"Children, please stop that," an old woman said rising from a chair in the corner. "Those are the wishes of visitors who came before you. Don't mistreat them so."

I chuckled to myself as an exasperated chaperone pulled as many boys off the fountain as he could while verbally lassoing the rest. "If you do not step away from the fountain right now, you can forget about pizza this afternoon."

Collectively, the girls decided on the best route to the Vermeer, then neatly folded their maps and put them in each other's backpacks. They looked at the raucous scene by the fountain with a mature, womanly contempt, though I imagine the most popular among them later pocketed a few wet quarters.

Ten minutes after we were supposed to meet, she texted to say she wouldn't be there for another hour.

I slid the phone back into my pocket as the voices of the children recessed into seventeenth century Holland. The cherub, now splotched with water spots, continued his pissing, and the attendant retired to her seat among the ferns. A timid stillness rejoined the room, amplifying the sound of water falling onto stone. I considered heading home but found myself walking down an empty hallway toward the traveling Turner exhibit.

I skimmed the introductory text posted at the entrance. Father, boy, master, paint; travel, enlightenment, industry, man; accolade, critique, isolation, death—the tortured life of an artist forced to paint fields rather than work them.

The first room was filled with verdant green watercolors, Arcadian landscapes, and pen-and-ink sketches, deftly done but predictable in their attention to line and to form. The monuments of Venice rose in strong, angular lines, resisting the deconstructed swirls of pink, purple, and blue. Capital ships sat at anchor while dockworkers toiled on the shore. Before a picture of a harbor at midday, I held my breath and leaned in to marvel at the construction of a plank through a single immaculate brushstroke. Was that length of wood painstakingly recreated through iterative attempts, its misshapen siblings buried in layers of concealing paint? Or was it created ex nihilo in a singular moment of chaotic inspiration, perfect at first sight?

The second room was luminous, and I delighted in images of suns slung low on their horizons, barely contained by nets of wispy ochre clouds. Schooners listed on swirling waves of topaz and turquoise. Storms condensed in ominous blackness on lofty mountain tops menacing the armies of mortals below. Parliament burned. Carthage fell. Pont Neuf faded into a bank of morning fog. Function followed form. Verb followed noun.

The walls of the third and final room were painted in somber burgundy, each frame lit by a single source. Here, the artist abandoned myth and legend, history and histrionics. All that remained was a resplendent communion with light. Horizons were obliterated by an ineffable curvature— of setting suns, of swirling clouds, of the painter's own eye reflected on the canvas. Was the boundless circle that emerged the jubilant liberation of a master considering no one's hand but his own? Or was it the senile paint pushing of an old man, a manifestation of the final point of punctuation awaiting him at the end of his hapless life?

"What a mess," a voice said from behind me.

I turned and saw a man six inches taller than me with porcupine spikes rising off the top of his flat head. He wore an ill-fitting blazer over an untucked shirt, his muscles below still in swollen recovery from their last set of reps. She was there too, but at first I didn't see her. For a young woman who burned so brightly at night, she was nearly invisible in the daytime.

"You don't like it?"

He leaned in closer, wrinkling his nose as synapses deep inside his block-like head fired for the first time ever. "No, dude. No, I do not."

She grinned, self-satisfied, as if she had just liberated her queen to command the center of the board. "This is Trevor. Sorry we're late. We had a late night."

She wore a baggy sweatshirt that fell from her shoulder, revealing the interwoven straps of her sports bra. The curves of her legs were hugged by iridescent yoga pants, her feet enrobed in spotless white kicks. Her bee-stung lips were lacquered in glistening pink gloss, and her eyes were shielded by dark-tinted glasses that had lost all association with the sun. By any measure, she was a most respectable lady of the modern athleisure class.

I moved to castle. "I think I like it, Trevor. I think it's brilliant. I think he's managed to capture the essence of the thing, without copying its form. In so doing, we're free to feel and not just see. To feel the warmth of the horizontal light. To feel the wind that brushes the sea and picks up notes of salt and seaweed and the cold of the ocean's waves. It's the end of a day, and we don't know what may come next, but we need not fear the darkness. Not just yet. We can simply exist in this moment, sharing it with a man two hundred years dead."

"Is it a sailboat?" He turned his head like a Victrola dog.

She giggled, looking up from her phone. Her thumb continued without her, bending and extending in an endless downward scroll.

"Yes," I sighed. "It's a sailboat."

"Cool." He nodded, well-assured he'd absorbed all the painting had to offer.

"If you two are done with the art appreciation lesson, can we go?" She put her hands on her hips and pouted. "You promised me coffee and new pics. There are some super pretty statues outside. Buy me a latté on the way?"

"Go? You just got here. I'd like to see more of the museum. They have a good number of impressionists in the permanent collection and some famous works on loan from abroad."

"Fine," she huffed. "But if I don't get a venti first, I'm never sleeping with either of you ever again."

She trailed behind me for the next hour, sipping frothed soy juice and compulsively refreshing her news feed. Occasionally, she would look up long enough to say, "Oh, I love her dress" or "Look, it's another Jesus." Trevor, to his credit, at least made an effort, but apart from the works depicting warriors or battles, he was hopelessly lost. In nineteenth century France, he stood in front of Monet and Seurat like a tourist in a Chinese train station, staring at a board of indecipherable timetables, not sure where he was, or where he was going, or where he had been.

"Why would anyone paint the same church over and over again?"

Trevor could probably pick me up and bench press me a hundred times, providing I had the ab strength to lie still, but there in front of oil on canvas, in front of oxidized iron and cobalt and zinc smeared with a knife or feathered with a brush, his gelatinous mind was mine to dominate. I summoned the most paternalistic tone I could. "He was experimenting with light. He painted the same facade over and over again to show how the world is beholden to the passage of time, how our perspective is mutable and ever changing."

He contemplated this for a few moments then waved her over. "Hey, babe. Look how he used different colors to show how time passes."

She snapped a picture with her phone. "I love that. Can we go now?"

I relented and followed the pair out into the sculpture garden. She handed me her purse and an empty coffee cup, and the two of them bounded across the lawn to take selfies with marble women and bronze men. She fluttered from statue to statue, and the hedges, tall and full, concealed her from me only to reveal her somewhere else, nestled against a plinth of lifeless stone, smiling at her own extended hand. It was midday, the sun at its zenith, and my eyes strained to stay open in the fullness of the light. It didn't seem to bother her.

She strolled back to me, leaving Trevor behind in the garden to attempt to recreate the pose of a club-wielding Hercules. "What do you think?" she asked, handing me her phone.

She favored a large aperture that disintegrated the world behind her into swirling color, light refracted and bent by the round lens to frame the lines of her painted face.

"What a mess," I said.

She grabbed her phone from me and slapped my arm. "What's with you today? I think I look cute. I'll probably add some filters, though, before I post."

"What are we doing here?" I asked.

"I have no clue. This was your stupid idea."

"Let me rephrase that: what is *he* doing here?"

"Who, Trevor?"

"Yes. Who the fuck is Trevor?"

She lowered her phone and looked out into the garden. "I met him at the club last week, and he gave me a ride home. I think he's sweet."

"He's a bumbling idiot."

"I'm not keeping him around for his mind." She turned back to her phone and started editing the photos she had just taken.

I walked over to a sun-drenched bench, and she followed. The stone slab was almost too hot to bear, and beads of sweat trickled down my back. She sat next to me and rested her purse on her lap the way her mother held a throw pillow.

"Today was supposed to be about us. I haven't seen you in ages."

"Yeah, you've been completely MIA."

I swallowed a riposte. "I thought, what could be better than spending a Sunday morning looking at beautiful art with a beautiful woman?"

The compliment bought me a quick smile, or maybe she was just pleased with the filter she'd selected. "A museum. What good is it anyway? Just cold hallways, whispering old women, and wall after wall of paintings getting increasingly blurry."

"What good is it? It's our cultural inheritance. The artists who came before us saw truth and morality and beauty, captured it in art, and left it for us to appreciate."

She scoffed. "The artists who came before us left us women with spherical tits and babies that look like old Frenchmen."

"Well, I like women with spherical tits."

She glanced up from her phone, her eyebrows raised.

"*In art.* And I like babies that look like old Frenchmen. *In art.* And I wanted to come here and see art with you."

"Oh, please. This was all foreplay. You just wanted to get laid in the afternoon without spending any money." She tapped her thumb one last time and dropped her phone into her purse. A few seconds later, my pocket vibrated. Another masterpiece hung in her gallery.

"I just..." I grasped at words I barely believed. "I just thought you'd like it."

"I don't," she snapped. "It's not me."

"It could be. There's more to life than going out to clubs and coming home wasted. We have to grow up eventually."

"You can do whatever you want. Go be an old man, puttering around art galleries if that's what gets you off. Just don't try to drag me down because you've hit rock bottom. It's not for me."

"I haven't hit rock bottom."

"Yes, you have. And everyone is talking about it—about how you just show up at parties to mooch off the bar before you disappear back home. It's kinda pathetic."

I sprang off the bench and crossed my arms. "If I'm so pathetic, why are you hanging out with me?"

She pulled a mirror from her purse and began reapplying gloss. "Good question."

"Well, please don't squeeze your eyebrows too tight trying to think up an answer. I'd hate for you to get a wrinkle."

She snapped the mirror closed. "I'm far more likely to get a laugh line."

Trevor ambled back to us, his heavy footsteps swishing the loose white rocks as if parting the water left behind by a receding wave. His simple, ignorant grin was proof enough he was incapable of sensing the tension in the air.

"So, what's next, sports fans?"

She popped up perky and twisted her arm around his. "Let's get out of here, Trev."

He pulled out his phone and opened a map. "You hungry? We could all go grab some grub."

She shot a quick glance back at me. "Nah. I'm kinda tired. Take me back to your place."

Trevor gave me a fist bump. She blew me a kiss that struck with the force of a closing parenthesis. Then they were gone.

I crossed the street and slunk into the modern art wing where white light echoed through an irregular, vacuous space. Gone was the triumphalism of our youth—the gilt frames, the soaring arches, the subtly bowed columns and marble floors. In their place, there was nothing. Blank walls, blank ceilings, blank columns, blank floors. Here, with our victory lost, with our ambition effaced, there was nothing to do but submit.

On the second floor I came upon a Rothko, some assemblage of paint swatches supported by nothing but consensus. It was weightless, and I tossed it aside to hang myself in its place. For the rest of the day, people stopped to view my installation, to consider the lines that defined me, to read on the plaque beside me the content of my constitution. They mumbled. They tittered. They coughed. They yawned. Then the sun set, and the tourists shuffled off to dinner, and when the guard locked the doors and turned off the lights, I was left alone in the darkness with nothing but my smug self-satisfied sense of beauty, of morality, of TRUTH.

****

—I think I'd like to stop now.

—*Absolutely not. You cannot remember the fall and forget standing back up. You must see the whole. Yin and yang, young grasshopper.*

—What if there's no standing back up? Isidora is flat on its back. What if that's the end of the story?

—*Isidora is inevitable. It will rise again. And you will be at the center, as you've always been. Just keep going.*

A week later, I heard someone shuffling about outside my bedroom door. Then a bony hand knocked *shave and a haircut*. It was clearly not one of my housemates. They were either kind enough to leave me alone or rude enough to barge straight in. I slid my head under the pillow and said nothing.

"Hello? Hey, buddy? I'm coming in, alright?"

The door opened, sweeping aside empty beer bottles and dirty laundry. The Mouth stepped in, followed by the midday sun that poured through the skylight in the hallway.

"Go away."

"Hey, chief." His voice was like that of a rancher calming a startled mare. "I tried calling but it never went through. Everything alright?"

"They disconnected my phone." I pressed my face against the fitted jersey sheet and inhaled the sweltering air of my own exhalation.

"Now, why would they do that?"

"I stopped paying them."

"I see. Capitalist pigs." The Mouth brushed a delivery wrapper off a metal folding chair, which he carried to the bed. He dropped a backpack on the floor and then sat, kicking his feet up onto my back. I groaned but remained still.

"We haven't seen you in awhile. You don't call. You don't write. You didn't come to Hawke's thing last week."

"Can you please leave?"

"It was a blast. Worth crawling out of bed for."

I wanted to remain buried, to submit to even deeper depths if I could, but it was getting hard to breathe. I threw the pillow aside as he unzipped his backpack. He pulled out a pack of loose-leaf tobacco and dropped a pinch onto a thin piece of paper.

"You're rolling your own now?"

"Yeah. It had a romantic, doughboy-in-the-trenches quality to it at first. Never again. What a pain in the ass. Now every time I want a smoke, I have to play arts-and-crafts first. Plus, I'm walking around town with a backpack full of pouches and papers like a goddamned itinerant tobacconist. It's a nightmare."

He licked the paper's end and twirled it into a tight cylinder. The flint of the lighter flashed white.

"You want one?"

I didn't, and I knew we weren't supposed to smoke in the house, but I couldn't resist the urge to watch him roll another.

"So, what's the deal? Did you find bigger assholes to hang out with?" His eyes were down, his fingers busy. The cigarette hung from his mouth burning impatiently.

"Of course not. How could I?"

"Well, that's a relief."

"I'm just going through some stuff."

"Like what?"

"Like . . . fiscal austerity."

"Looks like physical austerity to me." He slid the freshly rolled cigarette behind his ear and turned his attention to the lit one. "You know we don't have a problem treating you to a few rounds when you come out with us. Squire's got a direct line to his daddy's pocketbook. Regina is gainfully employed with something or other. I forget. I have my means. We got you."

I shoved his feet off my back and sat up. A nod and he handed me the cigarette from behind his ear and a lighter. The unfiltered smoke singed my throat, and the nicotine spun my head around.

"She's done with me," I moaned. "And already on to someone else."

"Mmm. I see. And this surprises you?" He exhaled an addition to the cloud collecting on the ceiling.

"And this depresses me."

"Aw, don't be like that. You know what they say—other fish, vast waters."

I had once thought we had a future together, that we would rage in reckless chaos under moonlit skies, burning through the last of our youth until we found tranquility in a banal middle age of game nights, movie theaters, chain restaurants. That potential future was easily sacrificed. What I mourned was the loss of a certain past—the weight of her Lycra-painted body, the glow of her summer skin, the racing of my teenage heart, each beat a firework in my chest—a baggy sweatshirt worn like a dress, her naked legs below tiptoeing to the island where we devoured frozen waffles, the soft pink light that bled through the skylight of her apartment as she looked up at me and said with the reassurance of a morning affirmation, "I love you." The weight of it all crushed me, and I wanted it gone.

"I'm sick of fishing."

The Mouth rose to pace the room, staring at old photos and high school trophies like an actuary building a risk table. At my desk his hand found a lunar model, the kind that floats above a magnetic platform, and he flicked it so hard it fell from its field and rolled under my bed.

"One bad relationship, and you throw in the towel. That's messed up, man. You hold onto things too tightly."

"No, I don't."

"Yes, you do. Look at you. I can see you white knuckling the past from here. You've got to let it go. She *was* your girlfriend. Was. Past tense. And now you *are* depressed? Present tense?"

"Sure. Cause and effect."

The Mouth shook his head in disappointment, and back then his disappointment stung. It's easy to get lost chasing the approval of an opinionated man. "We don't live in a deterministic world. There's only memory and action. Both are present-tense phenomena. You're suffering now because you're remembering now. Let it go. There is no cause."

"But the past is real."

"No, it's not. The one undeniable truth of the world is that we have free will. But it doesn't fit in any model. Theologians can't explain it. How can an atemporal god be all-powerful if temporal humans get a say? Thousands of years of dusty monasteries and gilded temples and the best they can do is shrug and shove an offering plate under your nose. Scientists are no better. Rather than accept free will, they posit a multiverse of infinite, deterministic timelines. Give me a break. Free will is obvious. So, how do you account for free will? How is it that the past isn't a constraint on the present? You realize it doesn't exist. And the more you recognize that fact, the freer you will be."

I swung my legs around and rested my feet on the warped parquet floor. "You're saying if I forget the past, it's no longer real?"

"How could it be?"

"And if I forget her, *she's* no longer real?"

"To be honest, dude, she wasn't all that real to begin with." The Mouth returned to the folding chair and placed both hands on my thighs. "And now she's just a painful echo of a past only you sustain, a figment of your imagination, and you're wrecking yourself over it."

"A figment?"

He nodded as he sucked the last bit of smoke out of his shrinking roach.

A figment. A wisp of nothingness caught in the web of my memory, a past that only exists by consent. It was clearly a sophism, a lie undercut by the testimony of stone and starlight. But it was a lie that hinted at agency, and at the time that was all the justification I needed.

"A figment," I said, dropping my cigarette into an empty can. "It's a start."

Chapter Three

I went into my chrysalis a butterfly and emerged a caterpillar, content to drag my somber bulk through the undergrowth, to never again feel the sunlight penetrate my stained-glass wings. Each night I slept a dreamless sleep. Each day I woke with nothing to do. My existence dissolved into a dizzying rotation, a plodding revolution, a looping trail traced through time and space like the path of a pen in a spirograph. There were days I never left my bed. There were nights I never came home. There were afternoons I sat for hours in the park, watching the leaves wither and fall, one by one.

I made no effort to find another job. And why should I have? The unemployment checks paid for my basic necessities, and though I couldn't cover rent, my monthly tithes were enough to delay eviction. Despite the clear drawback in befriending an inert mass of self-pity, the Mouth never abandoned me. As I got to know them better, Squire, Regina, and Hawke did the same. In an empty life, a single addition is definitional, and when I felt I had nothing and no one, this small group of outcasts and the worldview they shared became my existential clarion call. Soon, I awoke thinking only of Squire's apartment and the heated debates we would have, the plans we would put into motion, the speeches we would make, and the swords upon which we would fall.

Squire had been deposited in a charmless neighborhood across the river from the capital in an apartment he did not choose with an exorbitant rent he did not pay. His parents thought it best. The river was a moat protecting their innocent boy from the perils of a city full of loose women, street drugs, and ethnic food. And he couldn't afford any distractions. He was there to become a lawyer, like his father, without losing the docile piety of his mother. God willing, he might even come out of it voting Republican. Squire—short for esquire, an appellation as truncated as the JD he couldn't bring himself to finish. It was there, at the end of a mauve hallway, past ascending ordinals as welcoming as white-collar prison cells, that the dream of Isidora was born.

> —*Yes. But not right away. We weren't done with the capital yet, and it wasn't done with us.*

> —No. Before planting, the ground must be cleared.

> —*Slashed and burned.*

The group's ethos spoke to me, and when we discussed those wronged by a systemic injustice that robbed people of their dignity and the fruits of their labors, I counted myself among its victims. It was not quite socialism, not quite anarchism. At its core, it was the philosophy of the have-nots, the unlanded gentry, the holders of short straws and losing hands—same as it ever was. I felt it intuitively. For the Mouth, resistance was a spiritual act. He metabolized ritual and exhaled dogma. Hawke was his profane analog. Discontent pulsed through his veins and bubbled in his viscera. Squire possessed a finely articulated moral compass, guided by a motherlode of goodness at his core whose polarity repelled the privilege he had inherited by chance. In activism he found a salve for his perpetually guilty conscience. Out of all of us, only Regina had any common sense. She was five foot nothing—fierce, driven, and confident. While we drifted from one daily distraction to the next, her focus never wavered, forever fixed on our distant objective like an astronomer tracking the movement of the faintest glimmer in the night's sky.

—*You're stalling. We have to talk about it.*

—About what?

—*It's time to remember Tent City.*

****

Regina had the right of it. The flatbed Sam had borrowed from the bar *was* shit, but I still found her complaining off-putting. He didn't have to join us, let alone procure capital for the enterprise. Sam wasn't with us back then. He was just our regular bartender—dependable for a surprise round of shots and some jukebox credits paid from the tip jar when the evening started to drag. And yet here he was, pupils like pinpoints hidden under a raggedy old trucker's cap, a vampire among day-walkers risking immolation under the noonday sun.

"Seriously, this cart is awful," Regina continued. "Is this really the best you could offer?"

Sam looked exhausted, but he smirked as he lit a cigarette. "I fight with that thing every night. You use it once and you can't stop bitching?"

The tiny plastic wheels caught every break in the sidewalk, sending jolts up through the donated canned goods and day-old bread. I reached over to steady the load.

"Honestly," Sam continued, "I thought you'd bring more hands. Where are Dean and Squire?"

"Dean is deep in his newfound digital celebrity, and James is right beside him, clapping like a moron every time they get another follower." Her voice walked a tightrope between detachment and derision, but it was clear she loved them both.

Our movement had, until that point, deployed standard activist tactics. We drafted sweeping manifestos, we canvased sidewalks during lunch breaks, we rallied and marched and chanted and sang. We got into the occasional scuffle with acolytes of the new authority. We shouted obscenities at the police. The Mouth documented it all in posts that echoed across the Internet, and people started to take notice. It seemed that even in the most placid of waters there was a Brownian motion of dissatisfaction, a subatomic disquiet, a subconscious discontent, waiting to be organized and directed. Enter @Publius_Junior, a.k.a. Dean Fitzroy Fitzsimmons, a.k.a. the Mouth. They drank from his ever-flowing spring, nourishing that voice inside themselves that told them all was not well.

At the same time our serpentine economy, fat from swallowing an especially large bull, reattached its jaw and began shedding its skin. The weathered outer layers of our decaying manufacturing sector were scraped aside, and workers once promised pensions found themselves pitching tents, reduced to the status of veterans from that other war. If they couldn't be heard, they could at least be seen. That's what many of them thought, anyway, and the mall swelled with a tent city of the newly homeless. Food, we thought— easily demanded, easily procured. It was the least we could do. And in this way we found ourselves patrons of the dispossessed.

Our trolley rattled down still Sunday morning streets on what promised to be that most singular autumn day when the north wind breaks low and sweeps aside any hope of an enduring summer, when leaves wring themselves dry into shades of auburn and marigold, and the air, blown clean of clouds, swells with golden sunlight but not warmth. In March, at the end of a long gray winter, a day like this would be cause for jubilation. Women would dig through boxes of summer clothes and emerge into the afternoon light in billowy dresses and short skirts. They would crowd themselves on picnic blankets in the park, sipping spritzers concealed in Nalgene bottles, as shirtless men jogged around them in slow, deliberate laps. But in October, with our sun-drenched skin exhausted by the light, we wrap ourselves in cashmere and halfheartedly mourn our paradise lost. The parks were drained dry, the coffee shops overflowing.

We crested a minor rise above the Golden Triangle, and I took a turn at the helm, pulling more than pushing to prevent the cart from slipping away from us. As we descended, we saw the manicured lawn of the national mall suffocated by triangles of plastic, tents and tarpaulins hastily assembled in a sprawling, stochastic mess. Straw had been scattered about to absorb the rainwater and the crushed chlorophyll of the once-thriving grass. Trails of smoke striated the sapphire sky. We paused at a stoplight, and I raised a hand to my eyes.

"It's grown a lot this week."

A gust of wind rolled over the river, and the landscape before us buckled and churned. Trees bowed and shed their leaves, and my nose was filled with the faint smell of pressed apples and hay bales on a cold, starry night. Regina pulled a black newsboy cap off her head, revealing sandy hair that flagged behind her as her pale face split the wind.

The signal changed, but I didn't notice at first. Sam bumped me aside and began to push. "Onward," he said.

We crossed Constitution into the land of remembered men, now overrun by hoards of the forgotten, and proceeded along the straight sides of a man-made lake, feeling the eyes of hundreds track our long march to the canteen. In the water, a woman sat naked with a child nestled between her full breasts. The baby giggled and cooed, swatting at the surface and watching her reflection swirl and stretch. The woman was expressionless, lifeless, cold. We walked by in silence as if there was nothing to see.

The canteen was at the foot of the great memorial, inside a circus tent that swelled from the cookstoves like a hot air balloon. A crowd of people, common only in their degradation, milled about outside, shuffling ever closer to the stewing beef and rosemary potatoes bubbling away inside. Hawke said to bring it straight up, so we grabbed what we could and began to climb.

I raised my eyes and saw a man seated in his temple, surveying everything, remembering nothing. His hands rested on the arms of a marble throne, forever signing his own initials, condemned to an eternal egotism he would have no doubt rejected in life. Had the sculptor wished to honor the man rather than worship him, he would have carved one hand into the sign of benediction, two fingers extended to absolve the sins of a divided nation. The other would be clenched in a fist for any who dared threaten the hard-won peace.

Hawke was waiting at his feet, and he pointed each of us to the appropriate corner to deposit our load. Perishables at the back against the cold stone walls. Dry goods away from the entrance in case it rained.

"On the next trip up, put the heavy stuff on the lift," he said, pointing to a plywood chute that descended the stairs. A makeshift cart assembled from a few shopping baskets and a skateboard was attached to a rope allowing one to lower food directly to the back of the canteen. He dropped it in and let it slide.

"Genius," I said as the skateboard descended.

"A few wheels and an inclined plane. It's the best we could do." Hawke shook his head as he let out the rope, hand over hand, until the cart came to rest at the bottom. Beneath his worn RATM tee, his muscles choreographed every articulation, and I saw his body as nothing but a squeezing network of fibers made dense, impenetrable by repeated trauma and repeated self-repair.

We returned to the flatbed and loaded the cooking oil and some canned goods into Hawke's lift.

"Take 'er up!" Sam shouted.

The rope pulled taut, and the cart's contents fell against the lower side of the baskets. The wheels inched uphill, pausing a second only to climb another foot and then pause again as the man above reeled in the rope.

"He's really gotten into this," I said, heaving a case of baked beans up another stair.

"Hawke is a spinning top," Regina said. "He can focus an enormous amount of energy on a single point. But when he slows down, he tumbles and crashes into anything that gets in his way." She held two jugs of water, one at the end of each arm, like a servant girl returning from a well.

"You don't trust him?"

"It's not that." She set the water on the step in front of her and shook out her hands. "Hawke has a tendency to get lost in his convictions. He basically raised himself, you know? His mom was deported when he was seven or eight. His dad was MIA. He had to sort out the world on his own, poor thing. Sometimes he forgets he's no longer alone."

The light that breached the tops of the trees struck her slight form pure and revealed in a girl who was so irredeemably plain—who carried jewelry like a porter, who wore makeup like a mask—an eternal and effortless beauty concealed to all but a patient few. She turned toward it, then looked down at the misfortune below, the tails of her canvas jacket dangling in the wind, and sighed.

"What a mess."

We reached the summit before the cart and found Hawke there coiling and stretching, hand over hand, to bring it up the last few yards. He was breathing heavily, and sweat beaded in the creases of his brow. Sam dropped the case of cornmeal he was carrying at the statue's feet and rushed over to help.

"I got it," Hawke said, reaching to grab the basket. With one last exertion he pulled the cart over the lip.

A few more trips, and the work was done. We descended the stairs a final time and parted ways. Sam had a shift in the evening and hoped to get in a nap before work. Regina, not knowing where to direct the sympathy that overwhelmed her, simply wanted to be somewhere else. I lingered behind, and Hawke offered to show me the latest developments.

The idea of Tent City appealed to him, and he had been an early adopter, squatting on a quiet patch of ground south of the baths the same day Tent City spilled over Independence. He spent the first few days lazing on the grass beside his tent like a lizard, consuming sunlight and mass-market sci-fi in equal measure. Wave after wave of new arrivals filled in around him, and bit by bit his placid ruralism became densely urban. Now we twisted and turned through a maze of improvised shelters, the path eroded into a quagmire of mud.

"There's a central committee of sorts," he shouted over his shoulder. "But they're completely powerless. We have meetings twice a day, at ten and three. Used to be just once, but we found it wasn't responsive enough. Whoever shows up gets a vote. Nothing moves without a vote."

Tent City was a hum of chaotic energy. Men in lawn chairs argued about the injustice of national ID cards. Women in knit bikinis played a game of Twister with the enthusiasm of an orgy. A semicircle of drummers beat djembes in an asynchronous thrum, and beside them, in a circular clearing apparently reserved for such a purpose, a half-dozen bodies whirled and wriggled, light feet trampling straw into the soggy ground. Everywhere there was mud. Everywhere there was weed. And no one seemed the least bit interested in being anywhere else.

That's not to say Tent City was paradise. As much as Hawke would have disagreed, I saw the tents set farther back on the hill, as apart as apart could be. I saw the man in coveralls who sat on an abused suitcase, staring blankly ahead. I saw the woman looking down into her empty hands. I saw the young girl beside them chasing butterflies and moths, her soiled teddy bear skimming the few remaining shoots of green grass.

I followed, listening to Hawke rhapsodize about Tent City's perfect social order, until we reached our destination. The library tent was made for events, not for camping—the kind with roll-down walls that could be thrown above the tables of a modest wedding when a bride's perfect day didn't go to plan. It was filled with wooden crates stacked one atop another and a large shelf punctuated with books by Nietzsche, Spinoza, Madison, and Marx. As we approached, a man wearing a houndstooth vest above a beige T-shirt stood to greet us. He pushed round golden specs up the bridge of his nose and snapped his fingers.

Hawked snapped in reply. "Is it in yet?"

"Sorry, Hawke. Not yet. Gary is a slow reader."

"He probably hasn't even started it yet. The man prefers possessing books to reading them. Anything else new come in?"

"Doubtful. You've read all the sci-fi, and we're clean out of fantasy."

"There are a half-dozen copies of the Federalist Papers on offer," I said, pointing to the stack behind the librarian.

Hawke shrugged. "It's fine. I'll see if Squire can lend me some cash, and I'll run to Kramer's tomorrow."

We snapped goodbye and turned to leave. Somewhere in the distance a church bell rang once and then again.

"Two bells," Hawke whispered.

I checked my watch. It was 11:13 a.m.

It rang again, the same two hollow reverberations, and I realized it wasn't the clang of some far off steeple, but a much smaller bell struck nearby.

"Two bells!" Hawke yelled.

"Two bells!" the librarian gasped.

The words spread like a plague and in an instant they rang from the mouths of everyone in Tent City.

"Two bells!"

"Two bells!"

"Two bells!"

"But where?" Hawke rose up like a prairie dog, his eyes darting from one corner of the encampment to the next.

"Hawke, what is it? What's going on?"

The bells rang again.

"Northwest!" he yelled.

"Northwest!" the librarian screamed as he leaped across the table and disappeared down a trail.

Two bells and the djembes were abandoned. Two bells and the line at the canteen dissipated. Two bells and Tent City awoke from its languor and lurched toward the sound.

Hawke took off at a dead sprint to the north, staying on pavement where his feet fell solid and sure. I ran after him, huffing like a clydesdale.

"Two bells, Johnny!" he shouted as he passed a closed tent. The flap unzipped, and a kid poked his head out, rubbing sleep from his eyes.

"Two bells!" I yelled, flailing past.

I caught up with Hawke in a glade of trees on the edge of the encampment. Tent City's human contents converged on a man in a beret and woolen scarf, who stood beside a bell suspended from a frame.

"Two bells!" he announced.

"Two bells!" the group confirmed.

The man turned to confront a uniformed member of the Park Police who was flanked by a dozen sanitation workers in reflective yellow jumpsuits. Behind them three garbage trucks had jumped the curb and parked on the bare ground, their open hatches facing us like the gaping mouths of hungry beasts.

The officer removed his wide-brimmed hat and cradled it in his hand. "Look, I understand you're upset about this, but I have orders. This is public land, and it's illegal to erect artificial structures for the purpose of habitation without the expressed consent of the Park Police. You have not requested consent, and either way, we would never give it." He pointed with hat at the tents behind us. "These illegal structures must be removed."

Like a hydra, the residents of Tent City hissed back.

"We're not going anywhere, and we will not allow you to enter," the man with the beret said. "As you say, this is public land. We're the public. This is our land, and we are claiming it as our own."

The officer turned to the man on his left. "Alvarez, let's just get this over with. As much as you can carry. Everything goes."

Alvarez grabbed a pair of gloves from his back pocket and put them on as he advanced toward us. Hawke stepped forward to meet him but was grabbed from behind by a young woman who linked her arm with his. Another person stepped forward and linked with her. They were joined by another and another. The girl next to me, her thick black curls defying gravity, offered her elbow. I wove our arms together, and she pulled me in tight.

"Look, y'all. I'm the public too. Don't give me any right to throw that tree into my truck and plant it in my front yard."

We stepped forward as one, an unbroken shield of civil disobedience protecting Tent City.

"Shit," the officer said reaching for the radio on his shoulder. "Carl, we got a problem . . ."

We continued forward as one.

"I understand, but these fellas aren't paid to scuffle. You got any blues you can send our way?"

We marched forward again.

"No, you listen. We're calling it. I don't want this to turn ugly."

The officer released his radio, and for a second he just stood there, surveying the defiant crowd and the blight behind them that he was forced to let fester. The wind gusted through the trees, and his hair, unburdened by the weight of his government-issued pith helmet, frolicked in the breeze. He exhaled, swept his hair back, then screwed the hat down tight. With a tap on Alvarez's shoulder, the crew returned to their vehicles and left.

The crowd reveled in defiant victory. An encampment that flourished under the nose of power somehow escaped its grasp. And I had been a part of it. For the first time in my life, I felt powerful. Present. As Tent City flowed back into itself, I flowed with it. And the drums beat all night long.

Chapter Four

In the weeks that followed, the number of economic refugees seeking shelter in the capital swelled, driven by an anomalous rise in mortgage defaults and bank foreclosures. Every parent pulling closed the door of their child's bedroom for the last time, every aging worker lining up at the recruitment agency like a geriatric sow at the county fair, knew the full weight of our economic fragility. But for the rest, for those not personally touched by the seizing of single-family homes and the repossession of sputtering Nissans, the hardships of others were too abstract to generate much sympathy. Like the collapse of a distant star, it barely registered. No one sensed that their night was now a little bit darker. So, as Tent City waxed, enthusiasm waned, and those who could afford to tune out did so. The local news raved about the home team closer mowing down batters in the playoffs. The canteen served thin soup and hardened bread.

"It's getting rough," Hawke concluded. He had just showered and was patting his hair dry with the towel around his neck. "Every patch of ground is covered, and families are now forced to share tents. Everyone is covered in mud, everyone smells like shit, and everyone is fed up."

Squire reached forward with his chopsticks and grabbed another baozi from the center of the table. He dipped it into his saucer of soy, then placed it into his mouth whole, chewing delicately as if the act was an offense to the conversation in progress.

"What are we going to do?" I asked.

"What *can* we do?" Regina was the only one at the table having tea and she poured herself another steaming emerald cup. "Tent City sounds good on paper, but it's unsustainable. It's inhumane. Those poor people can't go on living in squalor and bathing in the reflecting pool until the end of time. It's not a permanent solution."

Hawke's expression grew pained. "It's civil disobedience, Regina, bolstered by an experiment in neo-progressive social order. Tent City exists to raise awareness of the possibility of an alternative to the shit reality everyone is living now."

"Awareness." The Mouth started circling the table, shoveling rice into his face from a lifted bowl. "That's the key word. My following has skyrocketed in the past few weeks. Everyone's talking about Tent City, how it works, how to join. It's working, but we won't have achieved anything if TC just withers away. We need something big. We need a win."

"Dean, it's just social media. None of it matters. And besides, you haven't even been down there in person."

"First, Hawke is my eyes on the ground, and no one is better positioned to report back. Second, who do you think is on social media? Cats and dogs? These are *people* following us, Reg. People being crushed by the big machine. People lost somewhere in the cogs and wheels. People waiting for us to lead them."

Squire reached for another dumpling, but the conversation lulled, and in the silence of the moment our eyes fell on him and froze his hand. "What?"

"Feel free to jump in here, Squibs."

"Oh. Well, good points all around, in fact." He returned his empty chopsticks to his plate. "*If* we were to act, we should discuss our options. There's a city council meeting next week with an open comment period. One suggestion is raising the issue there and starting a dialogue that could unlock new resources, maybe even get a natural disaster declaration."

"Oh come on, Squibs."

Hawke leaned forward over his untouched bowl of dan dan mian. "Squire, the city council doesn't want to help these people. The city council wants them gone. Who do you think is sending the parkies?"

"You see, the Park Police report to the National Park Service, which is a federal body," Squire explained. "The city council doesn't control them. In fact, the city is regularly opposed to the feds. They could be an ally in this."

"Not this time, Squire. The city wants them out and is giving the parkies free rein. They're even providing sanitation crews to help."

"Well, what do you suggest then?" Squire skewered a bun with both chopsticks and shoved it into his mouth.

"A march," the Mouth said.

"Oh, please." Regina took her bowl to the couch and switched on the TV.

"A march, Regina. A march to the capitol. The whole of Tent City on its feet, holding signs, demanding respect, cameras capturing their triumphant confrontation with power."

"They're primed for it," Hawke added as he moved to sit beside her. "They're a goddamned powder keg, ready to explode."

Squire dumped the rest of the soy sauce on the remaining baozi and carried the plate to the living room, perching himself on the arm of the sofa beside Regina. "Gentlemen, a march doesn't just happen. It takes weeks to organize. There are lots of considerations to address. Announcements to draft. Permits to apply for..."

"Jesus, Squire. Permits?" The Mouth said. "A march. Not in a few weeks after all the t's are crossed and the i's dotted. A march—ASAP—like this week. People will join us. All he has to do is say the word."

They turned toward me, and I raised my head from my bowl like a dog caught drinking toilet water. "Who, me?"

"Yes, you, pretty boy."

—*There's no way I called you "pretty boy."*

—You most certainly did! You pushed me into the spotlight, even then.

—*And look how you repaid me . . .*

"I just don't think it's the right move." Regina crossed her arms. "Tent City is a hot mess, and people aren't very sympathetic. Like you said, we have a good thing going right now, and you want to cash it in on a march for..." Her voice trailed off and her eyes widened.

"For dignity, like I said. For . . ."

"Hush. Look."

Regina raised the volume on the television. The talking heads disappeared, replaced by a black screen and a red line that moved left to right like surface water on a plains state. The chart refreshed, and the line plummeted down the Mississippi.

"It's falling." Squire pointed to the TV. "It's falling fast. A thousand points in the last fifteen minutes?"

"Is that a lot?" Hawke asked.

"Yeah," Squire said, almost holding his breath. "Twelve hundred."

The Mouth leaned forward to read the crawler. "'Dow drops fifteen hundred points as real estate uncertainty mounts.' What the fuck does that mean? 'As?' *As Squire stuffs another dumpling in his face.* 'As.' As is not an explanation. As is just simultaneous action. Why can't they ever just tell us what the fuck is going on?"

We held our breath, and the line continued its descent.

I may not have fully understood it at the time, but the money we all save in the bank is not saved in the bank. It doesn't just sit there collecting dust.

The bank uses it, loans it out as a mortgage perhaps, recording the potential that we may come asking for it back as a liability, an obligation. Millions of people, millions of accounts, millions of obligations. When banks lend out money for a mortgage, they don't sit around waiting for that money to return. They sell the hole in their pocket as an asset to someone else, packaging it as a security with a coupon based on the mortgage payments we make every month. Millions of mortgages. Millions of coupons. Millions of obligations. Maybe a pension fund buys that security but doesn't fully trust us to pay on time. They pay for insurance on that security, a small fee to guarantee they're made whole should we prove unreliable. The insurer takes a payment, gives an obligation. Millions of securities. Millions of policies. Millions of obligations. None of this is centrally managed. No one part can see the whole—a whole in constant motion, shifting like desert sands.

The entire financial system is a web of obligations written on an etch-a-sketch in a fault zone. In the end, it's only ever a matter of time.

"Three thousand, three hundred and forty-two points," Regina said with a long exhale. A man in a pin-striped suit celebrating the one hundredth anniversary of his family's polymer business rang the closing bell. He had the good sense not to smile.

"So, are we agreed?" Hawke asked.

"After this?" I rose from the table. "This is going to get ugly. Businesses will close, workers will be laid off, tens of thousands of families will suffer. People will demand a response. And we could be the first to manifest that demand. How can we not march?"

"Regina?" the Mouth said, his fingers at his temples, his voice almost a whisper.

"I need some air." She rose from the sofa and slid her feet into her pre-tied sneakers, pulling out the heels before wrapping herself in a scarf and long woolen coat. "It's still a bad idea." She slipped out the door. The latch took ages to fall into its cradle.

"Squire?"

"Just give me some time, fellas. A day at least. Let me talk to her. She prefers ideas to confrontations. Walking down the middle of a street in a crowd? Yelling at the top of her lungs? Merits aside, it's just not her way of doing things."

The Mouth stood and grabbed his jacket. "Take all the time you need. Show up or don't. The announcement goes out tonight."

Chapter Five

Following the crash, the political landscape roiled like the sea above an earthquake, and our movement, a paper boat set upon that sea, found itself riding high on a tsunami of disillusionment, grievance, exhaustion, and grief. Hundreds of thousands lost their jobs in that first week. Tens of thousands were evicted from their homes. Thousands turned to looting and crime. Hundreds found solace in suicide. When it was discovered that dozens of representatives sold stock in the days before the fall, there was only one thing left to do—walk to the foot of the capitol and remind our electors who held power in a government of, by, and for the people.

The Mouth's social media addiction turned into mania, as he sermonized, radicalized, lambasted, cajoled. He shared the saga of a people breaking free from the bonds of systemic unreality. And he always positioned me as its protagonist. I was the charming face he didn't have, the bold action he couldn't take, the hero he could never be—at least that was the role I was given, and I tried my best to play the part. We filmed agitprop in the tents, shot b-roll on the mall, and lacquered the Internet in revolutionary spittle.

It had the desired effect.

The day of the march we arrived at the ball fields to find a mass of protesters milling about in anxious anticipation. Tent City had been almost completely mobilized, if not in solidarity then to have a temporary reprieve from the boredom and the stink. Others came from farther afield, moths drawn by the incandescence of the Mouth's online persona. And despite Regina's pessimism, we were surprised to find some of the professional activists from her network there too, spiders cajoled into activity by the vibrations of a juicy fly stuck in their web.

As we walked into their midst, we were hailed with shouts and applause like a trio of storied gladiators. The unyielding dissident, the sweet-talking soothsayer, the local boy done good. In their eyes, we were their champions, but it wasn't until we moved amongst them, finding ourselves at the center of their Circle no matter where we stood, that the designation felt true. As I watched the Mouth pose for selfies and Hawke give each of the members of his adopted community a good-natured slap on the back, I realized this was only news to me. I was high-fived, fist-bumped, smiled at, and hugged. Somewhere along our journey we had fallen into celebrity. And celebrity felt good.

>—*It was never a popularity contest. It was only ever about the movement.*

>—Nonsense. You ate it up. You eat it up still.

>—*And what? You're now immune to the adoration of others?*

The representative council of Tent City opened the ceremony with a few words of inspiration followed by the reading of our list of formal demands. Then there was a public comment period, followed by voting, followed by the introduction of a few amendments, followed by more voting, and eventually, adoption. To close, the Mouth gave a short and uncharacteristically forgettable speech, and we were off.

As the mass formed up, I thought about Regina. She was always headstrong and stubborn, a characteristic we knew well, even loved her for. It was no surprise she wanted nothing to do with the march, but I wanted her there with us, nonetheless. I wanted her to see the giddy optimism on their faces, to try on giddy optimism herself for a change. I wanted her to feel the thrill of anticipation as we prepared to elevate moral consciousness over social obedience. I wanted her to take her rightful place at the front and feel the world file in behind her.

Squire's absence was felt too and much more acutely. He had been gone a lot. Only a few years out from retirement, his parents lost a third of their savings the day of the market crash, and with the shadow of forced financial independence looming large above him, Squire promised to finish his studies. He started auditing a tort class mid-semester and in so doing reclaimed his rung on the ladder he had previously been so reluctant to climb. None of us encouraged the decision, but it was hard to criticize. We would have found ourselves climbing too, had we a ladder laying around.

But we never discounted him, never questioned his place in the movement, until the day before the march when Squire told us meekly he couldn't join. He attempted to slide his alibi into a casual conversation the way a mother hides mushrooms in her kids' spaghetti. The Mouth unleashed a torrent of vitriolic rage, bursting like a squeezed sponge. Then like that sponge set down atop all that had spilled from him, he soaked the anger back in, letting the emotion evaporate to leave behind nothing but a lasting stain of betrayal. I tried to summon the same outrage, but the emotion wasn't my own. Mostly, I just missed having Squire around.

We had intended to move during rush hour, to interrupt commuters when they were most vulnerable to interruption, but the revisions to the formal demands—and a rather lengthy discussion of the importance of intersectionality—delayed us. When we finally turned east, the three of us unlikely generals at the head of a column of levied soldiers, the sun was already slipping behind a curtain of low-lying purple clouds. Having requested no permits or street closures, we slithered through the center of the national mall like a centipede. After a summer of ample rain and adult kickball, the ground had dried unevenly, like a field of plaster footprints, and we marched slowly toward that hill of power.

Living in the capital, one grew accustomed to protests. They all looked the same from the outside. Empty mouths shouting empty slogans that bounced off empty buildings only to return to the empty ears of their originators. It was an echo chamber actualized, mobile. Locals fled. Tourists gawked. Commuters in idling cars turned radio nobs and stared at the lingering red light. News cameras captured a homogenous clump of humanity putzing down the street or boisterously trampling perfectly serviceable grass on a perfectly serviceable afternoon.

It was, however, completely different on the inside. I felt alive in the dying light, replete with purpose, absent of desire, duplicated to the hundredth power. When I yelled, my voice burst from a thousand mouths. When I stepped, my stride moved a thousand bodies. When I looked, two thousand eyes saw.

"I can't believe Squire is missing this," I said. We had traversed the length of the mall, and the capitol grew in front of us, illuminated by warm yellow bulbs.

"He's going to regret it," Hawke said, his fist raised in the air.

"He's a moron," the Mouth added.

We didn't notice them at first. They weren't where we expected them to be. We thought the police would resist our march and erect barriers in front of us to attempt to block our path. Instead, we approached unimpeded, and they quietly filed in behind.

It was like the caw of a raven across the broken stalks of a harvested field. The call of a muezzin grinding the gears of the physical world to a sudden halt. The clap of thunder announcing a heavy rain to come. A wave of sound, crisp and pure. And then another.

Two bells.

Hawke's eyes bulged. No command was given. No command was needed. The chanting, the drumming, the singing stopped. We caught the breath in our lungs and listened to the silence grow around us.

Then it came again, a wave of sound, crisp and pure. And then another.

"Two bells!"

Like an immune system separated from its host but still able to detect a pathogen, the mass of protesters turned and faced west. The sun had set, and the sky above us had abandoned the last of its color. Stars were awakening in the darkened firmament. And yet the horizon was ablaze with light. Flames of orange and red consumed the hills of the encampment, and the monolith that stood in front was cast into relief, a great hulking beast the color of pitch, its eyes flashing blood red.

"Fire!" A wave of panic passed through me. "It's all on fire!"

There was no need for a vote this time. The residents of Tent City had lost almost everything, and what remained was easily enumerated in their minds. They could see the stuffed rabbit, spared the garage sale and dragged by their daughter through rest stops and gas stations halfway across the country. The fur didn't burn so much as melt, its glass eyes rolling back into blackening plush. They could see the palette of eyeshadow, last opened the night of their anniversary, two streaks of lavender above warm, familiar eyes. The metallic flakes sparkled and popped as the fires licked the pigments and singed the brushes. They could see the book of privileged words, revealed and willed to them by generations to soothe, to comfort, to uplift. The thin pages sublimated into pure white smoke. The hardbound cover burned for hours. There was no need for a vote this time. The residents of Tent City ran.

The activists ran too, not knowing what was meant by the sound of the bells, not needing an explanation, and we who had led the advance soon found ourselves trailing the retreat.

Hawke quickly caught them. His light feet and powerful legs propelled him over the uneven ground. His mess of curls reciprocated like a piston, and he carved through the fleeing protesters as if nothing at all united them. A woman tripped and fell, and Hawke leapt over her prone body, his mind unclouded by a single empathetic thought.

He was the first to see the wall. He did not slow.

They stood shoulder to shoulder in a line down the length of 14th Street, a maniple of body armor, shields, and helmets. Squad cars lurked behind them, their lights twirling red and blue. Park Police advanced along our flanks mounted on beasts that snorted and stamped the ground in anticipation. Like the legions at Cannae, we had pushed too far. Like the legions at Cannae, we were trapped.

The protesters froze, some of them feeling nothing, stupefied by the apparitions before us. Some of them felt everything, tears pouring down their cheeks. I ran through them and stood alone, my eyes tracking Hawke as he shot toward his own destruction, like a bomb in free-fall, its terminus inevitable.

He slammed into the line of plastic riot shields, not between them like the thrust of a rapier but square into one like the crash of a hammer. The officer, stunned by the brazenness and velocity of his approach, stood flat-footed, and Hawke with his shoulder lowered bowled him over and tumbled behind the police line. In an instant he was back on his feet, flying toward the fire, officers behind in incredulous pursuit.

The retort of the first salvo was deafening. A flash from the left and right, and canisters spiraled above us, trailing plumes of thick, acrid smoke before bursting at our feet. Taking a moment to recover from the shock of Hawke's charge, the center of their line fired last, not in the arcing lob of an artillery barrage but with barrels lowered and aimed. A projectile hit me below the ribs, sending a shockwave through my diaphragm and knocking the air from my lungs. I doubled over and fell onto my side, unable to breathe, unable to gasp. I clawed at my throat with one hand and stretched out the other, attempting to summon back the breath that had been stolen from me. Above,

Andromeda faded behind an expanding, black cloud.

When it finally returned, the air was a chemical cocktail that stripped my throat raw as it rushed to fill the vacuum of my lungs. I coughed and gasped, each cycle a pump of the billows that fanned the flames in my chest. My eyes burst. My nose opened. Every liquid in my head was squeezed from me. I rolled forward, found my knees, then my feet, and staggered in the only direction I could—forward. Out of the gas.

When he appeared before me, my eyes straining to see through the flood of burning tears, that was when I knew this was not about public order. When he appeared before me, in the only direction I could conceivably flee, that was when I knew this was spite. The fire still raged on the hillside, and he stood before it, not a man but an anonymous industrial shell, a silhouette of straight lines and sharp angles, hollow and black.

I raised an arm to shield my head, crouched, and clenched my teeth. The shadow grew before me, twisting and reaching skyward. Then it fell with the force of a monsoon. The hand held the baton. The baton shattered the ulna. And the pain spread like Brushfire. I swallowed it and planted my feet in the earth. And then I rose up, and there was only me and him and the contested ground between us. I knew he would do anything to clear me from that ground. It was his right, his duty. He would beat me until I collapsed, and once I collapsed, he would kick me until I stopped trying to rise, falling onto me and crushing me into the earth before dragging away my empty husk.

In an instant I knew there was only resistance or annihilation. I rose up and kicked forward with my heel, connecting with the shade's gut. He stumbled backward and fell into a pile of clattering plastic.

> *—It was revealed to you then—unambiguous and true. What have you done with that TRUTH? How did you lose it along the way?*

Then I ran.

I ran south. My sight was clouded, my face was covered with

translucent snot, and the skin beneath felt like it was melting. But I could still hear. I could hear the laughing horses and their braying riders. I could hear the concussive overpressure of flash bangs and the slicing of pepper balls fired in rapid succession. I could hear Tent City scream.

I ran south through closed-off streets and joined a panicked mob that spilled past barricades like water from the floodgates of an abandoned dam. With each step a jolt scraped together the splintered ends of bone in my arm. I cradled it with my right and dug my teeth into my bottom lip. Pain overwhelmed all else. Electricity raced up the bundled nerves of my spine.

Soon I was alone, running along an elevated street, following the brightest lights I could see—streetlights that stretched before me like a string of pearls into a vast darkness. I stopped on a bridge, and all I could hear above the recent past ringing in my ears was the sound of water lapping below. The peeling paint chipped as I swung my legs over the railing and looked skyward. The stars shone down without judgment. Then they receded from me, and the water became sky. Bubbles sizzled past my ears, and droplets rained down on the surface above. Then there was silence.

I hung there in the void like a specimen of myself, preserved. I made no attempt to surface.

****

I don't know how I got there, drenched as I was and chilled to the bone by the night air blowing from the north. Perhaps I flew. Perhaps the waxing moon plucked me from those brackish waters with its long gravitational fingers, tugging at my saturated garments like whitecaps. Perhaps it raised me up like the tide, up above the paddle boats beached for the season, over the dying embers of Tent City, between the lecture halls of the university where a new generation was slowly being wound like cymbal monkeys. The air thinned as I rose and grew colder, harder to catch. The sounds of the city submitted to the roar of my tinnitus. The glow below me dimmed. I landed in front of a backlit sign—"Emergency."

On the other side of the doorway a courtroom tried an entire day's docket all at once. Barristers in long black robes crowded the bench where they gesticulated and howled. Defendants fresh from the scene of the crime pulled out their eyeballs and dropped them into plastic bags. Exhibit A. Exhibit B. Judges stood before them unmoved, shaking their powder-white wigs and rapping their desks with overgrown claws. Jurors sat perplexed in disordered chairs, reading periodicals.

"Protest?" the bailiff asked me through her muzzle. Her eyes fluttered above like twin spiders.

Nothing would be gained by attempting to hide my crimes. "Guilty," I pleaded.

She grabbed my pink hands and wrapped her fingers around my wrists like handcuffs. I did not shiver. I could not feel.

"Jesus, they're like ice." She prosecuted my case before the judges with a single look. My fate was decided without deliberation. To the gallows, most certainly.

The executioner arrived with a rolling chair to push me through the mob and into captivity. The hallways were mirrors reflecting a harsh white light that pierced my eyes. I tried to hide them in my lap, but the executioner pulled me back to seated. It seemed disobedience would not be tolerated, and I wanted a good kill, so I sat tall and held my eyes open with my thumbs and index fingers. Tears rolled down my cheeks like mercury.

We entered a preparation room where I was told to stand. A henchman appeared, and the two conversed in a coded language made only of numbers. In front of me were two showers, one occupied by a quivering woman who pulled the water down on top of herself with one hand while attempting to cover her breasts with the other. Her eyes peered out behind curtains of black hair matted to her face by the torrent. She looked through me and shivered. The assistant unwrapped a pair of silver shears, and with a single cut down the length of my back I, too, was naked. I stood next to her, our eyes locked in a sympathetic gaze. The water enveloped me, though I do not know from whence it came. I was purified.

The delousing was over quickly, and they rushed to dry me with stiff cotton towels. I was dressed, reseated, and wheeled to the execution chamber— a small room warmed by an electric sun. The assistant smeared me across the top of the gurney like butter on brioche.

I was ice. She had said as much before. To kill me, they would thaw me. Servants formed a line in the hallway and entered one after another, bringing a change of blankets, each one hotter than the last. It was having the desired effect. My solid became fluid, and I felt it slowly drain from my chest to my shoulders and hips, down my arms and legs, and out my fingers and toes. I embraced death, but I had no energy to meet him properly.

If he wanted me, he would have to find me.

In sleep.

Chapter Six

I awoke in a hospital bed in searing pain. My arm swelled against the squeeze of a fresh plaster cast, and I cried out. The nurse came quickly. He had been waiting for me, he said. Medicine would help, and now that I was awake, I could take some. He would notify the doctor, fetch the pills, and be right back. Blankets were layered on top of me like geological strata, and at its core, movement, heat, and life had returned. Sweat bubbled along my skin as I struggled to unbury myself.

"Leave a few," a voice said as it entered the room. "They'll help support the body as it rediscovers its equilibrium."

"What happened?" It would take time for me to reconstruct the night of the protest and the strangeness that brought me to that hospital bed. In the moment, it was all still a blur.

"Quite a bit actually." She sat on a stool and rolled over to the bed, her white coat tails brushing the tiled floor. She peeled back the first page on the clipboard in front of her and read. "Bruised diaphragm, topical exposure to and ingestion of a chemical agent, multiple fractures in the lower left arm, and hypothermia. You checked yourself into the ER last night."

"I don't have insurance." The unbidden confession spilled from my mouth like the marital status of a man at a strip club. She laughed, crossing the room to grab the TV remote. A small screen mounted to the wall flicked on, and she scrolled through channels until she found a cable news network. The crawler at the bottom read: "Violence Erupts Between Police and Protesters at the National Mall: Homeless 'Tent City' Burned."

Off screen commentators jockeyed to claim a moral high ground that shifted between law and order and the freedom to peaceably assemble. In the corner, a looped video showed a single man in between a crowd of civilians and a line of police, caught in no man's land, alone. A yellow circle highlighted an object that moved toward him as the video crawled forward frame by frame. It reached him like the docking of a spaceship, striking below the ribs. He fell and was consumed by a creeping haze. Police in gas masks entered the shot, batons raised. He was struck down but rose again. He kicked, and the officer crumbled. Soon all was obscured by smoke. The video repeated.

"Is that. . ."

"It's on every outlet." She smiled at me before making annotations in my chart. "You know, we actually get quite a few celebrities through here, more than you might think—Senators, CEOs, world leaders. Most of them don't have insurance either, and we give them all the time they need to pay us back. Meanwhile our billing department hounds the shit out of every single mother who brings her kid in with a fever 'cause she had no one else to turn to." She clicked the top of her pen and pulled her glasses down into her lap. Her hair was silvered and dull, but her eyes shone with the vitality of youth. "I'm not sure where you fall on that spectrum, but I'm sure we'll get our money back. Nothing sticks like medical debt."

I laid in bed for a few more hours, sipping hot tea and bathing in a river of opiates. Eventually, the doctor handed me discharge papers and a discrete twenty to get myself home. I dressed in donated clothes and collapsed into the first taxi I could find.

It was a resplendent autumn day, and the capital shone triumphant at every turn. The cab rolled through late-afternoon traffic, stopping at every yellow as if in unhurried appreciation of glass and stone. The windows were down, and the driver kept the radio loud, blasting out the best of the 80's, 90's, and today, the looping soundtrack of the perpetual generation. The heart of the capital beat as it always had, pulsing pedestrians down broad sidewalks and cars through narrow arteries. Only the Mall looked at all abnormal, full of dump trucks and sanitation crews and a few lines of police tape for the tourists to circumvent.

We hadn't changed a thing. The gears of the great machine kept turning, the blood and tears ground from us the night before nothing but lubrication. If I had thought myself special, if I had thought myself transcendent, the view of the capital skyline recessing through the rear window exposed my folly. The capital was a lie that could not be made true, like an indefatigable mirage that recessed each time we advanced. It sat there rigid on the horizon as it always had, as it always would. I closed my eyes and turned away.

The stairs at Squire's apartment were punishing, and I paused often to catch my breath and slow the pulse that squeezed against the broken bones of my arm. At his door, my hand touched the knob, but I couldn't make it turn. What would I say to them? What combination of words could convey my sense of humiliation and shame? They trusted us—friends, allies, strangers. They trusted us and followed our lead. And for what? To be gassed, shot at, beaten, scorned, their possessions burned, their community scattered? I wanted to run, to flee down the stairs and never look back, but where would I go? There was nowhere left.

The knob twisted from the other side, and the door opened. Before I could see her face, it was buried in my chest, her arms squeezing my waist with all the strength she had. Five-foot nothing and bursting with tears.

"We thought you were dead," Regina cried. "No one knew where you were. We called everywhere—the hospital, the police station, the morgue. No one could give us a straight answer."

I wrapped my arms around her and felt her wet breath seep into my second-hand sweatshirt.

"I . . ." My throat was tight and hot, and the words struggled to break through. "You were right," I said. Tears fell freely.

The Mouth limped over to us. He had fallen on the sprint from the capitol and laid on the grass clutching his ankle when the first canisters of tear gas dropped in front of him. The flash bangs lit up the cloud like lightning. The pepper balls fell around him like hail. He was cut off by the storm. Alone. He smooched my cheek and wrapped his thin arms around us like twine, bundling us in his embrace.

Squire approached, a pained smile on his lips. "We didn't want to be right." His body enclosed us, soft and warm. His beard tickled my face.

"And Hawke?" I asked.

"Jail," Squire said. "They caught him near the monument trying to pull books out of the library tent."

Regina lifted her head and sniffed. Her eyes were pink and glassy.

Squire sighed. "They still haven't set bail."

Chapter Seven

For the longest time we held each other there in the doorway to Squire's apartment, shipwrecked survivors clinging to our only life raft. When we finally released, nobody drifted far. The Mouth and I said we didn't want to go home, but in reality there was no home left beyond those four eggshell walls. I took the couch; the Mouth took the loveseat. Squire pulled the mattress off his bed, and the four of us slept in the living room, everyone slightly displaced.

When the call from my landlord finally came—improbably on the Mouth's number—my eviction was a forgone conclusion. "Pay me my money, or get the fuck out!" He tried to sound intimidating, but I knew they weren't his words. They were a repetition; the words of the bank that held the second mortgage on his property—words he feared hearing more than he relished repeating. It was all dead air. He could have the room and everything in it. I stopped by long enough to drop off the key and fill a knapsack with essentials. I banished the rest.

Our protest had the good fortune of being followed by absolutely nothing of note, and the news cycle idled for weeks on the confrontation. The

Mouth ate it up. He changed his profile pic to an image of himself kneeling in front of the cloud of tear gas as it obscured the monument and the fires behind. He reposted the video of me getting struck by the rubber bullet, smashed by the baton, rising up despite it all and kicking an officer to the ground. His following quintupled. For a time I sat glued to the TV, my arm in Regina's lap as she slowly blackened my cast. But in the end there was nothing much to see, just echoes of ourselves caught in a spin cycle, growing increasingly sterile with every loop.

"Where the hell is Squire?" The Mouth's phone went black, and he rose to seated for the first time that afternoon.

Regina didn't look up from the row of hearts she was tessellating. "Like I said, he has class today."

"No, he doesn't. He finally took my advice and dropped that nonsense. I mean, where do they get off teaching anti-trust? Who do they think they're fooling?"

Regina and I said nothing.

"Anyway, we have a shuffleboard date." He stood and looked blankly around the room, then opened the door. "Don't wait up."

Then it was just the two of us.

"I think I'm done with this," I said, switching off the TV.

Regina capped her sharpie and returned my arm. "It's a lot, isn't it? It's OK. I have just the thing."

She disappeared into the bedroom and returned with a pad of low-grade recycled paper. The cover was bright yellow.

"Crosswords?"

"Yup," she said, smiling. She grabbed a bag of chips and returned to the couch to lay with her head on my thighs, then flipped past completed puzzles to the next clean page. "Oh! 'Spring Things.' You ready?"

I looked down at her, this cat purring in my lap. "I've never been more ready. Let's do it."

I was never very good with word games, so for a while I just watched her work. She read the clues, then thought through the answers out loud. *If this than that, but then what do we do over here? Certainly twenty-one across wouldn't start like that. Sixteen down must be something else.* Every so often she would stop and look up at me.

"What?"

"Chip?" Her eyes pleaded, and I placed another on her lips.

"OK, you got this one," she said. "Four letters. 'Perpetual confusion.'"

"Love?"

She dropped the book to her chest and rolled her eyes. "It doesn't fit."

****

For several days we returned to that position—me on the couch with snacks, Regina sprawled out with her head in my lap. Sometimes it was crosswords, sometimes a movie. Sometimes we drank beer and gabbed until Squire and the Mouth found their way home after bar close. Sometimes she would sleep, and I would lower the volume on the TV and sit there watching her chest rise and fall as she slowly slipped away from me.

—*God, the two of you were insufferable back then.*

We were in that position one afternoon, watching something I would never choose to watch myself, the Mouth beside us scrolling through clickbait, when Squire came through the front door with Hawke under his wing. He looked haggard, emotionally drained.

"Hawke! They let you go?" Regina rose but made no move to greet him.

"Something like that."

I walked over, and we embraced, slapping each other on the back like men always do, our chests echoing like drums. "It's good to see you," I said.

"In fact, they had to let him go," Squire added. "With sentiment what it is, no capital jury would convict him."

Hawke fell onto the sofa like a spent candle, his body soft wax, his fire extinguished. Squire grabbed him a beer, and we huddled around as Hawke recounted every detail of his arrest and detention—the heat of the fires as he ran through Tent City, the boot that kicked at the back of his knee, the unnecessary bludgeoning of the baton as he tried in vain to submit to his arrest, the glares of the officers at the station and the feeling he was not a suspect but a captured enemy combatant, the cold showers, the cold meals, the cold bars.

The Mouth sat silently, projecting himself into Hawke's story, imagining it had been him to barrel through the line, to weather the blows, to sleep on a suspended cot waiting for freedom. When Hawke asked us what happened, I told him of the gas and the flash bangs and the line of men advancing in riot gear, scattering us like rats. The Mouth made no move to speak.

"It was a trap," Hawke said. "They wanted us gone, and we gave them the perfect opportunity."

"I don't think your little stunt helped any," Regina said. "They might have let you disperse peacefully if you hadn't steamrolled one of their officers."

"It was a trap, Regina. They surrounded us. This was exactly what they planned." He looked to me for confirmation.

"They fired high," I said. "They blocked our exit with their first rounds of tear gas. And they were on top of us pretty soon after that."

She gave me a disappointed frown. "Yes. But only after he charged them. It was reckless, Hawke. You got a lot of people hurt." Regina went to the kitchen. I thought she might boil water for tea, but she threw ice in a rocks glass and poured herself some of Squire's Laphroaig.

"I acted, Regina. It was a trap. You would have seen it yourself if you hadn't pussied out on us."

"Acted like an ass." She took a sip of scotch, and if it burned on the way down she didn't show it. "How many of those books did they let you keep, huh?"

"Fuck you."

"You wish."

"Whoa!" Squire stood and held out his hands. "Let's all calm down. We don't need to assign blame here. What the police did was unjust. Period. The question is, what do we do about it?"

Hawke sank back into the cushions. "It's over, Squire. Tent City is gone. Everyone who lived there has scattered across the river, out of town, and back on the road. The capital rejected them. They're invisible again. What is there to do?"

The Mouth stood. "There's still a community online. And a lot of energy and media attention. We can still make something of this."

I shook my head. "Perhaps, but not here. This movement was about giving people visibility and a voice, but the capital is blind and deaf. We can march and protest and scream at the top of our lungs, but it won't change a thing. Here, we will always be invisible and unheard."

For a moment there was nothing but silence. Regina stood next to me and leaned her head against my shoulder. Squire squeezed her limp hand.

"The decision may already be made for us," he said. "I've been cut off, and my savings are basically gone. I have the apartment until the lease expires next month, but then we have to move out."

"Squibs, what happened?" the Mouth asked. "Why are you just now telling us this?"

"It's a fairly recent occurrence."

Regina dropped his hand and fell onto the loveseat.

"I'm sorry," Squire said as he sat beside Hawke. "I've wanted to say this ever since the night of the march, but our group has been incomplete. I'm sorry I wasn't there with you, in fact. I'm sorry I divided us. Maybe I haven't been as committed as I could have been, but I see it all so clearly now. We can't do this alone. We have to do it together. So, I'm glad my parents cut me off, and I'm glad I'm moving out of here. I'm tired of having my friends schlep up six flights of stairs and sleep on my floor like vagrants and vagabonds. I want to start over with you. I want a place where each of us belongs, something we all own together."

"Outside the city?" the Mouth asked.

"As far away as we can get," Hawke muttered.

The vision of Isidora flashed before my eyes, perfect and complete. Women in aprons hauling baskets of vegetables up from sun-drenched fields to the communal canteen where everyone eats together as one. Men in overalls wielding hammers and tongs and bending the world to their will on an anvil of justice. In the evenings, the braziers would be lit, and the people would gather under the stars and affirm a shared understanding of TRUTH.

—Today, for the first time, I see you. Today, for the first time, you are real...

"We need to go someplace new," I said. "Someplace we build ourselves. Everything I'm surrounded by here is fake, and I'm sick of it. When I look, I want everything I see to be real. The rest of the world can just fade away for all I care."

"Remind me to stay in your line of sight," Regina smiled, her cheeks flush.

"I mean it," I continued. "Everything we have we built ourselves. And they keep taking it from us or burning it down. Why do we put up with it? Let's build something where they can't reach us, not here but out in some fly-over state, in some already forgotten land. For us, for the residents of Tent City, for everyone this world overlooks, let's build a place where we all belong. An invisible city where everyone is seen."

"Like a commune?" Regina asked.

"Or a collective. Something like that. A place where we can put into practice what we've so far only dared put into words. We want to change the way we relate to one another. How can we do that without a fresh start?"

Hawke leaned forward. "We could be autonomous, self-sufficient, off the grid."

"Hell, we could be our own grid," I said. "Imagine empty fields waiting to be plowed. Imagine consuming only what you produce with your own two hands."

The Mouth walked to the fridge for another beer. "A lot of people are primed to join us. They had Tent City, but it was never really theirs. They're tired of being displaced. They need a locus, an axis mundi around which they can recenter themselves."

"We can give them some real stability," I said. "Not sticks and tarpaulins and idle time but houses and workshops and honest work." I turned to Squire. "And we can do it together. Out there where we're safe. Out there where nothing will ever come between us."

From that moment on, Isidora never felt like anything but an inevitability. We had inserted ourselves in the capital like a donated kidney, and despite the terminal illness that consumed it, the body rejected us. Renting a dilapidated group house on the outskirts of town, groveling for mindless work and base pay, printing lofty manifestos to have them thrown unread into the capital's storm drains, growing old and bitter and unambitious—this counterfactual was never really considered.

—The TRUTH has no counterfactual. It is singular, incontestable, self-evident.

In the month that followed, our plan came into focus. The Mouth took it upon himself to find a suitable location for our new home, and he received a steady stream of scouting reports from followers seized by the idea of self-determination. He selected three to visit personally—a shuttered car plant, an abandoned washing machine factory, and a derelict textile mill—all decaying in the gutted corpse of the country's industrial heartland. The latter was so long forgotten that the building had collapsed in on itself. The former sat in pristine condition on the outskirts of an idle town, waiting for a subsidy or stimulus plan that would peel the plywood off the doors and return everyone to work.

Only the washing machine factory held any promise. On returning to the capital, the Mouth assured us it would be the perfect place for our cleansing.

While he was away, we busied ourselves with preparations—pawning possessions, liquidating bank accounts, severing ourselves from the world we looked to leave behind. Time did not slow for us. Hours passed like hours, minutes like minutes, and when the day finally came, it was unheralded and plain. We swung camping backpacks onto our shoulders, and Squire turned the key to his apartment lock one last time. We moved in somber silence but felt no shame. Like a defeated army we knew that even steps taken in retreat carry one forward. The vision of future victories transformed our shameful expulsion into a glorious escape.

******

We abandoned the capital the way the Romans abandoned Carthage—superior to an enemy humiliated, poisoned, and left to its obsolescence. Never again would that city bear fruit in our minds. Never again would its gilded domes catch fire in the sun and beckon us home. Our small band clambered into the coach of a westbound train, and as we shot from Union Station like a bullet from a gun across the river and into the Shenandoah hills, the city and all its inhabitants, all its life, all its banality, and all its beauty were obliterated in our wake. The train skipped from rail to rail, the rough crashing of the wheels across gaps and imperfections smoothed by springs so that we might sway gently above as if palm trees in a salted gale, as if gliding on nothing but air. My head bounced against the frosted window as I dozed in perfect contentment.

Hawke paced the length of the car, catching no one's gaze and returning none himself. His mind, like the wheels beneath us, spun relentlessly, feeling every bump on our path, crushing every spot yet unsmooth. Like the springs of the carriage, Squire squeezed and stretched. He bowed his head low between his knees when thinking of everything that had just been cleaved off his life. But then as the weight rocked off his hunched shoulders and the future, pregnant with possibility, unclouded his mind, he rose and looked at the fallow fields streaking past the window and thought of thawed ground and the planting about to begin.

The Mouth was effervescent, bubbling incessantly about the factory that awaited us, its dimensions and its many superlatives. Regina sat beside him, gently smiling, asking probing questions, allowing herself to submit to the intoxication of possibility. We had shed the weight of the capital forever, and for the first time in many months, we were happy and free.

> —*And we're still free. Free in the Isidora we built.*
>
> —"But I'm cut off from that happiness. I nothing had, and yet enough for youth; Joy in illusion, ardent thirst for TRUTH..."
>
> —*I think that's enough for one day, don't you? Let's get some sleep and pick back up in the morning.*
>
> —Goodnight, Dean.
>
> —*Sweet dreams, O great Omicron.*

Part Two

Chapter Eight

The town that was Isidora was never a destination, so when you arrive it's difficult to know for sure that you're there. Dropped halfway along the great western migration route like a broken wagon wheel, Isidora was the town you settled in when you could not take one more step along the trail. Its founding was the surrendering of a dream of pacific waters and cities of gold. Its denizens were those content to sell you fatback on the road to paradise. But there was money in that, so Isidora endured. When the schooner ruts were memorialized in steel, the meatpacking industry flourished, dispatching pork raised on prairie grass to consumers on the coasts. It was a humble wealth, and for a time the town could coddle and comfort.

Still, the fact remained: Isidora was never a destination, though it quickly became an origin, a point of disembarkation for those who longed for more. Over time its children were scattered in search of promises Isidora could no longer keep, and the town languished, not in the magisterial refinement of those great continental cities but as a quintessential new-world upstart whose youth abandoned it prematurely.

Our train did not so much stop at a station as loiter for a moment in an empty field, there being nothing but a weathered pavilion and hand-painted sign to reassure us this was a proper node on the line. "ISIDORA." We threw our backpacks onto a platform overgrown with grass and waste and jumped down next to them. The doors slammed behind us. We stood and watched as the train glided over the horizon, transporting others toward western destinies. The December air was thin and dry and carried nothing but the sounds of the receding carriages and the faint smell of manure.

"Is this it?" Squire asked. There were no fences, turnstiles, newsstands, or food carts, not even bathrooms. With the train's departure, the station lost all meaning and was returned to pure form—four beams and a wooden roof rotting away in the middle of a field.

"Of course it is," the Mouth said. "Let's get moving. It'll be dark soon, and we have a ways to go."

A two-lane road intersected with the station, and my eyes followed it along barren ground dotted with cottonwoods to where it met a highway. Distant headlights raced through the growing dusk unimpeded by the bother of topography. I hoped one might slow and turn and come to ferry us to our new home, but I knew there would be no one there to receive us. Reality had been reduced to the size of five camping backpacks, and we could only rely on what was inside. I shivered and zipped my coat up to my throat.

The Mouth walked down the length of the platform and slid from its edge, then started following the rails, not west where the sky was aglow in the day's last light but east, back toward the darkness from whence we had come. He plodded along the ballast like a bloodhound on a scent, and we followed close behind.

"Why not take the road?" I asked, my breath condensing before me.

"This way is quicker. About a mile ahead there is an abandoned spur that once serviced the industrial park. Junemark 6 is on it. We can follow this right to the back door."

Hawke walked along the tracks themselves, hopping from tie to tie or balancing on the rails. We were alone, and the earth gradually fell away from us into fallow fields and drainage ditches. Nothing could sneak up on us, least of all a locomotive, but our absolute exposure, our unobstructed vision, only made me feel less secure. In our dislocation, our world had shifted into an unfamiliar plane, and I questioned if any of the previous rules still applied. If Hawke wasn't smacked in the face with a freight engine, might he not tumble off the rails into a thorn bush? Or float away into the naked sky, pushed by a new gravity that no longer pulled? And what if he was perfectly safe? What if he was standing on tracks where no trains would ever run again? What if the carriages that left us in Isidora, that clattered off into the setting sun, were the last there would ever be?

"Are we sure this place is completely abandoned?" Hawke shouted down.

"In fact, the Junemark company filed for bankruptcy a few years back," Squire said. "It liquidated its assets to pay off creditors and bondholders. I'm not sure who owns the facility now, but Junemark won't be asking for it back."

Twenty minutes later we found the industrial spur. The switch joining it to the main line had been removed, and its rails ended in a tangle of sumac and milk thistle. Night descended and brought with it a piercing cold and a sky full of stars that flickered above us like frozen flames. The Mouth stopped to pull a flashlight out of his bag. Hawke took a few strides off the path to piss on a bush.

"Have you ever seen so many stars?" Regina asked, her head raised to the heavens. "We never get to see them in the city. You almost forget they're there." She leaned into Squire who rubbed warmth into her arms.

The sky was bursting with pinpoints of light, in some areas so dense they appeared to be woven together with spans of celestial thread. I spun until I saw the hunter climbing the southern quadrant, his faithful hound trailing behind with Sirius hung around its neck like a radiant dog tag. His arm was raised above him, a club suspended, ever ready to crush. In front of him was the arc of a raised shield. At his back, shoulder Betelgeuse burned crimson like blood letting from a wound of betrayal. At least the sky was familiar.

"We don't always see them, but there's nothing more eternal," Squire said.

Hawke looked over his shoulder and snorted. "They die like everything else and far more spectacularly. Some of them are dying right now. Some of them have been dead for centuries."

"All the more reason to show them respect. I'd like to keep burning for centuries after I die."

"And so you shall." The Mouth swung his bag onto his shoulder. "Look, there you are already." He pointed to the hunter's constellation. "See? It takes three stars to hold up your pants. And your paunch shall proceed you for all eternity."

Regina laughed and wrapped Squire's hands around her chest.

"Very funny," Squire said. "But those stars are already taken. In fact, that's Orion."

"That's its old name, its pre-revolutionary name. Henceforth and forever more it shall be known as O'Squire, the wayward lawyer holding aloft a tray of gin martinis." He struck a waiter's pose.

I laughed. "Squire—heaven's advocate."

"What about you, chief?" The Mouth turned to me. "What will your constellation be?"

I rubbed my hands together and buried them in my jacket pockets. "I have no desire to keep burning after I die."

"You don't want to be remembered?"

"I've thought about it. I've imagined my funeral and what people might say about me. But no, I don't think I care, and I certainly won't care after I'm gone. Everything that outlives me is irrelevant."

Hawke zipped up his pants and jumped back onto the trail. "Perhaps

Dean can find a supernova to name in your honor. You know, something that ends in a catastrophic fireball."

I wasn't sure what Hawke meant, but his comment felt like a threat. He had been in a foul mood since his release from prison, fouler than normal, and though he supported our decision to move to Isidora, deep within him the fires that torched Tent City still smoldered, waiting to set the world alight.

"Sure. Why not?" I pointed forward, down rusted rails that disappeared into the blackness. "Let's keep moving."

Two parallel lines meandered through the darkness—across empty plains, through narrow ravines, over a shallow stream. As we entered the industrial park, minor spurs broke from the main, as if by mitosis, sending progeny toward barren concrete slabs and crumbling warehouses still haunted by the specters of rolling stock. When we finally reached Junemark 6, the world was dark and cold, and the spare, windowless walls of the Mines rose through the beam of our flashlights like a fortress. A wide train yard ran beside it, littered with boxcars, flatcars, and hoppers like the siege engines of some long-defeated host.

Only the Mouth had stood there before, and at the time that place was nothing but the backdrop of an unlikely daydream. Seeing it now, actualized with the four of us standing beside him, brought on a rush of unrequested exposition. The Mines—a cavernous, undivided production zone built to expand Junemark's operations—sat in the center of the compound punctuated with steam pipes, loading docks, and smokestacks. It was a blank slate, infinitely pliable, that could be subdivided to suit the needs of the revolution—workshop, canteen, greenhouse. Behind, an office tower—the Winter Quarters—could serve as a dormitory should anyone else decide to follow us to Isidora. The train yard that formed out of the industrial spur at our feet ended at a machine shed perched on the lip of a depression that rolled down to a pond and empty fields. Opposite the Mines—across the train yard on the northern edge of the compound—sat the Ark, Junemark's original factory and administrative building, ringed by an aging brick wall.

"The water tower is still functional, I think," the Mouth said. "Or could be made so with some minor repairs, though I don't know who among us is fit to repair water towers. Maybe Hawke. It's ringed by a catwalk and gives you a good look at the entire complex and Isidora proper. And the surrounding wooded areas and farmland. Wanna go up?"

"Tomorrow," I said, cold and exhausted. "When there's light. For now, where's home?"

"The old factory building. We can use the C-suite offices as bedrooms. There's one for each of us. Follow me."

The Mouth led us across the rails and along the walls of the Ark, which were topped with broken glass embedded in concrete. Halfway down they were interrupted by twin wrought-iron gates hung below a sign that spelled in arching letters, "The Junemark Co." A chain and lock held them closed. The Mouth dropped his bag and pulled out a key, which he handed to me. The chain fell at my feet, and the doors of our new home swung open for the first time.

The foyer was empty, and the hardwood floors and bare walls felt colder than the night air we had just left outside. Beyond, dust defied gravity in a drab receiving room. Through the haze, our flashlights caught the angular lines of armchairs upholstered in mustard cloth, ashtrays built into side tables, and an upturned bar cart. In the building's heyday, the room would have represented the threshold for some plucky lubricant vendor who would be asked to sit and cool his heels while the corporate boys downed martinis upstairs. He'd refuse the coffee that would only make him jittery during his presentation and douse his nerves instead in chain-smoked nicotine. But the gatekeepers were long gone, and our group moved ahead unobstructed.

We climbed a marble stairway that doubled back on itself left and right as it rose to the second floor. My bag had grown heavy, and I grasped at the thin metal railing to pull myself up. At the top, five doors with gilded nameplates punctuated a wood-paneled antechamber.

"Charming," Regina said. "Though a little corporate for my taste."

"Don't worry, Reg," the Mouth said with a grin. "It's a hostile takeover." He moved to the center of the room. "See? One for each of us. Hawke and I are on the left, COO and CMO. Squibs and Regina on the right, CFO and CIO. Chief, you're in the middle. Congratulations, Mr. CEO." He bowed and gestured toward the center door.

"I'll be chief janitor if it means I can go to sleep." I reached for the handle of the center door but paused and turned to look back at my friends. "I suppose it's only us now."

The Mouth walked over and put a hand on my shoulder. "Buddy, it was always only us. Only now we are free from that oppressive otherness. Only now we are able to build the just world we deserve. Only now we are..." He yawned and rubbed his glassy eyes. "Fucking hell. You get the picture."

"Only now we are free to sleep," I said. "Good night, friends. Tomorrow we build a new Isidora."

I pushed through the heavy wooden door and closed it behind me. Then I stood alone in the tomb-like silence of my new home, my flashlight touching on foreign objects buried in dust—an oak desk and receiving chairs, a glass-topped sideboard with mirrored doors, an armchair and bookcases, an area rug made of concentric orange and yellow circles. I would have my way with all of it but not that first night. Alone in that foreign space, I felt an irresistible deference to time—time that waited out the previous occupant, that claimed everything in his passing, that left the room and all its furnishings feeling unclean. In my first act as a citizen of Isidora, liberated from the past and all who came before, I touched as little as possible, rolled my sleeping bag out on the rug, and dropped into an uneasy sleep.

Chapter Nine

I was eight years old again—eight and three-quarters—back in the living room of the old ranch on Chaney Road, standing in the middle of the area rug as the adults spoke above my head. They had come to see Dad, and it took all the composure he had to play the role they demanded of him: to be the focal point of their shock and sadness, to let them hold his hand in theirs, to watch them weep into his tissues, to invite them for coffee in the parlor where they'd worry and whisper. The younger kids had no clue. They were simply excited to have cousins around, and they ran manic circuits between the scotcheroos brought by the pastor's wife and the jungle gym in the back. The older kids were despondent and locked themselves in the basement, convinced they were affected the most.

Seeing as it was her funeral, Mom had the least to do to prepare, and she sat quietly in her favorite chair, waiting for all the well-wishers to arrive and the ceremony to begin. I tugged at the top button of the collared shirt gifted by the Sunday school teacher the day before. Mom called me over and straightened my bowtie. *There now. That's better.* Tears welled up in my eyes, and I crawled into her lap. She ran her fingers through my hair, stroking my scalp and sending waves of calming tingles down my spine. She told me if I sat still during the service we could share a milkshake after, but she wore her own face like a mask, and her lips stayed still as she spoke.

I thought she should know, but my uncle warned me not to say anything, and everyone else pretended not to notice. But how could they not know? I knew, and I thought I should say something. She was dead. When the words formed in my mind, the thought panicked me, and I tried to wriggle free from her grasp. I wanted to scream it—to yell it into her face. "You're dead! You're dead! You're dead!" But how could I? It wasn't something a boy said to his mother.

Then we're at the kitchen table playing Monopoly, like we always did. She rolls doubles. She is finally free from jail. She goes to move, but her hand passes through the silver dog. I push it forward, and she smiles.

****

I woke with a jolt, gasping for air. When I finally caught my breath, I was doubled over the armchair, my sweat-soaked clothes in a pile at my feet.

It had been years since I had last had the dream—not since before the capital—and I felt angry and ashamed that it had found me again in Isidora.

So much for a fresh start.

I dressed in dry clothes and snuck outside to find the compound enveloped in morning mist. Condensate of the previous day's vapor frosted the grass that grew amongst the tracks of the train yard and blurred the blank walls of the Mines. The roof of the water tower caught the first rays of sunlight, and birds in the nearby cottonwoods began to rouse. I crawled onto the dusty floor of the nearest boxcar and in stillness waited for the new day to burn off the residuals of the past.

"You're up early."

Startled, I turned to see Regina's head barely visible at the boxcar's other door. "Jesus, you scared the crap out of me."

"I called out a couple times. You OK?"

"Sure," I sighed. "I just didn't sleep well."

Regina rounded the boxcar to stand below me. "Was it the ghosts?"

I rolled my eyes. Regina would be sympathetic, but she wouldn't understand.

"I'm just kidding. Help me up?"

She gave me her hands, and I pulled her into the car beside me.

"But seriously, this place is creepy. There may not be ghosts, but there's definitely a feeling. My room is full of old corporate furniture, and it's as if the souls of the people who used it before are still trapped inside."

"Mine too," I said. "It's unsettling. I don't even want to touch anything. Are the others up?"

I started to stand, but she caught my arm in a grasp she was not anxious to release.

"They were up late wandering around in the dark. Stay with me here for a bit longer. Let them sleep." She leaned her head against my shoulder, and I leaned mine on top of hers. Her hair was soft and smelled like vanilla, and the breath that entered my nose rolled like a calming ripple down my outstretched arms.

In the filtered foggy light, the factory appeared to be on pause, awaiting the morning whistle and the punching of timecards. But in the glimmer of dew on overgrown weeds and the darkness that hid behind broken loading dock doors, the dereliction revealed itself.

"Is it everything you hoped it'd be?" she asked.

"I didn't really hope for anything. In fact, I'd hoped for nothing. Tabula rasa. But it's amazing how much lingers on after something ends. I thought we'd start building on day one, but it looks like there's a lot of destruction left to do. The past still haunts this place."

She sat up straight and twisted her torso left and right, stretching the sleep from her body. "True, but we don't need to destroy *everything*. We may find we can put some of the remnants to good use." She raised her chin and yawned like a cat. It floated in the air, and I caught it like contagion.

"Maybe." The yawn rolled out my open mouth and passed back to her. "I guess we'll have to see what they left behind."

"Mmm." She sat back on her knees and stretched her arms above her head. The curve of her slender neck slipped below the hem of her sweatshirt. She pulled air deep into her raised chest and yawned again.

"Would you stop that?" I slapped her exposed belly. "You're making me want to go back to bed."

She grinned and pushed me to the carriage floor. "You'd have to take me with you."

"There's barely room in the sleeping bag for me. Where would I put you?"

She scoffed and rose to stand in the doorway. "Silly boy. You lack imagination."

Light seeped through the wooden slats of the boxcar. Outside the fog was already starting to lift, revealing to us the plot of land that would become our new home, the origin of a society that we would build ourselves, independent from the world of make-believe beyond its walls. We would be untouchable there. No one would block our ascent. But I also knew no one would catch us if we fell. Like a man stranded on a deserted island, I felt a sense of liberation—and dread.

"Regina, can I ask you something?"

She turned, her solemn eyes meeting mine. "Anything at all."

"Why did you come?" Her expression remained stoic and composed, but I felt something within her retreat. "Don't get me wrong—I'm so glad you did. Squire needs you here. *I* need you. But out of all of us, it felt like you had the most to lose."

She looked away from me. A flock of geese flew overhead in a V, two lines streaming behind an appointed leader. It was late in the season for them to be heading south, and the fields long harvested below would offer little sustenance.

"I'm here because I want to be. I'm here because I know that no matter what I had back in the capital, I wouldn't be able to hold on to it. Someone or something would have taken it away eventually. That's just how it is. Nothing seems to last. But maybe here, things can be different."

"Do you think anyone else will join us?"

"No. Not at first—I don't care what Dean says. No one wants to leave a place where they are cold and hungry to go be cold and hungry somewhere else. But maybe this spring when we can provide for them, when this place offers real security. Yes, I think they'll come."

I nodded as I stood. "Speaking of cold and hungry. I am both. They've slept long enough. It's time for breakfast."

We found Squire milling about downstairs in his PJs. I left Regina with him as I went to wake the others. Hawke was already descending the stairs, dressing as he walked, a cotton T-shirt rolling down the almond moguls of his abs. Hawke was the kind of man who wasn't bothered by cold, or at least he pretended not to be. He no doubt slept naked, and the image of his body sliding out of a vinyl sleeping bag formed in my mind uninvited.

The door to the Mouth's suite was still closed, and I didn't hear anything from the other side. As I approached, the gilded nameplate caught my eye. "Guy LaBouche—Chief Marketing Officer." I opened the door without knocking. He was on the floor, spilling out of a half-zipped sleeping bag, snoring softly.

—Our hero finally enters the scene.

"Buddy." I prodded him in the back with my big toe. "You overslept."

He groaned and rubbed his eyes. "What time is it?"

"I have no idea."

"Then how do you know I overslept?"

I kicked him in the ribs. "Because I'm hungry, and we can't eat until you get your ass up."

"Well," he said, yawning, "that's reasonable."

I left him to dress and returned to the receiving room where Hawke had already set up the stove. We left the capital knowing we would arrive with only that which we could carry, the sum of our worldly possessions jammed into our camping backpacks. But still, we found room for dry goods and bottles of drinking water—enough to last a couple of days. We had ridiculed Squire for packing a carton of eggs in rolled sweatpants, insisting he would arrive with a backpack full of yolk, but having transported them safely, none of us complained when he served us fresh omelettes that morning. We ate them in grateful silence under the front room's large bay window as orange light caressed the dusty parquet floors.

The morning was devoted to a tour of the grounds. The Mines and Winter Quarters would be essential for growing our community, being relatively modern and spacious, but we all agreed their reclamation would have to wait. By sleeping in the Ark, it had become our origin, the intersection of our x and y, the point from which everything else was measured. It had its advantages, of course. The bicycle lock that fell at my feet on the night of our arrival had replaced a heavier one cut by the Mouth, one placed there long before Junemark went into bankruptcy, and it seemed the liquidators assumed the building was empty when dispossessing the factory of its soluble assets. Like a museum, the mid-century furnishings remained and gave the building an immediate sense of home—if not ours then someone else's.

The most usable space, its vast factory floor, had sat neglected for decades and was littered with heavy iron fixtures and conveyor belts long rusted into immobility. Pulleys and long, hemp ropes hung from the exposed rafters. As we walked through the grand hall, light pouring in from a row of second-story windows, Hawke's mind assigned to the detritus an appropriate disposition—salvage, scrap, junk. The promise of future labor brought him a clarified energy, a pacific buzz.

"The chains and sprockets are obviously valuable. And maybe some of the sheet metal. Who knows what we'll need to build? Anything that articulates is likely too rusted to be functional. The replaceable parts—nuts, wing nuts, bolts. . ." He picked up a wooden cigar box and ran his fingers through small bits of metal. "Yeah. I wouldn't trust them."

Regina slapped a hulking press that had been bolted to the cement floor. "Hawke, do these things strike you as strange? They seem out of place. In fact, nothing here seems to be designed to make washing machines."

"Yeah, you're right. More suited to heavy machinery. Maybe engines or agricultural machines."

The Mouth pushed against one, attempting to rock it. "They're gonna be a bitch to move out of here."

"They may need to stay," Hawke said.

"Oh good," Squire added. "Our first statuary."

In the middle of the factory's length, in a clearing void of machinery and debris, a skylight in rows of tented glass let light tumble down into the room. Below, a circle had been worn into the floor like the path of a dog at the end of its rope. The apparatus that created it—no doubt some wheeled instrument that rotated around a central pivot—had been removed, leaving behind nothing but the dilated pupil of a fatigued iris.

We sat on the rim of that weathered curvature, legs sore and stomachs rumbling from just a half-day on our feet. Eventually, we would grow the strength demanded of us by life at Isidora, more even, but in those early days the mere act of being exhausted us. Sheltered from the winter wind, the sunbeams that dripped through the bubbled glass felt almost warm, and we stretched ourselves beneath them, letting the light caress our faces and outstretched hands. Regina pulled a loaf of bread out of her bag, Squire a jar of peanut butter, and we feasted.

"I like this place," I said to no one in particular, perhaps to myself. "It belongs to us."

The Mouth nodded vigorously, his face clogged with peanut butter.

******

We retreated to our bedrooms in the afternoon to rest and unpack. My door opened to a small sitting area, two armchairs in the familiar drab yellow facing a couch I had overlooked the night before. My sleeping bag lay splayed on the rug in between. A large oak desk faced the doorway, a high-backed chair sat behind it, and along the back wall a row of windows were obscured by metal slat blinds. The other C-suite offices had exterior windows—Squire's and Regina's catching the morning sun in the east, the Mouth's and Hawke's aglow with the setting sun in the west. Mine looked out onto the shadows of the factory floor, and I would find that even at midday in summer the room was haunted by a perpetual gloom.

I unpacked my clothes and dropped them onto the shelf of a bookcase in a single, sorry pile. The office had an ensuite bathroom, and I foolishly thought about taking a shower, but of course no water came. The miles we had traveled and the dust, layered like sediment on fossilized bone, clung to me, and I wanted to wash it all away. I settled for a handful of bottled water splashed on my face and a dampened towel run between my legs. I laid on the couch, and in my inertia the day caught up with me. I was hit with a wave of exhaustion. I closed my eyes and dozed in dreamless sleep.

I awoke as I had in the morning, disoriented. Through the window I saw pink light fall on the machines of the factory floor, pillars of pitch bleeding crimson shadows, and I knew I had only been asleep for a few hours. Music from downstairs rose through the vents, carrying with it the faint smell of butane and MSG. I descended to find Hawke over the camp stove, bouncing his head and rapping along to a tinny voice coming from his cell phone's blown speakers.

—*Music? There was music? Are you sure?*

—*In the beginning, yes. Don't you remember?*

"Chicken or beef?" he asked without turning.

"What are you making?"

"Ramen. Chicken or beef? And do you want me to drop in one of the last eggs?"

"Chicken. And save the eggs for Squire. He did carry them all this way."

"Fair enough."

Hawke's hands moved from bowl to bowl. He obviously had not slept.

The others soon joined us, and we ate like half-starved dogs, none of us willing to put down our chopsticks to strike up a conversation. When the noodles were gone, I guzzled the broth and then stared longingly into the empty paper bowl flecked with herbs and ringed with yellow fat.

"Do we have any more?" I asked.

Hawke shook his head. "Not of the ramen. And we should ration the other stuff. If we eat light, we can stretch things until the end of the week."

Squire stood and surveyed the pantry table, enumerating in sighs and shrugs the food we had left. "Corn flakes but no milk. A half-jar of peanut butter. Half a loaf of bread. Three cans of tuna. Mayo. One pound of peanut M&Ms. A bag of baby carrots. Celery. Five kilos of rice. Five kilos of dried kidney beans. And two gallons of water."

"Squire, throw me the peanut butter," I said. "I'll just take a lick."

He lifted the jar and discovered a silver wrapper hidden behind. "Oh, and this one-hundred-calorie chocolate pleasure bar, gluten free. Who brought this?"

Regina raised her hand. "Oh that's mine. I meant to eat it on the train."

Squire threw it to her, but the Mouth caught it mid-flight.

"Oh no, no, no. Like everything else on the table, we're sharing that."

"Dean, give it back."

I stood. "LaBouche is right. We're splitting it five ways. Twenty calories of gluten-free chocolate pleasure a piece."

Regina stuck her tongue out at me. "You guys are assholes."

"We're just joking, Reg." The Mouth tossed her the bar. "And anyway, I've got something better. But you'll have to follow me outside."

We wrapped ourselves in coats and scarves, hoping the Mouth would lead us to a pig roast or clam bake surreptitiously organized while we were sleeping. Instead, he took us through the iron gate and across the rows of parallel train tracks. The sun was slipping below the trees to the west, and a bouquet of color reflected off the chrome surface of the Junemark water tower, our destination.

"It's up top," he said, pointing to the ringed catwalk.

Hawke withdrew. "You know, I'm not really that hungry. You guys go up."

"It's not food."

Squire and I looked at each other, wide-eyed. "It's not?"

"Just. . . would someone climb the damn ladder?"

When no one else moved, Regina grabbed the rungs and started climbing.

Hawke reached his arms behind his back and tugged at his elbows. "Why don't I go clean up the ramen?"

The Mouth shook his head. "Hawke, you're coming. Everyone is coming."

Squire took the next turn, followed by the Mouth. Hawke hesitated, but in seeing I was not about to leave him alone on terra firma, he groaned and started the climb. He was the most athletic of all of us, but he lagged behind the Mouth, stopping often and panting heavily.

I leaned back into the metal cage that enclosed us and dangled my arms through the gaps. The cold air danced between my fingers. "Almost there, Hawke. Just keep your eyes on the ladder or up on Dean's skinny ass."

"I don't. . . need your. . . commentary." He squeezed the words out between quickened breaths, his legs trembling ever so slightly above me. "I'm just. . . admiring. . . the view."

When we finally reached the summit, Hawke crawled along the catwalk and sat pinned between the banister and the body of the water tank. He nodded, and I stepped over his vertigo-paralyzed frame to join the others. The Mouth was holding champagne.

"You do the honors," he said, passing me the bottle. "I've never been any good at opening the fancy shit."

The tower was the tallest point in the area, and from its catwalk we could see the entirety of the town that was Isidora and the surrounding farm lands. My eyes caught the point where the tracks of the train yard converged, forming the industrial spur, which I followed back to the junction. The main line we arrived on passed directly north of Junemark 6, separated by a mile of naked deciduous trees lodged in the earth like toothpicks. I nudged the cork up slowly until I was sure it would go.

"Ready? What am I aiming for?"

Squire pointed to the roof of a boxcar below. I lifted the bottle and, with a flick, shot the cork out into the void. It spiraled downward, not with the resolve of a rock but the absentminded flittering of a leaf in a breeze. When it finally struck the car's metal hatch, it bounced to the ground as if it weighed nothing at all.

Squire laughed. "An excellent shot."

We circled the catwalk, sipping champagne from dixie cups the Mouth had found in a supply closet. To the south the highway was ironed flat, running like a mirrored image of the rails at our back. When it reached the town that was Isidora to our west, it diverted away, enclosing the settlement like a fish in a net. When we first arrived, it felt like Junemark 6 was isolated, but between us and the warm glow of the town's fashionable suburbs and commercial districts, the Shambles sat crumbling in eerie darkness.

To the east, behind the machine shed, there was a large pond—its banks spotted with cattails and leafless weeping willows. Farther out there was nothing but darkness punctuated by the halogen porch light of a farmhouse or a solitary street lamp illuminating the intersection of lonely country roads.

By the time we finished our circuit, the sun had set. Hawke looked up at us from the anchored position we had left him in and held out his cup for a refill. Something about his helplessness filled me with hope. I put an arm around Regina's waist and another around Squire's as the Mouth refilled our glasses. Regina lifted her hand from the railing to push away a strand of hair blown across her face. She looked out at the horizon, then at me and smiled.

"A toast," the Mouth said. "To freedom. To self-determination. To a new society we can call our own."

As we drank, the air filled with the smell of forming snow—dried bark pressed into cassis berries. Soon after, flakes fell from the sky, fat and heavy. We stayed there, listening to crinkling air and catching the swirling white on our tongues like schoolchildren until it became too dark to see the ground. When we finally agreed it was time to descend, Hawke was already halfway down.

Chapter Ten

Days passed in the blink of an eye, and though we were always busy, we seemed to accomplish very little. Every door in the Ark was the lid to a time capsule, but things are forgotten for a reason, and almost without fail the contents of the storage lockers, broom closets, and cubby holes were trash. Still, the fact that anything remained—defiant after decades of neglect—obliged us to catalog it all, as botanists might the banal flora and fauna of a previously undiscovered isle. Every now and then we were rewarded with a new species, a butterfly with resplendent indigo wings, and it made the excavation worthwhile. A day of rummaging through Junemark's basement archives revealed boxes of useless pay slips, invoices, and timecards but also the compound blueprints complete with plumbing and wiring diagrams for the Ark. The detritus scattered across the factory floor was almost universally rusted beyond recognition, but occasionally a drawer would open to reveal a pristine hacksaw or functional hammer.

The excitement of our arrival and the thrill of discovery buoyed us for a time, but the vagaries of life in isolation began to take their toll. We woke each morning cold and sore, unrecovered from the previous day's labors and unenthusiastic about the day to come. There was no electricity, no running water, no communication, no heat. We ate a thousand fewer calories than we burned. We drank the melted snow.

One week after our arrival, we huddled on the factory floor to break bread, though the last of our split loaf had been devoured days earlier. Light ricocheted through the snowpack on the skylight above like pachinko balls, losing energy at each collision until it finally fell on us, diminished and cold. I looked down at a fistful of rice and beans in my bowl, then at Squire who dropped onto the hard cement floor beside Regina with a thud. Hawke groaned as he stretched himself along the length of the machinist's table before rising.

"Jesus, what's that smell?"

"It's hunger," the Mouth said, staring down into his empty bowl. "Expectation. Disappointment. Excess hydrochloric acid."

"No. I swear something is dead or dying in this room. I've smelled it before, faintly, but now it's something awful."

Regina stirred her rice and beans and took another bite. "It's *us*, Hawke. We all smell like shit. How are we supposed to get clean when the only water we have was recently frozen?"

Hawke slid off the table and walked over to smell the Mouth, who belched in his face. Then he moved to me, and I knew what came next. I hugged my arm to my chest. The smell was repulsive, for sure, but it was mine and so in some way comforting. I took a whiff every now and then, and it shocked my senses. Hawke looked like he wanted to puke.

"It's that fucking cast, isn't it?"

The plaster, darkened with Regina's doodles, had grown foul, and my emaciated forearm below squished about in a layer of congealed funk.

"What do you want me to do about it, Hawke? I can't wash it."

He marched across the factory floor to a row of storage lockers. "We're taking it off," he said, throwing open a steel door. "We're taking it off now, and we're burying it outside before some coyote comes 'round, thinking you're roadkill."

"In fact, it *has* been six weeks," Squire mused.

"Take it off with what, Hawke?" Regina asked. "Doctors have special tools for. . ."

"With this." Hawke brandished a hacksaw.

I cringed. I could think of no greater torture than to be picked apart by manual instruments—to be prodded, nipped at, sawed in two like some dark age heretic at the gallows. But the cast, which started as a comforting addition, had recently become something of a hangnail—itchy, loose, and decidedly putrid. My choice of physicians was limited, and Hawke had the steadiest hand.

I looked down at the cast, then back at Hawke. "Alright," I said, rising. "Where do you want me?"

I followed him to a workbench against the wall covered in metal bits and bobs. He cleared it with a swipe of his arm, sending a shower of parts crashing to the floor. The Mouth and Squire hurried over to watch, followed by a reluctant Regina.

The Mouth flicked on a flashlight and began inspecting. "Whaddya figure, nurse Squire? Cuts lengthwise? One on each side?"

"In fact, it's only attached at the wrist and hand. Your arm is so weak— no offense—there's a fair bit of space between the cast and the skin."

"Can you just cut around the circumference of the wrist and slide off the rest?"

"Guys. I got this." Hawke motioned for the Mouth and Squire to hold me still, then he set the teeth of the saw down along the length of the cast.

"You idiots are going to saw his arm off, aren't you?" Regina said as she slid in behind.

Hawke's first cut was a cautious pull, but he pushed back with force, and the teeth nicked Squire's hand at my elbow.

"Ah! Funyuns, that hurts." His pinkie bled immediately, and Squire thrust it into his mouth.

"I barely touched you. Back on it, Squire."

"No way. One appendage under the knife is plenty."

"There," the Mouth said, pointing to another bench across the factory floor. "A table vise."

"A what?" I exclaimed.

Hawke grabbed my cast and pulled me across the room. He dropped my arm into the vise, and the Mouth spun its jaw tight. As Hawke felt for the groove he had started, I sank down, trying to create as much space as possible between the plaster and my skin. I wanted to turn away, but I didn't trust him enough to fully relinquish control.

Then he sawed. Slowly. Back and forth. The muscles of his arm flexed, working against themselves—force and counterforce, pressure and control. The saw's teeth kicked out puffs of fine powder as the blade descended.

"You're close," I said, thinking I felt the faintest of strokes along my arm.

The Mouth shone the flashlight down inside the cast, and I saw a glint of metal from within, but Hawke continued.

"Hawke! You're through."

I reached up to stay his arm, but he pushed one last time.

"Hawke!" I cried.

A dozen teeth tore at the crest of my palm. In an instant, a stream of blood flowed down my fingertips. From my position below, I saw it fall on the workbench in a steady flow of dark viscous drops.

"Stop!" Regina cried, pushing Hawke aside. "God. You're such Neanderthals." She unscrewed the vise to release me and then, grabbing my good hand, led me back across the hall.

"Where are you going, Reg?" Hawke called out. "You won't get it open with only one side cut."

We walked to the Ark's front room where she dropped me into an armchair then began heating water above the camp stove. She grabbed a bucket of snow melt, still half-frozen, and placed it below my arm. While she worked, I pried at the cast with my good hand, but Hawke's incision had done nothing to weaken it.

"He's not wrong, Regina. It's still firmly attached."

"Hush."

When the water was steaming, she poured it into the bucket. The snow that remained sighed as it retreated into itself. She stirred, then dropped my arm inside.

I gasped. "It's still freezing."

"Hush," she said again. "I'll boil another pot."

The others came in as she was relighting the stove.

"Clever," Squire said, beaming.

Hawke snorted in derision, but her approach was having the desired effect. The water penetrated the plaster at my hand and elbow, and especially along the lengthwise cut. I could feel it softening, the squeeze giving way. The cold even clotted the blood in my palm.

Then the camp stove flame went out with a flicker and a puff.

Regina sighed. "There goes another one. Squire, can you grab a spare bottle?"

He shook his head. "There aren't any more."

"That was the last one?"

"The last one. No more hot meals for us."

The Mouth sprang to his feet and began pacing the floor. As he did, he catalogued what the loss would mean. No more French press coffee. No more ramen. No more sponge baths in what was at the best of times lukewarm water. No more rice. No more beans. No possibility of life whatsoever.

"Oh, don't be so dramatic." Hawke said. "We can always burn wood, though not nearly as often."

"No way," the Mouth said with a panicked quickness. "We're not regressing to cooking over an open fire once every fortnight. Our rations have been unbearable as it is, and I'm not about to eat this crap cold. It's time for a supply run."

"A supply run?" Regina had pulled my arm out of the bucket and was probing the softness. "We just got here. What happened to self-reliance?"

Hawke smirked, perhaps amused to find he and Regina had common cause. "We can engineer a solution. Maybe set up a firepit at the back of the factory floor."

"It's not just fuel, guys. We need food. *Real* food. I honestly can't keep going on pig slop and gruel. I'm not a Hyundai. I run on premium."

Squire scratched his belly. "We are running a bit low on nutritional diversity. . . in fact."

"And we have a day or two of good weather before it's supposed to snow again," the Mouth continued. "What happens if we're shut in, and our supplies run out? How will we survive?"

Regina dropped my arm back in the bucket. "Wait. What do you mean *supposed* to snow again? According to whom? Have you been online?"

The Mouth sat and fell back onto his elbows. "I check in on our followers once or twice a day from my phone, and I happened to look up the weather forecast. So, sue me."

Regina brushed her hair back and held her hand atop her head in bemusement. "With what charge? I'm tripping over furniture in the dark like a drunken Mennonite, and you're on the goddamned Internet?"

"I brought a spare external battery. It's for the movement."

"It's for your ego. And here you are lecturing us about isolating ourselves from the outside world. We're supposed to be in this together. And anyway, what happens when the spare loses its charge? Jesus, you're so short-sighted."

"Oh, get over yourself, Reg. This was an inevitability. What? Did you think we'd get here and grow a hydroponic cornucopia overnight? If we starve, there is no revolution. A supply run is a revolutionary act."

Hawke lit a cigarette. "The outside world is a fiction. There's nothing for us there."

"We've lived on fiction all our lives. It can sustain us a little while longer."

I pulled my arm from the bucket again and tested the cast. It was ready. I held up the gooey mess and looked at Hawke. "A little help?"

He formed a circle with his mouth then released a stream of smoke rings. "Not on your life."

Squire stood, and I gave him my arm.

"Ready?" He inserted the fingers of both hands in the crack and then pulled the cast apart like an egg. My arm slid free. It was light and weak and exposed, and, yes, it smelled horrendous, but there was nothing more satisfying than release. The thought that I should return to that captivity—that the security it provided was the better path—never entered my mind. The bone was healed. It would have to hold together on its own.

"Oh, thank god," I sighed.

"You're welcome," Regina winked.

I dunked my arm back in the water to clean off the residual filth.

"Guys, I think Dean is right," I said. "Or, at least, I don't think he's wrong. We reject everything about that capitalist, figment world we left behind, but until we're self-sufficient, we'll need to do supply runs to survive. So, we'll feed on it with all the tender fondness of a parasite. We'll suck it dry until we can stand on our own."

****

Leaving Junemark should have felt like concession, but all I felt was relief. As Squire and I walked south past the Mines and across the expanse of unsoiled white that concealed the barren parking lot, we were just as hungry, just as cold, just as achy, and just as tired as all the days before. But buoyed by the thought of warm food and perhaps a fresh change of clothes, it all weighed a bit less.

"Strange, leaving so soon," I mused as we arrived at the end of the compound's driveway. A row of stone letters six feet tall spelling "JUNEMARK" stood at the entrance like Daoist steles, announcing an immortality unrealized.

"Yes," Squire said. "But you were right. There's no point sacrificing ourselves for our principles."

"Well, when you put it that way..." I looked over at Squire who walked ahead contentedly, thumbs shoved under the straps of his empty backpack. "Anyway, it's only temporary."

I paused at the edge of the compound, the threshold between our new reality and the figment world beyond. It was an imaginary border, perhaps, but so were all the others I'd ever known and respected. He stopped beside me.

"Shall we?" I asked.

Squire grinned the only way he knew how, fully and without reservation. "Onwards and upwards."

The unmarked road of the industrial park connected to another that led to another that took us to the highway. There we walked beside cars returned to their full velocity by snowplows and chemical salts. I considered hitchhiking, but it seemed too big a breach of our self-sufficiency pledge, and anyway no one was likely to slow down. Motorists crossed this country the way the wagoneers did generations before them—at all haste for as long as haste was theirs, driven by a well-founded desire to be anywhere else when the tank ran dry. But the walk didn't bother me. The sun was high in the blue sky. The snow crinkled and melted as we crushed salt pellets beneath our boots. We were in no rush.

As we walked, we left behind the town's industrial exurbs and approached its decaying downtown. The highway avoided it all, curving to the south, but it still offered off-ramps of broken concrete that dropped like double-dog dares into a patchwork of empty lots and boarded-up row houses, shuttered off-brand service stations, and the repurposed shells of bankrupt franchisees. The Shambles. I'd be the first to admit my hometown was far from pristine. Every street had at least one house that was decidedly rough. But still, I had never before seen such urban decay.

We paused next to a billboard that promised the counterfactual. "EDEN VILLAGE. 250,000 sq. feet of Mixed-use Development at the Heart of Isidora. Pre-construction Leasing Available Now." Below was a picture of gleaming glass buildings drawn in forced perspective to tower above synthetic humans dressed in smart casual.

"It's amazing what people will try to sell you." I turned and rested on the guardrail. "Nothing more than an idea, a notion, a figment."

Squire dropped his backpack and scratched his belly. "In fact, Eden never sounded all that great to me. Ignorance, gluttony, boredom. Eve did us all a big favor."

"But that's what people want, isn't it? To know only pleasure, to close their eyes to suffering?"

"Her and that snake, I suppose. And being naked all the time?" He slapped the sides of his bulging belly. "I'm not built for fig leaves."

He chuckled, and I laughed. "Squire, you always see the big picture, don't you?"

"That's a big picture," he said pointing to the billboard. "And a lot of good it does."

I looked around. "Which way now?"

Squire pulled the Mouth's cell phone from his bag, and we waited for it to turn on. Before we left the compound, we had pinned the location of a BigBox.

"It's another half-hour if we keep following the highway, but we can save about fifteen minutes heading that-a-way."

Our eyes ran down Exit 6B, past the green astroturf stairs of the One

Grace Presbyterian Church and the barred windows of a 24-hour EZ Check Casher.

"I'm happy to have the exercise," I said.

"Me too."

Before we resumed, I pulled a candy bar out of my bag and tore open the wrapper.

"Regina's chocolate pleasure bar?"

I nodded as I split it in half. "To ignorance and gluttony."

He gave me an accusing look. "She gave it to you, right?"

"Of course. She said we might get hungry on the way."

"You two have gotten very close." He turned and walked ahead, tasting, chewing, swallowing. "She's very thoughtful."

"Does it bother you, Squire? That we've become close?"

He responded after a pause that probably lingered longer than he had intended. "No. No, of course not. I'm glad she likes you. In fact. I like you too. It's just. . ." He sighed. "There's history."

I could have responded right away, telling him there was nothing to worry about, that we were platonic friends and nothing more, words even I could not confirm were true. I could have pried the story out of him, coaxing reassurance into the chinks in his armor, only to twist it round to crack his protective shell. But instead, I gave him that which I valued most in a friend, silence and space.

The air was cold and empty, and the light—those few horizontal rays from our low-slung star—hit our faces full of warmth. Eventually, he spoke.

"In college there was this guy, in fact, and she fell hard for him. Organic chemistry, sophomore year. She still thought she wanted to go pre-med. They were lab partners, her and this monied pretty boy. And you know Regina. She's open. She's free, especially with guys like that. And there she was in thick-framed glasses and a sweatshirt from her high school science club." He smiled, his mind a decade in the past.

"Eventually, they started hooking up whenever he was lonely or bored. What he gave her, the space at the periphery of his life? It meant nothing to him. But for her it was everything. She melted with every fleeting kindness and froze solid during the long periods of silence. I told her she was being foolish. But she wanted to be foolish. Foolish felt good. Foolish held hope. Eventually, he started dating someone else, some six-foot-tall blonde girl trailing the latest fragrance from Dior down the hallways of the business school. And Regina was forgotten, wiped clean from his life. It was inevitable. But she was crushed."

"And you think I'm like that guy?"

"In fact, no. But on the outside, yeah. Handsome, charming, confident. I can see it when she's around you. She feels foolish again."

I was at a loss for words. The man he described and the man he thought he saw standing in front of him were both strangers to me. I wasn't Regina's college crush, the smooth-haired rake with a plastic girlfriend. I was the melancholy brat who pissed himself in traffic on the way to O'Hare and flew home in a pair of new Blackhawks sweatpants, the disappointment of his parents seared into him by averted eyes. I was the third wheel of a teenage love affair, chauffeur to a couple who made out in the backseat while I drove circles around the mall, not knowing what to do with the dull pain in my heart. I was never one to make a girl feel foolish. I was, in every instance I could remember, the fool.

"That's not me," I said. "She's not on my periphery. None of you are."

"I know," he said, then added again softly, as if the first iteration were incomplete, "I know."

"Look, Squire, the past is only real if we give it life. It only exists by consent. You're torturing yourself with it for no reason. The Regina that was? The Squire that was? The me that was? We don't exist anymore."

"I know we talk about it like that. Destroying the past. Being reborn in the present. But it's not that simple, is it? I mean, that's not really how it works? There's continuity. Memory."

"Memories are just scars on our cerebral tissue, neural pathways frozen in place, holding onto an idea or an image that no longer serves a purpose."

"You don't mean that." He kicked at a stone that skidded along the shoulder until it stopped dead at a guardrail post.

"I do. You remember the day Regina discovered the new girlfriend of this college crush. Maybe you can picture the setting—your dorm room or hers or maybe a desk in a quiet corner of the library, her tears stifled to avoid causing a scene. But do you remember what day it was? What hour? What you were wearing? What *she* was wearing? Was it sunny or snowing? You've already forgotten so much. Your memory is incomplete, selective. You hold onto some elements because subconsciously you think they may help you. Because someday you'll encounter another handsome, charming, and confident man who comes into Regina's life, and you'll be able to judge him because of the scar that covers that poorly healed trauma. And if you're wrong, what good is memory? It's just an anchor straining to hold you in a past that no longer exists."

"I'm sorry. I'm not judging you. I just don't want to see her get hurt. And maybe you're right. Maybe it's time to let some things go. To try to forget."

"Everything is gonna be fine, Squire. There's nothing you need to protect her from. Besides, she chose you, right? And she's chosen you every day since."

—Squire was not the kind of man to beat his chest, throw punches, and roar. He fought for Regina as a lawyer might, through a structured arbitration with the counter claimant. He needed her. I don't know why I put up any resistance.

—*You told him the TRUTH.*

—I weaponized the TRUTH, manipulated it, melted it down, forged a blade, and used it to pierce my competitor. I didn't even know I wanted her at the time.

—*To manipulate is to grasp, to hold. If you want the TRUTH in your hands, at your fingertips, this is the only way.*

An inscrutable smile formed beneath Squire's thick, ruddy beard. His gaze was glassy and long. "Are you cold? I hope we get there soon. I'm starting to feel chilled."

****

The next exit was ours, and we took it up and across the overpass to the far side of the highway. There in the middle of a sea of concrete, squat and eternal like a Soviet fallout shelter, sat BigBox. It was a chain I knew well. In fact, while growing up there were months when it was the sole recipient of my parents' meager income, supplier of Hamburger Helper, cap guns, underwear, kitty litter, the one-stop-shop fueling the middle-class pursuit of happiness. And so the parking lot in front of us—its raven-like street lamps perched above an unchoreographed dance of rogue shopping carts, minivans, and cankles in tube socks—was a sight both familiar and depressing. I knew for miles around bells hung in ghostly silence above the entrances to bookstores, grocers, hobby shops, and tailors as if tied to the fingers of the dead. But here the doors danced in continuous utility, sliding open with a *whoosh* to blast another pilgrim with a jet of perfectly conditioned air or to *whoosh* out another satisfied customer and their cartload of crap. The products were cheap, the store hours were long, the consumption asked little of the consumer and gave as much in return.

"What a mess." The chocolate pleasure in my stomach started to curdle. "Squire, are you sure you don't want to go somewhere else? Somewhere less. . . soul-crushing?"

"It's the only place open."

"But it's Tuesday afternoon."

He shrugged. "Still."

To our right, sitting at the edge of the pavement beyond the acceptable walking distance to the store's entrance, an old F-150—cherry red divided by a broad cream stripe—glistened in the sun as if glazed with rain water. In the front window a sign read "For sale by owner, dependable, $2k OBO" and listed a local number. The word "owner" had been struck through and replaced with "Earl."

"Squire. We're buying that," I said walking toward it.

"It's a good-looking truck, in fact. Maybe we can take down the number and discuss it with the group."

"Nope. We're buying that today. We're buying it and loading it up with a metric ton of shit, and we're never coming back here again. Call the man, (6-4-1). . ."

Squire circled the vehicle, cupping his hands over his eyes as he looked into the cab, bending low to check the progression of rust on the rear quarter panels, pointing out the torn upholstery on the long bench seat.

"Well, it's already got snow tires on it." He pulled the Mouth's cell from his pocket and held down the power button. "Alright. Let's do it."

"Do you think we can pay him later? Or maybe we all go back to the ranch together to give him the money?"

Squire pulled a worn security envelope out of the breast pocket of his parka as he raised the phone to his ear. He mouthed the words "five K," his bushy eyebrows dancing up and down.

"I thought we were broke. I thought you burned through the last of your money on rent in the capital."

"It's not mine. It's from Dean's online followers. It turns out they're good for more than just likes."

"Squire, you're a goddamned genius. I don't care what everybody else says."

"Hush. It's ringing."

He put the phone on speaker, but I let him do all the talking. It was a short conversation despite Earl's leisurely affect.

"We're interested in the truck."

"Well, that's just fine. Can I meet you on Sunday to give 'er a spin?"

"We have cash."

"I'll be there in fifteen minutes."

Earl, it seemed, was also a frequent BigBox shopper, and he covered the distance between the store's entrance and the lonely truck in a stilted skip, frequently hiking up his Wranglers and adjusting the camo baseball hat covering his thinning hair.

"Shit, you boys nearly gave me a heart attack, sayin' you want to buy the old gal today. And in cash, no less? I just put 'er here not two days ago now. It's a damn good thing I was here already, stocking up on salt melt and Coke Classic before we get pummeled again. Next day or two I hear."

Squire took a small step toward the cab. "Earl, do you mind if we take a look inside."

"Oh, of course. Go right ahead."

He made no move to open the door, and we glanced at each other in confusion.

"Oh, it ain't locked." He reached past us and pushed in the latch with his calloused thumb. "Ain't nothing to steal inside anyhow."

Squire pulled at the door, and it creaked and strained at the midpoint before flinging wide open. He pulled himself up, slid behind the wheel, and ran his hands along the spartan dash.

"And I got the keys here somewhere if you want to get 'er going." Earl patted his pants and then the button-down breast pockets of his flannel shirt only to find a pack of Marlboro reds and a Bic. He flicked open the top, grabbed a cigarette with his lips, and lit up.

"You boys. . ." He paused to take a drag and consider his next words. "Buying this together?"

I grabbed a cigarette from the side pocket of my backpack and put it in my mouth. "Oh, my cousin and I are opening our own business." I flicked a plastic lighter a few times in the concavity of my raised hand, the fire refusing to emerge into the frozen air. Earl looked relieved. "You see, our uncle Jim has this junkyard not too far from here—small yard but he moves a lot. He figures he could move a lot more but that his customers got transportation problems. They can't get it to him, and he's too busy running the auction circuit to do deliveries. So, with a truck we can do all that, take a small cut from the sale and a delivery fee from the customer. We'll get paid on both sides. Win-win-win."

Earl removed his cap and scratched his head with the brim. "Gee, that sounds alright. I tell you what, I admire you two trying to start something new at a time like this. Takes some balls. Everyone I know is sitting on their ass and cashing that unemployment check once a month. Living to wait, and that's about it."

"It's tough out there, to be sure. But we figure people will always need to get rid of shit."

"Heh-heh! You got that right. Maybe now more than ever. I tell you what; I like you boys, and I want to help you out. How's about two thousand dollars? Two thousand and you drive her away today with my best wishes."

Inside the truck, Squire lowered the sun visor, and a set of keys fell into his lap. He turned the ignition, and the old truck growled and hummed.

"Earl," I yelled over the squeal of a flywheel, "you got yourself a deal!"

An hour and a half later, we were barreling down the highway at sixty, the bed full of $3,000 worth of provisions paid in cash to the floor manager as a dumbfounded clerk stood nearby. The snow tires hummed on the tar-stitched tarmac, carrying us in minutes over ground that our boots took hours to traverse. The radio was still dialed to classic country somewhere in the gap on the thin tuning strip between 100.0 and 102.0. Squire stretched his hand out over the steering wheel to tap out the beat on the plastic dash. *You clap hands and I'll start bowing. We'll do all the law's allowing. Tomorrow I'll be right back plowing. Settin' the woods on fire.* The truck would be named "Hank" forevermore.

I cranked the window down and stuck my arm out into the jet of rushing air where my hand became an aileron. My arm rolled up and down, left and right, dancing in the dramatic repercussions of the smallest articulation beneath my skin. We flew along, banking into the long turn east, gliding out beyond the reach of the town that was Isidora, over farm and stream, meadow and wood, into the great nothingness of the glacier-leveled plains.

"Squire? Wasn't that our turn?"

He looked at me with a knowing smile. "Earl was kind enough to leave us a full tank. Let's burn a little more before we head home."

He dropped the throttle with a hoot, and we disappeared into the world beyond.

When we finally returned to the industrial park, the Junemark steles emerged from the darkness like startled deer in the truck's halogen headlights.

"Should we honk to get the others?" I asked.

Squire's gaze remained fixed straight ahead. "Not just yet."

We crawled up the drive and across the snow-quilted parking lot, the engine practically at idle. Then Squire jerked the wheel to the right and slammed his foot on the gas. The truck's backend jumped out behind us, sending the contents of the bed slamming into the tailgate and me, unbelted, flying into the crash pad of Squire's ample belly.

"Yee-haw!" Squire let out a bellowing laugh, his eyes aglow in the dusty orange bulb of Hank's flagging speedometer.

I don't think the others could have seen us, certainly not from the Ark. And as I watched the man's long-held anxieties dissolve into a swirling present, I decided I wouldn't tell them. They wouldn't have believed it anyway. Their soft, sweet Squire clutch-kicking an F-150 into endless loops on the snow-covered asphalt? Never. But behind the wheel of that aging truck, he was something else. He was a newborn foal prancing about the grass on day-old legs, and in the twisting, turning, laughing, roaring, I saw him blow away the past in a fine spray of spiraling snow.

Chapter Eleven

In those early days before Isidora felt like something we could reasonably claim to possess, we scurried between buildings and slinked along walls, trespassers in our own home. In the open expanse of the train yard or among the grasping prairie grasses in the field beside the pond, the faintest breeze felt like an accusation, the interruption of a car accelerating in the distance an indictment. But over time we came to realize we were not being observed; or if we were, the observers had no intention of uprooting us to reclaim the compound for their own. We stopped delicately disassembling junk that stood in our way and started crushing it with hammers and handsaws, chucking the remnants out open windows onto a growing pile of metal, rusting in the snow. Like impatient archeologists who abandon their brushes and trowels for pickaxes and shovels, we tore through the strata of Junemark, driven by the vague notion of utility hidden from sight.

On one such occasion, I trailed behind Hawke as he kicked in the door of the machine shop to discover that, like the Ark, it had been left untouched by liquidators. The three-room structure was nothing but corrugated sheet metal above a cement slab, and the hollow within, shielded from the snow but also from the sun, pulled the warmth from our chest and the color from our lips. Tools—most of which I could not identify and would never learn to use—hung from pegboards and wall mounts like sides of beef in a meat locker. My teeth chattered as Hawke bounced from object to object, reciting their names in turn—shear, planer, lathe, broach. He claimed it all, and the only way he could have made that fact more clear was to lift a leg and pee on it.

Each day he devoured his breakfast in silence, then trudged off to that metal shed to nest. After sweeping away cobwebs and layers of dust, he started on the tools, using one to improve another, his capacity increasing exponentially with each project done. Wire mesh pulled rust off a wrench, which bolted down the legs of a vise, which held a length of wood, sawed at and drilled by hand tools polished with salt and vinegar.

On the back side of the shop, behind an overhead door painted in chipped crimson, the landscapers' shed held a cornucopia of small engines—a ride-on mower, two push mowers, hedge trimmers, weed whackers, and a pair of leaf blowers. None of them would start at first, but that only furthered Hawke's excited preoccupation. For weeks he tinkered, and with each new day the sun rose higher in the sky and the blanket of snow slowly melted, giving way to awakening grass that filled with chlorophyll and stretched straight in the warming air.

One day at noon, as we put down our chores and made our way to the Circle for lunch, a low growl shook the machine shop and crawled out into the grass. We poked our heads through the Ark's wrought-iron gate to see Hawke riding along the ridge at a snail's pace, sat triumphantly atop a tiny tractor like Marie Antoinette in her pantomime farm.

"It's alive!" the Mouth yelled as he sprinted toward Hawke, then tripped and tumbled into a tuft of thriving Kentucky blue.

Regina sighed. "Squire, next time you're in town you better buy that idiot a helmet."

"Which one?" I asked.

Hawke attempted to drive up along the train yard but misjudged the tractor's turning radius and rammed it into the Ark's external wall instead. He turned the key, and the engine sputtered to a halt.

"You got her running," Squire said. "I'm surprised the drivetrain still works."

Hawke slid off the machine, pulled a rag from his back pocket, and wiped his hands. "It surprised me too. I was only aiming to get it to turn over, but all things considered, it's in good shape. I only had to flush the fuel lines, change the oil and belts, and rework the electrical. It's a well-built machine."

"Good thing," Regina said. "The grass is looking a bit long."

Hawke walked past her.

"What's it for, Hawke?" Regina asked as she turned to follow him. "You know I need more tools in the fields."

"It's not for the fields, Reg." Hawke said over his shoulder.

"Then what is it for?"

"It's time for Circle, Reg."

Hawke grabbed peanut butter and a loaf of bread off the table in the receiving room, then led us to the factory floor where we stitched our way through a maze of detritus that seemed to shift constantly but never shrink. I took a seat on the steel drafting chair I had placed in my spot on the Circle. Hawke hopped onto the machinist's table to my left, with Regina and Squire sitting on their armchair and stool to my right. The Mouth sat across from me, for the time being content to spread out on the cold cement floor.

"I call this Circle to order," I said.

The chairmanship had fallen to me almost by happenstance.

—No. You were the chosen one.

In the division of labor that accompanied our first days at Junemark, I became responsible for our water supply, a task well suited to my particular familiarity with the principles of scarcity and thermodynamics. Full bucket good. Empty bucket bad. Heat plus snow equals water. Fresh water was a constant preoccupation. We used far more than I would have ever imagined—to drink and cook, of course, but also to clean the compound and ourselves. In the beginning, lunch was just that—lunch. But I found myself regularly taking the opportunity with us all gathered together to discuss our water supply, to propose increasingly complex solutions, and to urge restraint.

"Water. We depleted Tank One yesterday evening and started drawing from Tank Two today. The settling tank has been at rest for about a week now, so I'll start skimming that soon. There's been no rain, so the cistern is still dry. Squire, could you go this afternoon to pick up a hand pump? I'm tired of skimming with the sauce pan."

Squire was roped into assisting me with supply runs and in so doing discovered his charge. His bond with Hank made him our errand boy, and I sent him to the Farm&Field almost daily to buy another water tank or length of PVC pipe. The trips off compound seemed to do him well, and there were more than a few occasions when I sent him out for a simple valve or box of O-rings and he would disappear all afternoon. I didn't know where he went, and I didn't ask. He returned empty of agitation and worry, which in a way comforted me as well. Regina and Hawke complained incessantly about the cost and our continued reliance on prefab solutions from the figment world, but they used more water than anyone else, and we all knew we'd die of thirst before starvation. It was a unanimous priority.

"Sure. I'm heading that way today anyway. Hawke was hoping I could load up the gas reserve."

"Are you going to haul that huge tank into town?" I asked.

Hawke scoffed. "It's a three-hundred-gallon skid tank made of twelve-gauge steel. It's not moving. I simply asked if he could bring back a few gallons, so I could keep working on the tractor."

"Speaking of the tractor, we're all ears, Hawke. What's the plan?"

"As you all saw, the tractor is running. It's mobile, but that's not what I had in mind when I started tinkering with it. I figured I could get it to turn over a couple times, and that would be enough to prove it was functional. I had no idea it would get up and walk about. The tractor engine is the second-biggest engine on compound that works—second to Hank—and I propose we use it for electricity generation. I can strip off everything but the basic components of the fuel and electrical system and use it to spin an alternator that will give us basic power."

"You just got it working, and now you want to rip it apart?" Regina looked sick.

"I want to convert it from a lawnmower, which as you pointed out earlier, we don't need, to an electricity generator, which we do."

"Hawke, I spend all day digging up the field by hand. Field—pfft—at the pace of one woman tilling, it's going to be a glorified victory garden at best. If we're serious about growing our own food, we need scale, which means we need a tractor. Either that, or Squire needs to buy me a water buffalo."

"Fine by me. Just keep the beast away from my wires. I need an engine—I made an engine—and it's going to be used for electricity."

This was typical of our early Circles—Regina and Hawke in violent disagreement. Squire hoping the squabbling would stop. The Mouth hoping it would go on forever. I was always the one to step in and play King Solomon.

"Regina, after you plow, could you sow and care for the fields by hand, at least until it's time to harvest?"

Regina pursed her lips and flared her nostrils. "I mean. . . I suppose, but you're going to have to work with me on irrigation."

"Hawke, can you wait a few weeks to build the generator and in the meantime work out a way for the tractor to pull a plow?"

"Your wish is my command."

"Wonderful. The following?"

The Mouth changed the cross of his legs and sat tall like a yogi emerging from deep meditation.

"The following. A quarter of a million aspirants are now following our posts from the figment world, and our first video since arriving at Isidora has over a million views. We continue to get requests from followers to share the details of our location so they can join us. Some of the most active followers are sharing theories of where we are, and they're getting pretty close."

"Should we be discouraging people from coming?" I asked.

"We're still buying all our food from outside," Regina said. "I could use more hands in the fields, but I'm not sure if we can feed more mouths."

Squire raised a finger, and we waited for him to finish chewing his last bite. "Our inventories are good," he said, wiping ketchup from his lips. "And we have plenty of cash on hand. It's coming in faster than we can spend it."

To finance our founding, the Mouth spent his days on social media blogging or posting videos about the progress we were making for an audience that was in rapt attention. He recounted with unfailing energy each time we cleared a room or kicked in a locked door for the first time, blending what felt like a stream of monotonous chores into a cocktail of creation and discovery. They drank it up and, in the process, sent, with no questions asked and no expectation of repayment, hundreds of dollars a week.

"Anyway," the Mouth said, "it's their money. I say we open the gates."

"Hawke?" I asked, turning to him.

"I'm tired of looking at the four of you every day. I say we do it."

I started spinning on the drafting stool, talking aloud as if only to myself. "The water supply is barely keeping up as it is. We have some catchment devices ready but no rain. If that changes, we could support more, but we'll have to ration."

"The tower?" Squire asked.

"The tower," I muttered. The schematics we found in the basement identified local valves connecting Junemark to the larger grid. They were closed when the factory was shuttered, and the water tower and the pipes below were dry. It lingered, an empty reservoir in the sky, waiting to be filled.

"It may be time to tilt at that windmill," I admitted.

Hawke popped off the workbench and refilled his cup from a communal pitcher in the center of the Circle. "A windmill is exactly what we need. Something to power a pump at the top of the tower to refill the basin— maybe drawing water from the pond."

"Well, I don't know anything about windmills, but it sounds like a solution. If you can build it, I can run the pipe, perhaps through the fields. When the tower is full, we can reverse the flow and use it for irrigation."

Hawke rubbed his hands together and twisted his torso right and left. After finishing his lunch, he had little appetite for lengthy discussions. "If I'm waiting weeks to build the generator, I can try to design a windmill. But someone else needs to figure out how to install it."

Squire nodded, knowing he was the only one capable of such an operation.

The Mouth unfolded his legs and stood. "If we're thinking about an invitation for aspirants in a month or so, I'll need you. . ." he said pointing at me, ". . . to make an invite video. Your ubiquity in the capital news coverage and disappearance ever since has caused unending speculation among the bloggers. If you welcome them, they'll come running."

—*You see? The chosen one.*

—You always wished it was you instead.

—*Wish? I only ever wished for Isidora.*

"Oh," the Mouth added, "John Galt came by asking to borrow some tools."

I gave him a blank stare. "Who is John Galt?"

"Oh, some hermit who lives nearby. I told him to fuck off."

Chapter Twelve

—You don't have to be here for this part.

—*What? Are you ashamed?*

—Just go ask the cooks for breakfast. You're hungry, right? Besides, it has nothing to do with Isidora.

—*Isidora is everything.*

—LaBouche?

—*Fine.*

The following day, Regina and I rose early and skipped through the iron archway of the Ark toward the unplowed fields beside the pond. It was a brilliant, dewless morning, and we shed our coats and rolled up our shirt sleeves to catch the unfiltered light on our fair spring skin. As we walked, we passed each other coded smiles, sharing a secret known to everyone—that we would spend the entire day together. The thought quickened our pace, and once outside the Ark's walls we ran the length of the train yard, chasing, catching, and escaping one another in an exuberant, child-like romp.

She ran ahead of me to the bushes that bloomed at the end of the train yard, then disappeared over the ridge that concealed the fields from the compound the way the curvature of the earth hides Calcutta from Bombay. She was at an effortless sprint when the ground retreated from her grasping feet, and I heard her tumble into the buffalo grass.

"Are you OK?" I ran to help, but before I could offer a concerned hand, she was giggling and spinning downhill like a barrel rolling over a falls.

"You nut," I called out after her. But soon enough I was on my belly too, then rolling down the gentle slope, the earth and sky playing their own game of chase as the world dissolved to a blue-green swirl. Even after our bodies slid to a halt on the pond's reedy embankment, everything was delightfully topsy-turvy.

She stood and patted the dust from her blue jeans before pulling me to my feet.

"I think I'm getting too old for that," I said, picking a blade of grass from the tangle of her hair.

She reached up to flatten my upturned collar. "Nonsense. We have plenty of years left for rolling down hills."

We dropped our lunches in the shade of a scrawny elm and headed back uphill to the spot where Squire had deposited lengths of pure white PVC pipe in piles sorted by diameter. We worked all morning dragging them to the water's edge and arranging them along the descent like the vertebrae of an enormous spine. A third and two thirds of the way down the hill we dropped valves and stretched out perpendicular ribs of smaller-gauge pipe among the weeds and prairie grasses to form irrigation lines.

In time, the plots demarcated by these channels would be split and seeded, the earth mothering leeks, snap peas, spinach, and kale that would burst through the rain-soaked soil in fronds of verdant green and purple. Tubers, turnips, parsnips, and carrots would cower under the surface, viewing the world above through leafy periscopes. From naked ground, Regina would bring forth a cornucopia of color, texture, and taste that would nourish our revolution.

The morning passed quickly, and by noon our breath was hot, wet, and heaving. Our brows were sullied by dirt left behind as sweat was wiped away, and I felt unclean, not just from the day's labors but from every other day since we arrived, unclean from months of thrice-worn clothes and feckless sponge baths with rationed rinse water. The calm blue of the pond, once locked away from us under a frozen shell, now rippled playfully, its depths unbarred and yielding. I dropped my uneaten sandwich back into the bag and put a strawberry to my lips. My hands worked down the buttons of my shirt as the juice of the red fruit burst sweet in my mouth.

"What are you doing?" she asked, recumbent in the elm's disappearing shade. A line of smoke streamed from the cigarette between her fingers.

I nodded toward the water.

The second bite was wholly different—tart, grainy, and puckering. I threw the top into the reeds and pulled my singlet up my torso and down the length of my arms. I tried to swallow the strawberry, but my body rejected it. I spit the half-chewed mass into the pond and started undoing my pants.

"No really," she said, sitting up on her elbows. "What are you doing?"

"Getting clean."

I closed my eyes and stretched myself tall, letting my head roll around my neck in slow, effortful circles. Months of rationed food and physical labor had chiseled me into a form I barely recognized, and when I moved I was no longer a brain floating in space; I was muscle pulling at tendon, tendon tugging at bone. My skin stretched over the ridges of my chest and rolled along the hills of my abdomen. My hips protruded, and two trenches carved their way down to the stone pillars of my thighs. In the past I would never have stripped naked in the open air. My body had been soft and dull from neglect, and I was everywhere ashamed. But the form I had discovered in Isidora, the form of hunters and gatherers, of shudras and kshatriyas, was older than shame, and my bare feet flattened to meet the ground like puzzle pieces finding their mates.

She tamped out her cigarette and stood. I took a deep inhale, dropped my underwear, and hurled my naked body into the pond.

The water was nothing but thawed ice, and I was shivering before I could reach the surface.

"Fucking hell!" I yelled, bursting back into the air. "It's so cold."

She laughed and shook her head. "You idiot."

But already she was moving to the water's edge, glancing over her shoulder before pulling her shirt up over her head. My eyes followed the dappled light as it climbed her ribs like the rungs of a ladder. She tossed it aside and smiled.

"Are you sure?" I said. "It really is cold."

She unbuttoned her jeans and shimmied as the stretch denim slid off her hips and rolled down her thighs. The fabric piled around her feet, and she stepped from it to dip a toe in the pond.

"You're going to regret it." My teeth chattered. My breath froze. My heart pumped frantically but not to keep me warm.

She shook her head and smirked. Her chest rose as she reached her arms behind her back to undo the clasp of her bra, which dropped from her lightly-freckled skin.

The water around me began to boil, and I found I played the frog.

Her underwear fell, and for a moment she stood before me enrobed in nothing but statuesque alabaster, her arms folded across her belly between the modest mounds of her breasts and the tangle of hair that grew wild between her legs. Her eyes ran down along the curves of her naked form and then darted across the surface of the water to meet mine. I hoped she would hear a twig snap or leaves rustle and re-dress in rapid humiliation. I hoped she would spring high into the air and swan dive on my face.

She did neither.

Taking a few steps back, she galloped forward, leaping from the embankment and curling her naked form into a cannonball.

"Geronimo!"

A wave of frigid water rose from her impact and slapped me in the face.

"Oh, fuck!" she gasped as she breached the surface. "It's so cold." Her arms and legs darted back and forth to keep her afloat. "Why didn't you warn me?"

"My mistake." I leaned back onto the pillow of air in my chest and kicked myself to the center of the pond.

She rolled onto her belly and frog kicked after me. "How was my dive?"

"What a mess," I said. "As graceful as a thrown watermelon."

"Pfft. Better than yours, twiglet." She leaned her head back and let the water pull the hair from her face. As she rose up, it hung heavy and glistening like the ebony grain of a polished hardwood. "Are you able to stand?"

I reached down and dug my toes into the muddy bottom. "Just barely."

"Good. My arms are getting tired."

She took a deep breath and buried her face in the water. The innocent white of her heart-shaped ass flashed above the surface, followed by her legs, and then she was gone. For a moment I was alone. The split tail of a swallow shot through the air above me, air that carried the faint perfume of a blossom burst too early, before the true arrival of spring. Below, Regina came at me like a torpedo.

When she emerged, it was not in front of me but behind. Her hand grabbed my sloping shoulder, and she pulled herself in, the curves of her body pressed into my back, her legs open wide to wrap around my hips. With her free arm, she reached around my side and squeezed a hand to my chest. Her head fell onto my shoulder and she sighed. "That's better."

I don't know how long we stayed like that, me erect like a telephone pole planted in the muddy bottom, Regina the flittering bird that balanced on my wire.

"You know, I've missed you," she said.

I smiled. "We've been with each other every day for months."

"Yes, but never alone. Never like our nights on the couch in the capital."

She brought her other arm around to my chest and slipped slightly down my back. I felt her legs tense, and I reached to catch her, placing my hands beneath her thighs and raising her up. She squeezed in tight. The water between us was pushed aside, and in our embrace nothing separated the racing of our hearts but our own flesh and bone.

I wanted her. In my room that night, on the banks of the pond that afternoon, right then and there in the depths. I wanted her, and no warning from the past or admonishment from the future could blunt the sharp desire of that present. I wanted her, and I wanted her to slide her hand down my stomach along a trail of skin that burned like molten lead and discover it for herself.

"Regina," I said—a calling, a command, a plea.

Her lips, an inch from my ear, parted, and a single syllable slid over her hissing tongue. "Yes?"

"Should we. . ."

A whistle from the top of the hill pierced the air, and the question I only ever dared ask once died unfinished and unanswered. We looked up to see Hawke pull his thumb and pointer finger from his mouth.

"Are you two serious?" His voice rolled down the hill like an avalanche. "I'm working through lunch to put a plow on this tractor, and you two are fucking about in the pond?"

My heart tumbled, but if Regina felt any shame in being found that way, she did not show it. She decoupled from my back and paddled toward the shore.

"This isn't how fucking works, Hawke," she said. "Why don't you come join us?"

"You know we're gonna drink that water, right?"

"Come swim with us, Hawke." Her voice was a playful plea.

He shook his head. "This is the last time I do you any favors, Regina." With that he stormed back to the machine shed.

"Jesus," I said when he disappeared over the ridge. "We're screwed."

"Oh, calm down. No one is screwed."

She reached the embankment and sprang from the water. A river ran down the length of her spine, fed by the draining of her hair, each strand a tributary.

I turned away and felt the pond pull from me every ounce of warmth.

"He caught us," I said hollow and cold.

"Mmm? Caught us doing what, exactly?"

I glanced over my shoulder to see her pat herself dry with my shirt. "I don't know."

I sighed and took a deep breath before diving down through layers of water, each one colder than the next, each more hidden from the light. The formless air that I inhaled at the surface streamed past my ears in a crackling procession of bubbles. Doing what, exactly? It was a question I couldn't answer and could not bring myself to ask her in return. What were we doing? What was this? The deep comfort of trusting friends? An innocent nose thumbing at monogamous social taboos? An unqualified invitation to sinful, scandalous sex behind the back of a suspicious friend?

When I surfaced, she was half-dressed and seemed in no rush to finish the job. She threw me my shirt with a beguiling smile, and I turned away to brush the beading water off my goose-bumped skin.

"So you're not worried about this? About him saying something to Squire?"

"Saying what, exactly? That I failed to be the virtuous kept woman who neuters her own desires in obedience to her partner? That I'm not the standard bearer of traditional monogamy?" She sat and lay back in the grass, leaving her shirt draped out of reach in the bush where it was thrown. Her hands skimmed the grass for her half-smoked cigarette, which she relit and held in her pink lips.

I pulled on my pants and singlet and sat cross-legged in the grass opposite her. "Not in so many words but that you're not as committed to being exclusively with Squire as he thinks you are."

"Or that *you're* not as committed to not sleeping with his girlfriend as he thinks *you* are? James knows who I am." She chuckled to herself. "Hawke too."

"What do you mean 'Hawke too?'"

"Oh, it's nothing. I'm just saying this isn't an issue for anyone but you." She patted the ground beside her. "Come sit closer to me."

I felt no urge to move. "Regina, what aren't you telling me?"

She pushed a stream of smoke out her nostrils in a relenting huff. "Fine. A few years ago, Hawke and I kind of hooked up."

The words hit my ears, empty and meaningless. "What do you mean 'kind of' hooked up?"

"We fucked in the backseat of his car." She sat up and hugged her knees to her chest. As she spoke, she took a series of short, agitated drags.

"He had a car then, and he drove me to this heavy metal concert. Real screamo. The kind of thing Squire hates. We snuck in a flask of this putrid grain alcohol and a couple of joints and just raged. At the end of the night, we were drunk and high and covered in sweat and . . . I don't know. It just happened."

"Hawke? You and Hawke?"

She shrugged and reached out to offer me her pack of cigarettes. "Yeah. Me and Hawke. But it's no big deal. It was years ago."

I pushed her hand away and stood. "What the fuck, Regina? How could you have slept with Hawke?"

She shrugged. "Like I said, it just happened."

"But what about Squire? You slept with Hawke behind his back?" I knew it shouldn't have bothered me. After all, I didn't even know her then. But with each word a tongue of fire crept up my throat. My eyes burned, and I felt my blood turn to bile.

"Really? This coming from the guy who not ten minutes ago had his hands on my bare ass?"

I squeezed my eyes shut and buried my face in my fists. "Fucking hell, Reg."

"No, really. I'm curious about that. It's OK for you to go sneaking around behind Squire's back, but if I'm transparent about having an open relationship, that's going too far?"

"What open relationship, Regina? You may be open and free, but Squire is as loyal as a puppy dog. He just loves you too much to put his foot down."

"His foot down? Right on my fucking neck." Regina tried to take a drag, but her cigarette had long since burned out. She threw it away. "What right do you have to say any of this, huh? You were the one who stripped naked during lunch."

"I just wanted to go for a swim."

"Well, so did I." She turned and grabbed her shirt from the bush and slid her arms down the sleeves. She fumbled with the buttons for a second before tying the tails in a knot at her navel.

"I can't do this anymore, Reg. I can't be this close to you and also keep away."

An unbidden tear rolled down her cheek, and she brushed it aside before pulling a fresh cigarette from her pack.

"Fine. It's fine. I understand."

"Reg, we can't do this. I don't want to sneak around behind Squire's back."

She flicked the lighter a few times and then pulled the cigarette from the flame, the cherry glowing hot orange. "No. No, clearly you don't want to do that."

"Reg, come on." I took a step toward her, but she turned and walked away.

"It's fine," she said without looking back. "It's fine."

She spent the rest of the day away from me, sulking cold along the tracks of the industrial spur or stewing hot beside the stream at the bottom of the ravine. I didn't know, didn't ask, didn't care. The thing that was born between us in innocent flirtation and daring touch as my arm healed and my heart wandered the world unguarded, that rode beside us on the train from the capital and shoved us both naked into the pond—it was time for it to die. The realization of this rebellious project, the actualization of this audacious act, it would ask everything of me, and I resolved to give it nothing less.

I returned to the top of the hill and started connecting the lengths of pipe, applying sealant to the rim of one and sliding the next into place. The smooth PVC, heated by the midday sun, warmed my hands like the length of her pale-skinned body pressed into mine in the frigid water, her erect nipples tracing aimless lines along my back as she rose and fell.

No. It was behind me, languishing in a non-existent past. The exigent present. The completion of my labors. A mantra, a forgetful meditation, a sutra sewing me to the now.

The spine assembled, I worked to connect the ribs. The long white pipes slid through the overgrown grasses, wild and woolly like the hair between her legs, coyly concealing the moment of our canine congress, she bent over in the underbrush and I behind her. The ecstasy of release.

Sweat beaded on my brow, and my breath pushed panting. But I was no longer working. I was inert, lost in a vision that never was and never would be, sinking deeply into an imagined past. I had to free myself of it, to make a clean break. I reached for the present, pulling back from the dream just long enough to fling my fully clothed body back into the pond.

The icy shock ran fingers up my back and quelled the raging of my reptilian brain like baking soda on a grease fire. I let out a long, slow exhale. Enough.

I pulled myself from the water, sopping wet and desirous of nothing but a meal and a warm bed. When the sun slid down the arc of the western sky, I plunged the last pipe into the pond's lightless water, prepared to drain it dry.

Chapter Thirteen

That night a bracing northwesterly wind brought an abrupt end to the spring that wasn't. Regina and I continued to work the fields together for the next few days, stripping the ground of the long grasses and weeds that would interrupt the passage of the tractor and plow. It was arduous, back-breaking work, and we did it in a mirthless silence. In her overcoat and gloves, the wind whipping her hair into a voluminous tangle of ringlets and curls, her cheeks flushed pink by the cold, Regina was beautiful—perhaps more beautiful than ever before. But I felt nothing. The responsive corner of my heart that once belonged to her alone was mine once more.

—*You're an even bigger idiot than I thought.*

—The eggs?

—*He'll bring them up. Do you see how you were trying to sabotage Isidora even then? Your judgment is flawed.*

—Perhaps. But Isidora was always threatened by more than just my wandering heart.

Once the fields were clear, Hawke and Regina began to plow, and Squire and I jumped into Hank and drove out amongst the country roads and homesteads surrounding Isidora to bring back a windmill. It was a squat thing, perched on a rise above a large steel watering trough near the boundary of a pasture where glass-eyed cattle grazed in the field or lazed under the outstretched arms of a lonely black walnut, lost in the ennui known only to livestock. The windmill had long been replaced by electric pumps, and the owner was happy to be rid of it.

It was no great effort disassembling the windmill, plucking the metal head with its circular rotor and long positioning tail from the skeletal body and breaking each component down to a size that fit in the pickup bed. A half-dozen trips and a couple days later we had the pieces laid out in the grass beside our water tower, ready to be cleaned, greased, and lifted into position. As we waited for Hawke to prep the machinery, Squire and I extended the PVC line from the pond up along the water tower's cage-enclosed ladder, securing it with metal bands that worked like oversized zip ties. The windmill would be bolted to the topside of the water tank and connected to the feeder line and the outflow pipe by a valve assembly, which would allow us to reverse the flow of the pump and either draw up from the pond to fill the tank or up from the tank to send water to the irrigation lines and a spigot on the ground. It was no great feat of engineering, more MacGyver than Eiffel, but it would save us the labor of carrying water by hand.

On the day of the windmill's raising, we broke from lunch to find the sky crowded in a thick blanket of cumulostratus that undulated in parallel bars to the horizon. The sun behind them was prisoner, pacing its arc like a beast in captivity, and we walked to the water tower amongst boxcars that cast no shadows. To the west a black smear rose above the plains, vapor stained by the topsoil of the great interior sea. Rain was on its way, and the thought of full cisterns and a swollen pond added urgency to our mission.

At tower's base, Hawke told us again how the parts should be positioned and affixed, information we knew well from a week of watching him scrape away rust and lubricate gears, yammering all the while. He was content and focused when working with his hands, happy even, but we would never get him up the ladder, so it fell to Squire and I to finish the job. He wished us luck and wandered back to the machine shed to start converting the tractor into an electricity generator.

We hoped the lengths of rope from the old factory floor would prove long enough to stretch from the ground to the catwalk and back again. Squire volunteered to pull from below, his body providing more ballast than mine even after months of poor eating, so I tied an end around my waist and began to climb. With each rung of the ladder more rope was lifted into the air below me, and when I finally reached the top, it took all the strength I had to pull myself onto the platform.

"Are you up?" he yelled from the ground below.

"Yeah," I replied, panting.

"Then start pulling."

I lay flat on my belly, my feet digging into a ridge of rebar at the lip of the stairs, my hands outstretched above me, clinging to the platform's sides. Like a chameleon's tongue, the rope had me at the waist and was trying to retract me into its gaping maw.

"Just give me a second!" I shouted.

I switched the position of my feet and twisted my torso through a series of handholds until I was on my back and stable. Then I pulled. Hand over hand. Yard by yard. Lifting the length up over the lip and piling it around me in disordered coils. Eventually, the weight lessened, and I felt the tail end swinging freely, banging against the ladder's cage like the chain of a clapper-less bell. My arms ached, and the last stretch of rope felt as heavy as the first.

With the job done, I fell back and let my head roll to the side. In the distance, the town that was Isidora sat silent and unchanging. I knew somewhere amongst the sterile office parks and suburban split-levels someone was reaching to open a tap that spilled forth an endless stream of clean, cool water, half of which would flow down the drain unused.

"What are you doing up there?" Squire yelled. "Pass it down."

I stood and untied the end at my waist and fed it through the pulley we had attached to the catwalk railing. The lowering was easy enough, but I did it cautiously, not wanting to let the entire length slip through my hands. When Squire had a firm grasp of his end, I kicked the remaining tangle off the platform and watched it slither through the air before it smacked the ground. It reached.

The first part to go up was the truss, or a third of it anyway. We split it into sections on the farm and decided we needn't reassemble it on the compound, the water tower being tall enough on its own. One section would serve to lift the rotors into the tired breeze that rolled endlessly across the plains. The gray steel lines of the truss framed nothing but polygons of empty space, and still Squire alone couldn't convince the assembly to leave the earth. We worked together, me jumping to grab the line, letting my body weight raise the truss, and Squire behind me, reeling in the rope and anchoring it between cycles. The truss climbed with the cadence of a dirge, swinging black against the overcast sky and whistling with each gust of air like the moan of a soul escaping a gibbet cage. When it reached the platform, Squire braced himself, and I scrambled up the ladder to roll the assembly over the railing. Then he joined me up top, and we muscled it up the remaining curvature of the tank's dome and bolted it down above the access hatch.

Next came the windmill. The rotor caught the wind as it was meant to, and even a few yards above the ground the contraption swung wildly at the end of the rope like a toy plane on a tether. To prevent the blades from crumpling from an impact with the tower, I climbed alongside the head, one arm grasping the ladder's rungs and the other jutting out from the cage to hold the tail and give the contraption clearance. The higher we climbed, the stronger the wind blew. The rotor, which we foolishly failed to secure, spun with the howling blur of a buzzsaw, the head torquing left and right in my hand, attempting to fly free or to spin around and saw off the arm of its captor. It took every ounce of strength to keep it restrained. With each step my shoulders ached and my quadriceps shuddered, twitching me upward in the staccato stop-motion of a claymation puppet. When the mill and I reached the catwalk, I was spent.

I fell onto the platform and leaned my head over the side. "I can't lift it alone!" I yelled down to Squire. "I need your help."

Even from the height of the catwalk his exasperated groan was audible. "Well, what do you want me to do about it?"

"Come up and help me. I'll hold it away from the sides while you tie it off down there."

His arms quivered as he walked slowly around one of the tower's legs. The weight of the mill squeezed the rope against the aged steel, and after a few laps he had enough of an assist to lessen his grip and tie down the remaining length.

Then a horn sounded, not the beep of a car but the blare of a truck, distant but coming closer.

I looked away from the spinning mill bucking at the end of the rope and scanned the horizon. Traffic moved on the highway, as always, but one vehicle had broken away and was coming down the frontage road and through the gates of Junemark. It was an undersized gas truck—filled with liters, not gallons—and it circled the parking lot before pulling to a stop in front of the chained-off access path. The horn sounded again.

Below me Squire looked south. He couldn't possibly see the parking lot through the Mines, but he moved away from the ladder toward the sound without a hint of distress.

The horn blared again, and I saw the door to the machine shed fling open. Hawke shot from the darkness at a two-bell gallop and circled the factory to the east, kicking up clouds of dust on the unpaved trail. Squire saw him bolt and ran after him, a saint Bernard chasing the greyhound's hare.

"Hawke, no!" he shouted.

In the distance I saw a driver get out of the cab, remove his hat, and wipe his forehead with the arm of his sleeve. He bent over and cupped a hand above his eyes, peering into the abandoned compound, probably wondering why anyone would order 200 gallons of unleaded to a place like this.

A gust of wind howled around me, and the windmill head lurched away from the tower. I held fast to the rope above as the force slid me to the edge of the catwalk and pinned me against the railing.

"Squire!" I yelled, my voice disappearing into the gale. "Squire, it's slipping."

Hawke rounded the building at a full sprint, spilling into the parking lot as the delivery driver recoiled in surprise. Hawke's unintelligible screams rang through the air. I saw him reach behind his back to pull something from his waistband. A wrench? A knife? He raised it at arm's length and pointed at the driver in the unmistakable gesture of modern menace.

A handgun. The realization came slowly, and before I could consider the weapon's provenance, Squire was skidding to a halt before the wild man and his quivering prey. He waved his arms and stepped in front of the driver. Slowly, the gun fell from its target.

That same instant the blackening sky turned green, and the wind changed direction, sending the windmill careening toward the leg of the tower. I pushed it away and braced myself against the wall of the water tank. I considered yelling for help but knew my words would be devoured by the torrent swirling around me. Below, Squire and Hawke stormed in wild gesticulations. The driver, all but unseen, snuck back into his truck and lowered himself behind the dash.

When the gale finally subsided, the windmill head lurched earthward, and the line, escaping the knot at the tower's base, went soft. I caught the weight in a jerk and spun the rope around my wrist, attempting to bind our fates together. My chest slipped over the catwalk's edge, and my head dropped.

Earth's indifferent gravity pulled at me, tugging the tips of my hair, pooling my blood at the top of my skull like high tide on the bay. The knuckles on my hand holding the catwalk banister blanched white. The others descended into a dark purple. The windmill, an idle pawn in this tug of war, stretched my ligaments and threatened to tear apart the freshly healed bone of my forearm.

"Squire!" I yelled. "It's falling!"

My voice grew hoarse as I continued to yell, willing the words through the rushing wind. Some syllable must have reached him because his head turned, and his eyes lifted, and he saw the mill hanging like an ornament from the withered branch of my arm, the rope behind the pulley dangling limp.

I saw him run to me, then I winced my eyes shut as another gust lifted the head and spun its rotors. For what felt like an eternity, there was nothing I could do but hold on.

Even with the rushing wind, I heard the sirens.

The squad cars barreled down the frontage road and lurched around the corner of the industrial park before sliding to a stop on either side of the gas truck. Hawke threw the gun to the ground and walked forward with his hands raised. The delivery man reappeared out the open door of his cab, waving a cell phone and pointing in embolden accusations. The police cuffed Hawke, bent him in half, and shoved him in the back of their car.

Then the rain slipped off the edge of the cloud front in sheets, a spontaneous deluge that buffeted the earth in a frenzied assault. With a single brushstroke, the storm repainted the landscape below me. Water matted the overgrown grasses and coursed through scars stitched into the ground in rushing rivulets. Trees that whispered and swayed in gentle breezes bucked and bellowed in a gale that stripped leaves and broke branches. I was drenched in an instant, and my eyes followed water that beaded on the tip of my nose and then fell in dancing orbs through hundreds of feet of empty space.

Then the windmill joined them, accelerating away from me until it was locked in a motionless harmony with the droplets around it. Down they went together, along the uniform slope of the Earth's gravity well, trailing a rope stained with blood from the freshly torn skin of my outstretched hand. The sound of the metal capsule bursting on the ground was lost in the cataclysm of a million drops of water hitting the earth all at once.

The rain must have sapped any desire for further investigation, because the officers jumped in their squad car and drove away. Red and blue lights faded into the storm as the police retreated with their catch. And the tanker left as full as it came.

****

Squire met me at the foot of the ladder, and we surveyed the destruction. It only took a few seconds, a few swipes of our feet through the metal that blossomed on the ground like a popped flower bud, to know the windmill was unsalvageable. We abandoned it there and escaped through the downpour across railroad tracks that balanced rainwater like bands of liquid mercury. When we reached the gate to the Ark, the first bolt of lightning struck the tower, energizing the dome in a current that would have cooked my flesh and melted away my memories, certain death but for the displacement of a few moments in time.

"Arrogant buffoon!" Squire yelled, as we burst into the Ark's receiving room.

"What was I supposed to do? You left me hanging off the edge of a water tower with a windmill tethered to my arm."

"Not you—Hawke. I'm fed up with that know-nothing dimwit." He slammed the door behind him and reflexively flipped the light switch, but the gloom remained. "Goddamn this place!"

Regina rushed in from upstairs and lit a few candles.

"Thank god you're OK," she said as she ran across the room to drape her arms around Squire.

They stood there squeezing each other. I kicked off my soaked sneakers and fell into an armchair.

"What the hell was that about, Squire?"

He looked at me over Regina's shoulder and then at the Mouth who entered from the hallway, the blue glow of his cell phone reflected on his face.

"Whoa, is it raining?"

"The driver, the truck, the gasoline? What were they doing on compound?"

The Mouth's phone went black and slid into his front pocket. "Where's Hawke?"

"I ordered it a week ago," Squire said, pulling free of Regina's grasp. "Two hundred gallons of gasoline to fill the sled tank. If we're going to be running a generator, I'm sure as hell not going to town every day to fill a plastic emergency canister."

I slicked my hair back and shook the water from my hand. "You have to let us know, Squire. You can't just surprise us with figments on compound."

The Mouth walked over to me. "Someone else was on compound? From outside the movement?"

I waved my hand at Squire and pulled a cigarette out of the pack in my breast pocket. The paper dissolved at my touch, and the wet tobacco that remained stuck to my fingers. I sighed. "Help me out here buddy."

The Mouth grabbed a cigarette for himself, then tossed me his pack.

Squire walked over to sit on the arm of the chair across from me. "Look, I'm tired of being handled with kid gloves like I'm some village idiot who needs minding. I don't need to ask permission from you or anyone else to get things done around here. I didn't leave behind everything I owned to come play errand boy to you four."

"Well, let's take a look at the consequences of that decision, shall we?" I replied. "We have no gas. Hawke is arrested again. And the windmill was crushed from falling off a five-story water tower."

"And whose hand did it slip out of?"

"Whose knot did it slip out of? For fuck's sake, Squire, if you don't want to be here then just go. No one's stopping you. But if you're going to stay, you gotta commit to this, and you gotta play by the rules."

"What rules?"

I stood. "Rule one: no figments on compound without warning."

The Mouth sat cross-legged on the floor between us, smoke slipping from his lips like a Lewis Carrol caterpillar. "Seconded."

"Rule two," I continued, "nothing but the essentials from the figment world. We'll have crops soon, and our water situation is almost sorted. We are here to be independent, so let's do it."

"Seconded," the Mouth said.

Squire glared at him through squinted eyes. "Rule three," he said. "Everyone does his or her share. No more hiding in your room all day on the Internet while the rest of us work."

"Seconded," Regina said, crossing her arms.

We sat in tense silence, long enough for a cloud of smoke to build in the room. The Mouth had switched to reds, and the smoke from the cigarette he offered me slid down my throat like sandpaper. Squire sighed, stood, and went over to crack a window. The breath of the room slipped out and merged with the final exhales of a sky about to tire.

"Look, Squire," I said. "It makes sense filling the tank all at once. If we can convince the driver to come back, let's get the gas and be done with it. He has our money already, doesn't he?"

Squire nodded.

"And I'm sorry about the windmill. We can find another one, right?"

He nodded and pursed his lips as he walked back to the chair. "I guess my knot tying skills are a bit rusty. It's been ages since Scouts. It's fine. If you'd held on in that storm, it would have pulled you down with it. That, or you'd have been zapped by lightning. We'll find another."

Regina turned to look out at the remnants of the rain. Night had crept into position behind the curtain of clouds, and now, as that curtain lifted, the ground shimmered, each puddle reflecting the light of a thousand stars and the glow of a gibbous moon. She sighed as if she were the only person on earth.

"You still haven't said what happened to Hawke," the Mouth said. "How did he get arrested?"

We lit a few more candles and told him everything. While we did, Squire ignited the stove and started cooking dinner. Slowly, our clothes dried and warmth returned to the room.

"Hawke's in trouble," the Mouth concluded.

"It's not good," Squire agreed. "By now his court date from the capital has come and gone. He's officially skipped bail. If the local cops look up his records, they'll likely find a warrant for his arrest."

"True, but it's the local cops I'm worried about," the Mouth said. "Or more specifically their boss—the Constable, they call her."

Regina rolled her eyes. "'They,' Dean?"

"Yes, Reg. *They.* The internet menagerie. They call her a psycho bitch."

"The internet menagerie calls all women psycho bitches."

"Sure, but apparently she deserves it. She ran for sheriff a few years back, promising to clean up the Shambles and get tough on crime. Real zero-tolerance bullshit. Her goon squad is a bunch of testosterone-hopped ex-military a-holes who drive through town like they're rolling through Fallujah. The mayor has been criticized for turning a blind eye to police violence, so he keeps the Constable on a short leash. But she would tear it down brick by brick if he let her."

"What does she have against the Shambles?" I asked.

"The same thing rich people have had against poor people for all eternity. Poverty is a moral failing. Morally fallible people are essentially criminals. They need to learn to pull themselves up by their bootstraps. But not *their* bootstraps, *her* bootstraps. And also, stay the fuck away from her bootstraps."

"Well," Squire said, rubbing his forehead. "Basically, he's fudged, isn't he?"

"Basically, we're all fudged," the Mouth replied. "The Constable doesn't sound like the kind of person to lock Hawke away and turn a blind eye to his squatter friends. What are we going to do when the police return for us?"

My mind scanned a mental map of Junemark. There was a fire exit at the back of the factory floor, and from there it was a short run through the trees to reach the main train line. We could hop in between the cars of a passenger train exiting Isidora or jump onto the ladder of a slow-moving freighter. We'd have to leave a lot behind, Hank and the piping and the split earth in the fields. But we could start over somewhere else. It would be difficult, but it could be done. And in the spring the going would be much easier.

The rain had stopped, and through the open window we heard water gather on the building's eaves and fall, bouncing off sheet metal in the yard like the yarn-wrapped mallets of a xylophone. Only Squire continued to eat, chewing in delicate apprehension as we listened for the sound of sirens.

****

It wasn't the sound of their sex that kept me awake, though I could have done without it. Normally, Squire slept in Regina's room, providing a buffer of two walls and an empty suite between me and their lovemaking. But after we finished eating and agreed on an exit plan in the event the compound was raided, we retired upstairs, and Regina made a grand display of pushing Squire back into his own room under an assault of kisses. For what felt like hours the single wall between us was nothing but a curtain, and I lay on the other side like an audience member seated in the front row, hearing each footstep and rolling wheel as the tech crew changed sets. In this case, though, it seemed discretion was not the goal.

I could forgive Squire his labored breathing. It was innocent and unavoidable, like that of a pug—more the result of physiology than anything else. And the furniture was decades old and bound to squeak. Regina's heavy moans and pleads for more, on the other hand, felt performative. In the weeks since the pond, the string that connected us was unplayed but no less taught, and I wondered if given the right pluck it might vibrate again. But mostly I tried to put her out of my mind. The time spent with Squire helped, and I made an effort to be near him whenever possible. But perhaps she took it as a threat—the usurpation of a jilted admirer conquering her conquest because I could not conquer her. Or perhaps my intuition at the pond hadn't been so far off. Perhaps this was a piece of theater designed to bewitch an audience of one—a full-throated demonstration of the could-have-been. The more I considered it, the less clear it became.

But in all fairness, it wasn't the sound of their sex that kept me awake.

"What a mess," I sighed. I looked up at the moonlit ceiling, my eyes tracing the water stains that tarnished the suite of the leader who had failed before me.

I spun onto my side and pulled the vinyl sleeping bag over my ears.

Eventually, the noises stopped, and the beasts next door dropped into sleep.

Eventually, I did the same.

Chapter Fourteen

The next morning my mind lingered in limbo between the clarified reality and an abstract dream. The vision that flickered my eyelids the night before had already been forgotten, but a sensation remained, that of being wrapped around a warm body, and I held onto it as long as I could. When my mind receded and sleep looked to conquer me again, I felt the press of a woman's shoulder in my embracing arm and smelled the vanilla in her hair. But hunger and the need to piss caught me like a hook in the gill and fished me from those unconstructed waters.

It was only at the top of the stairs, pausing in the silence of a day not yet begun, that I remembered the sword of Damocles hung above our heads by Hawke's recklessness. It had not fallen—not on me anyway—and if the others had been spirited away in the middle of the night, the police left no evidence of it. I wondered what it would mean if they had, if in addition to Hawke, the rest of them had been taken from me, rounded up and shoved into a paddy wagon, leaving me to fend for myself in that industrial ghost town. Could I survive on my own? Of course not. Without them, alone, confronting the privations of life in Isidora, I would be an ant separated from its colony, only then understanding the true meaning of "ant," the true meaning of "colony." The sight of the Mouth sitting on the windowsill downstairs slurping milk from a bowl of Frosted Flakes didn't completely dispel the feeling that I was, in fact, on my own.

"Morning," he said with a smirk. "How did you sleep?"

I groaned and started boiling water for coffee. "Are they still in bed?"

"I guess so. Haven't seen them." He stood and grabbed a handful of M&Ms from an open bag on the pantry table. "Are we still filming today?"

I thought about the dead windmill and the rainwater that pooled in its concavities, waiting to be taken back up by the morning sun. It would have to be replaced, but I would leave it to Squire to do the reconnaissance.

"I suppose so."

He threw an M&M in the air and caught it in his mouth. The sound it made ricocheting off a molar, like the chipping of porcelain, sent a shiver up my spine.

"Jesus. How can you eat those things so early in the day?"

"With my metabolism, I can eat whatever I want." He lifted his shirt and slapped a belly that looked unchanged from the day we left the capital. "Why deny myself a little luxury from time to time?"

"LaBouche, the gluttonous consumer. It's a new look for you."

"Yes, darling, but I wear it so well." He grinned at me with chocolate-stained teeth. "Buck up. We survived the night."

I sighed as I poured boiled water into the French press. "That's hardly a cause for celebration."

"Tell that to most of the world's major religions. We're on the other side. The danger is behind us."

"How can you be so sure?"

"What? Do you think the Constable would give us a head start?"

We finished our breakfast, dressed, and reunited in the courtyard. The silence from Squire's room continued, and I thought to knock to rouse them. "Aw, leave 'em alone," the Mouth had said. "Everyone deserves a day off from time to time." He gathered his filming equipment, the totality of which was a cell phone and a makeshift tripod, and we headed to the Mines.

Junemark's production building had been liquidated, leaving nothing behind but paper clips and dust bunnies. Like the Ark, the Mines had a suite of offices at the eastern end, but most of the space was dedicated to the expansive factory floor, open and empty like an aircraft hangar. Apart from traffic patterns worn into the cement pad by boots, trollies, and lifts, it was the blank slate we had hoped for, the perfect image of the nothingness that awaited our followers at Isidora.

The Mouth skittered about, shooting B-roll as I drew circles in the dust with my feet.

"Are you sure you want me doing this one?" I asked. "You brought us here. You're managing outreach to the following. Shouldn't you do the invite?"

"It wasn't meant to be," he said without looking up from his phone. "Turns out the chosen one can't also be the chooser. They want you." He paused as if to consider another path, another way, then shook his head. "Anyway, after a couple of weeks in Isidora they'll realize how boring you are and change their minds."

I laughed. "You're probably right."

"And that's when I'll step in to sweep them off their feet."

"Do you really think they'll come?"

"Absolutely. At least a hundred in the first crop. And do you want to know something?" He leaned in close. "Some of them will be women," he whispered.

"Right," I said, nodding.

"Women!" he yelled, the word echoing through the empty hall. "I mean real women made of nothing but legs and tits and hair. Women, not hundreds of miles away but right here in Isidora. Can you imagine?"

"Yeah, I guess. Can we start?"

He grabbed my shoulder, his eyes aflame with biological necessity. "Do you know how long it's been? Of course you do. We've been cooped up here together. It's been forever. Exactly forever. It's been so long even Regina is starting to look good."

I brushed his hand off my shoulder and turned away.

"Regina? Can you imagine? I mean, good for Squibs and all, but really." He shook his head. "No thank you."

"Christ, why are you telling me this? Can't you just lock your door and take one on the wrist like everyone else?"

"Nope," he said as if the idea contradicted natural law. "Not here. We didn't come all this way to clench our eyes shut and jerk off in the dark to a half-conjured fantasy. Isidora will be real. It must be real. Everything."

"I didn't realize we came all this way to start some kind of sex cult."

"We didn't come all this way to start some kind of abstinence cult either. We're merely setting the table. Anyone who wants to eat, can. As for me? I'm famished."

I crossed my arms and rubbed the bridge of my nose. "You are a truly disgusting creature."

He smirked and raised his eyebrows as if to challenge me to deny the same of myself or to deny it of any man who has ever lived.

"Can we do this already?"

"Fine," he said, and then added with a whisper, "Women."

We set up at the far end of the production floor, our backs pressed against the western wall, the great expanse of the hall in front of us.

"What do you want me to say?" I had run through the scene a couple times in my head, but the words never came. It seemed a silly thing to do, to film a welcome video for people who were already chomping at the bit to join us. *Just let them come*, I thought. But the Mouth insisted. Until it was deeply ingrained in them, the narrative of Isidora would have to be spoon fed to our followers in daily doses. Words would not just describe our reality, they would define it, affirm it, sustain it. For the Mouth, the only way to lose it all, to lose ourselves, was to stop talking.

"Just lie to them." He said it with such a nonchalance that I almost thought I misheard him.

"Lie to them? I can't do that."

"Of course you can. You lie all the time. Go" He pushed on the screen, and I heard the beep of a new recording begun.

"Whoa, hold on a second. I'm not ready."

The Mouth groaned and hit stop. "What's the matter?"

"I can't just wing this. It's important. I need to know what to say."

"Like I said, just lie like you always do. Go."

"Dean, stop." The eye of the camera felt penetrating, and I stepped out of frame. "What do you mean 'like I always do?' I don't always lie."

"Of course you do. Words are lies—little bubbles of deceit blown at our friends and loved ones. They rise high and expand in vertiginous glory. They sink low and shrink to near nothingness."

I gave him a quizzical look.

"Don't get me wrong. That's OK. Reality does the same thing. It stretches, it bends, it twists and turns. Nothing is permanent."

"That's not a very compelling welcome message."

"Sure it is." Sensing the delay would last longer than expected, he reached into his pocket for a cigarette. "Isidora will be an escape, not just from the vision of an objective reality forced on us all by the figment world, but from objective reality itself."

"Here. Give me one."

"You know how babies are said to lack object permanence? How if you take a toy and hide it behind your back, they think it's gone forever?

"Sure."

"We act like it's some great thing to recognize permanence in the world, like it's some sort of higher-level thinking. But of course, the little squirts had it right all along. The toy is gone. Maybe not right away, but in due time, its average state over the infinite expanse of everythingness? Shit, who's to say it was ever really there?"

At the mention of a child's loss, I had a vision of my mother sitting alone at our kitchen table atop a heavy hardwood chair whittled by the hands of an artisan in the Amanas. The rattan lampshade above conceals a solitary tungsten flame, the only lamp in the room, and as dusk descends, the kitchen falls into the pallid hues of mourning. A cigarette smolders, neglected in the ashtray, beside a much-loved tumbler of gin.

I knew the Mouth was right, because at some point I closed my eyes to that vision. And when I opened them again, she was gone.

He dropped his half-smoked cigarette and stamped it out under his heel. "So, like I said, just lie to them. Like you always do."

I blew a breath of used air through my nostrils, and my body shuddered. "I'll do what I can."

The video probably still exists, sitting inert somewhere in the depths of our collective digital memory, a derelict barn occupying a binary parcel in some far-flung server farm, accessible to anyone with the patience for buffering. The Mouth edited it to open on naked images of the Mines that slowly panned left or right, or crawled along the dusty concrete floor, making the steel beams above feel like the rafters of some great sanctuary. He set it all to the plodding snare of Ravel's Boléro. My voice came in with the oboe.

"Friends, welcome to Isidora. It may not look like much, but here on top of this barren concrete slab we will build a new society. And we've done so much already. Since our arrival, we've built the foundation of just and equitable living— clean, abundant water; fresh, delicious food; and stable, reliable power. All that's missing is you."

The shot faded to black and reopened on the pond. The camera traced the line of piping as it snaked toward the water tower. In the distance, barely captured in frame, a truss was perched, topless.

"Right now, Isidora may seem like a dream to you. But when you're here, nothing else will seem as real. The world outside our compound is an imagined reality where lies masquerade as TRUTH, where conspiracy theories are commonplace, and common sense is rare. Where power and money conspire to preserve themselves at your expense. Here in Isidora, when the sun beats down and tans your skin, it's real. When the rain falls from the sky and soaks your hair, it's real. When you spend the day at labor and sweat beads on your brow, it's real. And all that you think, and all that you feel, and all that you build is yours to keep, forever."

The scene faded again, opening on the water tower's catwalk. Behind me, the town that was Isidora faded to black in front of the radiant light of a setting sun.

"Friends, for the longest time you have felt invisible. You have suffered in a world of unreality where your labor is a commodity, your voice is a commodity, your health is a commodity, your soul is a commodity. No more. It's time for you to leave that figment world behind. It's time to be real. The preparations are complete. The gates are open. Come to Isidora and be seen."

Chapter Fifteen

We descended from the water tower, and the Mouth flew off to the Ark to start editing. I had no desire to join him, no desire to see Squire and Regina cuddling on a couch in the receiving room, no desire to climb the stairs and rattle around the confines of my suite like a violently thrown super ball.

Instead, I turned away and followed the train line back toward town, my body ambling as my mind sputtered in indecision. It was April, or perhaps already May, but the nights still brought the sharp chill of early spring. I was underdressed, goosebumps rising off my bare arms, and it felt wonderful. My mind was dead, but my body was alive, experiencing the long brushstrokes of the steady breeze, the rustle of infant leaves in the trees reborn, the give of ground swollen with rainwater.

Hawke had not returned. It wasn't what I wanted to think about, but it felt less self-serving than the other topics that begged for my attention. Hawke had not returned, which meant he was likely to never return. I pictured him at that moment, bouncing off a wooden bench in the back of a police van as they transported him back to the capital jail, chained like a steer on its way to the slaughterhouse. The image carried a certain sense of injustice, but I couldn't decide if he deserved better or if I just wanted him back.

He was our industrialist, and without him we were a hunter-gatherer, an agrarian, a water-carrier, and a demagogue, capable of subsistence and self-aggrandizement but not much else. We could continue to muddle through for a time, charging the Mouth's devices off of Hank's twelve-volt cigarette lighter, bathing in rainwater poured from a pot, and slurping down lukewarm Campbell's in the dark, but that wouldn't satisfy the hundreds preparing to descend upon us. We needed scale and efficiency. On both accounts, the Mouth was practically useless, and I wasn't much better. Regina was fastidious and dogged but untrained, and while Squire was blessed with the scout-like handiness that comes from growing up somewhere between Fond-du-Lac and Chippewa, to achieve what we had planned and what we had not yet dared to dream, we needed Hawke. He was a headstrong purist to a fault, but he was also necessary.

When I emerged from the thicket at the junction with the main train line, the stars revealed themselves in the black night sky. They were always a jumble at first, a beguiling chaos of light suspended above me as they must have been for the first humans to come down from the trees and look heavenward. How many nights were spent cowed by that fantastical display before they saw order? Years? Decades? Generations? I scanned the sky as I was trained to do, looking for a familiar formation. Then I reconstructed the heavens piece by piece with the shapes of legends known by heart. Start with Polaris at the tail of the minor bear. Cassiopeia, below, locked in chains above the northern horizon for her vanity and arrogance. The inseparable Gemini twins to the west, frolicking behind the black orb of a new moon. And in between, our hero, Perseus.

But he wasn't there. Instead, an orange glow emanated from the north Shambles, a million times dimmer than the constellation's burning balls of gas but a million and one times closer, so it was all I could see. I went to it.

A half-mile past the Isidora rail station, the inky blackness smeared across the horizon came into relief, and my eyes traced the line of the rooftops, bouncing horizontally from brownstone to brownstone before mounting the incline of a church steeple or falling into the void of a darkened playground. Nothing was illuminated, not streetlights, porch lights, or dining room windows. Nothing but an empty parking lot ringed by chain link, drowning in halogen poured down like floodlights on no-man's land.

But that was not the source of the glow. Ahead, set apart at the edge of the Shambles, like a gazelle that had strayed too far from the heard, a three-story building burned.

It was once a tenement or perhaps an old textile mill. Nothing of the façade was visible, not even in the spinning lights of the trucks that sat idle in front. Before the tempestuous fire, the walls were iron bars, and the caged beast that paced behind sent tongues of flame through the windows to lick the eaves and singe the stucco. As it raged it breathed, wheezing air through the boarded windows on the ground floor, belching smoke through holes in the crumbling roof.

It was not fire as I knew fire to be—that dull orange ember crawling slowly across a campfire log, refusing at first to catch and disappearing without hesitation at the slightest inconvenience. This was something else. It looked like an apneated explosion, a chemical ordinance combusting in slow motion. The possibility that this was nothing more than timber and oxygen suitably catalyzed, a scourge so ancient it was imprinted into the minds of the earliest humans, never occurred to me.

The firemen were calm despite the calamity unfolding before them. Perhaps this was all old hat. They milled about outside their trucks or sat and watched from inside the cab. One stood in suspenders and a stained gray undershirt, reeling in a dry, flattened hose. Nothing was being done to quell the blaze.

Across from them, a huddle of humanity leaned on itself and wailed with the fury of the inferno in front of them. They were all in various stages of dress, men in pajama pants, naked from the waist up, women in hats and dresses and trench coats, with a dozen necklaces around their necks and suitcases in both arms. There were a few children too, standing dumbfounded before the blaze, their teddy bears dragging in the mud.

I approached to within a few paces of the firetrucks, pulled out a cigarette, and prepared to watch the uncommon spectacle of a building turning to ash. The fireman reeling in the hose stopped and walked over to me and, without a hint of irony, asked me for a light.

"Is there nothing that can be done?"

"Eeh," he said, flicking the lighter in front of him. "These old buildings are mostly wood. They go up pretty quick. I thought we'd spray at least, see if we could bring it back down. But the chief said to let it go. A boarded-up building, all abandoned? It ain't worth the water."

"Abandoned? Then who are those people?"

"Beats me. Squatters, layabouts, junkies? They don't own the place; that's for sure."

"It looks like they lived there."

He glanced over his shoulder. "Eeh. I guess they'll have to learn to pay rent like the rest of us." He lifted his helmet and wiped sweat off his forehead with the back of his hand. "Hell, chances are one of them winners started this blaze. I wouldn't worry about them."

He thanked me for the light, then walked back to his truck. The firemen lingered for another half hour, just long enough to convince themselves the bulk of the fuel was spent and the fire was beginning to starve. Then they left.

The squatters left too, though not all at once and not all in the same direction. Some headed west toward town and the possibility of a hand-out from diners leaving the second seating. Others went south, back into the Shambles to find an empty alcove where they could bed down for the night. A few, like me, stood and watched until the flames gave way to embers. I thought there might be a climax of sorts, a moment of finality that marked the end of the building, the end of the fire. But there was nothing; no moment of implosion, no cave-in or collapse. The fire was there for hours and then it was not. The building was lost somewhere along the way.

It was after midnight by the time I returned to Isidora. My body was covered in soot, and I smelled vaguely of summer camp. I walked past the Ark's front gate and circled the wall until I came upon the cisterns, then stripped bare from the waist up and filled a plastic milk jug from one of the tanks. The frigid water ran through my hair and rolled down my back, and the breeze that rose from the west wrapped around me like a warm towel. Above, black clouds rolled off a pin-pricked sky. Then Perseus returned.

Chapter Sixteen

Squire must have risen early because by the time we descended the marble stairs and dragged ourselves to the receiving room, he had already prepared a full spread. Omelettes, yogurt, muesli, toast. One day spent in bed with Regina and the fat man came back to us like a pensioner from a month-long cruise, ready to devote to any and all quotidian faff the full measure of his devotion. The Mouth was well attuned to such energy and hijacked breakfast with a discussion of the welcome video. The two of them sat to discuss it as if it were the only thing in the universe, as if nothing else stood between us and the glorious future we dreamed we could share.

Of course, plenty stood in our way, not least of which was a lack of coffee, so I set the kettle on the camp stove and poured beans into the hand grinder. I felt them breaking apart in the silver cylinder as I muscled the handle through stuttering revolutions, but all I could smell was ash. I considered telling them about the blaze in the Shambles, about the apathetic firemen and the people evicted by misfortune as they must have been so many times before. But with Squire and the Mouth sucking all the oxygen out of the room, I decided to hold it all in. When the coffee finished steeping, I plunged the mesh filter through the colloid and poured two steaming cups.

Regina stood by the window, watching clouds billow and curl. I sensed that she was a bit restored herself, that perhaps her moat had been drained and her drawbridge lowered. At least I was ready for that to be so.

For generals, wars can end any number of ways—the annihilation of an enemy; a forced, shameful retreat; the coming to terms at a table of peace. But for soldiers it always ends the same. At some point the fighter comes to know that the man in the opposite trench, whose bullets he has dodged for days, months, years, will no longer shoot if he lifts his head above the battlements. At some point he knows he can walk across the barren stretch of ground that separates them and shake the other man's hand, or sell him wine, or buy his wheat, or marry his daughter, or screw him out of money, or any of the other infinite ways we have learned to be with one another when we are not at war. Most importantly he comes to stop seeing himself as a combatant, and the pacific life he couldn't even summon in dreams during those cold nights in the trenches, he awaits with unshakeable certainty.

I walked over to stand beside her. The air that seeped in through the drafty window carried the warmth of spring.

"Four letters." Her voice was neither aggressive nor conciliatory. Her eyes remained straight ahead. "Another word for you."

"A horse's ass?"

She turned with a disarming smile, her eyes like marbles, her cheeks like poppies in snow.

"It doesn't fit." She grabbed a coffee from my hand, and I wrapped my arm around her shoulder and squeezed.

We didn't know what to do about Hawke—whether to inquire about him or not; whether he would be returned to the capital or left in the local county jail; whether he would be set free with a slap on the wrist or lined up against a wall and used for target practice. It didn't really matter. As much as it pained us to admit, he was the cat incarcerated in Schrödinger's box, and whether he was returned to us or was gone forever, we had no choice but to push ahead.

We spent the morning distracting ourselves with various labors and reunited as we always did on the Circle at noon.

"Dean already has a bead on another mill," Squire said through a mouthful of lentils.

"On another farm?" I asked.

"A flea market, actually. In Dorothea. The lady spun it a few times for me on video, and the piston rod on the bottom reciprocates. Hawke would know better, but I think we can make it work."

"Can we pick it up soon? I'd like to have water going up to the tank before the first followers arrive."

"This afternoon if you want. If it's in good shape, we can install it tomorrow."

"It's supposed to be a beautiful day," the Mouth said with a grin. His spot on the Circle had evolved the most since our first day in Isidora. Every week or two a new pillow or cushion would appear, pilfered from abandoned couches and chairs dispersed around the compound. Now he lazed on a pile of fluff like the sultan's favored vizier.

"Speaking of our absent companion," Regina said. "Any news? Is there even a way to know what's happened to that asshole?"

Squire resettled himself on his stool. "In fact, I'm not sure there's anything we can do, at least not without drawing attention to ourselves."

I scratched my head. "How long can he be held without some kind of public action—a hearing or sentencing or whatever?"

Before Squire could answer, a voice called out from the door to the factory floor—a voice that reminded me that though we lived behind six-foot walls topped with broken glass, our front gate was wide open.

"Not long, it turns out."

"Hawke!" the fat man squealed. Squire—always slow to anger and quick to forgiveness—sprang from his stool with such force he knocked it to the ground.

Hawke rounded a black iron fixture with a triumphant, shit-eating grin. But he was not alone. Our favorite capital bartender was at his side.

"And Sam?" Squire said, dumbfounded.

This time it was Regina who squealed. "Sam! What the. . . I can't believe you're here!"

He hadn't had a haircut since we last saw him and hadn't shaved in at least a week. The bags beneath his eyes spoke to sleepless nights, the wrinkled corners of his mouth to weeks of worry. Still, when Regina ran to him and threw her arms around his waist, he beamed.

"How did you find us?" Squire asked, still perplexed.

Sam pried Regina off his chest and dropped his large russet backpack to the floor. "It wasn't too hard to piece together your location from landmarks in the videos. Besides, Dean told me where to find you before you skipped town. Am I the first?"

I shot a glance at the Mouth, but there was no emotion behind it. It didn't matter that Sam was clued in. He was one of us and most welcome. "It's so good to see you," I said. "You're the first." I walked over and gave him a hug.

"I thought it'd be more difficult, to be honest. I knew I was looking for Junemark, but I didn't expect it to be spelled out in six-foot-high cement letters on your doorstep."

The Mouth lowered himself onto his pile of cushions and searched his pockets for a cigarette. "Yeah, we should probably get rid of those."

"And then there's the Junemark Co. sign above the gate to this old part."

"Yeah, that too."

"How did you find Hawke?" Squire asked, righting his stool.

"I ran into him in the parking lot."

"Wait." Regina leaned forward in her armchair. "Hawke, where the fuck have you been?"

Hawke slid across the Circle and took his usual place on the edge of the workbench. He sat straight and tall, and where most people would feel displaced by the ordeal he had just survived, he looked exactly the opposite. If anything, he had become even more immovable.

"In jail. Y'all saw me get arrested."

"But how did you get out?"

"What does it matter?" I coughed, ash and embers still tickling my larynx. "He's back."

"It matters," Regina said, turning to me. "It matters for our security— for the security of the movement."

The Mouth held up a cigarette from his recumbent position, and Hawke slid off the bench to claim it. "The police are nothing to worry about. We're safe here. I heard it from the Constable's own mouth."

"You told her about us?" Regina jumped to her feet like a mother bear prepared to maul.

"Reg, I had to. They knew we were here. *I was arrested here.* But it's fine. She doesn't care about the industrial park. Everything east of the Shambles is empty farmland as far as she's concerned."

"And she just let you go?" Squire asked. "Just like that?"

"I just. . . yeah, basically."

I walked over to Squire and put a hand on his shoulder. "There'll be plenty of time to talk about all this later. For now, we have a new member who needs to be housed and fed."

The Mouth rose up off his pillows with a groan. "The second admin suite is still empty. Sam, you can crash there. Follow me."

As the Mouth led him away, Sam stopped in his tracks. "Oh, I almost forgot," he said. "There was this grizzled old guy milling about near the entrance to this place. He mumbled something about needing fertilizer."

"Oh, that's just John Galt."

"Who is John Galt?"

"Exactly." The Mouth rolled his eyes, put a hand on Sam's shoulder, and led him out of the room.

"Squire," I said, "can we throw together a quick lunch for Sam?"

"On it, sir," he said with a salute.

"And you two." I turned to Hawke and Regina. "Can you try not to kill each other today? We have a guest."

Hawke smiled. "Of course."

"No promises," Regina said as she turned to leave.

****

Sam was the first—the first to come, the first to expand the Circle, the first to transition from the figment world to the reality of Isidora. His primacy would later be a source of immeasurable pride, but even then, at his beginning, he felt the TRUTH of Isidora deeply, naïvely. He walked the compound with the Mouth like a man reborn, wondering at the branching array of empty irrigation pipes, clapping into the void of the echoing Mines, breathing our planet's inert nitrogen-rich air deep into his lungs as if for the very first time. With Sam, there were never any complications, not like with the others. He was one of us, and his arrival was the reclamation of something lost rather than the adoption of something new. Like luggage that had missed a connection he came back to us, and we took him in like he had never left our side.

> *—His love for Isidora was always pure, his devotion unending.*

In TRUTH, he had nowhere else to go. His bar in the capital was doomed after the denizens of Tent City scared off the regular clientele. When the Park Police torched Tent City, the place sat empty, racking up debt night after night. Like the great industrialists before him, the owner knew when to take the money and run. He sold the liquor license, broke the lease, and skipped town without as much as an email to inform staff. When the place was open, Sam had made a fraction of minimum wage, and after nearly a decade of mixing rail drinks and pouring flat beer, he had nothing to show for it but a couple new tattoos and low-grade alcoholism. For a few weeks he wore out the welcome of friends, then crashed for a few more on the stained mattresses of local shelters. When the weather was decent, he even slept outside on a park bench, something he said he would have almost enjoyed were it not for the fear of being robbed in his sleep. He was in free fall, and he came to Isidora hoping for a soft place to land.

That first afternoon Sam refused an offer of rest and instead went with Squire to lasso the Junemark steles with rope tied to Hank's ball-joint hitch. The two of them, wild eyed and giggling like misbehaving children, jammed down the throttle and spun the truck's tires bald, toppling the monoliths one by one. The wrought-iron script above the old compound, "THE JUNEMARK CO.," would go too. Hawke would menace it with bolt cutters, chisels, and hacksaws, managing only to scrape the paint and blunt a few good edges. But with time and the procurement of a welding torch, he would remove the letters "JUNEM" and "CO" and banish the company that had been. Junemark was dead. Junemark never was. And Isidora—the town that had been Isidora—was nothing but a mirage at the edge of our periphery. From that point forward, the compound was Isidora. And Isidora was everything.

Chapter Seventeen

A river flowed south of town, born high in the jagged western mountains of trickling snowmelt and morning dew glistening on alpine flora. It coalesced on itself like the fragments of a shattering vase viewed in reverse— inevitable in a way, preordained by gravity and timeworn channels stitched into the rock. As each piece reunited, the brook became a stream, the stream a rivulet, the rivulet a raging river, swirling and contorting as it tumbled seaward. In its furious growth, it tore down its cradle walls, littering the path with fallen slate and stone. And on it raged, crashing into boulders, breaking itself in fine, misty sprays that refracted the light above, painting the air in color where once there was only white.

It bounded through the foothills of those same mountains, arrogant and arrow straight, chewing on its banks and filling itself with iron-heavy sediments. The pig farmers and cowherds who settled there could do nothing with its racing ruddiness. It refused to be tamed by dock or dam, canal or levee. And so they deemed it unnavigable and left the river to its lonesome. Far from the eroding shore, they huddled on hilltops and spoke only of rain.

But on the infinite plains of the spare middle-west where the soft strata are layered as perfectly as a void, the river lost its way. Gone was the constricted verticality of its youth, and ahead there was nothing but imperceptible flow across the numbing horizontal. And in that unstructured space it began to roam, hunting north and south in long languid arcs for a path that had once felt unmistakable. It diverted in deference to every granite outcropping. It retreated from every minor rise. And the sea—that most urgent desire that pulled the water down through canyon chutes and valley floors? The river approached it with the coy indifference of a spurned lover.

The people of the great plains praised its docility and its temperance. Its length became their commerce, its width their law, its depth their leisure. They drew the river's water into hand-hewn canals and irrigation ditches, and erected on its banks marinas, flour mills, and dockside gambling halls. And while its companions overflowed with demands, the river kept to its shores, desireless and yielding. It gave all that was asked of it for the chance to be part of that community, to be useful, to be needed. It was a suitable arrangement, and at points where the river could have slipped away over rocky rapids, it lingered instead, swirling in on itself and spilling onto flat, reedy marshes where it stagnated and grew fat with algae and cattails.

From the top of the water tower, the surface of the meandering river glowed in the late-afternoon light like calligraphy scribbled on the land in golden ink. I sensed that somewhere in the to and fro, in the pause and flow, in the long stretches of empty contemplation and the frenetic moments of utility, the river had discovered what some might call happiness. I took in a deep, contented breath of that elevated air, blowing free above the layer of pollen and dust that hugged the earth. Perched on the truss above my head, a windmill turned in steady creaks, pulling water up those many stories to slosh into the tower's slowly filling tank.

Below me a patchwork canopy of tents erected on the lawn of the Winter Quarters recolored the land in blocks of auburn, marigold, and sage.

The billowing mass swayed with each passing breeze, and its inhabitants—the dozens of followers who arrived in Isidora in the wake of Sam's appearance—skipped in and out like children under an heirloom quilt. They were, like their makeshift shelters, a motley bunch—some familiar faces from the capital, others fruit fallen from farther trees. But they were uniformly committed, uniformly called and uniformly chosen, and for the time being uniformly joyous.

My eyes looked south again to scan the interstate. Sixteen-wheelers, gray minivans, and base-model subcompacts crawled along in an endless processional, prudently spaced at an unhurried sixty-five. The red F-150 cut through them like a football player running cones, the dusty yellow turn signal illuminated far too late to be of any use to fellow motorists, more a taunt than a tell. Squire hit the exit ramp at the speed of a first-time father. As he rounded the turn to come down the frontage road, the chassis listed on its tired shocks like a ship at sea.

"He's back!" I yelled down to Hawke.

"About time!" he shouted in reply. "Let's get these coals going."

I hurried down the ladder, sliding the final few yards like a fireman on a pole. Hawke hadn't bothered to wait for me, so I trotted alongside the train yard and rounded the machine shed to catch him. He'd set up the improvised grill there above the Green, a triangular patch of grass that sloped from the Mines and Winter Quarters down to the pond. It wasn't much—just an old steel drum cut vertically and mounted on legs—but it promised to cook a prodigious feast for our new arrivals.

"You do the honors," he said, passing me a carton of strike-on-box matches.

The first few refused to light or were snuffed out en route to the kindling. When I finally set fire to the bundle of twigs and paper at the base of the coals, it wriggled and curled, resisting the flame with puffs of complaining brown smoke.

Hawke shook his head. "I told Squire this Eagle Scout shit was no use. We need an accelerant."

Saying nothing more, he ducked into the machine shed and returned an instant later wearing a backpack pesticide sprayer. With a few cranks of the hand pump at his waist he pressurized the canister and then sprayed a fine mist of gasoline onto the coals.

"I'd stand back."

In one looping motion he flicked his wrist to run a match along the box and flung the sparking flame at the coals while it still ate phosphorus. The length of the grill burst into flame, fire squeezed from the air like toothpaste from a tube.

"You use that thing often?" I asked with a smirk.

"From time to time."

And yet the coals were still not burning. They sat inert, cold lumps of blackened rock below frivolous orange and yellow sprites, the heat projecting harmlessly skyward.

"It's a wonder that something can be so close to a flame and not get singed," I mused.

Hawke hit the grill with a few more bursts—a cowboy giving his stubborn mare the spurs. At each kick the fire leapt in gasps, then settled into an obedient burn. The bed below glowed hot orange.

He paused for a moment, looking at his creation with a self-satisfied smile. "There are only two types of substances in the universe—flammable and inflammable. In the end, everything burns."

"That's a strange pun, Hawke."

He patted my shoulder as he walked back to the shed.

To my right I saw Squire backing Hank up over the parking lot curb. As he slowly reversed toward me—the truck's tires straddling the too-narrow sidewalk that ran between buildings—the fingers on Squire's dangling hand tapped in time to a bouncy Travis-picked tune that spilled from the cab's open windows. Two chest-sized coolers, red and blue, spanned the length of the pickup bed, and a pair of aviators darted between the wing mirrors and the rear view. When the truck reached the crest of the hill, Squire ratcheted down the parking brake and waved with a left arm two shades darker than the right.

"You already got it lit?" Squire asked, falling from the cab.

"Sure, no trouble at all. Good solstice," I added as I lifted my right hand to cover my eyes.

"Oh, right." Squire straightened up and did the same. "Good Solstice."

Covering our eyes was the agreed upon gesture of greeting, devised by the Mouth to replace a handshake or a wave—both ways to demonstrate that one was unarmed and meant the other no harm. "What can be more disarming than denying oneself sight?" the Mouth had asked. It would take some getting used to.

"You get the goods?"

Squire gave me a wide-eyed grin as his bushy eyebrows danced above his forehead. "Did I?" He dropped the tailgate. "We hit the jackpot. Good weather and healthy herds. That's what the butcher said anyway. All the locals are selling this year, and he had more fresh meat than he knew what to do with. He was about to move all this to the freezers, so we got it at a discount. Nice guy."

Squire jumped into the truck bed and offered a hand to pull me up.

"Ribs, flanks, strips. . ." The lid of the first cooler sprang open—warm air crinkling shopping bags filled with ice. "Sirloin, T-bone, chuck. . ."

I swallowed a mouthful of drool.

"The sausages looked excellent too—bratwurst, knackwurst, kielbasas. A few dozen half-smokes for old time's sake."

"Squire, I could kiss you."

He closed the lid and stepped over to the second cooler. "Today is market day for the figments, so I loaded up on veggies too. Sweet corn, asparagus, red and green bell peppers, a huge sack of potatoes. . ."

Squire named it all in turn, holding each item up for me to inspect like Columbus introducing Isabella to a parrot.

"It's wonderful, Squire. Well done."

"Should we start grilling?"

"You just got back. Let's grab a drink first."

We strolled down to the base of the hill where Sam had set up bar. The task wasn't forced upon him. We actually urged him to experiment with a new identity at Isidora. But Sam wanted to experiment with booze, so he sat shotgun with Squire on his trips out of town to hunt for moonshining equipment in flea markets and barn sales. In Anastasia, they happened upon an antique copper alembic, and with it Sam distilled a potent hooch from sour mashed winter wheat and wild prairie grasses. He said it was white dog, but we all called it Brushfire, and there weren't cups small enough to make it safe to drink.

A spare workbench from the machine shop was moved into the middle of the field and on it sat a large terra cotta pot, its lid rimmed with an old T-shirt to help create a seal. A line of followers matted the grass in front, everyone bouncing and gabbing like vacationers in a taxi queue. Sam saw us coming and waved us over.

"Shouldn't we wait our turn?" Squire asked.

"We didn't shiver and starve all winter to sit at the back of the bus," I said. "We deserve a perk or two."

I pushed past him and draped an arm over Sam's shoulder. The people in front whispered to one another, but they didn't seem to mind. Squire shrugged. Sam beamed. And our loyal bartender ladled us a few cups of moonshine.

"Still no mixers, fellas, but Regina's mint has already come in full." Sam clapped a sprig of leaves in his palms then dropped it into the first drink. "It'll soften the bite."

"Don't lie to us, Sam," Squire said merrily as he reached for the cup.

Sam slapped again and delicately placed another mint. He offered me the glass with both hands.

"L'chaim," he said.

"Gan bei," Squire added.

I raised my glass to the crowd in front of us. "To Isidora!"

They responded with an enthusiastic applause, but as they could not yet return the toast, there was nothing to do but clink my plastic cup against Squire's and take a sip.

Brushfire made its way to my gut with the haste of a millipede and to my head with the subtlety of a sledgehammer.

Squire nodded his approval through stifled coughs and then plodded back up the hill. Hawke had reemerged and was slotting meat and diced bell peppers onto bamboo skewers, alternating between the red, the cow, and the green. But when Squire returned, handing him a near-full cup of Brushfire, Hawke moved aside without argument. Even he had the common sense to defer to Squire on all things gastronomic.

Every boy who's ever been camping learns to impale weenies on a sharpened stick and hold them in a fire until they blacken and pop. But Squire knew a better way, a more masterful way. He saw it once at dusk under the naked yellow bulb of a peasant farmhouse somewhere in the misty reaches of the Khans' conquered continent, the hands of his homestay father dancing above the coals—brushing, shaking, fanning, flipping. His mouth chewing syllables that rushed past the young Squire's ears unintelligible. Every sentence or two the man's face would crumple into a laugh, and Squire would smile, and the man would laugh again in response, harder this time, knowing the strange boy from the barbaric west understood nothing.

Almost nothing. He understood the mutton fat that dribbled down through lapping flames to sizzle on the coals, sending off plumes of seasoned smoke that clung to him like robes. He understood the magic of that first bite, his mouth awash in the silken notes of caravans stretched thin through high mountain passes, of bejeweled camels and their ragged riders, of sun-bleached tents flapping in the warmth of a moonless eastern sky.

How could he regress from that to Lawry's and A1? To retreat into the profane having once tasted the divine? It was unthinkable. The apple could not be uneaten. And so through cumin and coriander, cardamom and clove, Squire projected himself into the past, attempting to recapture those docile nights in his homestay family's ancestral valley when the world was ancient and he was young and there was nothing to do but sit and watch and learn. Time travel by taste bud, if only just.

As much as Squire failed to relive a life long lost, he succeeded in enriching our own. For hours, Squire's grilled feast flowed down the hill to our followers, forming new threads that tied our tongues to that happy place and time. Through the exotic cargo of eastern spice routes, we lashed ourselves to that Isidoran present, an indelible node of memory made of taste and smell, eternally accessible and medium rare.

Full bellies helped the Brushfire down and by the time the last of the day's colors had drained from the sky, the terra cotta pot was dry. We moved Sam's empty bar into the tall grass, and Squire released the parking brake on the F-150, allowing Hank to roll downhill and come to rest in the flat center of the Green. He popped open the doors of the cab, clicked on the electrical, and twisted the radio dial until he found a decent beat.

And soon we were dancing. As individuals at first, shaking ourselves, eyes closed and heads bobbing in a mass around the pick-up. But then a pair would look up and lock eyes and with parted lips fall into synchronized movement, edging ever closer, consenting in bashful glances, bonding like valence electrons. I found Regina first, her hair undone and her smile shared freely. The length of her body rolled against the length of mine, as light as a feather playing in a vanilla breeze. When the song ended, she squeezed my hand and then blew off into the crowd.

I must have danced with everyone, all of Isidora. And the score for the evening was as mercurial as my dance card. Every song or two someone would climb into the cab and pop in one of the presets or spin the dial up and down the backlit glass strip, landing us a decade further in the past or pulling us into the recent present. With the inseparable Kennedy and Quinn, I boogied to a disco classic, mugging my best Travolta, not that I had ever seen the film. Sam and I spit west coast rhymes, both tripping over our tongues when our memories failed us or the lyrics came too fast. No matter the tune, the Mouth spun like a whirling dervish, and I spun along with him in a lighthearted revolution that made melodrama of Mellon Collie. And I danced with the newcomers as well—a boot scoot with Mollie who hitchhiked from Topeka, a classic croon with Preston who flew in from New Haven. We coupled and decoupled in effortless fluidity. Like drops of water in the river south of town, the only bond that mattered was the one that united us all.

When Hank's battery finally ran dry, we retreated to the makeshift campground and bedded down together, two to a sack and no one complaining. Only Hawke chose to drag himself back to the Ark.

Chapter Eighteen

On that first summer solstice in Isidora, there were twenty-six of us. On the opposite side of the sun, there would be 130.

It was a dizzying expansion, but they didn't arrive all at once. They dripped into Isidora for months like electricity into a dead lithium battery, each one an electron amplifying our potential to do work. Eventually. When the charging was done, and we were no longer tethered to the wall. In the meantime, the list of projects to prepare for the coming cold kept growing. The Winter Quarters would have to be made habitable, the outer fields beyond the pond cleared and prepped for the spring sow. A rudimentary electric grid needed to be set up and attached to Hawke's generator, and the meager first crop from Regina's victory garden would have to be harvested, canned, and stored with the dry goods below the Ark's factory floor. The followers approached it all with the urgency of a freshman mid-semester.

Breakfast coffee spilled into a late-morning snack, and if no one made a move to dress for the day, lunch slid effortlessly into apéro. After a few days of getting to know one another, the restless enthusiasm of the newly arrived could be channeled into an afternoon of decent work. But then a new group would appear in the amber evening light lugging backpacks across the parking lot, and we would get drunk in welcoming celebration, and the cycle would start all over again.

When we did work, we broke as much as we built. We were, after all, amateurs in almost everything we attempted. Every day another pipe would crack or board split or window shatter. Once, in pursuit of god knows what, Preston melted down an entire spool of copper wire into a useless ring of metal. The world we held so clearly in our mind's eye refused to materialize before us. By mid-October the grounds were littered with failed experiments and misplaced efforts, and the last of the summer warmth was beginning to leave us. Something had to be done.

We agreed to meet at the Circle at dawn, long before the followers were awake, to discuss our options. Without a word, Squire disappeared to the reception room and made a pot of French press over the gas stove, pouring us each our preferred cup—Regina's with a drop of milk, the Mouth's with two lumps of sugar, Hawke's straight black. We took our natural seats around the Circle, and but for the easy addition of Sam, it was just as it had been in the beginning.

"I'm not sure we have a problem," the Mouth said, flopping onto his pillows. "Everyone's thrilled to be here, and we're pulling in new followers every week. This is what we had planned."

"But we're completely dependent on outside supplies and making no progress in the fields." Regina pursed her lips as she blew across the surface of her mug.

"I am running to BigBox every week," Squire added, twisting on his stool. "They greet me by name now."

The Mouth sank into a leisurely recline and fumbled for a cigarette. "Sure, but we were never going to scale up our agricultural production enough to feed the masses this fall. Regina, you're wonderful, but as far as I know you can't simply summon turnips from the earth. And besides. These new folks are arriving with money. We can't be hurting for cash, can we?"

Squire held the French press above his cup, waiting for the last drops to slip through the grounds. "We're spending an awful lot. But no, we're not hurting for cash."

"Well, there you are."

Regina set her mug down and crossed her arms. "That's not the point, Dean. Nothing is getting done. We're not preparing for the future. These followers are just. . ." She paused, waiting for the word to boil out of her. "Lazy."

"Oh, Reg, don't sell them short." Hawke leaned over the edge of his workbench seat, swinging his legs in unison. "They're also incompetent. The more they work, the more likely they are to kill themselves."

I looked over at Sam who was sitting quietly on a wooden crate beside the Mouth's pile of poofs. "Sam, you are the last of us and the first of them. What do you think?"

He leaned back a little and scratched his head with the brim of his trucker's hat. "I'd say give them a break. They don't know what went into this place. They're just taking it as they found it. If you guys expect more from them, they're going to need a bit more direction. On their own, they're just looking to enjoy Isidora. You have to teach them how to run it."

"How about teams?" Regina said. "We each head a team of followers to ensure everyone does their part."

"Not teams, Reg. We're not organizing a fucking little league here." The Mouth was fully on his back, his bulk buried in motley fluff, smoke wafting upward like incense from a brasier. "What about. . . contribution collectives?"

Hawke shook his head. "Getting colder."

"Productivity brigades?"

"Even worse."

"Look, what does it matter what they're called?" Regina sat up straight and twisted her torso. She was still warming up to the day and was in no mood to play the Mouth's word games.

Squire leaned forward with a raised finger. "A friendly amendment—work units?"

"Sure," Regina said through a strained back bend. "Work units. We each head a work unit, and we meet here once a week to ensure we're all moving toward the same goal."

"And who decides that?" the Mouth asked.

"We vote."

"No." Hawke slid to his feet. "No more voting. If it's not immediately clear then he can decide." He pointed to me with the butt of an unlit cigarette, then tapped it against his pack.

"Me?" The proposal caught me off guard.

"Sure. Four work units and a tie-breaker."

"Five work units," Regina said. "Don't forget Sam."

"Five then. Plus one leading the Circle." Hawke let the cigarette roll along his lips as he spoke, absolutely confident it wouldn't fall.

The proposal hung in the air as we rationalized our way to that same least-objectionable outcome. Sam was thrilled to be included as an equal. Regina happy to have promoted an ally. The Mouth was giddy that our movement was growing increasingly rich and textural. Squire was comforted by the prospect of having someone help him on supply runs. And Hawke? Maybe he thought if he scratched my back, I wouldn't claw at his. It was, for a while, a suitable arrangement. And besides, it was exactly what I wanted.

—*Don't shy away from it. Your supremacy was never questioned.*

I was glad to have the followers join us at Isidora. It added new life to our compound, new energy. But still, I felt there was a gulf between us—

between those who founded and those who inherited. Everyone who came after Sam was real, of course, but in a way, not fully actualized, and I wasn't yet sure I wanted that to change. To avoid having to ingratiate myself to a crew of followers? To be set apart—responsible for everything and also nothing at all? I couldn't have asked for better.

Five work units. One leader. Six yeses. Meeting adjourned.

****

Regina left the Circle that morning determined to pluck from amongst the chaff of followers scattered across the Green the grains of wheat that would form Isidora's most elite work unit. With the rest of us content to follow Squire back to the reception room for another pot of French press and a smoke, she had the pick of the litter. She walked toward the Green, drafting them all in her mind. Charlotte in the forest-green REI near the front. Roger—or was it Rory?—in the auburn Columbia at the back. Mac, the brute, in his canvas pup tent or if not there bedded down with Xiaomai in her rose-pink Quechua. Xiaomai too if she had to wake them both. But in truth, the selection wasn't that difficult. The fire she was looking for in the belly of her recruits was the same that compelled people to rise early and with purpose. Her unit was practically assembled when she reached the tents, anyone fit for purpose already vertical and caffeinated. She gathered them like a mother hen aligning her chicks and headed out to the fields. Alpha was born.

To be fair, it was not her appellation, though by proposing the idea and forming the first work unit she had every right to name it. But like she said, what did it matter what they were called? It was the Mouth's idea to use the Greek alphabet, and as Regina's unit was both Isidora's agrarians and the ordinal first, the name "Alpha" stuck.

That afternoon the Mouth formed his own unit out of the very same people Regina dismissed for sleeping late. Refusing to be Regina's Beta and having little interest in actual work, the Mouth called his unit Lambda and rejoined them all in bed.

Sam took Sigma and at first struggled to find recruits, but he was frank and good natured, and many of the later arrivals joined his unit with no regrets.

Squire and the few followers willing to venture off compound went completely rogue and named themselves the Cowboys, but the Mouth insisted on calling them Mus, and a week later no one knew them otherwise.

At best, Hawke considered it all a farce masquerading as industrial organization, and it was possible he resented the fact Regina could call herself Alpha. Out of spite or satire he pronounced himself the Omega and made no effort to take on followers. Still, they found him, those few attracted to his cloistered energy, his yeoman isolation, his callous indifference, his busy hands and ever-rolling eyes.

Within a week, everyone in Isidora was paired to a unit, everyone except me. To preserve my authority as final arbiter in the Circle, I couldn't be biased by loyalty to a unit. I was to be apart, segregated, alone. That that could be considered a privilege and a punishment made the arrangement acceptable to everyone. We all saw what we wanted to see. The Mouth said I was to be first among equals, and while he believed in the meaning of the entire phrase, I stopped listening at "first." When the units had all chosen their moniker, Squire asked if I would take a letter of my own. I considered it for a few days, but there was only ever one choice. Round and infinite. A point of punctuation at the end of every debate. A circle for the Circle.

The Omicron.

Part Three

Chapter Nineteen

The shower handle was caked in limestone scale and I suppose pond scum and god knows what else. It took all the strength I had to break through the calcified bonds and open the tap. When it finally turned free, only a few drops beaded on the saucer above my head. But then the pipes shuddered, and a groan echoed through the walls of the Ark as if the flow of rust-stained water stampeding toward me was being squeezed from the building itself. I bit my lip in anticipation of the frigid spray that would burst free in every direction but down.

"Ahh! Ahh! *Ahh*!"

Sixteen months on compound, now in the shrinking shadows of our second spring, and an ice-cold shower in my private ensuite was the height of Isidoran luxury. The windmill had spun all autumn long, pressurizing the pipes that stitched their way through the Ark with the weight of the depleted pond. But we weren't there to notice. We had joined the followers in the Green for what would prove our last spate of egalitarianism—the Mouth talking his way into the tent of a new sack mate every couple of days—the rest of us pitching one of our own amongst the fold. Only when a wind from the north glazed the ground in morning frost did the followers finally bunk down in the Winter Quarters and we retreat to the Ark to find we had inherited the miracle of indoor plumbing. The followers were jealous, especially so when they were forced to brave the subzero weather to collect snow for drinking water, but it couldn't be helped. Besides, it was exactly what we had endured that first winter in Isidora. Now that spring had burst forth in radiant warmth, I suspected the followers out on the Green, sponging each other down in the morning sun like neoclassical water nymphs, had the better of it.

I closed the tap and slinked out of the shower to stand before the unclouded mirror. The matted hair that hung limp before my eyes was still as dark as good earth, but the face below looked ashen and aged, weighed down by something long missing, once promised to return. For a while it only snuck up on me during quiet hours when I was alone and still. But like a cancer, that abstract longing continued to grow. I wanted to believe I was only burdened by the imperfect realization of our new world—that Isidora was the medicine. I had simply taken too little. But deep in the recesses of my mind, a question was left to fester: what if Isidora was not the cure but the disease and what I yearned for was concealed somewhere out in the nothingness beyond?

I threw a towel over my head with a sigh and moved to put on one of my new homespun robes. The heavy beige cotton was cut long and loose, the V-neck trimmed with colored blocks to symbolize the Omicron's role of unifying the work units. Cinched at the waist with a woven leather belt, it was more Moroccan djellaba than silk of Caesar, but I didn't really care how it looked. The Mouth intended for it to be ceremonial, but I found the flowing fabric so easy and comfortable it became my everyday affair.

At the Ark's front gate, I came upon a pair of Alphas waiting to deliver baskets of early spring lettuce. On seeing me they dropped their loads and covered their eyes in salute. I shaded mine with both hands as if peering through binoculars, the designated response afforded only to the Omicron whose sight, per the Mouth's ever-growing dogma, was never to be barred. But he didn't think it through. Unable to see my response, the followers never knew when they had been acknowledged, and the two of them stood there, backs straight, chests puffed, eyes covered, waiting for a message they would never receive.

I cleared my throat. "As you were, fellas."

They lowered their salute and continued inside.

"Oh, Simon?" I called after them. "Are you in for euchre tonight? We need a fourth."

The taller one, wispy thin with a melancholic face, turned to me. "Mu, Sigma, or Omega?"

"A Mu-Sigma duo."

He gave a knowing grin. "Piece of cake. See you there."

The compound was buzzing with the energy of an anthill, each follower clad in the assigned color of their work unit. As I made my way to the fields, I was stopped and saluted by Alphas in white, Omegas in black, Sigmas in red, and Mus in green. Individual Lambdas were a rare sight, particularly during the day, but they were otherwise hard to miss. Not only did they adopt the color blue, they seemed to adopt every clothing style ever designed. They wore nightgowns, petticoats, dickies, and trousers; slip dresses, ascots, culottes, and blouses; feathers and leathers and gossamer and lace. At times they appeared to be wearing their entire wardrobe all at once, buttoned up in impenetrable layers like Victorian prudes. At times they wore almost nothing at all, the curves of their bodies open to the world, painted or powdered indigo and azure.

I ran into the Mouth and a tail of Lambdas huddled under blue parasols at the edge of the pond and walked with them to the fields.

If the fall had been defined by lethargy and reluctance, the spring saw our followers erupt in an enthusiastic hustle that refused to submit to our command. Everyone wanted to do everything all the time, and like road builders dropping tarmac along the edge of a cliff, all the Circle could do was add a few guardrails and hope for the best. Despite Alpha's exhaustive planting schedule based on water management, shade coverage, and pest susceptibility, the other work units couldn't resist the urge to poke about the fields, hoping to claim credit for the security of Isidora's food supply. Against Regina's emphatic objection, the Circle decided to divide the fields in five, giving each unit a plot of their own. The Mus mono-cropped corn, the Sigmas wheat. The Omegas planted fire red piri-piris, orange habaneros, and yellow scotch bonnets. The Lambdas filled their field with heirloom tomatoes, staid rhubarb, gnarled gourds, and a single row of red carnations that the Mouth unconvincingly declared was more important to revolution than food.

In the end it didn't really matter. Half of what went into the ground that second spring stayed there, never to be seen again, and the seeds that did germinate, sending shoots through the cracked earth of the most innocent green, were ambushed by a late-season frost, a winter's echo that burst the cell walls and spilled the plants' organelles down their stalks in a viscous sap. Predictably, only Alpha's field grew anything resembling a crop, and as we pulled the last of our food stores from the Ark's basement, we looked forward with rumbling stomachs to a summer of boiled rutabagas and bitter kale.

The Mouth was particularly irritable, in part because Lambdas' failure upset the balance of his intellectual universe but mostly because Squire forgot to stock up on peanut M&Ms. He fumed and huffed as we surveyed the desolation of the Lambdas' shriveled tomato vines and bloomless carnations. In Alpha's plot, Regina weeded the base of her bounty, whistling a carefree tune from beneath the brim of a conical straw hat.

"You know, I have half a mind to take a weed whacker to those plants just to get smug Madame Butterfly over there to shut the fuck up."

"It'd be a waste of good cabbage," I mused.

"Good cabbage? Do you even hear yourself?" The Mouth pulled a withered stalk from the dirt, and a tangle of thin roots followed. "Jesus, what a mess."

"Not your finest work, but it's not a complete loss. Alpha's harvest should get us through a few more months, and in the meantime we can replant in the other plots."

"A few months of that rabbit food? Just kill me now, why don't you?"

I shrugged and continued walking along the trench between Lambdas' desiccated rows.

"Hey, I'm not the only one suffering," the Mouth called after me. "How long do you think people are going to stay here if we can't offer them more than root vegetables and rain water?"

If the Isidoran diet drove some to leave, they wouldn't have been the first. We lost dozens during the winter when the bitter cold set our jaws to endless chattering. We beat it back as best as we could with bonfires in the Mines, but the fire did little but return to numb fingers and toes the tingling of sensation, such that as we warmed we only more fully experienced the cold. Those early deserters must have felt a tinge of shame because they universally snuck out in the early morning through unzipped tent flaps and propped open doors, leaving nothing to mark their departure but a trail of glittering footprints in the snow. Taken on their own, none of the departures bothered me, but it was a troubling trend.

"What do you propose?" I asked.

"More followers."

"More?" I stopped in my tracks, and a cloud of dust rolled past my ankles. "We can barely feed the ones who are here now."

"More followers bringing more money," the Mouth said. "Like we did last summer. Another big round of recruitment, lots of new faces coming in and bringing cash with them. Omega has been talking about solar panels— building out the power supply to the Winter Quarters. Sigma could start a livestock program—fresh eggs, fresh milk, fresh meat. We can do it all with a bit more money."

"You can't farm the fields, so you'd have us harvest humans?"

"Every human who joins us adds to the reality of Isidora. Expansion should always be our goal."

I walked in quiet contemplation to the end of the row and turned. Behind the Mouth, the fields looked war ravaged. The few followers that bothered to return to their labors milled about the dusty ground like survivors in a ceasefire, combing the battlefield for signs of life, or if not that, something shiny to tuck into a pocket. Amid the destruction, Alpha's verdant Swiss hamlet grew in peaceful ignorance.

"What makes you think anyone out there still wants to join us? It's been over a year since we left the capital, and look what we've achieved—or rather, what we haven't achieved. Why would anyone else feel compelled to uproot themselves and be replanted in this sterile garden?"

The Mouth put his hand on my shoulder and smiled with the reassurance of an infomercial, promising to transform my exasperated black-and-white existence into an eternity of technicolor bliss. "The world is no different today than it was a year ago and no different than all the years before that. The people who weren't fired in January were sacked in June. The children who had school lunch in April went hungry in July. The junkies who dodged the spoon in May by December found themselves trapped under the lid of big pharma's childproof cap. Racism, inequality, misogyny, compound interest? Nothing has changed. The world still needs Isidora, now more than ever."

"The world may need Isidora, but it won't come without convincing."

The Mouth smiled and gripped my shoulder even tighter. "Don't you worry about that. I have a plan. I can pitch it to the Circle this afternoon."

I thought about the coming argument—the proposals and counterproposals, the friendly amendments, Squire's points of inquiry, the voting. No matter the subject, it always played out the same, and it always exhausted me. "Don't bother," I said slapping his shoulder. "Just get it done. Isidora's survival is not up for debate.

Chapter Twenty

I knew something was coming; the Mouth just wouldn't tell me what or when. After a week of anticipation, like a child going to the mailbox every day only to find it empty, my piqued curiosity began to spoil. On the morning Regina's curdled roar rang out from the adulterated fields, I had given up looking entirely and, therefore, had not noticed the dirt under the Mouth's fingernails or the way he slumped exhausted over the back of Squire's chair, downing a cup of joe in one long gulp.

Regina was livid, gripped by an unprecedented rage. She blew into the Ark like a tempest and threw her trowel at the Mouth's head with such force it stayed lodged in the receiving room sheet rock for a day and a half.

"You little shit."

She lunged at him, but Squire—alerted by the scream and enlivened by the trowel—caught her.

"That weaselly motherfucker stole my plants."

The Mouth pulled himself upright. "I didn't steal your plants, Regina."

"No? Well, you fucking. . ." She pushed off Squire in a huff, so flushed with anger the words had no room to flow. "Redistributed them."

The Mouth bounced an open pack of cigarettes in his hand until a single filter rose above the rest, which he grabbed in his lips and pulled. His words came out like smoke rings, round and soft, squeezed around the cigarette he struggled to light. "Yeah, I did do that. But let's be clear, Reg: they're not your plants. They aren't even Alpha's. They belong to Isidora, and Isidora needed them to be redistributed."

Squire turned to face him. "What did you do, Dean?"

"For fuck's sake, Squire. I redistributed them."

I chuckled from my outstretched position on the mustard sofa. "We may need more of an explanation than that, LaBouche."

"He and his band of lap dogs replanted my crop," Regina said. "*My* crop. They uprooted Alpha's garden and redistributed it in the plots of all the other work units, killing god knows how many plants in the process. Half of them aren't even plants anymore; they're just leaf clippings pushed into the dirt."

Squire stood dumbfounded. Regina slipped from his arms and marched up to the Mouth. "Give me that," she said, pulling out his cigarette and taking a deep drag before slapping him in the face.

"Christ, Reg," the Mouth said, clutching his cheek. "I didn't kill your damn plants. They are perfectly alive, redistributed not more than a hundred yards from where they were born. Calm the fuck down."

"Living beings don't work like that, Dean. You can't just pluck something from where it lives and plop it down somewhere else and expect it to keep on growing. They don't understand their new context. Their roots don't know where to find water. They get over-exposed with the change in sunlight. They get shocked."

"Really, Regina? Come on. Hundreds of millions of years of evolution, and you think these things are going to be shocked. . ." He pulled a hand to his chest to clutch invisible pearls. "*Shocked!* by being displaced by a few dozen feet. Your plants are fine, Reg. I asked them myself."

The noise that came from Regina was primordial and raw. An ancient speech that pre-dated language itself, inarticulate and pure. The sound of an overworked hunter-gatherer fecklessly swatting at swarming gnats. A long, exasperated *arrgghh*. She shook her fists and spun out of the room.

"Sure," the Mouth said, casually lighting a cigarette to replace the one she had pilfered. "Go see for yourself."

I stood up from the couch. "We're all going." I put an arm around the Mouth's shoulders and aimed him at the door, then added under my breath, "You're gonna need a better sales pitch than that, my friend."

When we reached the crest of the hill, my heart crashed into my stomach with the same wrenching reverberations as Regina's cry. I did my best to swallow it. The orderly green rows of Alpha's garden had been scooped from the soil like paint from a palette and splattered Pollock-like across the canvas of the fields with a commensurate disdain for tradition, talent, and taste. There were no obvious rows, and the distance between plants, once standard and appropriate, ranged from a few feet to ten times as many.

"Dean," Squire said with the failing reserve of a mother to a toddler. "This is absolute chaos."

"You're looking at it wrong," the Mouth muttered as he descended the hill in long falling steps. He circled the pond, leading us to the field's northwest corner.

From the level ground beside the pond, our perspective flattened, compressing the length of the field along a single width. As we approached the field's corner, the incongruous nodes scattered in front of us were pulled together, as if bound by the gravity of the Mouth's concerted vision, into a single coherent constellation. The rows, no longer parallel, ran diagonally across the field, wide at our feet and converging at the far corner.

"Kneel," the Mouth said, and we did. As we descended, the cabbages in front of us grew to meet a body of green and violet kale, crowned by the leaf tips of distant chard. A vision of Eden stretched unbroken to a seemingly limitless horizon.

"We'll film from here," he added.

"It's kinda beautiful," I said.

"Beautiful?" Regina rose and shook her head like a balance wheel. "Beautiful is hard work and know-how that grows actual food. Beautiful is not going hungry because we planned ahead. Beautiful was the crop we already grew. This isn't beautiful. This is a cheap trick, a Potemkin garden to feed egos, not bellies."

Squire squinted and rubbed the bridge of his nose with his thumb and middle finger. "Regina is right, guys. What the heck is this all about?"

"We can't recruit more followers with a video of a fifth of a field of crops. We needed a better image, and I made one."

Regina pointed at her redistributed plants. "This isn't a better image, Dean. This is an optical illusion, a lie."

"It's one hundred percent real, Reg. We grew all those plants in this ground on our own."

"But this isn't how things really look."

"This is how things look from here. What? Do you want me to film this field from every conceivable angle and let the world decide what's real? We put the camera in the best place and shoot the best shot. What else would you have me do?"

"Dean." Squire shook his head. "Who said anything about new followers?"

"It's necessary," the Mouth replied, explaining his desire for more cash.

"But we never discussed this at Circle. Where are Omega and Sigma in all this?"

"Who do you think helped me pull this off?"

Regina turned to me with fire in her eyes. "You knew about this too, didn't you? Why didn't you bring this to the Circle? Why did you keep us out?"

"I knew some things and not others," I said. "But he's right. It's necessary. And if you were out-voted at the Circle, would you really have moved aside to let this happen?"

With that I earned a slap of my own. Regina turned and huffed back up the hill, Squire trailing behind her.

The Mouth rolled from his knees to his ass and sighed. I slid an unlabeled bottle from the back of my waistband and dropped down in the grass beside him.

"What are you packing, chief?"

I pulled the cork out with my teeth and spit it into my hand before taking a cautious sip. "Sam made it for me. Special order. Omicron's Reserve."

The Mouth grabbed the bottle from my outstretched hand and drank. We exchanged pulls, passing the Brushfire between us without saying a word, letting ourselves get lost in that constructed vision of agrarian perfection as it rustled in an early summer breeze.

He shot the scene later that day in the tired afternoon light and then again the next morning at sunrise. The resulting video was dropped into the stream of a binary monologue that consumed no oxygen and therefore flowed uninterrupted, an endless filibuster in a digital senate where nothing ever came to a vote, but somehow everything was decided. The engine of popularity commerce sprang to life, just as he said it would—views begetting likes, likes begetting followers, followers begetting money. Regina was right too; many of the redistributed plants were casualties to the Mouth's gambit, but with new cash flowing in, we never ran short of food. The Mus were back at BigBox before the rutabagas lost their charm.

Chapter Twenty-One

—*Why did you stop?*

—We were wrong to have done that. . . to have gone behind Regina's back.

—*We saved Isidora that day. You and me.*

—We saved *an* Isidora. We destroyed Regina's vision to rescue our own.

—*There is only one TRUTH.*

—Maybe. One TRUTH that stands victorious above the corpses of all the other truths that could not prevail.

—*What else would you have had us do? Take them all in like strays? Feed them saucers of milk until they were big enough and strong enough to claw us in the back?*

—I'm not scared of ideas, LaBouche.

—*Then you haven't been paying attention.*

—. . .

—*You can't quit before the conclusion. The necessity of Isidora is still in front of you, unavoidable. Keep talking.*

—. . .

—*Goddammit! She's not coming back. None of them are coming back. Isidora is the only TRUTH. It's that or oblivion. It's that or annihilation. Keep talking or all of this is meaningless. Keep talking or we're all lost.*

—Solstice Day.

—*Yes, Solstice Day. They all came, just like we planned. They were all there on Solstice Day.*

I never really understood where the money came from or how it made its way to us. The figment world was a blur to me, locked in the attic of my mind under eighteen months of dust. The Mouth, whose cell phone bill remained a monthly liability on Squire's books, kept his finger on the pulse of that nowhere "for the good of the revolution." He said the schism between labor and capital had never been healed, that while the former had been casually dumped at the first sign of distress, the latter now waited expectantly for her return—a date in heavy cologne, a wilting flower in his lapel, asking the server to let him keep the table for ten more minutes. Meanwhile, labor was at a club on the other side of town in a tight new dress, rejoicing in the epiphany of a freedom she didn't know she'd missed.

For many, Isidora was that freedom, an avoidance of an obligation that no longer felt true, an alternative to a return to the used-to-be. And where many of the first wave followers had come out of desperation, the second wave came by choice. Coders from the coast, chewed and excreted by bosses newly infatuated with Hyderabad. Double-breasted financiers doubled over from double time, content to jump before they'd secured their parachute. Electricians, mechanics, plumbers, servers, clerks, cleaners, farm hands, ranch hands, letter carriers, bus drivers, long-haul truckers, short-haul commuters, call-center receptionists, and even a disgruntled glass blower. They all came, cash in hand, prepared to abandon the innumerable lies of daily life for the chance at discovering the new TRUTH in Isidora.

Lambda set up an orientation of sorts and paraded the new followers about like know-it-all sophomores during welcome week. They toured everything but the Ark, which was increasingly off limits, and ran through a rudimentary recruitment process for the work units. Initially this was managed by the Circle, but in time it fell to secundi—followers who worked tirelessly to justify their rank and normalize the power they wielded on our behalf. Once they felt secure, they would anoint a secundus of their own. And on and on it went. In this way we became ascendent, not by muscling up the rungs but by standing still as a ladder was built beneath us. The further my vertiginous assent, the less that was asked of me, and boredom became my most common companion. When Hawke said he needed my help with a surprise for the followers on Solstice Day, I jumped at the chance to give of myself for Isidora.

—You did a great service that day.

He dispatched me to the Winter Quarters, and while I worried I had no good explanation for sneaking through the followers' dorm, the sound of laughter and singing layered over the easy beats flowing from Hank's tinny speakers on the Green reassured me. Sam was serving a new concoction that night—a slippery clear liquid not unlike gin that he called All-Weather—and it appeared to be having the intended effect. The solstice party was well underway, and there was no reason to be anywhere else. I poked my head around the corner. Seeing no one, I galloped to the front door.

Apart from the elevator bank and the stairs at the center, the atrium of the Winter Quarters had been a vast, empty space, the bulk of the building perched on pillars above a slick, seamless floor of black and white tiles. I flicked on my flashlight to find the followers had hung tarps and stacked wooden pallets to carve from that continuity discrete functional space. To my left, a canteen had been set up with unfamiliar objects formed into the familiar shapes of tables and chairs. In the back, gas burners sat on a folding table attached to a propane tank below, and diced onions—scattered and overlooked—browned on the adjacent workspace. A bright orange slop—lentils, perhaps, still fragrant of cumin and curry—was crusted along the rim of a tired pot.

I weaved my way through the maze of improvisations, less sure of each space's function the deeper I progressed. A dining hall? A pantry? A cobbler's bench? A tailor's stall? A workbench for whittling? A table for vice? A sanctuary for a soothsayer? A redoubt for spiritual retreats? It was a subsistence economy built of rag and bone; a shanty town inside a corporate shell, all of it lacquered in candle wax.

I was still alone when I reached the central staircase, but if I were to encounter anyone, it would be there in those constricted vertebrae. I took a deep breath and began the climb. Sigma had done the most to reclaim the Winter Quarters, tearing apart the old cubicle dividers and chucking them down the fire escapes, and they claimed the top floor as their prize. Alpha joined them at the top, and Lambda and Omega begrudgingly settled on the fifth floor below them, with Mus scattered throughout. That left the rest of the building unoccupied, untouched, and ready for expansion.

The fifth floor was as chaotic as a fire sale, but I could tell everything that littered the floor or swung from the ceiling had been recently and intimately touched. Lambda and Omega had erected tents on every square foot, not discrete bubbles of air as intended by their maker but exploded absurdities pinned to every available surface like the skin flaps and entrails of a dissected frog. I started on the windows, retracting the blinds where they still existed and pulling down the sheets of blue tarpaulin shoved under the ceiling tiles where they did not. At the back of the room, I found the electrical box and verified that all the switch and fuse positions matched Hawke's crudely drawn diagram.

On my way back to the stairwell, I leaned into an unobstructed window to look down on the party below. A mass encircled Hank and rippled like the surface of a pond every time a musical beat fell. At the top of the hill, unattended coals glowed soft orange as smoke rose and disappeared into the depths of the blackening sky. Above the Green and across the train yard, candles in the Ark's second floor windows were extinguished, one by one.

I hurried up to the sixth floor, which was in the same state as the fifth, and cleared the windows before checking the electrical box. My mission complete, I was free to return to the party, but I instead slid a desk chair to a window, popped it open to the OSHA-approved limit, and lit up a smoke.

In the fields, a half-dozen flashlights swept the ground as followers prepared the evening's celebratory fireworks. I knew they would be Alphas, Regina having banned any other work unit from setting foot on that ground following the Mouth's visual arts project. Restoring the mistreated earth to a state that could support a summer crop was a herculean effort, especially so without a tractor, and I spent many afternoons perched on the hillside above, watching rows of Alphas drop hoes in an unrefined syncopation or Mac, the ox, wrap his arms in leather straps to pull the plow.

The southern border of the fields was lined with Sigma's goat pens and chicken coops. Sam agreed to take on animal husbandry, needing no encouragement to embrace things soft and fuzzy, and the wire mesh enclosures and wooden shelters sprang up at his command. We all came running the day Squire hopped the curb and navigated Hank between buildings, the crate-filled bed of the pick-up erupting in squawks and hay and feathers every time the tires bounced along the uneven ground. When the truck stopped, Sam sprang from the cab with an ear-to-ear smile, clutching a baby goat like he'd just birthed it himself. Everyone stood for hours watching the hens claw at the ground of their new home, erupting into cheers when one dared to set foot inside her coop.

Alpha began with an overture of bottle rockets and Roman candles, which no doubt caused some commotion in the henhouse. When the first movement began with a mortar barrage, sending up whistling shells along trails of golden sparks, there must have been absolute pandemonium. Followers grabbed hands and pranced up the hillside to lie in the grass in twos and threes. The shockwave of the fireballs brushed their skin as night blossomed into day. Surely, the sky was falling. Finally, the sky was falling.

As the fireworks burst above the building, I stood, my arms gripping the metal frame, to lean into the window well to see. The second salvo came slowly, hands cradling explosives, lighting fuses that felt too short, dropping orbs down tubes that also felt too short, plugging ears as feet scurried away. *Thwump!* Off it went, getting smaller and smaller, quieter and quieter, until . . . *Blam!* It was the only thing in the world.

One by one they shot up into the night, all of them beautiful but none of them feeling as magical as they did when I was a boy lying in the grass at the fairgrounds as balls of light filled the sky, emerging from nowhere like presents on Christmas morning. These shells were well known to me. I could trace them back to their origin, from the wet summer air to the precariously balanced tube to the quivering hand of a giddy Alpha to the militaristic packaging wrapped in plastic to Hank's truck bed to the lonesome drive down I-something-or-other to the firework stand set up for the season in the parking lot of a sex shop, both open on Sundays in case you wanted to come after the sermon. From there to a box to a container to a ship, across an ocean, to a country that knew nothing of freedom or independence but wasn't above breaking a few backs to line a silken purse. There was power in these fireworks, each and every one, but no, not magic.

When the individual shells were spent, the Alphas moved on to the finale, a second row of tubes pre-loaded to be lit all at once. To cover the transition, some started shooting Roman candles again, and red and green orbs sprang from the ground as the fuses sizzled away. This was the signal Hawke was waiting for as he sipped smoke in the doorway of the Mines. He dropped his cigarette and moved inside to flip the switch. *Thwump!* As the fireworks shot skyward, electrons raced through lines of copper strung from the generator to the Ark and the Winter Quarters. Above my head, noble gasses began to stir, rapping at their tubes with ionic fingers until, sufficiently agitated, they burst into radiant light. *Blam!*

The followers erupted into applause, but no one was looking to the sky. They stared wide eyed and opened mouthed at their home. For nine long months, it had been a cold refuge. Now, bathed in an electric glow, it was a six-story monument to their incandescent perseverance, gifted by Isidora, visible for all the world to see. Their heads swelled with visions of light bulbs and radios, electric blankets and vacuum cleaners, washing machines and televisions, microwaves and blenders, computers and cell phones, sex toys and CPAPs, the Internet. A century of technology enabled in an instant, a windfall nothing short of magic. And standing in silhouette in a window overflowing with light, his arms raised in a T, seemed to be none other than the magician himself.

Me.

Chapter Twenty-Two

Like love, electricity changed everything and changed nothing at all. Those who wanted to work did so with a bit more enthusiasm, knowing their evening leisure would not be curtailed by the prudish chaperoning of night. And those who wished to do nothing at all found themselves with a million and one nothings to fill their day. Radios, cell phones, laptops, and tablets, crawled like zombies from the bottoms of knapsacks and the back of closets, with a single bolt of lightning their purpose restored.

With no internet access, devices were frozen in the state in which they came, and those younger followers who had previously pushed the cutting edge of technology, treating their objects as sluices for content streams flowing through cyberspace, found themselves left holding an empty tube. Their older luddite companions, who still remembered the practice of buying and owning a thing, were slightly better off, with hard drives full of downloaded music and videos. But even the largest library would eventually grow stale. It was, in the end, the truly grizzled among them—those old-soul analogs who had extended silver antennae to listen to the game while they putzed about the basement—

who held the most valuable asset in Isidora—radio. That unidirectional mana of information rollicking through the airwaves, an invisible bridge that collapses both time and space. In a sense it became the hot new thing, and Isidora filled with the sound of symphonies, talk shows, top 40, and country.

It was the latter that Squire had blaring in the Ark as we filed in on that mid-August day. At Hawke's request I had spent the morning shadowing Omegas as they installed solar panels on the roof of the Mines, not being helpful in any way, just thankful for the distraction and a bit of elevation. But sweat burst through my pits all the same, and I arrived at the Circle as grimy as the cowherds and troubadours sang about in Squire's songs. I took a cup of All-Weather from the steward—a plucky young Sigma honored with access to the Ark—and had him run to my room to fetch a clean shirt.

"Is LaBouche joining us today?" I asked, falling onto my metal stool.

Squire flipped off the radio and moved to take his seat. "He's bringing in our guests."

"Let's work through the rolls while we wait, then. Reg? How are things in Alpha?"

In the summer growing season when the sun brought energy, the sky brought rain, and the soil asked nothing of Alpha but to pull weeds, Regina found a meditative tranquility in the fields. She flowed down the rows in an undyed linen robe that clung to her naked skin below with every passing breeze. After a morning's labor she sat at the Circle with a conical hat in her lap as clean and composed as the moment she woke up.

"Alpha. We're about three weeks from the main harvest, though some rows could probably be collected a week earlier. I'd ask the Circle to direct each work unit to contribute a dozen members to the fields on harvest week, more if they can spare it."

"Any objections?" I asked, scanning the room. "OK then, a dozen each when Alpha calls for harvest. Squire, Mu may want to verify that our canning and storage materials are prepped and purchase anything that's needed."

He nodded. "We started this morning, in fact."

"Wonderful. Do you have anything for us, Squire?"

"Mu. The Omega solar project consumed nearly eighty percent of our savings, and new contributions have tapered off over the last few weeks. Relying less on dinos to run the generator will help, but at this rate we're going to run out of money again before Thanksgiving."

At that moment the Mouth strode onto the factory floor, head high and steps deliberate like a king entering his throne room. He hadn't yet talked someone into heralding his entrance, but I covered for this oversight by blowing trumpets in my mind. *Do do-do-dooo!* Two women followed him into the room but stopped at the Circle's edge. They were not among his standard hangers-on, and while they seemed uneasy walking through the Ark, they were not obviously cowed by living legend LaBouche.

"Every day is a day for giving thanks, Squibs," the Mouth said as he rounded a metal pillar and paraded through the center of the Circle. He was dressed in a newsboy cap, suspenders, and silken culottes like he'd just emerged from a Dutch casbah, and he fell onto his pile of cushions with a self-satisfied chuckle. "Besides," he said, pointing to the women, "thanks to these two we'll be awash in cash before we reach *figment* Thanksgiving."

"Glad you could join us, Lambda." I looked over to our guests. "Welcome. Please come in. I'm sure Dean can spare you a pillow."

They stepped to the center of the Circle but remained standing, facing me. From their quick glances at Hawke, I got the impression it was a joint effort.

"My name is Marianne, sir. I'm a . . . I *was* a computer systems engineer in the Bay area before coming to Isidora. This is Kristen. We used to work together, and we've been watching your videos since you first arrived at Junemark 6."

She paused ever so slightly as one would when attempting to bribe an official for the first time, not sure if it's done in these parts or how exactly—not sure if the display of Isidora's history she had just slipped me under the table counted as legal tender. I gave her a reassuring smile and nodded.

"You all were building something new here, something special," she continued, "and when the start-up we worked for went bankrupt, we knew we had to come. We arrived in early June, just before the solstice party."

"Are you Lambdas?" Regina asked.

Here Kristen took over. "Omegas, ma'am. We've been assisting with grid functionality and performance with . . . with . . ." She looked over at the metal workbench where the leader of her work unit sat.

"Hawke," he grinned. "You can say it."

"With Hawke."

I leaned forward, charmed by the two but growing increasingly impatient with my now empty cup of All-Weather. "So, what do you have to share with us today?"

"There's a power problem, sir." Marianne again. "More accurately, an excess power problem. The gas-powered generator runs at a constant speed, burning a constant rate of fuel and producing a constant supply of electricity no matter how much is demanded. It's either on or off, and when it's on, we rarely—I think I can say never—consume the full load. Solar panels and power storage can limit the times we run the generator, but when it's on, a significant amount of power, fuel, and, therefore, money is wasted."

"We have a solution," Kristen said. "We could route all the excess power into a computer array that mines for Block Coin."

"Excuse me?" Out of the corner of my eye I saw the steward standing sheepishly with my new shirt. I waved him over and handed him my cup. "Only half way this time."

Marianne took a small step forward. "Block Coin, sir. It's a digital token currency based on a blockchain architecture."

I blinked a few times and looked at Squire with a face as blank as the science chapter of an evangelical textbook.

"It's a computer thing, right?" He squirmed in his chair. "Like a digital investment account?"

"Kind of," Kristen lied. "Block Coins are digital assets, and you hold them in a digital wallet, which is like an account except there are no banks controlling transactions. Everything is recorded on a blockchain held in common by everyone."

"It's the future of just currency," the Mouth added, sitting tall on his pillows. "No banks, no feds, no finance charges, no late fees. Everyone sees the entire market, and no one is inferior to anyone else."

I was intrigued. "And we need computers for this? Computers that will suck up all our extra power?"

"Any old laptop can be used to manage a Block Coin account—to hold the digital wallet," Kristen explained. "But a more sophisticated arrangement is needed to do the mining."

"Mining now?" I lit one of the cigarettes arranged on the tray beside my chair. "LaBouche, I don't think we're properly zoned for this."

Marianne stepped forward. "It's the word we use for how the Block Coins are made, sir. Because everyone holds the record of every transaction in the blockchain, the security of the system must be maintained through complex cryptography. Computer arrays, like the one we're proposing, churn through mountains of data in this cryptographic space, trying to solve the puzzle required to create the next block of data in the blockchain. And when they do, everyone's blockchain receives a new block, and the winning computer receives a Block Coin."

The Mouth laughed from his belly. "Couldn't be simpler, right?"

"Marianne, Kristen . . ." Squire said stroking his beard, "if I could attempt to summarize; everyone who has Block Coins holds Block Coins in a digital wallet. When Block Coins are exchanged, it's registered on a block, a block we all see in our chain, our blockchain of blocks. Computers solve puzzles to add blocks to the blockchain and are awarded with Block Coins, ownership of which is recorded, again, on a block in the blockchain."

The Mouth rolled onto his side, giggling. "Jesus, Squire. How much coffee did you have this morning?"

I stood up and arched my stiff back. "OK, so we turn on some computers, lights flash, hard drives whirl, and maybe at the end of the day we earn one more Block thing than we had that morning. But why? Why do this?"

Kristen stepped forward to deliver the long-awaited punchline. "Block Coins were first issued in April at parity with the US dollar. One Block Coin for one dollar. Four months later, and now you can trade one Block Coin for five dollars."

Hawke chimed in. "That's over fifteen hundred percent annualized growth."

Sam, who had sat glassy eyed and mouth agape through the presentation like a Shih Tzu observing a Nobel acceptance speech, let out a long, receding whistle.

"We won't even need to sell the initial Block Coins," the Mouth added. "If we can tighten our belts for a few months and build up a stockpile, we can support Isidora on the growth alone."

I laughed. "And how is your belt doing these days, LaBouche?"

He slapped his paunch and grinned. "Tighter than ever."

I dismissed Marianne and Kristen, and the Circle took up the proposal. Apart from Regina, who knew enough about boys and toys to realize her opposition would go nowhere, the Circle was in agreement. The only issue at stake was the matter of degree. Should we rely on the new solar panels for daily use and only switch on the generator, and thus the Mines, when demand was high or the weather was bad? Or run the generator constantly to ensure the Mines operated around the clock, with the solar panels providing supplemental power to the rest of Isidora? Here, Regina won out, and we decided on the former. The Mines ran in the drowsy hours of dawn and the dreamy hours of twilight when the solar panels couldn't keep up. But when Marianne, Kristen, and their newly formed cadre of Blacklungs informed us that our first Block Coin had landed in our digital wallet with a satisfying ping, it was impossible not to step on the gas. The low rumble of the generator, the same small engine Hawke had pulled from the rusty recesses of the machine shed and rode straight into the Ark's front wall, became a constant companion. It sounded like money, and money sounded like freedom.

Chapter Twenty-Three

Every ten minutes. The race for a Block Coin is won every ten minutes. Not always by you. Rarely by you. But every ten minutes someone somewhere rides their digital thoroughbred over the finish line and is awarded a shiny gold token. And if it isn't you, and it probably isn't you, there's no time to lick your wounds in the stables. A new race is starting. In fact, it has already begun. The instant someone breaks the plane, you're back in that starting gate, a gun going off and the doors flinging open. You're not tired. In TRUTH, you expended nothing but energy, so you run again. Two minutes to the first turn, another two to the second. Three minutes down the back straightaway. Turn three. Turn four. Another minute to the finish line. You lift off the saddle, knees bouncing like bellows. The horse takes the whip, but he out sprints the pain, leaving it behind in the flying mud and spraying rain. A few more paces. Grow the neck long . . . stretch . . . and . . .

Nothing.

Damn.

You're back in the gates. The gun is going off. The doors are flinging open. There's no time to lick your wounds in the stables. You're not tired. In fact, you expended nothing but energy, so you run again. Another ten-minute footrace has begun. Ten minutes. Every ten minutes. Six times an hour, 144 times a day, 1,008 times a week, 52,416 times a year. There is nothing to do but run.

****

The mining felt easy at first, so easy, in fact, it wasn't so much mining as it was picking up diamonds from barren ground. The Blacklungs' computer array was purpose built, wired to do nothing else, and placed in a relatively limitless physical space. It was competing against crypto hobbyists mining in the background on their personal PCs and desktop-powered day-traders trying their luck on the next sure thing. To their artisan guilds and handicraft cooperatives, we were a steam-powered woolen mill, and for a short time we were absolutely dominant. The first week we started mining around the clock, we captured nearly half of the newly-made coins.

At the same time interest in Block Coin skyrocketed. All autumn long the Mouth trotted into the Circle, announcing the next big news story or front-cover spread that speculated Block Coin was the future of currency. From hedge fund managers with oceans of assets to blue-haired pensioners with pockets full of funny money, everyone descended on crypto exchanges, bidding up the price of Block Coin by thousands of percent. Five dollars a coin became $50, and $50 became $200. Up, up, up it went, and the seeming inevitability of it only drew in more buyers.

The dizzying assent emboldened our competition, and we soon saw more thoroughbreds join us in the starting gates. Those who didn't have the capital or energy supply to set up an array like ours joined mining conglomerates that pooled computing power and distributed in equal measure the ore and the slag both—horses stitched together from a thousand spare parts, but boy could they run too. Our win rate slowed to a trickle, but by the winter solstice we already had a stockpile of 4,326 coins. In other words, we were already millionaires.

Chapter Twenty-Four

Millionaires, I thought to myself as I awoke shivering in a nylon bag on the floor of my darkened suite. *The shabbiest millionaires in history.*

Having spent two years in the Ark's innermost chamber, my body was attuned to the differences between the raw black of midnight and the rounded dark of pre-dawn. I was somewhere in between—in the inky void that is 3:00 a.m. where stillness, as thick as oil, weighs down the world and silence holds its breath. And yet the cold dared move, dripping through the warped glass of the Circle chamber's skylights and creeping in the big picture windows of my suite. The heater at my feet, whose round silver parabola reflected electric fire, stood inert like a well-bribed sentinel betraying his king.

"Worthless piece of shit." I swung my bound feet at the disk like a flailing caterpillar, and it rolled onto its back.

I closed my eyes, hoping sleep would still my chattering teeth and save me from the cold. When I opened them again not more than a few minutes later, the steam of my breath clouded my pillow, and I knew there was nothing to do but get up and get moving. I dressed in all the layers I could and slipped down the stairs, past the snoozing steward in our reception room, and out into the night.

The air slept upon the ground, heavy and still, while above the firmament blinked and beamed through a million pinholes in the celestial sphere. The moon was full and low, sharing a bit of residual daylight that slipped past Asia and bounced off the barren planes surrounding the Sea of Tranquility. As the moonbeams fell on Isidora, they broke into shimmering colors on the blanket of crystalline snow that crunched beneath my boots.

I always felt immortal in starlight, not in the sense that my body would never die, but that by walking quietly beneath those predictable wanderers, I could shed my mortal form and commune with the world eternal.

At the base of the water tower with my head to the heavens, I saw a night indistinguishable from the last, indistinguishable from nights millennia past. A swirling starry field above, air that billowed or gusted or paused, the earth underfoot covered in arctic tundra or Aegean sand. Stillness and starlight revealed an immutable world, and in that world I felt immortal because I felt I had always lived. The low thrum that emanated from the Mines—the generator and its reciprocating pistons looping endlessly through time and space—only heightened the sense that everything that ever was and everything that ever will be lived with me in that moment.

I climbed toward the stars, up the familiar rungs of the water tower, rungs so cold they seemed to be drained of all tactility. When I reached the catwalk, the blood in my veins ran simmering hot, and air puffed from my chest like a locomotive. The world looked no less stark from the top of the tower. Isidora's dark, angular buildings rose from mounds of snow that hugged frozen train cars and bleached the pond out of existence. Beyond, the endless expanse of farm and field melted into a monochromatic blur like the background of a wet plate photograph. In the past, I would have seen in that serene portrait Isidora, the precarious. But with our Block Coin wallet full of tokens, the Winter Quarters teaming with followers, and my friends sleeping behind the glass-topped walls of the fortress Ark, I had never felt more secure.

I circled the catwalk, surveying the warehouses and factory showrooms that huddled next to the Junemark compound, and for the first time since our arrival I thought of expansion. If we followed the pavement from the parking lot past the toppled steles along the road, the next building over was a defunct construction supply store. We walked through it once in the early days and found it completely gutted. The building was in good shape, as I recall, but the upstairs rooms were the size of closets—much too small to be used as dormitories. In the other direction, along the rails out the back of the train yard, there was a crumbling tannery and overgrown grain depot, but I struggled to think of how we would put them to any use.

Beyond that, there were the Shambles. I walked to the tower's western rim, prepared to squint into that ill-fated ichor smeared across the horizon, only to find its northernmost reaches ablaze. Fire. It was only one building, or perhaps two, but it burned with the fury of the warehouse that first spring. It burned with the fury of Tent City.

Hawke, I thought. I knew.

But why now? There were no debts to be repaid, no favors to be asked, nothing to be gained. We were safe.

Before I could ponder the question further, my eyes fell on two shadows emerging from the tree line. They walked casually along the ties of the railroad tracks, not speaking but also making no effort to conceal themselves as they entered Isidora like overconfident thieves or long-married homeowners. I had never asked Hawke about his connection to the first fire or his seemingly miraculous deliverance from the hands of the Constable that same night. Better to let sleeping dogs lie, I thought, especially when one feels vulnerable to attack. But another fire so long after the first was inexplicable, which meant it was time for Hawke to explain himself.

Between my gloved hands and the slippery rungs, I moved slowly, and by the time I reached the ground I was practically on top of them. It was Hawke porting his pesticide-sprayer backpack and another man—a kid, really, despite his bulk—that I didn't recognize. If Hawke was at all surprised by my sudden appearance, he didn't show it. The look on his face, half in moonlight, half in shadow, was that of a jester, amused. The kid, on the other hand, looked like he was about to have a heart attack.

"The Omicron," the oaf gasped as he rushed to salute.

"Out for a late-night stroll, Hawke?" I asked. He walked right past me, so I turned and followed him to the machine shop.

"It is a pleasant night, isn't it?" he called over his shoulder.

"A very pleasant night, sir," the kid said as he lumbered beside me.

"We need to talk about this, Hawke."

"I don't think we do."

"I know about the fires."

"I figured you did." Hawke stopped in front of the machine shop and set the sprayer on the ground before digging through his pocket for keys.

"And I know they have something to do with the Constable."

"They do, indeed." The padlock sprang open, and Hawke unhooked the latch.

"Then tell me what's going on, Hawke. Are you working for her?"

He pulled open the door—a corrugated metal skin nailed to a wooden frame—and slipped into the pitch-black shed. The kid and I stood outside as Hawke traced by memory the steps through the darkness that took him to the pull chain in the back. With a click and a flicker, the glass tubes above his workbench awoke revealing Hawke's sanctum, flooded with machine parts and hanging tools but fastidiously cleaned and organized.

"You don't need to worry about it," Hawke said as he rearranged his arson kit. "It's just something I have to do."

"It's just something we have to do," the kid repeated.

"But I do worry about it. If someone in the Circle is a stooge to a figment cop, I should be very worried about it."

"I'm not a fucking stooge," Hawke erupted. Then he let out a heavy sigh. "It's an exchange of favors, that's all."

"What favors? What could we possibly need from the Constable?"

Hawke grabbed a cigarette from a pack on his workbench and raised a lighter to his lips, but after glancing at the sprayer on the floor, lowered his hand. "Outside," he said. Without waiting for a reply, he crossed the room and pushed back out into the open air.

"Outside," his Echo repeated as he trailed behind him.

I grabbed two cigarettes from Hawke's pack, putting one in my mouth and the second behind my ear, and followed them out. The moon had slipped off the horizon and fallen behind the earth, and the world was now darker than when I woke. I pulled a heavy, wind-proof lighter from my pocket—a token from a doting Sigma who insisted he couldn't keep it while I was still flicking Bics—and lit up. "Well then, speak."

"The day I was arrested, the day of that massive storm, the cops took me straight to the Constable. They did all the talking at first, describing what they saw on the compound—Squire and the truck and the huge order of gas being delivered. They weren't too concerned about the handgun, but they insisted we were planning some kind of attack with all that gasoline. Anarchists, they called us. I kept my mouth shut, and the Constable, for her part, seemed unconvinced. When the clerk brought my record and noted the outstanding warrant from the capital, the Constable just smiled. She said if I liked playing with gas so much maybe we could make a deal. So we did. I get my hands dirty in the Shambles, torching an abandoned eyesore, and she lets me—more importantly *us*—go free."

"That wasn't an abandoned building, Hawke. You know that, right?"

He took a long pull from his cigarette. "Looked abandoned to me."

"It was full of people, Hawke." I took a step toward him, turning my back on Echo, halving the distance between us. "Families. Kids."

He shifted his weight, rocking away from me. "What would you know about it?"

"I was there, Hawke. I stood next to the firefighters and watched them do nothing. Next to stunned men, sobbing women, and screaming kids. It wasn't abandoned."

Hawke spun on his heel and began pacing, as if searching for a machine that needed grease. "Mmm. What does it matter anyway? They're outside Isidora. They're figments. They're nothing."

"Figments are nothing," Echo repeated with a knowing nod.

"Hawke, those are the people we came here to help, to see when no one else sees them."

"You can't see them if they don't come, can you?" Hawke said, raising his voice. "No one on earth has had more of an opportunity to join us in Isidora than whoever is squatting in the Shambles. They're not just figments; they're the worst kind of figments. They're figments who won't lift a finger to challenge the world that's keeping them down."

Hawke flicked away his cigarette butt and began patting down his pockets looking for another. I put a hand on his shoulder and slid the cigarette from behind my ear. "They may be figments, but we don't need to attack them. We know these people. They could be the same families we marched for in Tent City."

Hawke snatched the cigarette and thrust it at my face. "Do not speak to me about that."

"Why not?" I asked, standing firm. "Was Tent City yours? Were you the only one that lost something that night? Was it your personal tragedy? I was there too, remember?" I raised my left forearm and shook it in his face. "Me and hundreds of others."

"Because it's in the past, oh great Omicron. Isn't that why we're here? To forget the past? So, let it go."

I took a deep breath and sighed through my nose. "Fine. But you burned a building tonight. Not in the past. Not to get out of custody. Not to escape the Constable. Why, Hawke? Why tonight?"

"Escape the Constable? You can't be that fucking naïve. There is no escape from the Constable. As long as we're here, she's watching us. As long as Isidora stands, we are under threat. I'm not torching warehouses in the Shambles because I like it. I'm doing it because it has to be done."

Every fiber of my being wanted to resist the man, to call him a self-serving masochist and a liar. But try as I might to contort my conscience and justify those words, I knew deep down there was TRUTH in what he said. The figment world had let us be, but that did not mean we were not exposed.

"It has to be done?" I said, kicking a pile of weightless white powder.

Hawke nodded. "It has to be done."

"It has to be done," Echo repeated.

"Why?"

Hawke let out a heavy, defeated sigh. "It has something to do with Eden Village—that development project from the billboard outside of town. The courts won't let them displace the squatters, and they can't move ahead on the project until they demolish the old buildings. There's a lot of money tied up in it, and you know some shithead billionaire is leaning on the local officials to do something about it."

"So you've been called in to burn them down instead?"

He bit his lip and tilted his head. "I was told to get them to move. Clear the Shambles, and they'll overlook what we're doing here. I figured fire was a pretty good motivator. Hell, it moved us halfway across the country."

"Only because we had the dream of Isidora to run to. Where are they supposed to go?"

"Here," Hawke said. "They should be coming *here*. That's what I said."

I scratched my head. "Then let's make an effort to recruit them. If the Constable will let us be when we drain the Shambles, then let's do it. Let's give them a proper welcome. Not fire to flee but a new home to join."

Hawke puffed out a breath of steam as his mind circled consent like a boxer waiting for the round to end. "Fine," he said in time. "But recruitment isn't really my thing. You'll have to convince Dean to help. And if you fail . . ." He let the words linger as his gaze dropped to his half-burned cig. He shook his head and threw it into the snow.

"If we fail, you can torch the whole fucking city. But we won't. Isidora is the only TRUTH."

Hawke discharged Echo, and the two of us walked back to the Ark. A bank of clouds had rolled in overhead, and the snow beneath our feet, once luminous and bright, now crunched like volcanic scree.

"Are you happy here, Hawke?" I asked as we passed through the Ark's wrought-iron gate. It felt like a question I needn't have asked until that point.

"Happy? I don't hold out for happy. But there's no place I'd rather be than Isidora. I would do anything to protect it."

And I knew he meant what he said.

****

There was no point in going back to bed. It would still be hours before the winter sun breached the horizon, but neither Hawke nor I wanted sleep. We wanted coffee, and we roused our beleaguered steward, who in his somnambulant state had the audacity to look annoyed. But only for a moment. When his bearing returned, he sprang from the couch and shuffled off to the spare secretarial office-cum-pantry with his head penitently lowered. He returned a moment later, empty handed.

"Sirs, there's no power."

Hawke rose from his armchair with a yawn, went over to the wall, and flipped the light switch, to no effect.

"Damn," he muttered. "Is it the generator?"

The three of us instinctively held our breath and listened. It was still on.

"The Ark's circuit must have failed then." I expected Hawke to rush out the door and begin trouble shooting the issue, but he instead fell back into his chair, the breath puffing out of him. "Just use the gas stove if you can find it."

The steward hesitated.

"What is it, Brandt?" Hawke called over his shoulder.

"Yes, sir. It's just that it won't be espresso. You see, I'll have to use the French press."

"That's fine, Brandt."

He lingered again. "Because normally you only take black espresso and a pingado for the Omicron."

Hawke put his hands on the arms of his chair, preparing to vault out of his seat and throttle the poor kid.

"It's fine," I said. "Just get it done. And light a few candles, will you?"

On my word, the steward ran like a dog unleashed, and we both fell into our chairs, laughing.

"That kid doesn't know how good he's got it," I mused. "Full access to the Ark, sleeps in the front room, gets to sit in on Circle . . ."

"If he did know, we'd probably have to replace him," Hawke replied.

We sipped coffee until dawn, sharing what would be the closest thing to a heart-to-heart I would have with the man. He told me about his childhood—how his mother got deported during an ICE raid at her factory and how his father, twice her senior, flew back to the islands and returned with another. How he passed his rebellious preteen days in the shadow of older boys bound for drugs or juvy or both. He grew tired of it all before it consumed him, and when for the first time in his life he was ready to choose something for himself, a high school shop teacher—whose wisdom was wasted on preserving the digits of teenagers as they first encountered bandsaws—introduced him to the two great loves of his life: engineering and speculative sci-fi. A natural gift for mathematics, some catch-up summer classes in physics, and a silver medal in a state robotics competition earned Hawke enough of a scholarship to drown himself in student debt. And it was there, in a freshman year seminar on the works of Orwell, that he met Squire and Regina. They didn't much care for George, but they liked each other well enough, and by the end of the semester they were practically inseparable.

"I wish I'd had friends like you guys in college," I said after Hawke finished.

Regina, who had slipped in unnoticed, wrapped her arms around me from behind and kissed my cheek. "You'd have fit right in."

Hawke rolled his eyes and stood. "We'd have been homeless a lot sooner." He went to the table to refresh his coffee, and when Regina moved to join him, he put an arm around her shoulder and poured two cups instead of one. Then with a grunt he trudged back into the snow, overfed by the world of men and content to pass his morning neck deep in machine.

Chapter Twenty-Five

That afternoon the Circle's attention turned to money—namely the fact that we both had it and didn't all at once. The dizzying Block Coin balance in our wallets gave us all a thrill, but there was no practical way to use it. In cyberspace, it was as illusory as the figment dollars it represented. In the meantime, Isidora's economy was sputtering under the weight of bartering and benevolence. The most erudite followers earned through their labors the same belly full of gruel as their leisurely compatriots, and some in the community began to question if that was what was meant by Isidoran fairness. When rumors of limitless wealth started to circulate, it became impossible to motivate anyone to do any work at all—shy of whipping them, and I hadn't the arm strength for that. We needed a way to recognize effort, and followers needed a way to store that recognition. In short, we needed money. Isidoran money.

"Why don't we just use dollars?" Squire asked, stuffing a napkin in the collar of his shirt as the steward handed him a plate of sausages. "At least we know how many of those we have."

"Fuck off, Squibs," the Mouth blared from between the two earflaps of his ushanka. "Have our followers pass around greenbacks with 'In God We Trust' printed next to a figment president? Have you lost your fucking mind?"

"Besides," Regina added, "we would have to liquidate our Block Coins to purchase those dollars. If we want to keep them and let them grow, we need a proxy—something we already have in bulk."

"Cigarettes?" Sam said as he paced the circumference of the Circle, which had become his custom when he wasn't too drunk to stand. "It works in prisons, and we have a ton stockpiled in the basement."

"No," Hawke said emphatically. "I don't want to feel like I'm burning cash every time I go out for a smoke."

"Aren't you, though?" Regina said with a smirk.

"Point Regina." I chuckled before sipping from my glass of Brushfire. "Whatever we choose, it should be durable and, I suppose, not too useful in its own right."

We sat for a few minutes, stumped, until Sam stumbled into a desk and knocked a crate to the floor. With a crash, hundreds of pieces of metal spilled like shattered glass on the concrete slab. Nails, screws, bolts, nuts. Durable detritus, and we had it in spades.

"Displacement!" the Mouth shouted.

Eureka, indeed.

The next day the Circle announced the Nuts and Bolts Campaign, and every Alpha, Lambda, Sigma, and Omega was tasked with scouring the compound for Junemark's residual spare parts. They brought wooden crates, cardboard boxes, and coffee cans heavy with rusted metal to the Ark's front gate, where Mus would receive them and carry them to the Circle for cleaning and sorting. When it looked like that wouldn't be enough, we sent scouting teams of three or four off compound to ravage through the neighboring warehouses like locusts. By the end of the day we had tens of thousands of industrial odds and ends.

With the Circle's blessing, Squire sold the first dozen Block Coins at over $300 a piece and took our windfall to BigBox to buy cans of gold, silver, and bronze paint complete with metallic flake. We discarded all the nails and screws—they were too small and too sharp to be practical currency—and started with nuts. One Isidoran nut, dipped in bronze, was at the outset worth roughly a dollar. One silver Isidoran wing-nut was worth five nuts. And one gold Isidoran bolt was worth twenty-five. We minted them in the appropriate proportions so that the entire value of our Block Coin wallet was reflected in the stock of Isidora's currency. Then we started distributing them through a universal allowance—twenty-one nuts a week for every follower, enough for three square meals a day at the canteen. The Circle also set wages above the minimum allowance for routine labor. Our steward, for instance, made an extra two nuts a day, and the Blacklungs earned five. Discrete activities like planting or harvesting earned a wing-nut a week.

The canteen in the Winter Quarters was joined by a community store, both of which purchased supplies from the Mu-run Treasury at a floating exchange rate, essentially the ratio of all minted nuts to the dollar balance in our Block Coin wallet. Because we kept mining coins and those coins kept selling for more dollars, the nuts and bolts in the hands of our followers kept increasing in value. Every day a bronze-painted nut could purchase more than the day before, and if a follower could save that nut for one day more, it was seemingly guaranteed to purchase more still. Each day, Isidora's wealth grew, and more important than that, every day followers *felt* Isidora's wealth grow. If the Circle was liked or even admired before the Nuts and Bolts Campaign, that unambiguous sensation of expanding potential, that feeling of exponential wealth, pushed our followers past love and into a state of exuberant adoration.

Of course, it's possible to have too much of a good thing, and some followers saw in constantly depreciating prices a reason to save at all costs. People started skipping meals to hoard nuts, and there were complaints of nepotism in the division of paid chores. The store and its magically falling prices was an enigma to most, but few transactions actually took place, and bartering continued to be the preference for followers looking to exchange favors amongst themselves. The Circle decided, in the interest of Isidora, to take some pressure off the exchange rate, and as we didn't have an unlimited number of nuts and bolts to add to the money supply, it was only natural that we would target the other side of the equation.

As the value of Block Coin rose, Squire was directed to sell a percentage of the growth, and we used it to improve the Ark. We cleaned out the first-floor pantry and made a proper dining room, complete with flatware, porcelain place settings, and a real table and chairs. To accompany our new crystal, we stocked the Ark's cellar with crémant and Burgundy and brought two followers into a custom-built kitchen to serve as our personal chefs. We outfitted our suites with high-pile rugs, wooden wardrobes, and glass-topped coffee tables, and by mid-March I could retire to my room with a belly full of pork roast and sparkling wine and fall asleep—for the first time in years—on an actual mattress, in an actual bed.

Of course, it needed to be done. It was all in service of Isidora, and Isidora was everything.

Chapter Twenty-Six

Our third spring in Isidora was a spring of plenty, a spring in which we wanted for nothing, a spring in which our cups raneth over. And yet it seemed the only thing anyone could talk about was the stain on the rug. How quickly those impossibilities long desired became frustratingly insufficient. The water routed to the Winter Quarters was too cold, the lightbulbs powered by that miracle of electricity the wrong shade of white. Isidora was born from suffering, and the more it responded to that suffering the more we manufactured hardships that were not really there. Yes, work was still being done. Alpha plowed and planted. Sigma incubated and hatched. Omega bent and welded. But in TRUTH, there was nothing they could produce in a season that couldn't be purchased from a week of burning gasoline and pushing electrons in the Mines.

>—*I don't remember complaining.*

>—Your entire being is a complaint.

The malaise affected the Circle as well, perhaps even more acutely, as the weeks, months, years spent in Isidora all stacked up and weighed upon us. We still met at noon, as we always had, to sort through the quotidian faff, but beyond that we lived in suspended animation, following the patterns of life worn into the Isidoran soil.

We suffered, according to the Mouth, from excess leisure, a condition against which he seemed fully inoculated. The followers were irritable because the followers were bored. Having banned the consumption of figment entertainment, there was a cultural void at the heart of Isidora, a void only Lambda could fill through the creation of Isidoran literature, music, and theater. With the Circle's shrugging consent, the Mouth established the Writer's Guild in March and had a wooden stage erected on the Green in April. Soon thereafter, Lambda held weekly performances of original plays and melodramas, and in between they organized poetry readings, concerts, and far too much improv.

It was all fine, and I tried to stay engaged, but after a few weeks the agita returned. More often than not, I found myself dozing on the banks of the pond or reading Hawke's latest recommendation of contraband sci-fi on the water tower's catwalk, my feet dangling in the breeze five stories removed from the commotion below.

        —*Isidora was thriving, but it wasn't enough for you.*

        —Isidora was stagnating in its own success.

        —*If it stagnated, it's because you stopped loving it. Your affection is fickle—easy come, easy go.*

        —What do you know of love, LaBouche?

The boredom fed my restlessness and returned to me that deep-set yearning for more. At some point in May the idea that I could leave Isidora—that the barrier between Isidora and the figment world was self-imposed and thus self-violable—caught in the synapses of my brain and refused to shake free. I was in many ways the incarnation of Isidora's rejection of the figment world. That I was present to observe Isidora gave it life. That I was absent from the figment world cast it further into the dark recesses of obscurity. And so, to sneak away from one to join the other, if only for an afternoon, an hour, a moment was on some level the greatest form of betrayal, a sin I had not dared commit since Sam's arrival a year and a half earlier.

—You see? You can't help but see the TRUTH.

For a week I ambled about consumed by thoughts of elsewhere, suppressing the desire to dart down the tracks at the back of the train yard or fling myself like a high jumper over the nearest hedge. But the indecision only lasted a week. The following Saturday night, I resolved to sneak out. I abstained from Brushfire and All-Weather and went to bed early, and the next day I awoke before the morning sun in a clarified sobriety that was beginning to feel foreign. I dressed in my old clothes from the capital—jeans, flannel, and a sun-faded Cubs hat—and made my move.

I crept through the dawn shadows like an escaped convict, but nothing was moving in Isidora save the starlings. By the end of the train yard, I was walking erect and carefree, west along the tracks of the industrial spur, then straight through a thicket of trees and forgotten scrubland to the charmingly improbable Isidora Station where our new reality began.

My heart was light and curious, open to the world and what it had to offer, but it quickly sank when I reached the Shambles. Whatever purpose was calling to me out in the figment world was certainly not there. The Shambles were the manifestation of everything we had rejected by coming to Isidora; the consequence of the repressive elsewhere suffocating a community until the fire of its life was snuffed out. It wasn't war ravaged, but it might as well have been. Time can bring down buildings just as easily as bombs, and a people that once delighted in open-air horseless carriages now scurried about like rats in the shell of their former glory. I turned away from it all and walked south along a moribund stretch of concrete stitched together with black pitch, then ducked beneath the interstate and wandered out of town.

Nature. The restorative breath of a fresh air swirling through wild grasses and constant pines. An open field. Boulders on a hill. A sip of water from a mountain stream, untouched by man.

Instead, I came upon a strip mall.

It sat at the outskirts of nowhere, anemic, its cinder-block walls smeared against the pastoral backdrop like the ruins of a civilization that collapsed before the advent of good taste. I had forgotten about strip malls—rows of retail coffins reused by dreamers who devoured the mythology of the small businessman and believed that volition was a sufficient determinant of success. Entrepreneurs went there and saw in empty windows and dusty shelves opportunity and resurrection. They went there and saw in the clear and undeniable failure of the one who came before nothing but success. Every sale was money earned, and every expense was an investment. They were almost there. It was almost working. What was one more price cut? One more check for a TV ad? One more mortgage? For as long as they could, they diligently counted their product. They never counted their loss—until one day that was all there was left to be counted. And in this way the dignity of the man was reduced in equal measure with his coffers.

This was supposed to be act one in the two-act play, *Creative Destruction*, and there was supposed to be another wide-eyed worshiper of the cult of possibility behind the first ready to set up shop. But some years ago an invisible finger on an invisible hand tipped the scales that held in balance those ever-dueling forces of death and resurrection. The returns to amassed capital became too great, the supply chains too long, and the impersonality of online shopping too suited to the mores of the modern world. The retailer found himself in the doldrums of professional obsolescence behind the cobbler, the cooper, the haberdasher, and the journalist. We barely noticed, so mindless was our belief in that cycle where only the obsolete dies and only the needed is created. We diligently counted our product. We never counted our loss.

Before I even recognized the impulse, I had a rock in my hand, and I threw it as hard as I could at the storefront window. It rocketed through, scattering a trail of glass that broke apart the light around it, glass that skittered at the feet of the naked mannequins and slipped amongst the dust bunnies below the empty metal shelves. The crash launched a huddle of crows off the rooftop and into the pale blue air. It tinkled for a moment longer, then was gone.

I felt nothing. No thrill. No humor. No tragedy. No remorse. I felt nothing because I knew, in that moment, there *was* nothing. Nothing beyond Isidora. The strip mall was nothing before I arrived, and it would be nothing after I left.

> —*Today, you are rescued from the darkness. The reality of Isidora is revealed.*

I felt a fool for expecting better, for thinking some ready-made solution to my malaise would be waiting for me out in the figment world. Life isn't a series of serendipitous events to be surprised by and delighted over. Possibility is finite, predictable, self-made. I decided if Isidora was insufficient, then I needed to make Isidora more. With that realization, I felt an urgent need to return.

The road ahead joined a stream, and both flowed east toward a small wood that flanked the interstate south of Isidora. I followed them for a while, thinking it would be quicker than going back the way I came. When the pavement stopped at a dead end, I continued along the water as it cut across fields of overgrown grass and trees huddled together in shady copses. I soon found myself in the woods themselves, where the air grew moist and cold, and the shade of the full canopy blocked out the sky. The trees thickened around rich beds of ferns whose prehistoric fans thirsted for sunlight. When it became too difficult to trudge through the undergrowth, I slipped off my shoes, tied the laces together, and threw them over my shoulder, then stepped into the cool water of the stream, which slid impatiently around my feet. I still remember the feel of the river stones, smoothed by ages of rushing water and softened by a layer of imperceptible life. I walked downstream with the swish of my clumsy ambling an analog to the wind rustling the leaves above.

At one point I came upon a solitary flower rising from the decaying bark of a fallen log, a pink cattleya quivering at the top of a long stalk as if about to fall, as if about to cease to be entirely, its ruffled petals cradling a bell of pollinium. I came across another, this one in white, then another in radiant yellow dancing in a shaft of light carved through the canopied sky. In the concavity of a long, slow bend in the stream, a clearing of tall grass and underbrush emerged, ringed by the fragile flowers. Dots of pink, yellow, and red. They burst forth in the penumbra of the forest's edge, seeking the light but fearing the sun. And I stood there too, at the edge of the clearing, still ankle deep in the clear stream. The water hushed. The air settled. A bird called, and its song, rather than interrupting the stillness, accentuated it.

Then she rises, emerging from I know not where, perhaps made in that very instant, birthed from the grass and the earth below. She's on her knees at first, or so it seems, her back to me, picking the miscellanea of nature's Velcro out of the onyx of her hair. Her fingers pass through it slowly, stretching the strands into parallel black lines as she hunts for thistles and burrs. She finds one and pulls it out brusquely, impatiently, and casts it aside. Then, with a startling jolt, she flips the mass of her hair over her head and bends with the weight of it so that it dangles in front of her face like a mourning veil. Wisps of hair at the top of her slender neck arise delicately, the light-starved underbrush of her forested mane now electric.

I see her shoulders, narrow and bare, and the plunging valley of her spine as it stretches the cotton of a simple white tank top. Below, her skin is a golden tan. She reaches to her forehead and skims her hand back, drawing the hair into a tight bundle, and as she does this she stands and smooths the top of her head with the palm of her other hand, coaxing each strand into the fold. In this intimate moment—her hands busy about her head, her chest raised, her back straight—I participate, silently; the uninvited observer hiding in plain sight. And I feel guilty for this participation. I should turn and go and leave her to her task, to her clearing, to her anonymity. But in doing so, the sound of each step dropped heavily into the stream would shatter the stillness. She would turn and see me, the bulk of me and nothing more. Horrified, she would run from this place leaving forever the clearing, the brook, the cattleyas. No, her solitude *depends* on my presence. This moment *depends* on my participation.

She snaps a black hair tie around her captured hair. It is all unspeakably beautiful.

Then she reaches down into the grasses and pulls on a shirt. It's nearly transparent, and it glimmers in the sun as if made from nothing but woven dew. It billows around the soft curves of her torso, occasionally lifting to reveal the large stitched-on pockets of her army-green canvas pants. She walks straight ahead, past the stump of a felled tree and between two overgrown ferns, finding the most imperceptible of trails. A moment later she is surrounded by the darkness of the forest. A moment later she is gone.

I was standing in a stream with my pant legs rolled up and shoes thrown over my shoulder. My feet were cold and wet.

Chapter Twenty-Seven

Of course the Mouth would suggest a party. It had become his solution to everything. Get drunk, dance, hook-up, screw. If emancipation did not lie somewhere in the slurry of that hedonistic cocktail, the Mouth would never find it.

"Yeah, a party!" he yelled over the pulsing generator. "If you really want to recruit out of the Shambles, why not throw a party? We're already planning for Solstice Day. It's going to be epic. Why not invite the Shambles?"

We followed the delicious cascade of Marianne's auburn hair out of the generator room and into the open expanse of the Mines. As the door closed behind us, the popping pistons muted into a familiar thrum that echoed through the vast, open space like war drums.

I nodded like a grinning bobblehead as Marianne explained the latest upgrades to the Mines, her manicured nails tracing the interconnections between the CPUs of the old array and our newly acquired units, the computational path on which our existence depended.

I leaned into the Mouth. "We've overlooked them for too long, don't you think?"

"Like I said, all god's chidrens," the Mouth whispered.

It had bothered me since Hawke's revelation, and when I wasn't thinking about the woman and the clearing and the cold water rushing at my feet—and I often was—I was thinking about the Shambles. If the alternative was to consume it by fire, by Hawke's own hand, we needed to do all we could to provide refuge for the poor souls who lived there. That's not to say the Circle needed to know Hawke's predicament or the stakes if we should fail. And, thankfully, the Mouth wasn't one to ask questions.

—The world always underestimated me. You should have known better.

As Kristen began explaining the impact of increased computational power on electricity consumption, the Mouth strayed from the larger inspection party and wandered into Sigma's nursery where a different sort of mining was taking place. White light funneled into solar panels on the roof and dripped down through transformers and extension cords and bulbs suspended by thin chain links to fall black on dozens of cannabis plants. The Mouth ran his fingers along the pointed purple leaves with the wet-lipped avarice of a lecher. Not waiting for a command, Sabrina, the most recent, most favored of his Lambda hangers-on, opened a silver cigarette case and handed the Mouth a joint.

"You're a treasure," he said as she flicked the flint of a lighter before his face. He exhaled a fog of half-consumed smoke in a constricted wheeze. "A goddamn treasure." She nestled under his arm, and the two walked conjoined for the remainder of the tour.

"In short, there's a divergence between the expected power supply and our upper limit on consumption." I glanced away from Kristen to Marianne, who winked at me as the Blacklung deputy handed her a cappuccino. "It's like some of the power is disappearing, and with us piggybacking on the old circuits, it's hard to tell where it's going. We are seeing blackouts when demand is too high and the failsafe trips. With the new UPS on the array, that should no longer stop operations."

We nodded as all bureaucrats do when being briefed on something short of an emergency and made our way back to the Ark for lunch.

****

On the morning of the summer solstice the sun rose but struggled to penetrate a layer of thick black clouds that promised to drown the world. The festivities were planned to start in the late afternoon with a performance of Lambda's newest play dramatizing the founding of Isidora, but almost everyone was thoroughly drunk by noon. When the first of the invited guests from the Shambles arrived, they were greeted by the fullest expression of Isidoran debauchery, or rather not greeted at all, as many walked straight on to the compound unnoticed.

Brushfire and All-Weather were particularly good at loosening tongues and amplifying egos, and as followers began letting both run free, an argument between a few Alphas and Omegas about which was the most favored work unit devolved into a brawl that flared like the grease-fed flames of Squire's barbecue. It took the joint protestation of Regina and Hawke to break up the scuffle, but rather than denying either unit was favored above the other, they took pains to praise the delicious quality of Sigma's eggs. Tempers still at a boil, a few combatants joined forces to attack the chicken coops, which it turned out were relatively easy to flip. When the panicked hens bolted through an open gate, the entirety of Isidora was plunged into an hours-long chicken chase.

I had a good bead on Gloria, a plump little thing that moved remarkably quick for having such short legs. A group of followers cornered her on the east side of the Winter Quarters, but when I approached them to assist with her capture, they all saluted me, and Gloria bolted through the legs of a follower with a hand over her eyes. As I chased her back to the pond, I found myself on a collision course with Antoinette and a pair of panting Sigmas hot on her tail feathers. With nothing but a knowing glance exchanged, we swapped prey, and I pounced on the unsuspecting hen as the others scooped up Gloria.

When the play finally started, two hours late, we were all drunk, winded, and covered in feathers. Half the actors were unable to stand in one place without swaying from side to side, as if performing on the deck of an ill-fated cruise ship, and the other half couldn't remember their lines. The hero of the tale, the Mouth playing himself, spent so much time feeding the other Lambdas lines that it started to look like a one-man show. This wasn't helped by his self-serving soliloquies, which went on for so long the audience had a hard time following the plot. When the skies finally opened and both audience and actors ran for cover, no one knew if the play was over or if we'd only survived act one.

In short, it was a miracle that any of the figments from the Shambles decided to stay. Those who felt rejected by the imagined world and hoped Isidora was the next evolution in progressive, inclusive social order left the compound on sight. But those who were looking for a bit of libertine chaos fueled by subsidized booze and a generous helping of smoked meats were not disappointed. When we finally decided to pump club music through the various loudspeakers installed across the compound for the Solstice Day celebrations, the followers and remaining figments melted into a homogenous whole, bouncing as one as they sheltered under the eaves of the Mines or among the shop stalls of the Winter Quarters. I wound up at the latter, sitting alone among upturned milk crates, feeling the blood pulse through my ears as the downpour filled the air with must.

"What a mess," she says as she sits down beside me, her voice like purified mist rising from a waterfall. From the directness of her approach, the lack of deference and prostration, I know she is not a follower, but it's not until she pulls a black band from her wrist and smooths her hair back into a ponytail that I realize she is the woman from the stream.

"It's not exactly going to plan."

She smiles, her dimples floating to meet her high cheekbones, her eyes open and bright. That smile—it is her most beguiling characteristic, at once cutting and comforting, vulnerable and confident. It arrives with the flash of lightning and stays etched into your vision long after it's gone.

"It's the most fun I've had all year," she says as a strand of jet-black hair falls from her bangs and brushes her naked lips. Her white T-shirt is dappled with rain.

"Are you living in the Shambles?" I ask.

"The what?"

"The Shambles." My cheeks fill with embarrassment, but my mouth keeps ignorantly pushing forward. "The run-down part of town near the interstate."

"I live on Swann Street in the Historic Quarter," she says, sitting straight and folding her arms. "Who told you it was called the Shambles?"

"I don't know." The word and the place came to me at the same time, and I questioned neither. "It's the only way I've ever known it."

"It's a very unkind term. It makes us sound like a bunch of hobos standing around trash can fires."

"I'm sorry."

"Sure, there are trash-can fires, but do I look like a hobo to you?"

She smiles again, that same incandescent smile, and in that moment the lights of Isidora sparkle to life. The rain that fell as formless sound hidden in the darkness now surrounds us, a curtain of ocean scooped from distant shores and dropped on Isidora in waves. In the amber glow of the exterior lamps, she is radiant—not beautiful, but beauty itself, the platonic form in relation to which all other women are false.

"I see you," I say. "And you're definitely not a hobo."

She uncrosses her arms and slides closer. The taught spring of her body unwinds. "Was there ever any doubt?"

"Look," I say, hoping to regain my footing. "Can I get you a drink?"

"If you have the nuts for it."

The confusion must be written on my face because she reaches into her pocket to reveal an assortment of metal nuts, black and silver and rusted brown. "You can pay with mine if you want. I've got no use for them after tonight."

I grab her hand in mine and fold her fingers over the counterfeits. "That won't be necessary."

I stand and Isidora stands with me. As I move through the crowd, followers careen off the bubble of my inviolable personal space, its radius expansive, like kudzu, undeterred by pruning. One of the newer Sigmas is tending bar, and in his rush to salute me he slaps a newly mixed drink from the hands of the follower at the head of the line, whose anger evaporates like the grain alcohol soaking through his sleeve when he sees it is the Omicron cutting in front of him.

"A Brush and soda. An All-Weather fizz."

I return to her, past statues blinded by their own hands.

"So, you're kind of a big deal here, huh?" She peers over the rim of both cups and decides on the Brushfire.

"You could say that."

"Funny. I would have put you more on the hobo end of the spectrum."

She takes a sip and leans back to look at the rain, as if only noticing it in that instant. And in that same instant, I'm filled with a million yearnings. I want to sew my life into a silk tapestry and hang it on her wall, so that she may know me. I want to abandon sleep and sustenance and sit motionlessly for hours to hear troubadours sing her praises. I want to chase her through dawn-lit meadows and let morning dew soak the hems of our robes. I want to pen her letters slipped into glass bottles and throw them from the deck of my wave-battered schooner into the sea. I want to scribble words of affection in mud sodden trenches and kiss her photo as the bullets crack overhead. I want to load up a station wagon and drive her west through painted canyons and empty deserts until the radio turns to fuzz and the dusk drowns us both in purple. I want to sit beside her in matching rocking chairs and creak in unison before a golden sunset. Unreasonable, illogical, inexplicable yearning—in that moment, I want to love her in all the ways lovers have ever loved.

We sit there for an hour, sipping cocktails that refill themselves, talking, laughing, whispering, sighing. The rain falls steady as if caught in a loop. The world stops demanding we pay attention to it. Still, I can feel a different sensation passing through the crowd of followers around us, an agita, a jealousy, a desire to pounce. She is the cuckoo chick in the nest of the thrush, and the flock is beginning to sense something is not right.

In one of the easy pauses in our conversation, I stand.

"Where are you going?" she asks.

"To get clean."

"To get clean?"

"Join me."

Without waiting for an answer, I step out from under the building's eave, and a torrent of warm water mattes my hair. I smile an irrepressible smile and shake like a dog, and she giggles as she recoils from the thrown drops. And then I am galloping over the rim of the depression and down into the Green. I am drenched in an instant. The water weightless. She pauses only to release her bundled hair and chases after me.

At the bottom of the bowl, I leap onto Lambda's stage. She bounds the stairs behind me and slides into my outstretched arms. I hold her for an eternity.

Two drops of water are birthed above of dust and the vapor of rains that came before. They grow until their cloud nursery can no longer hold them and then they fall, each an orb in empty space surrounded by others but locked in the isolation of a parallel descent. Down they slip alone, pulled along a collision course to the earth from whence they came by a force they cannot comprehend. Free fall is like a void, and it's impossible to tell if it's they that are tumbling and twisting or the world around them as they idle in frozen stillness.

An instant before hitting the cold wet ground, one drop lands on me and one drop lands on her, and they roll from our hair down our foreheads to our noses and our lips. And there, after an interminable isolation, in defiance of all probability, they are united.

Soon all of Isidora rushes to join us. The music grows louder, and bare feet glide and step over the trampled grass or rap across the wooden planks of the stage. She throws her wet hair about, face to the sky, eyes closed, letting the music wash over her like the warm rain that soaks her blue jeans and turns her white T-shirt into a second skin. In a sea of darting glances and whispered words, she is the only one of us who is truly free, beholden only to herself, to the music, to the weeping sky and the flooded earth. My hands encircle her waist, but I do not draw her in like captured prey. I come to her like a ship finding unexpected harbor in the middle of an endless sea.

We dance until the sky and the Brushfire vats are both drained dry and the clothes that cling to us are filled with chills. As I grab her hand to lead her back to the Ark, the lights flutter and the speakers hiccup and then all of Isidora is returned to the darkened silence of midnight.

"Stay with me tonight," I say ignoring the blackout.

She smiles and shakes her head. "No thanks. I can shiver in the dark at home."

We move through a crowd of followers reluctant to let the night have its way. Bonfires are built wherever a patch of dry ground can be found. Blankets are wrapped around twos and threes. Guitars appear and are plucked with the dulcet wandering of a deer tracing a trail on a forest floor.

At the edge of Isidora I stop, and her final step pulls her hand from mine.

"I can't go any farther, not with everyone watching."

She lowers her head and steps to me, taking my hands in hers.

"Stay," I plead. "Isidora can be everything you need it to be."

She raises on her toes and kisses me, not in love or lust but in sympathy.

"But it can't be, can it? Not everything."

She turns and walks away from me down the tracks into the darkness. At the edge of the impenetrable black, where she is nothing but a pillar of violet haze, she turns.

"If you ever break free from this place . . . you know where to find me."

Chapter Twenty-Eight

When I awoke the next day, it was bright enough in my suite to warrant a groan. I ladled some water from the tank in the bathroom, just enough to splash on my face, and plodded down the stairs with my open robe trailing behind me like the drooping wings of a fruit bat roused at noon. Halfway down I heard the door of a suite open behind me, and the Mouth bounded to my side, chipper as an ad for laundry detergent.

"Woof. What a rager, huh?"

"Sure," I said through a yawn.

We entered the dining room to find Regina and Squire sipping the last of their coffee over plates smeared with yellow yolk, and immediately the Mouth played to a larger audience.

"I was actually getting a bit bored with the rain. Sabrina and I were in the Mines smoking a J and thinking about calling it a night. And then all of a sudden this madman"—He slaps me on the back—"goes bolting down the Green like the feds are after him."

I wrapped the wings of my robe around me and cinched them with the cord. "Good morning, Regina. Squire." She raised her brow as she sipped from her mug. Squire gave me a courtly nod.

"But it wasn't the feds, was it, Squibs? It was a hot piece of ass. A tartelette from the wrong side of the tracks. A strumpet from the Shambles who this old dog threw a bone."

"Christ, Dean," Regina muttered.

The Mouth crossed his arms and nudged the air with his forehead. "So?"

"So what, LaBouche?" I sat, and the steward slid a foam-topped cup and saucer in front of me.

"So," he said sitting beside me. "How was that gorgeous Gamin?"

"Gamin?

"Yeah, Gamin. That girl from the streets with fire in her eyes. I bet she was pneumatic as fuck."

I rubbed my forehead and took a long sip of coffee. "We are not having this conversation."

"Oh." He lowered his voice to a whisper. "Is she still here?"

"She was never here, Dean. You're the only one who breaks that rule."

The Mouth dropped a silver teaspoon into his freshly made mocha. "Well, did you at least sneak off to the machine shed with her?"

"He probably threw her into the pond," Regina said with a cutting smirk.

"She left, guys. The Gamin left. She didn't want to stay, and I can't leave. So, she left."

The Mouth stirred slowly. *Tink. Tink. Tink.*

Regina rose and circled the table. "Them's the breaks." She patted my shoulder and then headed upstairs.

"In fact, she may still join us," Squire said softly.

"Maybe." I nodded, but I knew better than to hope. Isidora had been a diversion for her, an opportunity to experience something new, if only for a night. But she had no plans to abandon the life she was living on Swann Street. There was something there worth holding on to, and I desperately wanted to see it. I had no intention of abandoning Isidora either, but it took all the reserve I could muster not to throw on clothes and run off to the Shambles to find her. If only as a diversion. If only for a night.

She wasn't the only figment who came to Isidora with no plans to stay. By mid-afternoon, as hunger conquered hangover and life returned to the compound, it became clear how unsuccessful our recruitment drive had been. Of the fifty or so figments welcomed from the Shambles, only a dozen stayed the night, and most of them were gone by noon. Hawke whipped Omega into an indignant fury, claiming the Shambles had used us as a playground and a meal card and then discarded Isidora like so much trash. When we discovered they hadn't left empty handed, that half the plants in the Mines had been harvested and a fair amount of canned goods lifted from the Ark, that fury turned to rage.

"What did you expect to happen?" Hawke asked at that afternoon's Circle.

The Mouth sat cross-legged on the bare ground in front of his pile of cushions, hunched over and sipping smoke from a cigarette like hot tea. "I expected we would welcome them like every other follower who showed up and joined us. I don't know what the big deal is. So they didn't stay. So they smoked our weed and ate our food. Wasn't that the point?"

"Of course you don't get it, Dean." Regina sat at the edge of her chair, a coiled viper ready to strike. "You don't get any of it. You don't get how much work went into growing the food your honored guests walked off with last night."

Sam scoffed. "What about the work that went into building the coops that your Alphas trashed for no reason?"

"I'm sure they were Omegas," Regina replied cooly.

"Sure," Hawke sneered. "It can't be Regina. It's never Regina."

As the Circle devolved into petulant bickering, I turned to the steward, who was watching the scene with a bit too much interest, and sent him to the basement to carry up the heaviest thing he could find.

"What about Lambda's play?" the Mouth asked. "You don't think I put a lot of work into that? You don't think I'm bummed we never got to finish? But whatever. It's no one's fault."

I couldn't help myself. "God forbid we don't get to hear about the tortured soul of Dean LaBouche and how he single-handedly founded Isidora."

"Because I did. I discovered this place by myself. I planted the flag—not that any of you remember that."

Squire sat stoic, unbaited by the blood-letting. "We all built this place. We all made sacrifices. Isidora is ours. Equally."

"Yes, it's ours," Hawke said, his anger cooling to pointed resolve like iron cast. "It's certainly not theirs. Not those barbarians from the Shambles who returned our hospitality with theft. We were defenseless."

"We were unprepared," I replied.

"And what happens when they come back looking for more?" Hawke asked. "They know what we have now; they know the compound. We're completely exposed. And not just to the Shambles, but to figments everywhere. The more Isidora thrives, the more we become a target."

We all paused to consider the implications, and for a moment nothing could be heard but the last of yesterday's rainwater dripping into our cistern. Whatever Hawke was planning for the Shambles, I knew it wasn't recruitment. Not anymore. Hawke was not one to risk failing twice.

Squire cleared his throat. "What do you suggest, Hawke? Security cameras?"

"We had security cameras in the bar," Sam said. "They're very helpful if you want to *watch* people steal from you."

Hawke rose and lit a cigarette in a single motion, the tobacco cold and lifeless one moment and flame incarnate the next. "I'm not talking about cameras. Maybe we put some up, but that's not the point. I'm talking about an army."

"An army?" Squire exclaimed.

"Or a militia. We need to be able to defend what we've built here."

"From enemies foreign *and* domestic," Sam snapped.

Regina yawned through a stretch and then leaned forward. "A bit more law and order around here wouldn't hurt."

"No," the Mouth said, crab-walking back into his pillows. "We do not need an army rounding up all of Isidora's teenagers before the goo in their frontal cortex is set, giving them rifles and a vaguely southern accent, and shipping them off to war. We did that before, don't you remember?" His voice began to quiver and strain. "Don't you remember that endless war—that vortex that sucked up the youth of our generation? The lies, the cover-up, the corruption, the deceit? They bled us dry chasing mirages in the desert— figments even then. And what do we have to show for it? Bad checks written everywhere, a blood debt that will never be repaid."

Hawke took a short sip of All-Weather, then raised his open palms as if he was attempting to settle a startled mare. "That is not the goal. I'm not talking about offense. I'm talking about defense. No civilization, just or unjust, here or elsewhere, has existed long without a means of defending itself. If someone or something comes to take Isidora away from us, we can't simply talk them out of it. We'll have to meet force with force."

"In fact," Squire said, clearing his throat, "we should not let Isidora become Melos."

"Defense," the Mouth said, savoring the words as he talked himself through the idea. "To defend the freedoms of Isidora, not restrain them. To nurture the revolutionary experiment underway, not hijack it. A guard corps, not an army. Isidora's revolutionary guard corps."

It wasn't what I was expecting. I thought Hawke would propose hellfire, an apocalypse brought down on the Shambles to punish them for proving him right. A defensive force was meek by comparison and almost . . . rational.

"A shield for Isidora," I said. "And a sword for the Circle. But who will lead it?"

We needed someone physically imposing, someone who projected strength. But at the same time someone loyal, compliant, and above all, unambitious. In short, we needed an idiot. When Hawke suggested Echo, we could think of no one else.

Chapter Twenty-Nine

The next day the Circle announced the formation of the Committee on Unity and Isidoran Oneness, which separated followers from their work units and assigned them to unity groups, forcing Alphas, Omegas, Mus, and Sigmas to work beside one another to clean up the destruction wrought by the Solstice Day celebration. I was encouraged to walk amongst them as they righted the chicken coops and swept out the mines, but the constant saluting was more hindrance than help, so I retired to the top of the water tower and stared longingly at the Shambles. When they finished tidying, we turned our attention to Isidora's defenses.

Hawke directed a band of followers to establish a perimeter out of anything they could find, and they ravaged the compound like wild dogs on carrion, stripping boxcars down to their wheels and tearing apart cubicles to construct ramshackle barricades on the western edge of the compound. Mack and Rory lashed themselves to the derelict rolling stock and pulled a few cars to the neck of the industrial spur with a dozen followers pushing from behind. Sheet metal was cut and clamped to two-by-fours or directly to still-growing trees. Sofas were sawed in two and stacked onto dumpsters like da-da parapets. The end result was an impractical hodgepodge of crap more likely to deter invaders with its obscene appearance than its defensibility, but it made everyone feel safer, which is, after all, the only reason anyone builds a wall.

At the same time Echo began assembling his brute squad. Coached on theatrics by the Mouth himself, he donned a long gray trench coat and a black bandana tied around his bulbous forehead and stood on milk crates in the center of the compound, barking about duty and honor and the threats arrayed against us. A cadre of young men, their egos as brittle as honeycomb, gathered around, howling and beating their chests before the image of Isidora's first soldier. Each one fantasized it was actually himself raised above the rest, receiving the ritualistic submission of his peers, the only act of true love permitted among honest men. By mid-afternoon, two dozen of these paper tigers, these Wooden Boys waiting for the world to consent to their manhood, were drilled up and down the Green, mimicking the soldiering they had only ever seen on TV and in movies. That evening the first shift took watch on Isidora's western flank, armed with nothing but a supreme sense of self-righteousness and pointed sticks.

They are easy to evade.

Under a sky scorched umber by the dying light, I slip from Isidora's grasp, heading north through the toothpick forest until I reach the tracks of the main line. Then I scurry west past the withering station and the peripheral scrubland that separates farm from city, a field mouse and Isidora the hawk above. Only when I reach the edge of the Shambles do I allow myself to stroll.

Swann Street, I remember. She said to find her there. I don't know it, so I start at the northern-most reaches of the Shambles where land was leveled flat by the debt-fueled ambition of developers and then neglected, the weeds and thistles weaving a thick scab on the wounded earth. A warehouse, its heart burned to ash, its walls black as cinder, stands alone, ringed by a road that the city never attempted to light. For a moment I stand beside it and remember the time I stood there before. In the presence of humanity and the absence of humans, the world is preternaturally dark.

I head west into the Shambles. The inert street lights hang dumb above the pavement at the first intersection, and I climb the base of their pole to squint at the perpendicular road signs. Winnebago and Third. I pass another block of blue-collar flotsam—Mackey and Sons Carpet and Upholstery, well upholstered itself with particle board and two-by-fours. Theo's Garage and Restoration, long overdue for a spot of self-care. Unnamed plumbing, unnamed tax preparation, unnamed jerk chicken—tombs without headstones, reliquaries of forgotten saints.

At Winnebago and Fourth, I turn south down a broad boulevard split by a row of trees growing full and lush and wide. Stately row houses line either side, condemned by the authorities, boarded up by slum lords, and broken back into by their former tenants. Every so often a house is ringed by a chain-link fence as if its contents were particularly offensive, a hazard to public decency at risk of breaking free. Fourth and Virgil. Fourth and Upanishads. Fourth and Timbuktu.

Fourth and Swann.

The road to the west is dark and quiet, but to the east there is a light, and I walk toward it. At Seventh and Swann, the huddled townhouses withdraw to reveal a square ringed by the marble friezes of municipal buildings and the wooden spire of an Anglican church. Amongst the bushes and trees of a small public garden stands a bronze man, a lesser general from our bipolar war, on a plinth of stone taller than any man, illuminated by the mercurial flames of a half-dozen trash-can fires. Shadows prance around its base, coalescing like water on a window pane and then separating like cells. Coalescing, separating, uniting, dividing. One together, ones apart. The figments pulse through their organic dance to a gypsy tune squeezed from the reeds of a polished black accordion and the thrumming strings of a chipped guitar.

As I approach through the trees, a shade among shadows, the burble of the figment sea rises to meet me. Talking. Laughing. Sighing. Moaning. Complaining. Consoling. Remembering. Forgetting. The score of banal humanity plays on a loop, repeating itself indefinitely. I pause at the threshold between the light and the dark and scan the scene.

The figments are a motley bunch, dressed in a mishmash of faded fabrics and worn leathers like thrift store mannequins come to life. Near the base of the statue, a woman in a beige muslin dress hops on the heels of her lace-up boots, a mess of frizzled red curls hiccuping up her back as she trots in place. Beside her a man in a gabardine vest and flannel shirt taps his toe and hollers, a row of jagged teeth smiling below a bulbous red nose fixed on the bosom of his partner like a birddog. To their right, a couple in matching corduroy dance something like a jitterbug. Beside them, men draping bottles over each other's shoulders sway and slide like seasick sailors. A gaggle of women stand at the periphery, fists on their hips, arms flapped wide, clucking and scratching at the ground as they gab.

In the center of it all she rings the rosy, hand in hand with a circle of figment children who spin in the delirious delight of a bedtime broken. Her feet clap the time-worn cobblestones. Her hair dances in the air. She laughs, and the children giggle. She is nowhere else but there.

I breach the light and go to her, but I don't make it far.

"Well, hello stranger." I've caught the eye of the woman in muslin, and she trots to intercept me, her bouncing breasts assaulting the space between us like pile drivers. "Never seen you before."

"Never seen 'im," the man in gabardine agrees.

"Why you sneakin' around in the dark, hun? You don't gotta be afraid. Come dance with mama."

She reaches for my hands, and before I can react I'm pulled into her cloud of talcum, brandywine, and Chanel No. 5. Our hips are feet apart, but her bosom still hits me in the chest with a force that takes my breath away.

The man whistles, his toe still tapping. "Don't break the boy now, Marjorie."

"Oh, hush, Georgie. Young, sturdy lad like this? It'll take more to break him, alright." She leans in and slows her trot to a jiggle. "Don't you worry, hun," she whispers and winks. "Mama knows how."

She laughs and spins and smacks me in the face with her tangled red mane. I fall back out of her reach and cast a pleading glance toward the Gamin.

"Oh, leave the boy alone, Mags," Georgie says. "He ain't here for you."

Marjorie turns to look at the youth. "That little hussy. She catches all the big fish."

Georgie rubs the unkempt whiskers on his bony chin. "She got good bait."

"But she ain't got the biggest pole." Mags grabs Georgie by the shoulders and squeezes him to her breast with the hoot of a can-can dancer, and the two trot in time back toward the accordionist.

The gypsy tune ends like a train clambering into a station, and as the circle of children stop their dizzying spin, she looks up and sees me there, standing alone in a world that reluctantly settles back into place. She steps out of the circle and clasps the hands of the children behind her. The guitarist cracks his knuckles, rolls his shoulders, and then sets in again on his furious strumming. She comes to me. Behind her the children revolve again, faster and faster, unmoderated by her presence, until sweaty hands slip from sweaty hands and they tumble to the ground in fits of laughter.

"Your highness." She snaps erect and covers her face with her hands.

"Stop," I say, pulling at her arm. "What if they know what that means?"

She rolls her eyes. "Relax. Your reputation is no good here, oh great Omicron. The only thing you need to worry about is catching Marjorie's eye."

"Oh, I caught more than that. She was very . . . hospitable."

"Hospitable? I've seen her crush a man with her tits. No joke. Georgie used to be eight feet tall."

She grabs my hand and twirls, wrapping herself in my arm like a silken scarf. "So, are you out?"

"I don't know," I say over her shoulder. "I'm here now."

She shrugs. "It's a start."

She leads me away from the dancing out into the grayness of the residual light. At tenth and Swann we turn up an alley where blankets and sheets have been strung between the buildings in a makeshift roof that shelters a row of street vendors and their disheveled patrons. Woks and skillets, saucepans and soup cauldrons sizzle above heaving gas flames, illuminating the alley as if it were daylight. The air swells with sweat and steam and spice. A man in a threadbare apron drops a pile of freshly chopped onions into a saucer as wide as an embrace, sending up a cloud of vapor to assault my nose and squeeze my eyes. I rub the healed bones of my forearm as they pulse in a rhythm half-remembered.

"What are we having?" I say with a sniff, trying to hold back tears.

"Stew, I think."

I watch as the man empties a jar of tomatoes into the pan, a jar similar to the hundreds Mu has cloistered in the basement of the Ark. She grabs me and leads me away.

At the end of the alley, a woman with auburn waves and a gentle, time-worn smile stands before a blackened pot. We approach her with empty bowls in our hands, a queue of hungry pilgrims, and with a slow, deliberate sweep of her arm she ladles out our blessings. Lentils, carrots, rutabagas, thyme, parsnips, potatoes, parsley, chives. It waters our tongues and warms our hands. We give her nothing in return.

We carry our soup through a thinning crowd, down a second alley and then a third to a set of articulating fire escape stairs held down by tires. She climbs, ahead of me and I smell—between the stock and the herbs—a scent. Her scent. Something ethereal, eternal, otherworldly. Neither animal, nor vegetable, nor mineral. Celestial perhaps. The smell of pink nebulae blossoming in the void. I strain to focus on the curves of her form as they sway like a pocket watch dangled before my eyes.

We climb past open windows, past darkening rooms, past shirts hung on the back of chairs and dishes left dirty on vinyl tablecloths.

"This one's mine," she says, pausing at an open window where wind billows a white sheer curtain into the darkness beyond. We keep climbing.

At the top floor she hands me her bowl and, with a single, effortless motion, leaps to grab the ledge above and pull herself onto the roof. I hand up the stew and then take my turn. My arms are weak from disuse, and my legs kick desperately against the bricks. I launch a toe at the ledge and roll my body up onto the dusty cement. There, flat on my back, I see her look down on me, her head cocked slightly and a bemused smile on her face.

"What?" I ask.

"You look like a powdered donut."

"I'll get better at it," I say rising to brush myself clean.

She returns my bowl then brushes the hair from her face with her newly freed hand. "Only if you come back."

In the center of the roof, a single folding chair waits for us, the kind made of unpolished metal and woven green nylon that folds into a cumbersome flat rectangle, the kind my mother would plant herself in when we first arrived at a campsite as my father dispatched the older kids for firewood, the younger ones for kindling, then turned his own attention to cursing at tent poles.

"I'm sorry there's only one," she says. "I wasn't expecting company."

"Oh, it's fine," I reply, sitting cross-legged beside the empty chair. "I'm already dusty."

She holds her spoon in her mouth and drags the chair a few yards away, then returns to sit down beside me. For a while, nothing need be said. A soft breeze blows over the rooftop, that mid-evening air, unheated by the sun. It is the temperature of darkness. We breathe it in and blow it back over the rims of our bowls, kicking up condensate, a tribute for the sky.

"It's good," I say, muscling down a mouthful still too hot to eat. "And free?"

"Not always. But if the community garden is doing well or we run into some good luck, they try not to make money a reason to turn people away."

Her building is one of the tallest in the Shambles and from the roof we can see out in every direction—the soft, sterile glow of the western suburbs, the candle-lit tenements that lurk beside us in the darkness, and to the east the faint glow of Isidora puncturing the horizon like a rising sun. But the real show is overhead. I set my bowl aside and lean back to take in the celestials, wandering above in a cloudless, moonless sky.

"I love the stars," she says as if reminding herself. "They're so far away and yet so present. You know how sailors used to use the stars to navigate?"

"Yeah, sure."

"I feel like they help me navigate too, not across oceans but in life. If I'm ever feeling lost and alone, I come here and look up, and there's the north star . . ." She reaches up and points to Polaris. ". . . and all the constellations in their place, and I feel like I'm right where I'm supposed to be."

"Do you know their names?" I ask, preparing to take her on a tour of the heavens, conducting the music of the spheres as she sits in awe and admiration.

But instead, she nods. "Circling Polaris is the Little Dipper. It's actually a bear, you know—Ursa Minor—the little bear. Mama bear is not far behind."

Ursa. Lyra. Cassiopeia. Draco. I lay on my back, and she rests her head on my chest and names them one by one. Her hands trace the invisible lines in the sky, lines I see just as clearly when I close my eyes.

She speaks and I listen, just like the first time I learned to name the constellations reclined on the hood of my father's Oldsmobile in some pasture outside of town. Without cause or explanation, as all things are when you're a child, he told me to grab my coat, and we got in the car and drove into the night.

Just the two of us. And in leaving behind that ugly ranch with the broken screen door, the chaotic energy of five children, and a wife increasingly fond of gin, he left behind his characteristic anger too, and I saw him for the first time as he perhaps saw himself—wistful, wise, and a touch whimsical.

When we stopped in the pasture, all I wanted to do was throw my army man up as high as I could and watch him parachute through the beam of the car's one functioning headlight. But he grabbed me by the armpits and placed me on the hood of the Olds, then climbed up beside me. We laid there together, father and son, the way he had laid in the grass with his father as a child so many years before. Stargazing and teaching the constellations were part of his narrow idea of fatherhood. Like spanking and shouting and working as many second shifts as you could, it was just something you did when you were dad. He told me how the stars moved but moved together, how you could rely on them if you learned to read their signs. When a meteor lit up the sky, I asked why some stars didn't have to stay in place.

"Look," he said. "Look how quickly it disappears while all the other stars keep shining." I told him I wanted to be a fast star, to burn brighter than all the rest. He grunted that ambiguous grunt I always took for disappointment. Maybe, once, he wanted that too, but he knew enough about the heavens to know not to wish on shooting stars.

I fell asleep there on the hood of the Olds and woke up the next morning in my bed. I never considered how I got there, time for a child being a staccato flurry of moments isolated from one another by oblivion. But lying there on the roof of her apartment building, her voice long silent, her breath falling into a low, rhythmic purr, I saw my father slip down from the car to carefully open the back door, sliding his arms under my still form and dropping me gently on the bench in the back, my head beside the split in the seat where the kids would pick at the foam before depositing our car in pinches out the window along the highway. And then he drove, the radio off, the windows cracked, the cab illuminated by the two-watt bulb of the instrument display and the patient cherry of his Winston, the stars above and he below, rolling along as they always had and always would.

Before her, I was only ever tortured by the past. If a remembered event was sad, I would recall that sadness, and it would come live with me in the present. If a remembered event was joyful, memory did nothing but underscore the gulf of time that separated me from that joy. But on that night, with her peacefully dozing on my chest, my eyes lost in the stars, the past came to me sterilized by an even more powerful force that grew in the present—a feeling of deep contentment, of tranquility, of love.

Chapter Thirty

I said I would return to her once a week on Saturday night when the fires were lit and the band played and there was dancing in the lesser general's square. But in practice, I made it far less often. The Wooden Boys, whose numbers swelled with the rise of their reputation, soon learned to patrol our borders in all directions. They armed themselves with BigBox .22's and whiled away the long hours on watch, firing fecklessly at tin cans and two-by-fours. In that way, Isidora transformed from a cuttlefish camouflaged on the sandy sea floor to an urchin at all times projecting its spines outward. In sneaking away, the Omicron now risked more than identification, questioning, obfuscation, and suspicion. He risked being struck in the back by an errant bullet intended to pierce the heart of the Jolly Green Giant.

Still, I went, slithering through shadows, hugging the trees. When I was caught, which happened once or twice and only ever as I attempted to leave, I dropped my sneaking disposition and approached confidently, declaring a surprise inspection of the troops. Their recognition came slowly, often with a flashlight in my face, and when it finally arrived, I was forced to remain stoic as the man with a rifle pointed at my nuts hurriedly buried his face in his hand.

It was worth it. It was always worth it. Swimming in the stream of time as it flowed over the rooftop of her building. The smile of her eyes caught fleeting over her shoulder as she jigged with the roosters or clucked with the hens. The blissful isolation of that darkest block forever unchanging between Swann and Timbuktu. The lightness of the air, unbreathed, unsullied, blowing through the trees just beyond the confines of our cult-like conceit.

I only ever dared go to her at night and never made any attempt to sleep over. Each visit to the Shambles ended with her dozing in my arms as I grew increasingly panicked by the spinning earth and the approaching sun and the me-shaped hole left behind in Isidora. I lingered long enough at her window with my eyes closed and her tongue on mine to forget it was possible to exist anywhere else. But as soon as she ran a finger along my cheek and disappeared into the darkness, I scampered down the fire escape and bolted for Isidora like a flying fish that had lingered a moment too long in the open air. The Wooden Boys were always asleep on my return, nestled into the cushions of their parapets or propped up beside an unfortunate oak conscripted into our wall. The real challenge was reentering the Ark without rousing the steward or the cooks, but if I propped open a fire door and snuck in through the Circle chamber, I could usually collapse into bed without raising alarms just as dawn broke in the east. If I was lucky, I could grab a few hours of sleep before the Viewing.

Recruitment skyrocketed that summer as soon as the Mouth told the entire world we had discovered an endless vein of free money. To no one's surprise but his, the calibre of people who uprooted themselves to flock to Isidora on the promise of unlimited wealth for little work was entirely different from that of the initial followers who arrived expecting to hustle. Some came from the Shambles, others from neighboring towns, but the majority were vagabonds from nowhere in particular washing up on Isidora's shore like human flotsam. They were young, petulant, lazy, covetous, and generally unpleasant—shadows on the cave wall—figments, still, in all but name, and I made no effort to befriend any of them.

To break these shades and try to mold them into something resembling productive members of Isidoran society, they were prevented from having immediate access to the full rights granted previous followers. They were not assigned to work units, not afforded a basic income, and prevented from socializing with members of the Circle. They couldn't live in the Winter Quarters and were, therefore, unable to access electricity and running water. Instead, they camped in the parking lot, turning that empty slab of cracked concrete into a sort of halfway house straddling the figment world and our own.

With a month of good behavior apprenticing for a work unit or patrolling with the Wooden Boys, a shade could become a follower through a ceremony the Mouth called the Viewing. For the shades, it was their first time meeting anyone from the Circle and their only time being allowed into the Ark. For the Omicron, it was a dreadful Sunday morning charade where I would sit blindfolded as the Mouth prattled on and on about the momentousness of their transition from the figment world to the reality of Isidora. If there wasn't a cappuccino in my hand when the Mouth finally removed my blindfold so I could look upon our new followers for the first time, I could burn holes in their stomachs with the ferocity of my glare. If I hadn't fallen asleep during the spectacle, that is. Afterwards, the new followers could officially join the work unit they were apprenticing or be given their own rifle if joining the Wooden Boys.

It was a straightforward process, and we expected all of the shades to go through it in their own time. What we did not expect was for shades to work a few weeks, deprive themselves in order to stockpile nuts, and then live for months off the favorable exchange rate. But these were people accustomed to privation, disinterested in climbing the ranks of Isidoran bureaucracy, unfazed by being outcasts among outcasts. If anything they reveled in it. So, the parking lot became a shantytown, and Isidora became a class-divided society.

Trouble sauntered into the Circle chamber in October in the form of a nineteen-year-old kid recruited directly into the Mines by Marianne. He was tall, gaunt, and had rakishly wild shit-brown hair that Marianne couldn't keep her hands out of. But beyond that, he knew a thing or two about network optimization and had supposedly reworked the array in the Mines to improve our computing power. Throughout September the Block Coins rained into our virtual wallet, and he strutted around the compound like some kind of digital messiah. I hated him from the depths of my amygdala.

"Our win rate last month was two to three times what it's been all summer," he said, pacing the Circle like the headliner of a lecture circuit. "We've probably spent more than usual with the arrival of all the shades, but certainly not more than we've earned, right?"

He looked to Squire who returned his glance with a scowl. "Our expenses have gone up. We've had to sell more Coins to compensate."

"But certainly not more than we earned last month, right?"

Squire glared at Hawke and crossed his thick, hairy arms. "Look, if Omega wants to take over the treasury, be my guest. But until you do, why don't you tell your toady to stop questioning Mu's math?"

Hawke calmly lit a cigarette. "Squire, we're not questioning your math. But prices in the canteen have gone up."

"On *some* goods."

"On *most* goods, Squire. And people are starting to complain."

"Look," the rake said, attempting to exert an authority no one recognized. "If we have more coins and the same number of nuts and bolts, then the exchange rate should go up, not down. We should have more money, not less."

Squire sighed. "Yes, but we don't have the same number of nuts and bolts, do we? Mu has been minting new nuts in proportion to our holdings of Block Coin to maintain parity. In addition, there has been a huge influx of counterfeits since the Solstice Day party and the arrival of all the shades. All these people with all these nuts trying to buy a limited number of goods? Yeah, prices have risen."

"But it doesn't make any sense," the rake said, stopping his pacing. "There can't possibly be enough counterfeits to offset the number of coins we're winning. It doesn't add up."

I set my coffee down and rose from my chair. "I suggest you stop talking now. You've brought this issue to our attention, and for that the Circle is grateful. But you are on the verge of accusing Mu of something you yourself do not fully understand. Mu has explained the problem we have with counterfeits, and the Circle will address that problem. You are excused."

He stood for a second in stunned silence but recovered himself before appearing disobedient. He saluted and walked from the room.

"So, what gives, Squire?" I asked, returning to my seat. "Is this really just a counterfeit problem?"

Squire had always been a bad liar. He didn't have the stomach for it. And anyways he was rife with physical tells. He sweat profusely, and his sweat stank, so he stank profusely. And knowing that he was sweating and stanking, he would pace profusely. But every now and then, he could hold it together. And the thing about bad liars is that when they finally manage to pull one off, the whole world believes them.

"Yes." One word. One word and the die was cast. The asshole. "We could always sell more coins to lower prices, but why should Isidora impoverish itself because the shades don't respect our rules?"

"So, what should we do about it, Squibs?" the Mouth asked from his pillows. "Kick them all out?"

"In fact, we need to take a census. A monetary census. We need to know how many nuts and bolts are in circulation, and we need to adjust the supply to match the value of our Block Coins. In the process, we can clear out all the counterfeits or re-mint them as official nuts and bolts."

"Is that really necessary?" Hawke asked, flicking his cigarette butt into the center of the floor. "We must be millionaires two or three times over by now. Just sell the coins."

Regina took a sip of tea and cleared her throat. "Let's not cut corners on this, Hawke. We do this once and the problem will be solved." Sam agreed, and I added my support.

"Fine," Hawke said. "Let's just not make this a witch hunt. Amnesty for anyone with counterfeits."

The Inter-Work Unit Committee to Abolish Counterfeits and Promote Isidoran Prosperity began the following week by setting up a counting station in a quiet corner of the Mines and asking shades and followers to bring every nut, wing nut, and bolt they owned to be reviewed. The money was counted twice, then the Mu representative swapped out any counterfeits and recorded everything in an official ledger. The oldest followers naturally came first, their sense of duty deeply engrained, their faith in Isidora's bureaucratic machinations automatic. Counterfeits were rare and individual holdings high. They were doers, inclined to sign up for extra work and disinclined to indulge, and their savings reflected that. But even amongst the overachievers, Simon the quiet, erudite Alpha's total was a bit staggering: 142 gold bolts, 312 silver wing nuts, 1,202 bronze nuts, almost none of it counterfeit. It was over 300 weeks of basic income, and it took him four trips to bring it all into the Mines.

The Committee promised secrecy, but Simon's total quickly leaked. Those who knew him believed he had earned every nut, but most of Isidora hadn't met the affable wallflower. Hadn't seen him that scorching day the previous summer finish weeding his assigned row of rutabaga, only to walk over and start weeding the next. Hadn't been there that aimless second winter when he caught the flu working to clear snow from Squire's path, so Mu could make an overdue supply run. Hadn't hid in the dark on the second floor of the winter quarters waiting for Mac and Charlotte to convince him to come—hadn't flicked on a flashlight, burst out from behind a cubicle divider, and shouted in joy at a man so embarrassed to be the center of attention he nearly passed out—hadn't slapped him on the back and offered him a shot and said, "Happy birthday, old friend. We were so worried you wouldn't come."

They assumed the worst about him, and rumors circulated that Simon stole his wealth or was working with a Mu to create perfect counterfeits. No matter the reason, they felt his nuts were theirs for the taking, and the fact that he was stupid enough to drop his hardware before the committee only further proved he didn't deserve it.

For days the eyes of Isidora followed Simon, weighed upon him when he was in a crowd, gawked at him when he strolled the Green, bulged at him when he went to the canteen, his pockets heavy with iron. Someone started a recitation, an incantation, enumerating Simon's savings as if to dissolve the bonds of ownership in a noxious bile of mass intimidation. And soon all the shades were saying it. "Simon has a thousand nuts, but Simon has no gun. If Simon wants to keep them all, then Simon better run." He heard it from across the canteen. He heard it in the fields. He heard it while taking a piss and when dropping off to sleep. "Simon has a thousand nuts, but Simon has no gun. If Simon wants to keep them all, then Simon better run."

And then they came for him.

I was on the water tower that morning, nose deep in a book about terraforming, and at one point I looked up to see them huddling in the parking lot, a half-dozen shades working up the courage to impose their will upon the man. Some were apprenticing with the Wooden Boys, and they carried their borrowed hunting rifles on their shoulders as if marching off to Lexington and Concorde. Up from the parking lot they went, sliding between the Winter Quarters and the Mines, searching for their prey. In their wake, other shades followed like dandelion fuzz caught in a slipstream.

A commotion broke out when they entered the fields. I dropped my sci-fi and watched as four of them grabbed Simon, the armed ones waving off Alphas who tried to intervene. They yelled commands at him, commands he couldn't possibly fulfill, restrained as he was with his arms pinned behind his back and a hand at his throat. He must have agreed to something because they pulled him to his feet and paraded him across the Green toward his bunk in the Winter Quarters. Shades and followers both amassed around the abductors who shouted about Simon's illegitimate wealth as they tried to justify their actions to the crowd.

I sprang to my feet and leaned against the water tower railing, but then I froze, barely able to make out the pleading wails of Alphas from the crescendoing jeers of enthusiastic shades. As the mob reached the crest of the hill above the Green, the shade that was restraining Simon slipped and fell, and in that instant Simon saw amongst the taunting faces a patch of daylight, and he ran to it as if salvation was just beyond the ring of his tormentors. He was lean and quick on his feet, and he shot through the mass faster than the gaping jaws realizing his escape, faster than the outstretched hands grasping at his shirt, faster than the bloodthirsty screams demanding his head, faster than the shoulder that held, the hand that lowered, the eye that aimed, the finger that squeezed. But he couldn't outrun the report of the rifle as it echoed off the Ark, the Ark he flew to, his knees buckling, his chest falling, his arms limp in the air, unable to stop his cheek from slamming into the earth, the earth that squeezed the breath from him in a short puff of dust.

—He was the first martyr for the cause of Isidoran—
—Stop. Just. . . stop.

We buried him beside the pond in a grave marked with a cairn. It toppled during the first snowstorm that winter.

Chapter Thirty-One

"Hello? Are you in there?" A tuft of ruddy hair peeked around the crack of my open door, followed by a savannah of scaly skin and parched lips only marginally improved by their bushy concealment. It was Squire, and the door had to open a lot farther to let in the rest of him. I squinted at the flood of daylight that wasn't blotted out by his bulk.

"I'm here," I said as much to the ceiling as to Squire. "Where else would I be?"

"Did Dean tell you? We're all meeting for an ad-hoc Circle to discuss the incident."

"The incident?" I balled my pillow up between my hands and chucked it in his general direction. "For fuck's sake, James. A man was murdered yesterday. A man was murdered by a mob here in Isidora."

Squire gently closed the door. He picked up the pillow and held it to his chest. "I know." With his submissive, puppy dog whine, one would have thought he had pulled the trigger himself. "We're all dealing with it. That's why we need to talk."

"Talk?" I rolled over with a sigh. "I don't want to fucking talk."

"Well, what are you going to do then? Lie here in the dark for the rest of time?" He threw the pillow back at me, accurate and true. It hit me in the head with the weight of a grapefruit.

"Christ, Squire!"

"Get off your butt." He flicked on the light. "The Omicron doesn't have the luxury of closing his eyes to Isidora's problems."

"Then I hereby appoint you honorary Omicron."

He laughed and sat on one of the armchairs by the door. "Please. They'd burn this place to the ground."

He had the breath of a man twice his age, an effortful, ever-present wheeze. His cheeks were flushed from the flight of stairs.

I sat and lit up a cigarette from the tray beside my bed. The sheet around my waist was still heavy with midnight sweat. "Assuming they didn't. Assuming everyone downstairs and clawing at the gate and huddled in grubby tents scattered across our parking lot was waiting for *you* to act. What would *you* do?"

Squire itched at his beard like a dog scratching its jowl with a hind leg. "Only the Omicron can give the followers what they need. Only the Omicron can interpret reality and give them TRUTH. So, I'd probably come to your room. I'd probably tell you to get your butt out of bed and make a decision."

"I'm serious, Squire. What if I wasn't here?"

"If you weren't here?" He paused as if considering the possibility for the first time. "Jeez. If you weren't here, I'd probably walk out that door— straight out of Isidora—straight to the station to jump on the first train heading east. I'd call my parents somewhere on the far side of the Quad Cities and tell them when my torment was at its apogee, when I was about to be consumed by scotch, sex, and socialism, the Lord found me and called me back to the fold. That's all it would take, all they ever really wanted—for me to live some kind of Old Testament cycle of depravity and salvation that reaffirms their faith. Their pastor would say something about the power of prayer and sit them on his right hand at Bible study, and for however long I needed it, I'd never miss a rent check. I'd take my credits and go finish my JD at some cut-rate school on the Gulf—someplace where homely girls wear bikini tops under their shirts, waiting for the frat boys to invite them to ditch class and get high on the beach. And in their eyes I'd be some old guy, not quite a professor but definitely not a student. I'd eat hot wings at a sports bar where a scantily clad waitress would ignore me when she realized I wasn't ordering a second beer. And maybe, if I was lucky, I'd defend my thesis and get a job teaching at that same no-name school. And every fall the students would show up with the same fleeting optimism, and the administrators the same myopic focus on the endowment, and I would work twice as hard to muster only half the enthusiasm I had the year before. And the sun would shine, and the waves would lap the shore, and nothing would change but me. Then eventually I'd get sick of it all, put on the nicest suit I own, and walk straight into the ocean."

"God, Squire, that's horrible."

"I know, which is why the Omicron needs to get his flat butt out of bed and fix this."

"Fix?" The Mouth pushed into the room, accompanied by the sickening snap of industrial beef jerky trapped between his molars. He took the armchair opposite Squire and fell so deeply recumbent he could barely see us over his crossed leg. He was already drunk or high or maybe both, but that morning I didn't fault him his coping mechanisms. "We need to do more than fix things. We need a revolution."

Squire squinted at him. "A revolution? What are you talking about? There are four shades locked in a supply closet in the basement. What are we going to do?"

The Mouth ripped off another bite. "I don't know," he said between chews. "Let them go? Maybe thank them for standing up against mercantilism and the gentrification of Isidora?"

"You've lost your mind."

"No, I haven't. What was Simon doing with all those bolts, huh? It doesn't make sense. We didn't found Isidora to recreate a classist society of haves and have-nots. His savings threatened the very foundation of our society."

"Like always," Hawke said, entering in front of Regina and Sam, "Dean is one hundred percent full of shit." He slid onto the sofa, followed by Sam. Regina jumped up next to me in bed.

I sat cross-legged and bare-chested with the sheets wrapped around my waist like a fallen toga. "I guess we're doing this in here, then. Sam, tell Brandt to bring up coffee and close the door."

"Wealth disparity is the fundamental weakness of modern society," the Mouth continued, "exploited by oligarchs and the political elite to repress and disenfranchise the body public. We cannot let the seeds of classism germinate in Isidoran soil."

"Simon was not an oligarch," Regina protested, her eyes still blood red. "He was a builder, a doer, someone who made Isidora a better place. He earned those bolts and earned the right to keep them without getting a bullet in the back."

"What if someone came for you?" Squire added. "With guns drawn, ready to steal your wealth."

The Mouth rolled himself to seated and hunted through his pockets for a joint. "What I have can't be stolen."

Regina scoffed. "Or cured, apparently."

A meek hand wrapped on the door, and Squire rose to let in the steward and his tray of steaming espresso. "We need to focus on the shades in the basement, Squire said. "A crime was committed—a murder—and the culprits are in custody awaiting justice. What we do now will set a precedent for everything that comes later."

"Kill them all," Hawke muttered from the sofa.

"Oh, don't be ridiculous," Regina chided. "We are not executing people in Isidora."

"A man was already executed here, Reg. Here in Isidora. And the worst part is his killer used a rifle given to him for Isidora's defense."

"*That* is the worst part? *That* is what bothers you the most?"

Hawke shrugged. "The legitimacy of our guard corps is at stake. We have to make an example of them."

"By killing them?"

"Sure. After a trial or something if you want, but yes. Zero tolerance. They deserve what they gave."

"Thank you, Hammurabi." Regina looked around at the group. "Anyone have a solution that doesn't involve us killing people in cold blood?"

"We should hold a trial," Squire announced.

A splash of acidic coffee slid into my already sour stomach. "I want them gone," I growled. "I want their very being extinguished. I want their memory erased. Why should we waste time with a show trial when half of Isidora saw what happened—can't unsee what happened?"

"We all have a right to be judged by a jury of our peers."

"What peers, Squire? There are no such things as peers. Are you telling me if I went down to the basement and hacked those assholes apart with a machete, you could find a dozen peers to put me on trial—a dozen unbiased equals who could fairly judge my actions?"

"Well, of course not for you . . ."

"Not for anyone, Squire. We're all living behind the prison walls of our own consciousness, shaped by experiences that no one else can possibly understand. Justice is a sham. There is only action and reaction. They acted on Simon, and now it's our time to react. I hate to say it, but Hawke is right. They took life in Isidora. They've forfeited their own."

Regina recoiled. It was subtle, but I saw it out of the corner of my eye. She jumped away from me as if she had just learned I was no longer alive—as if

I were an animated corpse that stood and smiled and ambled about, only to open its mouth and let loose a stream of resident cockroaches.

"You can't possibly mean that," she croaked, the lump in her throat a ball of disappointment and contempt.

"If you kill them," the Mouth said with the coolness of a retired actuary, "we'll lose them all. Every last shade will leave. They'll pull up stakes and empty the parking lot in a day."

"So what's the problem?" I huffed.

"That's the future of Isidora gone. Hundreds of future followers. Poof." The THC was already dense inside him, climbing up his carotid artery like a sherpa on his umpteenth ascent. He burst into a childish giggle that ended in a coughing fit.

I rolled my eyes. "Isidora isn't about numbers, LaBouche."

"Isidora is nothing but numbers. Two years, eleven months, thirteen days, one compound eight hundred and thirty-four steps wide, two thousand six hundred and forty-five steps long, one Mines, one Winter Quarters, one Ark, five working groups, one Circle . . ."

"One Omicron," I said firmly, hoping to interrupt the spiraling of his smoked-out mind.

"And nothing. Nothing beyond what the Omicron sees. Nothing before and nothing after. Nothing awaiting us if this all falls apart. Nothing to protect us if hundreds of shades decide not to scatter but run at the Ark instead, tearing at the walls like Zulu warriors."

"If Cheech is done, may I suggest exile?" Squire shifted in his chair, his belly bouncing between the arms. "If acceptance in Isidora is being seen, then maybe punishment is being unseen. The Omicron turns his back on them, and they are told to leave. They've forfeited their right to live in Isidora, and if everything beyond Isidora is nothing, then isn't exile the same as death?"

I pictured Squire banished from Eden, armed with understanding and a double-breasted Super 110, walking slowly toward the sun as it slipped into tranquil water. Maybe it was the exhaustion of a night unslept or the tranquilizing dose of secondhand weed slowly filling the room, but I couldn't summon the energy to deny him. The bonfire of rage I felt at Simon's murderers had burned down to ashes of sadness, shame, and regret so easily disturbed and set aloft by a passing breeze.

I assented. Squire nodded. Regina sighed in relief. The Mouth tore open another beef jerky. Hawke fumed. And Sam sat there, silent as always, his eyes on me like those of one of Agamemnon's men watching the corpse of Achilles be carried away from the walls of Troy on the curve of a large golden shield.

Chapter Thirty-Two

It was the banners that bothered me the most. Not the Mouth's theatrical performance as public defender, his buttery words sliding recklessly between the crimes of his clients and the menace of inequality threatening Isidora as a whole. Not Squire's ham-fisted prosecution, the peppering of witnesses with stilted cross-examination, eliciting nothing more than "yes," nothing less than "no." It was the banners—bolts of black cloth hauled up the water tower's ladder behind the purpose-built parquet where I was enthroned, the ends secured to the railing, the bulk of them thrown earthward. They were cut where they met the ground, but they didn't stay there. Unfurled and unsecured, they danced in the wind. Ten stories of somber black fabric, a textile dirge, joyously free. For the duration of the trial, they flapped and snapped behind me like flies in my ears while I, draped in heavy white sailcloth, had to sit perfectly still, resolute, somber, as calm as death itself.

The condemned were made to stand blindfolded as I would be during a Viewing, though there was no intention to ever give them sight. They had endured five nights in the Ark's basement—one locked in a supply closet while we dithered and slept and four more in a larger expanse of the cellar as the preparations for the trial were underway. Echo volunteered to personally supervise their internment, and they undoubtedly suffered more as a result.

The day before the trial, Hawke went to them and told them their sentence. If this was going to be a pantomime, we needed to ensure all the actors knew their parts, and while Squire reasoned that exile was tantamount to death, we couldn't risk them celebrating if it turned out they had a preference in the matter—which, of course, they did. On hearing they would not be executed, Hawke said they tried to kiss him, a lapse in judgment that cost them food for the rest of their imprisonment. By the midafternoon trial the following day, they were dejected, weak, and delirious with hunger, which was generally the condition we were going for. The audience that gathered—followers and a fair number of shades drawn to the spectacle of it—saw broken men, and that was all that mattered. Still, they had the strength to stand.

"But what really is murder?" the Mouth opined as he circled the stage like Cicero, a foot above the heads of the onlookers, miles above in his own swollen ego. "Is it not a force that acts on men, that seeks to extinguish the individual? Must it be committed by a single person, or can murder be the act of a society, a collective, a community that lets fester the rot of inequality and in that way is complicit in the moral death of a man? And if it is a collective crime, then these men before us are guilty but only to a degree. They contributed their fraction to the guilt we all must bear, and so their punishment must be but a fraction of that befalling an individual that commits murder alone."

At that point, the Mouth returned to the script as he stopped his ponderous ambling in front of my chair, put a hand to his chest, and humbly knelt. "Just and fair Omicron, I beseech you to show these men their due mercy. For their crimes, they should be excommunicated, banished from Isidora, cast away from your sight and in so doing be doomed to the waking dream of the unseen. You should wipe them from your memory, their existence therefore effaced. They will be less than shades, less than figments. They will be nothing. They will be oblivion itself. Just don't kill them, OK?"

I raised my hand, and the still crowd grew stiller—feet went unshuffled, weight unshifted, voices unwhispered. Only the banners disobeyed, rolling carelessly in the steady breeze. I stood and looked out over the expectant faces, over the Green and the depression that hid the pond, over the endless miles of farmland, the crumpled Appalachians, the frigid waters that separated old world from new. The inner sea, the cradle of civilization, the wild lands that robbed that cradle. The uplifted mountains that broke the sky. The terraces, the floodplains, the paddies filled with rice, an upturned tuna slit along the belly, an expanse of water as foreign as a star. Golden mountains, golden valleys, golden arches, Golden CO. Then it occurred to me, with the circle finally complete, I was looking at nothing but the back of my own head.

If there was any anxiety in me, any apprehension in playing the role that I had been given, it left my body in that next exhale, and when I inhaled again, I felt nothing but clairvoyance.

"For the killing of a follower, a crime for which the four men before me have been charged and found guilty, I sentence them to death."

At that word, the breath caught in the lungs of the crowd in front of me. Regina gasped, the Mouth went white, and one of the blindfolded defendants collapsed to his knees.

"Death, by exile," I continued. "For, after all, are these not one and the same? We came to Isidora to escape a world of illusion, a world of delusion, a world where TRUTH is lie, where reality is fantasy. These men have proven themselves unwilling to shake off that fantasy, that lie, that delusion. They assaulted a member of our community, a man whom I saw, a man who was taken from my sight. So, they will be cast out. Just as Simon will always live in the eyes of my memory, so will they forever go unseen. I cast them out, back to the fantasy they came from. It is not that I believe nothing in the world beyond Isidora is certain; it is that I am certain the world beyond Isidora is nothing.

And to that nothing they will be returned."

With that I sat. And no one moved. And no one spoke. There was perfect silence, and perfect stillness, and perfect reverence.

Then a banner smacked me upside the head.

Chapter Thirty-Three

The exile of the shades was a temporary solution, a seal thrown over the puncture wound in the chest of Isidora, an attempt to hold back the pressure of the figment world and keep our community from collapsing like a shriveled lung. While it held, we were all content to go about our normal routine, but no one believed anything had been durably solved. The rift between the followers and the shades was now an open wound, exposed for all to plainly see and at risk of turning septic.

Simon's murder sat sour in my stomach, and I felt at once an obligation to defend Isidora with the fullest measure of my ferocity and a shameful desire to escape. It was clear to me the shades were the problem, and I told the Circle to maximize oversight. Apprenticeships in the Wooden Boys were eliminated (along with the loaning of firearms), and soon the shades only path to the Viewing, to full status in Isidora, was recruitment into a work unit and Lambda's rigid reeducation curriculum. As for the Viewing itself—that weekly pantomime I once found tedious and inutile—I returned to it with a renewed sense of faith. If the path to becoming a follower was to be more laborious, then the culmination of that journey—the threshold over which shades would cross—needed to be grand. I ordered new robes in striking black-and-white monochrome and had the Circle chamber prepped each week with columns of hanging crimson cloth. When it was time to perform, I did so enthusiastically, sitting blindfolded, rod straight, attentive with hands folded, ready to ensure they were truly seen.

But still, I went to her. That fall, I went to her every Saturday night. And in some way she was healing that which I only covered up. I was better because of her, and Isidora was better because of me. And that was all the justification I needed for my evening escapes. Every Saturday as I crept round the Wooden Boys, the tensions of Isidora at my back propelled me toward her, to a newfound freedom discovered in the Shambles. We danced in the general's square—spinning with the children, hiccuping with Georgie and Mags, filling our bodies with a levitating warmth that we expelled in cloudy breaths to the cooling air. We stargazed on her roof, now furnished with a second chair, taking in the celestial parade as it marched in revolutions above our heads. We walked hand in hand down to the river and spread a blanket on the shore and read books to each other by flashlight.

For weeks she had anxiously awaited the Saturday of the winter solstice when she said the Shambles would show it was capable of more than frivolity and a hot meal.

"A spectacle befitting the elevated tastes of your royal highness."

"I should hope so. I wouldn't come all the way into town for less."

That appointed evening she grabs my hand, buzzing with excitement, and leads me south to Main Street where the titans of yesteryear slowly decay from neglect. Hammerstein Savings & Loan, R. F. Dodge Actuary & Assurance, Confederated Pacific Rail. Amongst the flat brick façades of these derelict headquarters, the theater is indistinguishable save for a gilded marquee that juts out from the second floor, spelling "Orpheum" in rattling tungsten bulbs. It is a vestige of the town's glory days, a time when waistcoat-wearing men, mustachioed and behatted, strolled in the glow of gas lamps beside well-coiffed women in bustles and lace. The horse-drawn carriages deposited them on the red carpet, and there they clucked and rumbled with excited energy until an usher, dressed in a tired velvet suit and paper collar, ambled through the crowd ringing a hand bell, letting everyone know the spectacle was about to begin.

The front doors of the theater had been boarded up, then chained shut, then plastered over, then pissed on. Garbage had built up in the unused emptiness under the marquee as snow does in drifts next to fence posts in the wind. On the street, the husks of cars—abandoned by their owners, beached by tire thieves, and drained of all fluids—await death by oxidation.

She parts from them, saying nothing, and leads me down a narrow, labyrinthine airspace between the buildings. The darkness is almost impenetrable, but she reaches back for me, knowingly, and leads me by the hand. The sky above is a canvas of stars scattered on the demure orange din of streetlights lit somewhere beyond the Shambles. The glow floats there above our heads the way the surface does above a diver on the ocean floor. And down below we swim through asphyxiating air, fetid and foul. I long to bound up the heavy iron stairs of the theater's fire escape, breach that radiant firmament, and cleanse my lungs with the atmosphere above.

We come to a wall, and I look to the right, expecting to see another corridor, but there's nothing but brick. She turns and faces me. The glacial white of her eyes is almost entirely consumed by the wild darkness of her pupils.

"So, this is where you store your amontillado?"

"It's around here somewhere." She smirks and turns to slide open a small window that I had overlooked.

"Are we still going to the theater?"

"Of course," she says lightly. "Hop."

I clamber up until I'm seated on the window frame, my legs dangling inside. I pause and look back at her.

"What? Are you scared?" she asks, her tone mocking.

"No, of course not," I reply. "I love sneaking through creepy old buildings."

She smiles, confident in the power she has tonight, pleased with my vulnerability. She shoves me into the dark.

The room is shroud in somber violet, but even without a flashlight or flame our night-shifted eyes can see. I am surrounded by faceless mannequin heads supporting dusty wigs of white curls and brown locks. Draperies, tapestries, and heavy canvas murals hang crowded in the back, and barrels filled with prop swords and lances huddle like pincushions in the corner. Among the trappings of false knights and fake kings, the claustrophobia of the air shaft gives way to the expansive fantasy of make-believe. I pick up a halberd made of a broomstick and tin foil and thrust it at the shadows. She slides into the room and walks among the clothes racks, pausing to run her fingers across the silks of Cressida, the bodice of Juliet.

"I can't believe all of this is still here," I say, stabbing at another specter.

"Most of it goes unused," she says mournfully. "But it's still one of my favorite places. All the great stories we've told and retell, they're all deconstructed and stored here. Your pike fought on Saint Crispin's Day. That sword pierced Mercutio, bleeding him dry. That gown crumpled under the fainting Hero."

She walks the room, touching each object in turn and others that she does not describe but whose history I know she remembers.

"It's a bit dusty, but it's still here." She shakes her head, then bounces over to the row of busts and grabs a modest crown to put on my head. With a smile she kisses me.

"I am coronated in your glory," I say with a bow.

She kisses me again, but her mind has already withdrawn.

"Let's get moving," she says. "The show has already begun."

I take off the crown and replace it on the figure head, then grab her hand. Light seeps into the interior corridor from the broken doors of the hall. We crunch the chalk of fallen molding and pass wallpaper curling off the walls like leaves of palm. Ahead I can hear voices yelling, whooping, and crying out, in delight or madness I cannot tell.

We reach an empty foyer with two large chandeliers suspended at the end of long velvet ropes. A thud in the distance, monstrous like the boom of a cannon, sends waves through the walls. The shards of cut glass above us shudder.

"Hurry," she exclaims, grabbing my hand and flying me through the entrance to the great hall.

My eyes go immediately to the stage where an enormous patchwork sheet has been hung from the rafters and pulled taut, illuminated from behind in the most brilliant white. Like a cross hung above the altar of some ancient cathedral, it captivates, opiates, dominates. On its surface, the shadows of two men gesticulate in forceful, deliberate movement.

"My hour is almost come; When I to sulfurous and tormenting flames must render up myself."

We seat ourselves at the end of a row, behind the silver domes of a dozen audience members, transfixed. One of the shadows appears clad in armor, gargantuan and commanding. The other recoils like a fearful child.

"What am I seeing?"

"Hush," she chides. But then, as if regretting the sternness of her voice, she whispers into my ear. "Isn't it splendid?"

"Cut off even in the blossoms of my sin, unhouseled, disappointed, unaneled; No reckoning made, but sent to my account with all my imperfections on my head."

A moment later the hulking shadow flees the scene, and as it departs, it grows larger and more ominous, consuming the stage and all the other players on it until it vanishes and what remains is diminished by consequence.

By the end of the act, I recognize the piece, though I wish I hadn't. In knowing, I convince myself I am guarded from the performance, safely ensconced in a familiar space where I am free to nitpick and critique. In ignorance, there is nowhere to be but at the liminal edge, stuck between the mundane and the make-believe, exposed to the howling gale of the sublime. Of course, I had never seen it like that—men like marionettes casting shadows on the screen; they are poisoned, they are run through, they are fell, one by one. In bloodless monochrome, it is the most vivid spectacle I have ever seen.

I turn to her, and see she is softly crying. Having been found out, she leans in to me and places her head against my shoulder, drying her other cheek with a small square of cloth.

"Have you not seen the ending before?" I ask.

"You stupid man." She sits back up with a sniffle and in that moment abandons sorrow for joy. The curtain falls and a rush of air sweeps across the audience. The figments are standing now, clapping vigorously and yelling, beside themselves, drunk on the same cocktail of tragedy and profound wonder. She stands with them, is one of them, and I stand with her, applauding. The actors are nothing but spectral shapes in front of the halogen lamp, now unfiltered and shining directly at us. For a moment our eyes burn, and we're forced to look away. But then it is unplugged, and the light goes out, and we blink and see nothing, clearly.

Chapter Thirty-Four

When we return to her apartment, a cold wind is whistling through the woven iron of the building's fire escape, and she clings to me as if she might just be blown over the side. At her window she stops for the first time ever and turns.

"It'll only be worse on the roof," she says with a shiver. She pauses, and for a second the air pauses too, as if contemplating the role it will play this evening. My heart begins to race. Then the wind gusts, and the two of us jump through panicking curtains into the darkness beyond.

I pull at the stubborn windowpane until I get it down, and when I turn, she has already stripped off her coat and placed a flame atop a tall white candle, the kind cathedral goers buy if they're feeling extra penitent or particularly sinful. It sits and burns, and for a time the wax refuses to run. An auburn light clings to us like vapor on a misty November morning.

It is a single room, a rectangular box, nothing more. A row of cabinets line a wall, interrupted by an oven and range. They are covered with books and magazines, and she explains to me that since she found the place, there's never been gas. There are no dishes, no glasses, no pots, no pans. The shelves are full of sweaters. The drawers full of socks. In place of a dining table, there is a ripped leather armchair and beside it a small coffee table spotted by crusted paraffin. In the far corner, there is a mattress lying on the floor, covered in an heirloom quilt and a pillow. Bras and underwear are scattered about, but she doesn't race to conceal them. I am not some stranger that's come to fix a leak or an unexpected acquaintance stopping in to use the toilet. In this, her most intimate space, a space clearly designed for one, she makes room for two.

After the obligatory tour, she kisses me with a smile and leads me to the only place where two people can be at the same time—her bed. We sit together, but then she pops back up and darts over to the cabinets to grab an old radio from the counter. As she returns to me, she lifts the telescoping antenna on the receiver and slowly twists the tuner until it picks up a string quartet from somewhere out in the ether. Then she sets it on the floor and stretches out onto the bed like a cat in a midday sunbeam.

"Do you believe in god?" she asks, as if the question were a soap bubble, lighter than air and easily blown in my direction.

"I believe in me."

She reaches her hands behind her head and twists to nestle herself deeper into the quilt. The taut skin of her neck flickers in the candle light. "That's hardly the same thing."

"Isn't it, though? They say god created the world. Well, so do I. I create everything. Every string plucked, every neon sign lit, every grain of sand rubbing between my toes. It's all sensation, divided and categorized by me alone. Beyond that? There's nothing. It's all born in me."

For a second she rests her hand on her cheek and stares into empty space. "Sure. In a way. But at best you can only claim to have *recreated* the world. If you lick strawberry ice cream, you've seen it, felt it, and tasted it, but you didn't create it."

"Who's to say I didn't? Who's to say if you take the next lick you'll have seen, felt, and tasted the same thing?"

She sighs and scrunches her face into a frown.

"And anyway, if some lowly mortal can *re*-create the world with five measly senses, what use have I for god?"

She grunts. "Well, what about after you die? What about heaven and hell?"

I stretch out next to her and let my gaze caress the crenelations of her popcorn ceiling. "Hell is other people."

"Thanks a lot, Voltaire." She punches my shoulder and turns away from me.

"Easy," I laugh. "*Other* people. Not you. Besides, I was quoting Sartre."

She flips back with a wry smile. "You're one to care. Fine. But Monsieur Sartre may be surprised to learn that heaven is other people too."

"Oh, is that so?"

"So I've heard."

Yes. That's the promise anyways, the so-what at the end of the thirty second welcome spiel they give you on your first day of Sunday school. All your loved ones returned to you, forever and ever amen.

I turn to her and lose myself in the chocolate eyes only inches from mine. "Well then, I guess Sartre was fucked either way."

She kisses me with a peck and falls back with a self-satisfied smile. "I'm sure he got what was coming to him."

Another gust of wind howls outside, rattling the window panes and rustling the canopy of trees along the street below.

"So, you don't believe in an afterlife?"

I pause, trying to coalesce years of suspicion and mistrust into words. Life after life was always an appealing message, but I never could trust the messenger. Flawed institutions pronouncing the ineffable in paternalistic soliloquies and disingenuous lamentations. When I was a child, I accepted the concept without question. When I was a teen, I rejected it with reckless confidence. And now, I don't know. I don't even know if I'm supposed to know.

"I find infinity a bit intimidating." I sigh. "I don't know what I would do with myself forever."

"Do? It's not about doing." The radio falls into a low static as Vivaldi gives way to the background buzz of an empty universe. She flips onto her belly and crawls to the end of the bed to mess with the tuner. "The promise is of eternal life, not eternal chores."

I close my eyes and let my mind slip back to Isidora. "I'm not sure I can tell the difference anymore."

"Then you're doing it wrong."

"Which one?"

"Both."

She twists us through pop songs and country, talk radio and newscasts, each popping from the receiver like the air squeezed between passing trains until muted trumpets and a slow-walking double bass fill the room. Satisfied, she crawls back to me and sits cross-legged, clutching her pillow in her arms.

"Besides, if you reject the infinity of an endless afterlife, aren't you forced to embrace the infinity of an endless death? You wind up in the same boat as Monsieur Sartre."

"How's that?"

"Either way, you're fucked."

Somewhere at a distant radio station—a concrete box in the middle of nowhere lit by a lonely flood light—the jazz standard fades back into its wax sarcophagus, and a different platter starts revolving. Endless loops at a predetermined speed. A needle drops into a narrow ravine and vibrates with unfathomable precision over two minutes and twenty-three seconds of compressed and captured time.

"I don't know how you can find infinity intimidating, anyways. It's all around us."

"Is it?" I ask.

"Every moment is infinitely divisible. We take a day and divide it by hours, take hours and divide them by minutes, take minutes and divide them by seconds, and so on and so on."

"I suppose we're measuring the flow of time, not the volume."

She smiles. "Yes, but the volume is still there, and it's the volume that counts. We do the opposite with space, which is the other side of the same coin. Always measuring its volume, never measuring its flow."

I laugh. "The Bard sure puts you in a funny mood."

"I'm serious. You claim to be some kind of authority on what is and what isn't, and maybe you've got the kids in Isidora fooled, but it seems to me you're barely paying attention. There is an infinity of time in every heartbeat to be in awe and adoration of the world around you. And an infinite number of ways the space that separates you from the rest of the world can twist and turn and put you into a position to see it all differently."

I rise up to sit across from her, our eyes level, our hearts level.

"I think you're right, but I'm not sure I like it. Every heartbeat I'm with you feels infinitely full, but when I leave, every inch between you and Isidora feels like an infinite gulf I may never bridge again. I don't know how long I can sustain this dual existence."

She gives a short acknowledging hum. "It's all just space and time. Space you create. Time you let slip away."

The words hit me like buckshot, but before they sink in, she grabs my hands in hers and pulls me to her lips, lips that are full, lips that kiss fully. "Let's dance," she says, her eyes flashing.

I laugh. "Oh, I don't know . . ."

But she's already standing, and Lady Day has already started in. An infinity later, I've crossed the infinite distance between us, my hands are at her waist, and we're slowly rotating, our naked feet gliding across the worn Moorish fractals of her area rug. Her head falls to my shoulder as I package her in my arms.

Maybe he's not much...Just another man...Doing what he can...But what does she care...When a woman loves a man.

As Billie's voice lingers on the curves of those twice-rounded consonants, she stops and takes a step away from me. And I see her fully. I see as she crosses her arms at her waist to pinch the fabric of her cotton dress, to lift it slowly up along the length of her being, a curtain withdrawn to lay bare the incontrovertible presence of the form within. It glides along the fields of her belly. Clings to the hills of her breasts. Rushes along the river of her hair. And then she lets it slip through her fingertips and drop to the floor, empty. Her skin is aglow in the flickering candle light. The wind now howls within me.

She sees the want in my eyes, and it thrills her, and she grins, spinning slowly in front of me before prancing to the bed on the balls of her feet as light as the goosebumps rising from her uncovered skin. At the foot, she bends and begins to crawl, feline as before, on hands and knees, and then she stops and lowers herself to her forearms, the tips of her breasts tickling the sheets, her ass full and inviting, creased by the curve of her spine as it slips below.

I come to her, unbuttoning, unfastening, arriving bare, a trail of clothes behind me. My finger lands on the sole of her foot, rounding her heel, feathering her calf. I grasp at her knee and race my palm up the length of her hamstring. For a second, she squeezes me between her thighs, not to prevent but to reassure. And then she releases, and my fingers find among wild hair, matted and wet, a stream overflowing its banks, overwhelmed by a sudden deluge. I dive in, and she moans.

She wants me this way—all of me—and pulls at my arms in anxious expectancy. For a short while, I consent, my hands bouncing along her back ribs as the space between us expands and contracts. But my avarice grows, and I push her to the sheets and turn her to face me, pausing there only long enough to run my hand along her heaving chest, to capture forever in my mind that bit lip and those pleading eyes.

At first I sprint, like an untrained foal from its first starting gate, overwhelmed by the chance fulfillment of unlimited desire. But she reaches up to touch my face, her finger in my mouth the bit that steadies me, and I find I want for nothing. We lock eyes, and for innumerable infinities we float in rhythmic union, nothing between us, and the world beyond an unobserved void.

Then she turns from me and closes her eyes, her head rolling back and forth, writhing as an undeniable pressure builds inside her, a pressure that grows with each quickening pump of my heart. She begins to moan, her hands outstretched, fingernails digging into the sheets as she strains to fight back the disequilibrium she had so desperately invited. Until, in a flash, in an irreducible moment of pure time, she bursts, the pressure like a torrent rushing from her heart to her fingers and toes. And I feel her—the contracting quiver that passes to me, that grows my spine, that electrifies the hair at the back of my neck. Unsteadied, I charge in a maddening, headlong rush. Like the released hammer on a gun, I dive toward the percussion cap of a chambered bullet, striking it with all my force. The powder shudders, ignites, explodes. I exhale in panting breaths, sweat beading at my pores, and collapse on the bed beside her.

For a moment, we lay there formless and still, empty apart from the rushing of infinity in our chests.

******

And then we sleep. A long, deep sleep. And while we sleep the earth carries us like swaddled babes for nearly half a rotation in empty space, away from the cold pull of the expansive universe toward that singular celestial object that warms us and gives us day. From across the room, golden fingers of light reach through her uncovered window to wake us in gentle, patient nudges. And still we rebuff them and pull each other closer, the pillow placed above our head blocking the sun and catching the breath that's shared between us.

When I am finally fully awake, her eyes are on me, those bright brown eyes. She kisses my lips and says it is already morning, and at first the thought is comforting—an affirmation that touches the ancient human in me, the beast grateful for the night survived and the fresh day to come. But modern panic quickly follows.

"Oh, shit." I say, throwing off the pillow and quilt and springing to my feet. "This is not good."

She rises gently, wrapping the quilt around her breasts like the neckline of a homespun evening gown. "What's that?"

"I'm not there. It's already morning, and I'm not in Isidora. Shit. What time is it?"

"Let's see." She yawns and leans over the bed to grab the radio, turning the knob until she hears voices. I give her a puzzled look. "Just wait," she says. "They'll say the time eventually."

I scoff an involuntary scoff and hop into my blue jeans.

"What's the big deal? So you're not there. Aren't you in charge? Why should they have any power over you?"

"Isidora doesn't exist without me," I reply. "It doesn't function. I'm the Omicron."

It was her turn to scoff. She drops back onto the pillow and stares at the ceiling, listening to the radio.

It is only then that the full rush of the day's obligations come to me. "Oh, shit. The Viewing," I mumble as I drop onto her chair, a shoe in each hand. "They'll have to know now. There's no way they won't know. The Omicron betrays Isidora to sleep in the Shambles. Dozens of shades left unseen. It'll be all anyone is talking about."

"It's ten thirty-four."

I turn and see a woman sitting on a bed, but all other context escapes me. "Huh?"

"They just said it. It's 10:34. Well, maybe 10:35 now. And it'll be forty-two and sunny today." She returns to the radio and scrunches her face as the orange needle climbs the wavelengths. She pauses on the jazz station from the night before but then reconsiders and spins us to a frequency experimenting with Japanese city pop. "And how many times do I have to tell you, it's not called the fucking Shambles," she chides with cheerful nonchalance.

I fumble with my shoelaces, tying messy knots on my ragged trainers. She wraps herself in the heirloom quilt and walks to the window. Beyond, the world is red-shifted. Brick buildings glow vermillion, topped by pink marble and a yellow sky. I know it's cold still, but the world feels vibrant and warm, as if heated by color itself.

"I want waffles. Can you go out and get us waffles?"

"Darling. I have to get back."

"Go out and get us waffles, and then you can feed them to me while I lie here naked."

She throws the blanket aside, and my heart jumps into my throat. I groan and squint my eyes closed, searching for the sleeves of my winter parka. "I . . . I have to go. Isidora doesn't exist if I don't observe it."

She stalks me, a lioness creeping up on an ignorant gazelle, and the floorboards squeak beneath her paws. I feel her warmth on my cheek. My spine tingles as she purrs into my ear. "And what happens if you don't observe *me*?"

"If I don't observe *you*?" I open my eyes to kiss her neck, to run my fingers down her bare back, to lash her to me in an embrace. "If I don't observe you, I'm pretty sure *I* won't exist."

She leaps into my arms with a squeal, and I carry her back to bed, and for another hour Isidora fades into oblivion.

Chapter Thirty-Five

When I finally extricated myself from her apartment in a goodbye that verged on tearful, the way it always does when love is young and unreasonable, the world was a luminous gray, the kind of gray that stings your eyes even though the sun is buried behind a solid sheet of clouds. Streets that I had only ever seen in empty darkness were haunted by blank-faced figments who stared at me as if I were a ghost, billowing about in a half-existent state, waiting for some unresolved trauma to be set right. I walked quickly, trying to outrun their gaze.

I had no strategy for reentering Isidora unnoticed. All I knew was that I desperately wanted to avoid encountering a Wooden Boy at the periphery of the compound and skip the "Halt! Who goes there?" rifles-at-the-ready nonsense, but I didn't see any other way in. I could always lie to them—make up some story about an early morning scouting trip to prepare for the expansion of our compound. Or I could say I was inspecting prices in the figment world to verify Mu's exchange rate and put the inflation crisis to bed. My mind spun, but my feet kept walking, carrying me out of the Shambles, past the burned-out warehouse and the overgrown train station, down along the ravine beside the tracks of the industrial spur—the most predictable of paths.

He was waiting for me on top of a railcar just out of sight of Isidora's sentries, his legs dangling free.

"Good morning," he said. "Or should I say, good afternoon?"

"Hello, Hawke," I mumbled in disappointment.

"Out for a stroll?"

I kept walking, hoping to force him to jump down and trot to catch up as he had done to me so many times in the past. But he just sat there, legs dangling, eyes scanning the western horizon.

"Did you enjoy your night in the Shambles?"

"I'm surprised I didn't run into you there," I called over my shoulder.

He laughed like a millionaire who had misplaced a twenty. "You sure you just want to saunter up to our guards like that?"

I stopped and sighed. "Do you have a better suggestion?"

"Not a suggestion. A solution."

He climbed down the iron rungs welded to the side of the boxcar and walked away from me, away from Isidora. He said nothing, and once again it was incumbent on me to scurry to catch up. Hawke led me back along the industrial spur, back to the junction with the train line that first carried us to Isidora. There, he climbed the low ballast of loose gray rock and turned east, his stride falling effortlessly on the railroad ties. I followed, unsure if he was my guide or if I was his prisoner, if we would sneak into Isidora through some hole in the fence or if he would parade me down to the Green through throngs of followers anxious to devour me like a pack of hungry dogs.

"Is she worth it?" he finally asked over his shoulder. "The Gamin?"

I knew better than to equivocate. For Hawke, nuance was a weakness to be exploited. "Yes," I said.

He shook his head, willing his legs to keep moving, to push him through the disgust, but he couldn't do it. He stopped dead.

"I can't believe you," Hawke said, turning. "I really can't believe you. You have everything you've ever wanted in Isidora—money, power, respect. Christ, you have people who believe your very sight validates their existence, and you risk it all on a piece of ass from the Shambles? What the fuck are you thinking?"

"What makes you think you know what I want, Hawke? Do you think I like being sequestered in Isidora? Do you think I like being isolated by the constant deference, the constant kowtowing to the Omicron? It's insufferable. For fuck's sake, no one even looks at me anymore. They literally blind themselves when I approach." I covered my eyes in our now universal salute.

Hawke crossed his arms, his eyes fixed on some distant object over my left shoulder, his face drained of expression. "I *do* know what you want. I know what you want because you're not special. You're just like everyone else. You want everything. And when you have everything, you want more, because everything is not enough for you. Isidora is not enough for you."

"Maybe," I replied cooly. The air was still, and the steam of our breath, pulled from us by the cold in short, labored puffs, commingled and floated skyward to join the low ceiling of clouds above. Isidora *was* everything I'd ever wanted, an exhilarating and vibrant dream. But somewhere along the way I woke up. Try as I might to fall back asleep, to summon again those same sweet visions, I knew I was just tossing and turning. Part of me wondered if it was better to just get out of bed and get on with things.

Hawke sighed, as if intuiting in that one word all the thoughts that came after. "It's been a long time since we were out there, out on the other side. It's easy to forget how wrong it is, how deeply broken the figment world is. It's like an alien beast that feeds on people's souls, chews them up and spits them out. And it elevates others to sing its praises and protect it. Isidora defies that beast, but we haven't destroyed it. It's still there, hoping we fail, hoping we stop seeing the TRUTH, give into daydreams, and come floating back."

"I could still recruit her. She could still join us."

Hawke rolled his eyes. "It's not about the Gamin. It's about what your feelings for her means for *us*. If what you need most is out there and not in Isidora, then the figment world controls you. And if the figment world controls you, it controls all of us. Isidora is doomed."

"And what about you, huh? What about your deal with the Constable? You're just as guilty of colluding with the figment world as I am."

"I'm doing what's necessary to deal with a threat. You're slipping away from us out of lust. Compared to the Constable, the Gamin is a hundred times more dangerous." He crossed the rails, letting his feet slide as he descended the ballast to return to the tall grass below. "There's a figment train coming," he called over his shoulder. "And whether you see it or not, you're standing on the tracks."

His paranoia was tiring. "She's not out to get us, Hawke. Isidora is safe. I know what I'm doing."

He turned and smirked. "No, there's literally a figment train coming. And you're literally standing on the tracks."

I spun to see the angular metal face of a diesel locomotive barreling down on Isidora station, its squat yellow headlights squeezed to a menacing squint. The horn blared a short blast followed by a long, insistent reproach. *Get off the tracks, you lunatic, or I'll make you the bug on my windshield.* A hundred cars of pitch-black coal following behind ensured it was no bluff. I sprang from the ties in a leap that carried me all the way to the foot of the ballast where I landed at Hawke's feet in a cloud of white dust.

Hawke started counting. "One one thousand. Two one thousand. Three one thou . . ." The train rushed by, scattering stones that rained down behind me. Hawke hid his head in his upturned elbow. I curled into a ball and shielded my face. And the heartbeat of the figment world raced along beside us. *Ra-tic-tic-tic. Ra-tic-tic-tic. Ra-tic-tic-tic.*

When the train passed, he reached down to help me up. "You played that close."

"Jesus, Hawke. Maybe a little more notice next time!"

He grinned and turned to continue alongside the tracks. "You're the one with the all-seeing eye. I just build stuff."

We walked for another twenty minutes until we had passed by Isidora on the north. Then he turned right and led me through the toothpick forest, arriving at the compound's northeast corner. The wall had been extended around the full perimeter of Isidora, and Wooden Boys stood watch over every inch of it, but no one stirred at our approach. Hawke found a gap where a rusted out washing machine housing had been pushed aside. I crossed the threshold, and he kicked the hollow box back into place.

"You cleared the walls?"

"I saw you 'sneaking' out last night." He turned to show me the air quotes. "And when we found your room empty this morning, I knew exactly where you were. I told the Circle we were running a drill simulating an attack from the Shambles—that you had fled to a safe location. Echo pulled boys from the eastern walls to double the guard on the west. Then Dean canceled the Viewing, and the followers were told to either pick up arms or shelter in place. I had a relaxing cup of coffee and then came to collect you."

"How thoughtful."

He grunted. "More than I can say for you. You kept me waiting on that damn boxcar all morning."

Fifty yards from the wall, the woods gave way to our fields, and though nothing was growing we circled the barren ground like children skirting graves in a cemetery. The more we walked the more it dawned on me that I was in his debt, and the relationship I needed for its independence from all things Isidora was now dependent on the restraint of a man I did not trust. I was to be the falcon with the hood over its head, standing on Hawke's gloved hand, waiting for his permission to hunt. It would not do.

"I do appreciate you covering for me," I said after a long silence.

"Consider it a reminder. This is what it costs. This is what's at stake."

"I'm going back. This isn't the end of it."

"I figured as much." He sighed as if preparing to say more, but the words never came.

We trudged up the hill from the pond, following the PVC artery I had dropped into the ground those many springs before. At the crest of the hill we could see them there, in a semicircle embracing the Ark, four ranks deep with their rifles pointed west. Echo was at the deepest part of the bend, in the center of the fictitious fray, his open trench billowing like the red cloak of Alexander. To our left, a similar formation of Wooden Boys protected the western approach to the Mines.

"Should they breach the walls!" Echo yelled, his voice barking from his barrel chest in an effortless baritone. "We will take this position—first row on your knees, second standing, both lines ready to fire. Lines three and four, you're in reserve and will be deployed to the left or right flanks depending on the location of the enemy's advance."

Hawke approached the center of the formation and put a reassuring hand on Echo's shoulder.

"Well done, men. You may stand down. Our exercise is over."

Echo beamed with his master's approving touch. "Well done, men. Stand down. Our exercise is over."

The Wooden Boys turned from their position, and a few started to break ranks. But when they saw me, when they saw that the Omicron was there and also approved of their performance, they stood erect and covered their eyes in a proud, dutiful salute. Echo joined them, his elbow out higher than any other, his eyes engulfed in the blackness of his muscular paw.

I cleared my throat and summoned the most commanding voice I could muster. "Well done, everyone. Well done. The threats arrayed against us have been neutralized. Isidora is secure once again. You may return to your normal duties."

They stood motionless, expressionless, blinded by their own hands. I was once again talking to no one but myself.

Hawke chuckled and then turned to the Ark. "Coffee?" he asked as he walked on ahead.

Chapter Thirty-Six

The figment world had been teetering on a cliff's edge since our time in the capital, and after the new year the ground below gave way. Looking back, I'm not sure what happened, and I certainly wasn't paying attention at the time. Some Eurasian man-child must have started playing with rockets, or perhaps some hapless chaiwala sneezed and gave the subcontinent a cold. Either way, the global economy tumbled into the abyss. Of course stock prices plummeted, and equity managers lost their shirts. Those are things most people recognize as always in the realm of possibility, always anted on the table as the wheel spins and the ball dances above the numbers. But inflation—rapid, rampant inflation—that is always unexpected. That is the over-served gambler toppling the whole table, scattering everyone's chips and launching the silver ball halfway to the high-stakes baccarat room. You can't just resume play after that. Even when the guy is restrained, it takes time to sort everything out, mollify the aggrieved, and get the game going again. Meanwhile, everyone clings to what they can grab and looks at their fellow gamblers like strangers in a darkened parking lot.

When inflation hit the figment world, the nothing that was there before became even less—and twice as expensive. Prices drove panic, which drove compulsive stockpiling, which drove shortages, which drove prices even higher. And this happened everywhere, not just in the struggling middle west. Like film that catches in the projector and burns on screen, this all-too-human, base and shameful, and yet somehow forgivable cycle of frantic consumption revealed the reality behind the spectacle. The figments' animated existence was nothing more than a litany of light, color, and sound flashed in their faces—the illusion of progress, industrial sleight of hand. All of it had happened before. Many times, in fact. History repeats itself, after all. But who has time for history?

To be honest, I had as much opportunity as anyone to see that trouble was brewing. I continued sneaking off to the Shambles as many nights a week as I dared. A simple tweak to the standard operating procedures of the Wooden Boys—a requirement that Echo observe and record shift changes at his HQ in the workshop—created a predictable hole in Isidora's defenses with every changing of the guard. I could come and go with little fear of being noticed.

As the winter winds gave way to spring showers, the Shambles seemed to descend into a malaise that could easily have been mistaken for lethargy and laziness but was probably just hunger. The tarpaulin roof of canteen street hung limp, there being too few fires below sending up steam spiced with rosemary and thyme. The thick stew I enjoyed my first night in the Shambles thinned to a tepid gruel as if inundated with the rainwater that also soaked the silent queue of vacant faces stretching back to the general's square. The poor always suffer first and suffer the most. The proverbial canaries in our economic coal mine, when those with the least find they have nothing, it's time for those with the most to start asking for handouts.

None of that contagion should have ever reached Isidora. We lived apart in our own reality with our own economy and our own currency. And yet it felt like we were catching the figment world's cold. All winter long, prices in the Mu-run canteen inched upwards, and goods began disappearing from the shelves. Followers started mumbling, then gossiping, then complaining out loud, and we had to divert some Wooden Boys from the walls to guard the shop when the shades turned to shoplifting. The Circle directed Mu to sell more Block Coins, to do more supply runs, to flood Isidora with nuts and bolts, to do anything that might restore balance. But nothing seemed to work.

And then one exceptional Tuesday in late February, when the sun shone brightly and the streets were flooded with snow melt, Squire sputtered away in our aging red pickup and never came back.

It wasn't unusual for him to go out alone. There was always some other Mu at his side ready to take the keys at a moment's notice and dart out to anywhere he would send them, but Squire hated the idea of someone else driving Hank and usually did even the smallest errands himself. After months of white-knuckling it through rutted snow drifts and perilous black ice to ensure we had a constant supply of carbonated sugar water, it was only natural he would step into that glorious early spring day and decide to cruise the figment world until the tank ran dry. I would have gone with him, had he asked. But to not return? To carry on with a bit of self-indulgence for so long that someone else noticed or even worried? Squire would have had to bear the weight of generations of reproachful Lutheran ancestors to do something like that.

Worried, we quietly sent the steward and a few trusted followers out that night to check the frontage road up to the highway, but they saw nothing. The next morning, we sent a team of Mus to BigBox to see if Squire happened to break down along the way, but by then the news of Squire's disappearance had spread through Isidora, and the four faithful Mus selected for the task left on foot through hordes of jeering shades. They scurried away, huddled together with their heads lowered like the few remaining acolytes of some temple-less god. In the early afternoon, they returned with arms full of junk food and nothing to report.

The longer he went missing, the more convinced I was he was halfway to Chippewa. But there was one last place I wanted to check. Regina insisted she go with me. She said she was the only one who truly knew Squire, the only one he could talk to. But I knew his decision to disappear without telling her was evidence enough she was not the right one to bring him home. Hawke had Echo call an impromptu meeting of the Wooden Boys to put them on heightened alert, and in that moment of inattention I jumped over Isidora's southeastern wall and started for the farm.

Everything from our early days was still imprinted in my mind, and I had no trouble retracing our previous path from the compound to the frontage road, to the narrow underpass that ducked below the interstate. From there I followed the long planar highway, skirting guardrails and mailboxes and sun-faded Pontiacs valued in soap script. In a depression surrounded by woods, signs zip tied to rusted barbed wire greeted trespassers with the promise of a round from an AR-15, and in the lot that followed a child in a polyester princess dress seated on the steps of a trailer home brushed the hair of a naked, doe-eyed doll. It was a world I recognized but had only ever seen before in streaks through a car's rear window. Prolonged observation did nothing to improve my opinion of it all.

At the intersection with a country road overshadowed by a majestic white oak, I turned east, and there on the top of the rise, silhouetted against the pale gray sky, was a man on a fence post, a Rodin pensively statuesque, curated next to a glossy red pickup truck.

I trudged up that final hill, panting like a donkey. If Squire heard me coming, he made no effort to receive me. He just sat there, his head in his palms, his elbows on his knees, the heels of his boots clipped into the fence plank below. In the pasture before him, a brown cow sauntered across the pockmarked ground to lap water from a corrugated steel tank. She stumbled a bit as the mud gave way to a cement foundation where four red iron bolts projected skyward. A thin electric pump gurgled water up from an aquifer below. A smattering of solar panels decorated the fence posts, humming merrily as they sucked up the day's full light.

"I couldn't make it any farther than this," he said without turning. "In fact, that's not true. I made it 150 miles farther than this, but I couldn't go on. I had to turn around."

His voice was like that of a child after a tantrum—weak and vulnerable and pliant.

I mounted the fence post to his left. "Where were you going?" The cow lifted its head to take in the new presence, then swatted her belly with her tail.

"I don't know." Squire sighed. "Nowhere. Anywhere. What does it matter? It's all the same outside Isidora, isn't that right? Just darkness over the surface of the deep? I couldn't go on, but I couldn't come back."

A mild breeze blew across the pasture. To me it smelled like cow. The brown cow in front of us, the spotted cattle beneath the walnut, the frolicking calves covered in shit. But I knew for Squire it was something more. It was crushed hay in a gloved hand. It was a leather saddle atop a flannel blanket. It was dogwoods and snakeroots and sugar maples and milkweeds. It was sky-blue asters and golden-centered forget-me-nots. It was the popping embers of a campfire as it died beneath a starlit sky.

The cow, having drunk its fill, returned to the herd. The mud sucked at her hooves as she walked.

"So, here you are," I finally said.

"Yep. Here I am. I'm kind of surprised you found me, to be honest. Glad you did. I wasn't sure what came next."

"Why did you leave, Squire?"

"What's that?"

"Why, Squire? Why did you leave Isidora? Why is the store empty? Why isn't Mu making supply runs? Why are the shades up in arms?"

Squire answered all my questions with a single reply. "Because we're broke."

"What do you mean, broke?"

"We're broke. We have no money."

"We have tens of thousands of Block Coins. We're not broke."

Squire slid off the post and walked into the pasture to scoop up a pile of wet earth. He held it out to me, pushed it at me like unwanted medicine. "This! This is what our Block Coins are worth."

"Please," I said, rolling my eyes.

"Shit!" he said, as if I'd never before encountered the brown substance in his hand. "Jack shit!" He reached back as if to throw it at me, but then slammed the load onto the ground. "Our invisible magic money is worth visible figment shit."

"Do we need to relaunch the Inter-Work Unit Committee to Abolish Counterfeits and Promote Isidoran Prosperity?"

"God help me. It was never about the counterfeits. It was something out there." He turned and gestured to the empty air. "Something out there changed. Something you claim doesn't exist because you don't see it."

"There is nothing out there. Nothing we need." I knew the words were disingenuous, but they tasted good on the way out. "We have a machine that turns sunlight into money. It's practically photosynthesis, and it's made us rich. Tell me, Squire, how on earth can we be rich and broke at the same time?"

"I don't know why," Squire said, pacing the ground, "but the world doesn't want our money. Midsummer the rates were good, but then they turned on us, and I had to sell more and more coins just to get the cash we needed for supply runs. And then, poof, it's like all the buyers in the world just disappeared. I couldn't give a Block Coin away. It's like I was a merchant going to market, but instead of spices and rugs I had loaded up my donkey with . . . with shit!"

"How long?"

"Excuse me?"

"How long has this been happening?"

"Like I said, rates started turning in the middle of the summer."

"And your response was to lie to the Circle—to the Omicron—about counterfeits?"

Squire threw his hands up. "Well, yeah, in fact. With the value of our portfolio plummeting, there were too many nuts in circulation. We had to remove excess metal, and targeting counterfeits seemed like the best option."

I sprang to my feet, intending to cross the pasture, to push the fat man to the ground and rub his face in the mess he had made, but the mud froze my feet. "Goddammit, Squire. How could you let this happen?"

"Let what happen? I had no clue why everyone stopped buying coins. What was I supposed to do?"

"You could have told us. You could have been honest instead of having all of Isidora go through that stupid counterfeit campaign, that pointless counting exercise that put Simon in the ground."

Squire's voice caught in his throat, and he pointed a defiant mud-soaked finger at me. "I am not responsible for Simon's death."

"Then who is? You failed us. You failed Isidora. You did a half-ass job like you've always done, and now we're screwed."

"I thought you would understand." Tears of exhaustion and raw emotion fell from the corner of his eye.

"I understand how pathetic you are. I understand how little you care about Isidora."

He grabbed another handful of mud and threw it at my head. I dodged, and it smacked off my shoulder, leaving behind a foul streak.

"You're a child, Squire. A big, bearded baby. I can't believe we ever trusted you with something as important as Isidora's money."

"Money? Whose money got us here? Who spent every last cent he owned to get us out of the capital in the first place?"

I crossed my arms. "You don't honestly want credit for being too broke to pay rent, do you?"

"Christ. You have no clue. You're so damn blind. While you were sleeping on my couch and playing footsie with my girlfriend, I was liquidating everything I owned to pay for Hawke's bail. I got him out of jail. I sacrificed everything for the dream of Isidora."

"Well, it wasn't enough, was it Squire? You spent all that money but never bought a shred of common sense, and now the dream you had of Isidora has become a nightmare. We're broke because of you. Followers will starve because of you. Simon is dead because of you. You're off the Circle. I'll find someone else to run Mu."

To be a man is to spend your life on the whetstone, sharpened by constant friction as fathers, brothers, strangers, priests push your head into the spinning wheel, grind you down until you're free of all imperfections, prepared at a moment's notice and without stopping to think to fell your fellow man, to find on him that last piece of soft, uncovered flesh and plunge the blade in. Squire toppled like a redwood, his knees in the muck, his face buried in his hands.

I turned and jumped to the other side of the fence, then kicked my feet against a post to free them from the mud. "Get up, Squire. We're going home."

From the pasture I heard nothing but the muffled sniveling of a grown man sobbing.

"Enough, Squire. It's time to leave."

He rubbed his cheek against the shoulder of his sweatshirt. "The keys are in the ignition. Go."

"If I leave here without you, you're never coming back. You'll be exiled. A figment. Dead."

He stood, wiping his nose with the back of his hand. "It's fine. The friend I once knew died long ago."

I turned and jumped into Hank's cab. The heavy steel door slammed behind me, shaking the windows and rattling the mirrors. I stomped on the clutch and lit the ignition. The motor roared to life, but when I plunged the shifter into first and released the pedal, Hank choked and died in a sputtering fit.

"Goddamn it!"

I could feel his reproachful eyes upon me, but I didn't dare look back. I popped off the emergency brake that I had forgotten to disengage, and Hank began crawling forward, slowly picking up speed as we moved off the crest of the hill and down the steep grade, wheels spinning faster and faster, hearts motionless, inert. Our descent was preordained, a gravitational necessity, the release of an altitude briefly grasped. We plummeted together into the ravine. My foot floated carelessly above the brake.

I left Squire standing in the middle of a field, his boots covered in mud, his eyes red with tears. I left him standing there, parting in silent motion like a soul leaving the body. He is standing there still.

Chapter Thirty-Seven

At the base of the hill, I restarted the engine and dropped Hank straight into second. He shuddered in the hands of his new master but didn't stop, and by the time we turned in a wide arc around the defiant white oak, we were in third and charging ahead. The radio blasted a mournful cowboy tune, and I punched at the dash until it fell silent. The road ahead was wide and open. The prosaic figment world I had crawled through hours before dissolved into satisfying streaks of pure motion.

We roared onto the compound through throngs of gawking shades, and to avoid slamming on the brakes, I leaned on the horn. Mu had a path to navigate the haphazard scattering of shelters, to come and go without uprooting shades on every supply run, but I didn't know the way, and I soon found myself boxed in by weathered tents and plywood shacks. As I skidded to a halt, the parking lot shades descended on the truck, hands replete with throwable objects destined for Squire's fat head. But when the first of them saw it was someone else behind the wheel, they dropped their detritus and crowded in for a closer look. Fate forced the shades from the shadow of my reality into the spotlight. Hundreds of them, strangers every one, had camped on Isidora's doorstep for months, and now it seemed there was no choice but to let them in. I took a deep breath and stepped down from the cab. My robes fell behind, scraping the pavement as I circled the truck. I dropped the tailgate and jumped up into the bed.

"Friends," I said, raising my arms. "For many months a cancer was growing at the heart of Isidora, but you kept the faith. Today I rid us of that cancer, and it is now time for your loyalty to be rewarded."

A voice concealed in the crowd rang out, crisp and clear. "Who the fuck are you?"

I lowered my hands to adjust my vestments. "Perhaps I've got ahead of myself. I . . . I am the Omicron."

"Is that so? Then fuck you."

The mob began to titter and stir.

"Friends," I continued, "you have toiled at the footsteps of Isidora, but today the gates will open for you."

"We toiled for money. Where's our money, jackass?" another voice called out.

A chorus of dissent chimed in. "You lied to us. We believed in you. Where's our money?"

I closed my eyes and continued, reciting the well-worn verses of the Sunday Viewing. "Today for the first time, I see you. Today for the first time, you are real. Today you are rescued from the darkness. The reality of Isidora is revealed."

"We see you too, asshole."

A thrown piece of metal ricocheted off the truck bed. Then another.

"You have come in from the cold. Let Isidora be your fire. A moral society founded in TRUTH where freedom and right conspire."

"Where's our fucking money, O?"

The next probing throw struck me in the shoulder. Then another bounced off my leg. I looked down to see two Isidoran nuts clink to rest on the ribbed bed of the pickup truck. I could feel the energy of the mob abandon civility and lurch toward barbarism, and a moment later the sky opened up, and it began to rain money. The horizontal hailstorm of Isidoran currency loosed by the crowd pelted me from every direction. Bolts boxed my ears and bruised my head. Wingnuts sliced my forehead and jabbed at the lids of my squinting eyes. Nuts rained on the steel truck in a deafening roar, shattering the windshield, denting the doors. Unsatisfied with their monetary stoning, the mob grabbed wooden planks and metal rods and assaulted Hank, bashing out his headlights, crushing his hood, puncturing his tires. I crumpled to his bed and curled into a ball, wrapping myself in the heavy black-and-white robes of the Omicron. Above me a swarm of metal gnats blotted out the sun.

For an infinity the metal fell on top of me, all around me, in a steady drip-like ping, in an intermittent flaring thrum. Metal striking metal. Metal striking glass. Metal striking flesh. The truck convulsed with every impact like the death throes of a rodent in the jaws of a snake. I didn't think to call out. I didn't think to do anything. I held myself and squeezed my eyes shut like I did so many times as a child beneath that musty old afghan, hoping the violence of the world just beyond the borders of my being would disappear.

The first gunshot sounded like a door slamming somewhere off in the distance. Above me I heard the air tear apart. The metal stopped falling, and the truck stopped shaking, and the mob stopped yelling. A second shot, then a third, a fourth. Each one was aimed high, unzipping the atmosphere above our heads. Shuffling feet began to scurry and then began to run. There was a different sort of crashing now, the felling of plywood trees, the tumbling of tin canopies, the whole of the shades' makeshift camp being scraped off the parking lot like dried eggs from a pan.

I could hear Echo, barking orders in his burly baritone. The scattering of panicked shades receded. The heavy footsteps of marching soldiers approached. They surrounded me, clicked their heels, and then fell silent.

I shook off the metal debris and shifted to my knees. My head felt like it had been split in two, its contents running down the ribs of the truck bed and out the open tailgate. I tasted blood and snot and stifled tears, but I knew the Omicron must rise up, rise above, casting off the feckless missiles of the figment world to reveal himself unharmed, unchanged. I swallowed a deep breath and stood, raising my arms like the wings of a phoenix.

When I opened my eyes, I saw shades streaming away from Isidora, carrying backpacks, sleeping bags, whatever they could grab. Well-formed lines of Wooden Boys marched behind, shoving down stragglers and firing warning shots at regular intervals. They flattened the shade settlement like a tornado, and in their wake there was nothing but bare concrete, sagging tents, snapped plywood, and the scattered remnants of a hundred lives. The unit that rescued me stood at attention surrounding the pickup, feet together, backs straight, hands over their eyes. My face was sticky. I tasted blood. And a hundred thousand dollars lay piled at my feet.

The Mouth, Regina, and Sam appeared around the corner of the Mines, along with throngs of followers interested in the spectacle. They came to me, and I went to them, and when we met, Sam wrapped his arm around my back and helped me to the Ark. When we were finally back behind our battlements, behind an iron gate and cement walls topped with shards of glass, behind a heavy door and spun-off deadbolt, back in the quiet security of the Ark's front room, I collapsed on the armchair in the antechamber, a ragged, battered mess. Sam sent the steward to fetch a bowl of hot water and some gauze. The Mouth lit up a J.

"Funny them attacking you like that." He plopped into a yellow armchair and kicked his feet up on the coffee table before blowing on the cherry. "What did you say to them, anyway?"

"The Viewing 32:12"

"Today for the first time I see you. Today for the first time I am real . . ."

"*You* are real," I groaned. The steward returned with an emergency first-aid kit, the look on his face a mix of concern and terror, the most genuine thing I'd seen in the Ark in ages. Sam pulled out a wipe and started cleaning the cuts on my forehead. I longed for it to be Regina instead, to have her sympathetic eyes see my pain, to have her gentle hands anoint my wounds. But she was standing cross-armed before the window, her mind pacing a farmstead miles away.

"Oh, yeah. *You* are real. I don't know your part as well as I do mine." The Mouth took another deep drag and let the smoke roll out of his mouth in tranquil waves. "Funny them attacking you like that."

"There's nothing funny about it, Dean." Sam's hands moved brusquely, wiping at the blood that flowed from my head as if wiping away the shades themselves. He was not without compassion, but it was clear I was not getting the same treatment as one of Sigma's newborn lambs.

"Not laugh-out-loud funny, no. But ironic funny. All these months camped out in our parking lot, waiting for a chance to have the Omicron see them and welcome them into Isidora. And then one day the Omicron appears before them all, as if outta nowhere. He drives right in amongst them. And what do they do? They pelt him with spare change." The Mouth chuckled and coughed. "It's actually laugh-out-loud funny too."

"Maybe they weren't waiting to be seen," Sam mumbled.

"Please. Everyone is waiting to be seen." The Mouth took a long, self-satisfied drag and let himself slip deeper into recumbency.

"How's Hank?" I asked.

"Devastated. Windows broken, tires flat, dented all to hell. That thing's never driving again."

Sam taped a final bandage to my head and gave my shoulder a reassuring tap. "All set." I nodded, and he walked over to the bar to pour two glasses of Omicron's Reserve.

"Where's James?" Regina asked, her nose still pressed against the glass.

"Not that any of you assholes care. How is it that you returned to Isidora with Hank and not with James?"

"Squire's dead," I said. "I left him in a field outside of town."

Regina turned with a gasp.

The Mouth chuckled again. "He means he's exiled to the figment world." Then he paused and turned to me. "You didn't actually kill him, did you?"

"No. It was muddy."

Regina let out an exasperated grunt and started walking toward the door.

"It was self-exile, actually. I asked him to come with me, but he refused. He lied to us, Reg. He lied to us, and now we're screwed."

Regina stopped. "What do you mean he lied to us?"

"He lied about the counterfeits. He lied about our money. All the shortages, the price increases, the anger of the shades . . . hell, what just happened to me—it's all because of Squire's lies. We're broke, guys. We're fucking broke."

The Mouth tried to right himself, but the armchair slid away behind him, and he landed flat on his ass.

"What do you mean, broke?" Sam asked, handing me one of the glasses he had just poured.

"He said we're broke. No one wants to buy Block Coin anymore, so the value in our wallet is basically zero. He lied about the counterfeits to try to buy time, hoping things would magically work themselves out. All the while the value of our savings fell lower and lower. And then when it reached a breaking point, he tried to steal Hank and run away."

"No one wants Block Coin?" the Mouth said as he stood to go find his phone. "That's impossible."

Regina shuffled to the couch and lowered herself on to the cushions. "Why would he lie to us . . . to me?"

Sam put a hand on her shoulder. "He's a prideful guy. He doesn't mind losing, but he hates to fail."

"He's a fucking asshole," I snapped, gesturing for the steward to bring a cigarette.

"He's our friend. Or does that not mean anything to you anymore. He sacrificed everything for us, for Isidora."

"Yeah, yeah. He gave me the same story. But when things got tough, he ran away and left us behind."

"Tough?" Regina pushed away Sam's comforting hand and leaned forward. "Everything has been tough. Every minute of every day since those first nights when we all slept together in a ball for fear of freezing to death has been tough. It's only since we built the Mines that we've had any comfort, and still, watching you all descend into a bourgeois stupor has been tough. I'm sure James did the best he could, and you—his supposed friend—you just left him in a field and stole his truck?"

"He put himself in the field, Regina. He literally put himself out to pasture. And he whipped cow pies at me to keep me away. There's no way you can't smell it. So, don't act like he's the big victim here. I told him to come back to Isidora, and he refused. So I took *our* truck, and I came back home."

"That's not good enough. Go back and get him."

"Are you kidding me? We're in the middle of a figment riot, Hank is totaled, and in a couple of days Isidora is going to run out of food. Squire is the least of our worries. If he comes back with his tail between his legs, so be it. He can join you in the fields. But for now we need to secure the compound and figure out how to feed everyone."

"He was right." The Mouth reentered the room with his phone in his hand, his face morose, his joint long extinguished. "We *are* broke." He began to read. "Cryptocurrency Block Coin Plummets after International Sex Trafficking Ring Indictment. The shining star of the digital currency fad . . . Fad? Block Coin lost ninety-five percent of its value yesterday after a multination judicial action interrupted a global sex-trafficking ring. Members of the accused group used the cryptocurrency to conduct transactions supporting the prostitution and forced migration of hundreds of women and girls, some as young as eight years old . . . Oh, Jesus. The women were trafficked to the group's base of operations in Eastern Europe, whereafter their passports were confiscated and they were forced to work in private brothels. Along with this judicial action, parliaments around the world passed resolutions prohibiting trade in Block Coin . . ." The Mouth raised his head, his face blank. "Have we been . . .?"

The question evaporated, unfinished, unanswered. But none of us struggled to connect the dots of causality that led back to the Mines. Isidora sustained itself by plucking from the digital ether ephemera that was sold to Transylvanian pedophiles. Far from transcending the figment world, Isidora had tethered itself to its most despicable underbelly. It reverberated in our heads, each echo more intense than the last. We ran the gold mines of the conquistadors. We pumped the oil of the lecherous emirs. We cashed in our funny money to buy Tic-Tacs and caviar, and in some dank Soviet-era basement a child was groped by a man whose breath smelled of a substance she was too young to drink. A glass-eyed teddy bear filled with tears from the night before sat on the nightstand, waiting its turn.

The news squeezed the air right out of us. And when we were hollow, when our lungs burned and our eyes bled and our hearts exploded in our chests, it squeezed even harder. Sam sprang from the couch and stuck his head in a trashcan. The rest of us sat slack-jawed in a stunned torpor, listening to him wretch, feeling ashamed of being empty and having nothing to wretch ourselves.

Tears stained Regina's ashen cheeks. "Monsters," she whispered.

"Us or them?" the Mouth asked, though of course he knew.

We sat there in silence. For a minute. For a day. I can't remember. Regina was the first, but we all took turns crying. Not the wailing sobs of personal tragedy, but the tranquil, measured tears of souls trapped in a mortal world filled with an evil they are powerless to suppress.

In the midst of our grieving, Hawke entered, elated with his troops' performance. We told him, and he left.

Chapter Thirty-Eight

After two nights of intermittent gunfire, I called Echo into the Ark to explain himself. I told him the Wooden Boys needed to knock it off, that they were shooting at shadows. He said shades were testing our perimeter, so on some level we were in agreement. But as I leaned on the railing of the water tower on the third and final Day of Isidoran Reflection, I could see them stalking us. They crept through the abandoned factories between Isidora and the Shambles, then they disappeared beneath the canopy of verdant young leaves painted across our western horizon. While I watched, one rushed the walls like a wild dog, hoping to nab a few rifles, as they had done the night before. A half-hearted volley of errant shots erupted from our parapets, and the figment scampered back into the woods.

"We're under siege," I declared an hour later. "And it's only a matter of time until we run out of food or bullets or both."

"This is absurd," Regina fumed. "We should have packed up and left days ago. Isidora is a failure." She crossed her arms, wrapping herself in the billowing sleeves of Squire's homespun auburn sweater. It hadn't left her body in three days.

"We agreed to take this time of reflection in order to approach this decision with clear heads," I reminded her.

"Nothing is clear!" she shouted. "Nothing! It's all a mess."

"Is this the end?" Sam asked plaintively.

"Why should it be?" The Mouth dragged a folding chair from the corner and sat down in front of his pillows. He was eerily sober, disquietingly lucid. "Why should this be where we fail?"

"Because we've already failed, Dean. We didn't change the world. All we did is close our eyes to it. And in so doing we financed evil."

"We didn't finance evil, Reg. We didn't cut the Romanian pervs a check. We created value in one commodity and traded it for another. End of transaction."

"What's the difference?"

"If you go to a bakery and buy a loaf of bread, and the baker turns around and uses that money to buy kids crack, you're not a drug dealer. You just bought a loaf of bread. You're not responsible."

Regina lowered her head and rested her eyes in the palms of her hands. "We made the money they used to imprison little girls. How do you not get that?"

"It was going to be made anyway, Reg. We just captured it and sold it along. When it left our wallet, it was perfectly neutral. Who knows? Maybe we kept Block Coin *off* the market by mining so many ourselves."

Regina sighed. "I wish Squire was still here."

I picked up my cappuccino and began to stir. "He made his choice. It's time for us to make ours."

Regina stood and paced behind her chair, preparing her final arguments. "We shut it down. Clearly, we shut it all down. No more mining. No more coins. We roll up our sleeves and we make what we need ourselves, right here in Isidora, like we should have been doing all along."

Sam leaned forward and adjusted his cap. "I don't know how we can, Regina. We've come too far. My chickens alone eat more than you harvest all season. Even if Alpha grew nothing but feed, we still couldn't support the herds."

"And why should we take down the Mines?" the Mouth added. "They're the most valuable thing we own. Maybe Block Coin isn't good anymore, but there are other currencies out there."

"Other currencies? Why?" Regina asked. "So we can keep mining dirty coins to sell to criminals who use them to commit unspeakable tragedies on the other side of the world?"

The Mouth smirked. "What currency *isn't* linked to unspeakable tragedies on the other side of the world?"

She stopped and glared at him. "We don't need money. We can make what we need."

"What's the difference? We do it ourselves? We pay others to do it for us? Either way, we are consumers. We clear cut an old-growth forest to grow fucking turnips. We round up baby calves and slaughter them for a nice veal dinner. We pump petroleum out of the earth and mold it into a clamshell, so we can carry a cheeseburger around for a couple of blocks and then throw it straight into the goddamn ocean. Consumption requires unspeakable tragedy. That's the deal. The best we can hope to do is spread the tragedy around enough so that it's nothing more than an annoyance for the guy living next to us." The Mouth pulled a fresh pack of cigarettes from his breast pocket and started rapping it against his palm. "Besides. It's all figment. It doesn't matter."

"Isidora is a figment! It's a lie, and it always has been." Regina sat, her body shivering with anger. "You act like something special is happening here. You act like we've transcended the evils that weigh down the world, but all we've done is recreate them. Greed-fueled exploitation, mindless consumerism, systemic injustice; that's what Isidora has become. Only now, we are in charge. Only now, we only have ourselves to blame."

"None of this is our fault." The Mouth pulled the foil out of his freshly opened pack and flipped over a cigarette. He lit a second and then tossed me the box. "We are not responsible for—"

"We are the *only* ones responsible. You've denied the existence of anyone else. It's our fault. And it's always been our fault. Even in the capital."

Hawke scoffed.

"Even in the capital!" Regina glowered. "We bitched and moaned about the world holding us down, but it's only ever been us. Just people. People making decisions. One after another. All stacked up. That's all there is. I thought if we came here, if we isolated ourselves and rallied around a common ideal, we could make better decisions. But you assholes kept driving us toward the same mediocre end. Isidora isn't special. Isidora is banal. It's predictable. It's boring. We've failed, and I can't even say I didn't see it coming."

"Ah, Reg. Always wanting to play the martyr." Hawke slid off the workbench and crossed the circle to grab a cigarette from the Mouth's pack. "If Isidora's a failure, then you're just as much to blame as any of us."

Regina raised her head and sighed, a deep, heavy sigh, releasing in that one breath a weight she had born for years. "I think I'm OK with that."

I sipped my cappuccino, then licked a row of foam from my lips. "No offense, but this is a pointless discussion. We live here. Isidora is ours, like it or not, and it needs us to save it. We're going to keep mining because the Mines are our greatest asset. If it's not Block Coin, we need to find another currency and quickly. A bit more money and people will be satisfied again. And the shades? If they insist on attacking us, we need to be prepared to meet them."

Regina stood and looked around the room in somber reflection. The afternoon sun peeking through the skylight fell like snow on her winter cheeks. "I'm leaving," she said. Then she turned and walked out of the Circle chamber, stopping in her room only long enough to grab a bag packed three days prior. When she descended the stairs for the last time, I was standing at the bottom, waiting for her.

"You can't go," I insisted. "Isidora needs you. I need you."

Her eyebrows laughed across her forehead. "I'm pretty sure Isidora doesn't need me anymore. And I'm positive you don't."

"I've already lost Squire. I can't lose you too."

She rolled her eyes and looked up at the drop ceiling above our heads. "When we first came here, everything was so exciting. It was empty, blank, and there was nothing for us to do but build and create. I felt this intimate connection to life, organic life, that I'd never felt before. And we were free. Hawke was focused and productive, almost sweet at times. Dean was always a quirky asshole, but here he was color on those frozen grayscale mornings. Squire . . . and you. You had a vision. A vision that felt just and true, and everything we created seemed to embody that vision, to come alive right before our very eyes." She shook her head. "I don't know why it took me so long to realize you can't see farther than the tip of your own nose."

I reached out to put a hand on her shoulder. "I can make it up to you, Regina. I can help us go back."

"No," she said. "You can't. You don't believe in back."

She ducked my hand and turned to the couch where her blue hiking backpack lay bulging, as if she had opened the drawstring and stuffed down every memory from our years in Isidora. I wondered how she would carry it all with her. But then again, perhaps she only chose to pack clothes. She slung it onto her shoulder, and the weight of it made her stumble. But only for a second. She buckled the waistband and cinched the straps. The door closed firmly behind her.

I shared a moment of shameful indecision with the four naked walls of the Ark's receiving room, the faded ochre furniture, the cold mauve tiles, the silver tray of cigarettes on the sideboard, neatly arranged. Visually, little had changed since we first unsealed the chamber—the room remained an afterthought trapped in time. But the air I breathed in shallow, troubled sniffs had lost all memory. Gone was the dust and the must and the mold. The window was open, pulling in the scent of dew evaporating off fresh spring shoots and the searing of tofu in the kitchen of the Winter Quarters. It brought along birdsong and radio and muffled conversation. It was alive with the life being lived there and then.

I swung open the door and burst out into the full afternoon light. She was walking away from the industrial spur, away from the Shambles, away from any of the infinite futures that would pick her up at Isidora station and spirit her away. Instead, she went toward the fields, disappearing behind the earth as it dipped into the Green. I gave chase and caught up to her as she rounded the pond. Her hand was outstretched, dreamily caressing the cattails.

"You won't convince me," she said over her shoulder as I approached.

"Where will you go, Regina? There's nothing out there."

"I don't know," she smiled. "But that's never stopped me before."

"Do you remember that first spring when we came down to the pond? It was a day kind of like this—sunny, newly warm."

"I'm not stopping to go skinny dipping with you, if that's what you're getting at."

"What was it, Reg, that thing between us? Was it love?"

She sighed and looked out at the tranquil water as if somewhere down in its cloudy depths we were there still, our naked bodies spinning together in a whirlpool of trapped time. "Love? Of a sort."

She stopped walking, and I circled around to look into her onyx eyes for one last time. "Was it wrong?"

"We were young and free, and the space between us was fertile. When it felt like something was growing, I encouraged it. The thought that it might be a weed, that I might need to pull it and throw it away, never even occurred to me. It was a bud, and I wanted to let it blossom, to let the world be a bit more beautiful as a result." A gust of wind blew across fields dotted in green. She reached up to brush the hair from her face, then she kissed my cheek. "But flowers are temporary things. Only a fool loves a flower."

She rolled her shoulders to resettle her load and continued walking ahead. "Now an oak . . ."

My chest throbbed, and my face pulled into a smile indistinguishable from a wince.

"You can love an oak forever."

We rounded the fields in silence, and I could feel her attention touch upon the rows of budding greens, the well-ordered plots, the memorized irrigation schedule, the expected harvest window for every varietal in the ground. Then she let it all go and lifted her gaze to the woods at our border, to the scissor-tailed swallows zipping through the air, to the newly returned robin puffing out its brilliant solarian belly, to the budding trees and bushes building up the courage to pop. She grabbed my hand and gave me a smile and led me to the walls at the southeast corner. A handful of Wooden Boys snapped into unseeing attention. I told them to piss off.

The wall on that side of Isidora was nothing but bulk trash spread along our arbitrary border. She climbed a toppled cubicle divider and stood, now as tall as me, now taller. Her hair caught the wind like a weather vane, pulling her into that alignment she bore so naturally—face to the rushing air, certain her destiny lie somewhere beyond that unyielding resistance. She was and had always been that way, that monumental woman. I felt the urge to capture her in my arms, to carry her back to the Ark and drop her into my bed, to tell her— to tell myself—that we were enough for each other, that we would never want for anything so long as we had each other, fully and without distraction. But even in my mind, the words felt hollow. I could attempt to capture her and bind her to me, and maybe in the beginning it would feel honest and good. But love is a poor prison guard. It smothers. It neglects. The cyclical freezing and thawing of our hearts would crack them, like roads suffering iterative winters. I knew there was no future in which she did not eventually climb that wall and disappear.

"I'll miss you," I called to her.

"No. You won't."

"Just give me this one, Reg. Let me lie to you sweetly."

She chuckled. "Fine"

I raised my eyes to meet hers. "I'll miss you, Regina."

"I'll miss you too."

She turned and walked away from me. And then she was gone forever.

Chapter Thirty-Nine

"She's dead, then." I had expected Hawke to be elated, to feel the visceral sense of relief one feels when pulling out a splinter, when the affected area stops its throbbing, and the body calms to its base state of unfeeling. But there was no respite in him. He dropped back on to his elbows, and the head of the lit cigarette at his fingers grew grizzled from inattention. His feet hung limp in the alcove of the desk that had forever been his seat at the Circle.

"And then there were four." The Mouth waved his hand in the air as if conducting the symphonic calamity. Sam had served Brushfire, and the Mouth—returned to his state of affected normalcy—had done away with the folding chair and nestled back into his pillows. He stretched out, unbothered by the prospect of having to take up a bit more space. Squire's stool lay toppled against the wall. Thrown or kicked, I could not tell.

I grabbed the glass of whiskey left at my chair and sat. "There was only ever four." I took a sip of Brushfire and coughed to clear my throat. "Like I said this morning, we are under siege."

Sam sat cross-legged on a tall stool. I didn't know if he wanted to stay or if he simply knew he had nowhere else to go. "It seems like the shades are slowing down. I heard less gunfire today, anyway."

Hawke sat up, flicked the ash off the tip of his cigarette, and took a short drag. "They're gathering their strength, preparing for something big and organized. Echo sent out a small scouting party this morning, and it looks like most of the shades we scattered have made their way to the Shambles. But there's nothing for them there. They want Isidora, especially the Mines, and they're preparing to take it by force."

I thought of her alone in her apartment watching from the window as the plague that we had scattered to the wind descended on her community, dropped tents on the dance floor of the general's square, and swelled the already swollen lines for rations in the alley. The shades wouldn't suffer privation long. Discontented, they would search the Shambles for a fire escape like hers that led to a window like hers that led to an apartment like hers that led to a bed like hers. They would take all they could, consume all they could, destroy all they could.

The thought of it turned my stomach. But at the same time, I knew I could never go to her, not while the Shambles was full of shades. If they recognized me, they would do worse than they had done in the parking lot and without hesitation. They would tear me limb from limb, and if they recognized that she was with me, they would do the same to her.

"Should we reinforce the wall?" Sam asked.

"No," I said. "We need to get rid of them. Their presence in the Shambles threatens everything we hold dear here in Isidora."

"Attack?" Hawke asked, his eyes gleaming in expectation.

"Yes. Preemptively and with overwhelming force. We need to drive them away and instill in them a fear that keeps them from ever coming back."

"Attack the Shambles? Are you sure?"

"Tomorrow at noon. We need a night to prepare."

Hawke leaned back with a knowing smile. "Yes, of course. Let's make sure everyone is where they're supposed to be before this kicks off."

"Are we going to kill them?" The rocks in Sam's glass trembled against the side.

"Some, maybe." Hawke flicked away the cigarette butt and sprang to his feet. "Not many. They stole a few of our rifles, and some may have been armed before, but most of them aren't. Not yet anyway. If we go at them quickly, they probably won't fight back."

"Precisely. The goal is to make them disappear, not to drown the Shambles in blood."

The Mouth sat up and reached for the bottle of Brushfire. "We'll need medals."

"Medals?"

"Yeah, medals. We'll need to recognize the soldiers who fight for Isidora, who die for Isidora. Tomorrow will be glorious."

Sam gulped. "And the police? Surely a bit of urban warfare will get their attention."

Hawke began rolling his head, twisting his torso, arching his back. "We'll make sure it does. Tomorrow the Constable will get everything she's ever wanted—a reason to crack down on the Shambles and raze it to the ground. Anyone that doesn't flee will get arrested. We'll be the bait. The police will be the trap. We just need to get out before the jaws slam shut."

"Won't they come for us here too?"

"They promised me they won't. This will prove our worth to the Constable. Isidora's independence will be assured once and for all."

Sam looked shaken and confused, but he didn't protest—didn't turn and flee.

We broke to begin making preparations, but before he left the chamber, I grabbed Hawke by the shoulder and pulled him back in.

"She has to be warned," I whispered. "She needs to get out tonight."

Hawke shrugged. "Then warn her,"

"I can't. The Shambles is crawling with shades. They'll eat me alive."

Hawke crossed his arms. "So, what do you want me to do about it? Send a carrier pigeon? We're fresh out."

"Send Echo."

"No."

"Send a Wooden Boy."

"Absolutely not."

"Then you go. You know the Shambles. You go there all the time. I can draw you a map to her apartment."

Hawke frowned and rubbed his forehead. "What makes you think she'll come?"

"She has to. She has no choice."

He sighed. "If she stays, this has to end. If she chooses the Shambles over you, that's it. Isidora cannot have you groveling for the affection of a figment."

"Agreed." I hugged him and patted him on the back. "Thank you, Hawke. She'll come. I'm sure."

We went up to my room, and I grabbed a piece of paper from my desk. In between annotated rectangles, circles, and squares, I drew a line that ran from Isidora straight to her front door.

Chapter Forty

At dusk I was seated on the water tower dais before the long black banners. This time their ends were resolutely secured, and though they struggled against their constraints, they could not break free. The light from the retreating sun skirted the billowing cloth and illuminated the rows of Wooden Boys before me in scorching orange and umber, gilding the rifles in their steady hands. Behind them, followers stood apprehensive. Some doubted our decision to attack the Shambles, but after three days of raiding, no one denied the need to act. They were told to stay behind and serve as Isidora's rearguard, and this they could do in good conscience.

To my left, Hawke and Sam sat in their usual place—one stern, one solemn—but the other half of my constellation was composed of different stars. Charlotte had forever been Regina's secundus, but she was vocal in her opposition to the attack and was as likely to leave Isidora as she was to lead it. When Mac volunteered to join the offensive, Alpha was his. His bulk dominated the stage, but the thousands of eyes before us made him squirm in his chair all the same. We gave Mu to Marianne and the Mines to Mu, consolidating our income and treasury into one work unit. Some Omegas grumbled about the loss, but Hawke didn't object. Marianne sat there poised and confident, her face on her hand, her fingers rapping at her cheek. Lambda's chair was empty, as the Mouth paced the platform delivering a dissociative soliloquy bordering on fugue.

"And were we not generous? Did we not welcome them to Isidora? Did we not give them a pathway to share in our riches, to join in our fraternity, to be in our being? We did all of that and so much more. We set them on the path, but they refused to walk ahead.

"This saddened the Omicron, as it saddened all of us. He wanted to receive them, as he had received all of us. And so, in an abundance of generosity and goodwill, the Omicron decided to go to them. And in going to them, the Omicron knew he must part from us. He knew that to serve as their bridge, to bring them over the gulf that separates our reality from the figment world, he must depart from our shores and land on theirs. For a time, Isidora would have to be left unseen. But still he went to them.

"It was a decision that upset many. A decision that broke bonds of friendship. A decision that led ex-Alpha and ex-Mu to leave Isidora, their hearts cold and their sights short, and extinguish themselves far from the Omicron's benevolent eye out in the nothingness of the figment world. But still he went to them.

"As he prepared to leave, he held Isidora in the reality of his mind's eye. His brow beaded with sweat, his vision blurred, and he stepped into the void.

"A cold wind blew that day. Do you remember it? A cold wind blew that day. It started when the Omicron left us, and it blew constant all afternoon. It blew until the moment of his return.

"He came back to us. He returned on a chariot of fire, gliding over the uneven ground. And like a bridge, when he came to us, he also went to them. Not to their periphery, but to their core, to their center, to their heart. And there he rose to speak, to tell them that for the first time ever, they were seen.

Can you imagine? For the first time ever, they were seen.

"But what did they do with that gift? Did they fall to their feet in awestruck penitence? Did they rejoice in the glory of his miraculous apparition? Did they open their hearts to the spirit of friendship he had brought to theirs? No.

"They asked him who he was. They questioned him. They verified in their minds what they must have already known in their hearts. And then they attacked him. They assaulted him with the same blessings he had brought forth for us all. They rained down a flood of vile rejection and vitriolic contempt, hoping the Omicron would drown.

"But he did not drown. You, brave Isidoran soldiers. You came to his aid. You ran off the heretics, and you rid us of their heresy. And when the Omicron rose again, the first words on his lips were words of gratitude.

"But the heretics are not truly gone. Those figments worse than figments, they who rejected the Omicron's sight, who rejected being itself—those mirages, those voidlings, those disappeared—they are still menacing Isidora. Even now they are there lying in wait, building their strength in that half-seen periphery that suits them so well, that half-built, half-decayed barnacle clinging to Isidora's side. The Shambles.

"When you march, you will rid us of that barnacle. You will pluck that withered hair. You will pull that thorn from our heel. When you march, you will assure the very survival of Isidora.

"Along the way, you will meet resistance, but when did you not meet resistance in the figment world? You will come under fire, but when were you not under fire in the figment world? You will be asked to sacrifice, but when were you not sacrificing yourself in the figment world? You know this. You have done this all before. But this time things will be different. This time you will be observed. This time the Omicron will witness your deeds. This time your sacrifice will be real.

"We *are* in the eternal Isidoran present. In the eternal Isidoran present, we are. And in so being we must act. You, brave Isidoran warriors, are the seen, and the brilliance of your sacrifice will glimmer in the eyes of the Omicron. There can be no delay, no hesitation, no procrastination. We cannot assume to forever be in the light. Go while the Omicron's eyes are upon you. Fight while the Omicron's eyes are upon you. Sacrifice while the Omicron's eyes are upon you. Only through this will you be forever real in his memory."

When the Mouth finally sat, he was drained, and whatever hypnotic elixir he thought he was squeezing out of himself was received as an energizing tonic, a vial of iridescent jet fuel injected straight into the veins of our men at arms. The mob erupted in zealous fervor. Wooden Boys growled and barked and brayed. They butted heads and bumped chests and jostled energy into one another. They stamped their feet and pounded the earth with the butts of their rifles, creating a rhythm that reverberated off the corrugated walls of the Mines like the beating of iron war drums. The followers behind hooted and hollered, clapping their hands and jumping up and down to add to the cacophony.

Then Echo blew a whistle, and the disorderly rows of Wooden Boys were transformed into columns, ready to march.

"What are they doing?" My words were swallowed by the cheering of our rearguard gathering at their flanks like dockside well-wishers.

Echo strode past row after row of surplus trench coats, gum-rubber ankle boots, and billowing plaid neckerchiefs. When he reached the head of the column, he blew the whistle again, and instead of leading them back to their bunks in a harmless bit of impromptu pageantry, he took a deep breath and marched them straight down the industrial spur.

I jumped from my seat. "What are they doing?"

Hawke put a hand on my shoulder and forced a smile. "Easy, oh great Omicron," he whispered. "Your troops are marching off to war, and they expect you to watch over them."

"Tomorrow. It's supposed to be tomorrow. You haven't—"

"Up-bup-bup. Let's give them a nice salute, shall we? You're not the only one who sees."

I wanted to bolt. I wanted to drop my heavy robes there at my seat and sprint naked through the woods ahead of them, arriving at her door like a harried doomsday prophet. I wanted to trample Echo into the ground and blow his whistle until that piercing vibrato scattered our troops like a Maxim gun. But Hawke was right. I had a role to play, and this piece of community theater was only just entering Act III. He had played his cards perfectly, and there was nothing left to do with my empty hand but stand at the edge of the dais and affix it to my forehead.

"We agreed they would go tomorrow," I muttered through an empty expression.

"Why give them another night to fortify themselves?"

"You promised, Hawke. You promised to warn her."

"Yes. But it's better this way."

He gave Mac a nod, and the two of them walked down the dais stairs to flank the rear of the column like sheepdogs leading the herd off to slaughter. As they entered the blackness of the canopied woods, shaded from the dying light above, Hawke took one final look back and grinned. The column rounded a bend in the spur and disappeared.

The rage that was percolating before boiled over, flooding my senses. I dropped my salute and vaulted the edge of the stage, cutting a direct path to the Ark. The rest of the Circle scampered behind, attempting to reconstruct on the fly and in double time the orderly recessional envisioned by the Mouth.

At our front gate, a pair of towering Wooden Boys stood at attention. A burgundy crushed-velvet sash was draped over their trenches, and as I approached they failed to cover their eyes. A new honor guard of some sort. Isidora metastasized beyond my command. I flew between them, and they followed.

"You can wait here!" I called over my shoulder as I blew past the steward holding open the Ark's front door.

"Those are not our orders, sir." They trailed me inside and up the stairs.

"Who has a higher authority than me to give orders?"

"No one, sir. We are the first regiment of the Omicronian Guard promoted by your edict this morning. Protect the Omicron. Protect Isidora."

I scoffed at Hawke's brazen manipulations, but there was no time for debate. "You can protect me from outside the suite." I entered and slammed the door behind me.

Trapped.

Or so Haweke had hoped. The new chaperones were a minor annoyance. What troubled me most was time. The Wooden Boys had a head start, and I desperately needed to catch up. I dropped my robes in the ensuite and pulled on some work clothes and an old ball cap. Then I tied two sheets together into a baroque escape rope and secured one end to my desk. I pushed one of the armchairs over beside the door, not up against it but close enough to only allow it to open a foot. I returned to the window and looked down on the Circle chamber. The old Junemark machinery stood like pillars of salt, but the room was otherwise empty and quiet. I closed my eyes and took a deep breath. This had to work.

I bent down to tie the free end of the rope to the legs of my heavy wooden desk chair. Then I wrapped my hands around the seat's faded forest-green upholstery and in one movement sprang up and hurdled the chair through the window. It shattered like candy glass. The sheets pulled taut, and the knots held. I bounded away on the points of my toes and hid myself in the ensuite shower.

A sentry threw open the door, and a head floated into the room. "Sir? Are you OK?"

Before he could throw his weight behind the obstruction, the guard saw the shattered window and the sheet strung through the frame.

"He's gone out the window!" he yelled back to his associate.

The head disappeared back into the hallway, and the voices beat a panicked retreat down the stairs. "If he gets off the compound, Echo will slit our throats."

I emerged from the bathroom but stood motionless in the shadows of my room. A few moments later, I heard them burst into the Circle chamber below.

"Shit. He's not here. Is there a back door to this place?"

"Hell if I know." Their voices roamed the room like hounds that had lost the scent.

"Anything?"

"I can barely see. Where are the lights?"

"Focus. There must be another exit."

"Here."

They pushed through the rear fire escape, and a beam of tepid orange swung into the room from the floodlight outside. A moment later the door latched shut, and they were gone.

I ran after them, down the stairs, through the darkened chamber, and out the same fire door into the night. I knew there is no better place to hide from someone than where they've already looked. The world was full of people grasping at things in front of them, assuming their past was permanent, a constellation of objects inert and fully catalogued in infallible memory. Why bother looking back when nature had dedicated both our eyes to face forward? It never occurs to us that what we seek is somewhere behind.

I didn't know what Hawke had told them, the reason they should be prepared to protect me from myself, but I imagined it involved me escaping to the Shambles—to join in the glorious fight if he was generous or to run like a coward into our enemy's arms if he was not. My protectors, anointed in velvet, were nowhere to be seen, but I assumed they would start their search at the industrial spur, hunting silently, telling no one of their mission. To avoid them I could have gone north to the train tracks to follow the cleared ground along the rail's ballast in a wide loop to the Shambles outer reaches. It would be safe but slow, and I needed to make up ground.

Instead, I skirted their gaze and ran to our northeast corner to vault the defenses abandoned by the charging troops. For a half-mile, I trotted through the thickening forest until I reached the creek, already swollen with a spring surge, which I followed back south to the industrial spur.

On that wide ground I was able to sprint, overtaking with each stride the steady, plodding footsteps of hundreds of Wooden Boys. Echo would have already known the way. He was the disciple walking in the well-worn footsteps of his master. Where the industrial spur bends to join the main line, Echo would go straight, plowing uncomfortably through a few hundred yards of shrubs and thickets to reach open ground on the other side. There, the streets of the Shambles would lie before him like open doorways, each path an incision on the body of that decaying district. He would march his troops down the widest of those cuts, the one that led to a bronze man illuminated by firelight against the backdrop of a black starry sky, the one that bisected the heart of the Shambles. Swann.

I fell from the thicket with my heart beating at my throat—a throat I elongated as I craned my head skyward, hands up, elbows out, in the supplication of the fourth-quarter athlete praying for the return of a breath so thoroughly squeezed from him. I had sprinted thus far, assuming I was nipping at the heels of our column, but the empty warpath before me was a reminder of the long minutes spent frozen still, saluting the same offensive I now desperately wished to stop. The rage of betrayal and the adrenaline of evasion both burned off in that initial jettison from Isidora's atmosphere, and as I floated through the dark, timeless void of the outer Shambles, where there was no evidence of a Wooden Boy onslaught, no ground worthy of defense or capture, it was the gravity of my concern for her that pulled me forward.

By Fourth and Swann my pace quickened. Ahead of me, the general's square was illuminated by the flickering of savage, unfamiliar flames. At Fifth and Swann, I could smell them—youthful sprites dancing across timber beams as they metabolized the body of a tree dead two hundred years. At Sixth, I saw a cloud of smoke and ash hide the stars as time once trapped took flight. I found the Square at Seventh in suspended chaos, tents crushed and contents scattered. The casings of cartridges tinkled at my feet, but there were no bodies, no viscera, no bile, no blood.

Inside the Anglican church to my right, the devil raged against its stucco walls, igniting the pews and combusting the pulpit in contemptuous, oxygen-deprived flames. His fingers stretched through the cracks in the heavy oak doors to feather the faces of martyrs and saints. His breath melted the lead filigree of the rosette window, sending the sapphire-dipped glass plummeting to a shattering death on stones below. Energized by a gasp of fresh night air, he leapt to the spire, now turned pyre, engulfed in liberated flame as if a matchstick struck against the sole of the devil's shoe.

A steady wind blew from the south, shuddering the leaves in the trees above me, fanning the flames that threatened to leap from the roof of the Anglican church onto the municipal building next door. But the fire needed no natural intervention to spread that night. Its acolytes rampaged through the Shambles, proselytizing everything flammable and inflammable in their way. Hawke would have put her in their path or their path on her. An electric panic sparked through my body, and I ran again.

The canteen street was an ensnaring mess of fallen canopies and tangled ropes, so I sprinted ahead to loop around the backside of her block. As destruction gave way to the Shamble's base spareness, I knew I had crossed to the other side of Echo's advance, and a small spring of hope bubbled inside of me that that night's incursion may be limited, precise. The first sight of her building froze the source solid.

The patch of grass in front was trampled into a muddy mess, and the small tree that had grown there was uprooted and run into the building's boarded up entryway like a battering ram. It lay there beneath partially broken plywood, both burning to reveal the articulating lattice barrier closed firmly behind. The first-floor windows had all been shattered, the projectiles that missed their mark pebbling the ground below. But if the Wooden Boys had thought to build ladders to climb up, they discovered the rear fire escape before making the attempt.

The base of the stairs was littered with broken furniture as if residents had attempted to bar the way, but as my eyes ascended a trail of smashed shelves and upturned drawers it became evident the crumpled wooden mass had simply been pushed down the final flight or thrown from a higher floor. I looked up at the shattered windows and began counting the stories.

First, second, third. . .

Each one cracked like peanut shells, their content looted from within.

Fourth, fifth, sixth . . .

A black cloud billowed from her apartment's open window.

"God, no."

I jumped toward the fire escape but was arrested by the raspy drawl of a woman behind me. "Don't you go get yourself killed, now, hun. There's nothin' for it. She ain't there."

I spun to find Marjorie limping up they alleyway, the weight of her full figure supported by Georgie, her diminutive crutch.

"She went with the others," Georgie said, his voice tired and flat. "Down to the Orpheum to avoid the fighting."

Marjorie stood tall and pushed the man aside. "Now why you go an' tell him that, huh? He ain't with us."

Georgie stretched his back and rubbed his forehead with the brim of his cap. "Maybe he can help."

"Oh please. Stupid man. He don't care 'bout us. He's only here for her. Probably sent these hooligans here in the first place."

"What happened, Mags?" I asked, reaching out to grab her hand. "Are you alright?"

"You think I was born yesterday, child? Please." She pushed my hand aside. "You know damn well what happened, and I know you don't wanna help. You wanna do what you day-dreamin' discontents always do. You wanna pluck from our garden the prettiest little flower you can find and then spray the rest of us with weed poison. You wanna carry her up into your ivory tower and stand on top, pissin' down at everybody else. And it's never enough. You wanna go further, climb higher, do more. You the kinda person who thinks you gotta go to the stars to be somebody, never realizin' all this time the stars been coming to you."

"Mags, take it easy on the boy." Georgie came over to put a hand on my shoulder and spoke straight into my ear as if it were a tin can on a string. "You see, we was down at the Square, as we always are, trying our best to make merry, though it's been hard with all the newcomers about. We know how to be hospitable. That we know. But they had other things on their mind. Schemes and such. But like I said, we was there anyway, trying to be hospitable, and all of a sudden this army of soldiers comes marching down Swann. At first we didn't know what to do, but then they started shooting—not at us but warning shots, up in the air. And then we knew *exactly* what to do. Everybody starts a runnin'—Mags and I too, though she trips on one of them tent poles and sprains her ankle out front of the old savings and loan. So, we just lay there on the side of the square, and we watch as these so-called soldiers forget their discipline and just run amok, like dogs off leash. They pay us no mind, but they set fire to the church and tore apart practically everything in that square. There was a whistle. Then as quick as they appeared, they were gone. We come 'round seeing if anyone's left, but nobody's left. Everyone's gone to hide out in the theater."

"And you say you saw her. You're sure it was her?"

"Yessir. No mistaking that one," he said with a wink.

"Georgie!" Marjorie scolded. "For Pete's sake."

He shrank back, and she grabbed him by the shoulder and pulled him into her breast. When he came up for air, he flashed me a second wink and then positioned himself at her armpit next to a foot balanced on the toe.

"What a mess," Marjorie sighed as she surveyed the littered street. Embers fell like fireflies too fat to stay afloat, and the flames that burned next door appeared to entangle themselves in the messy knot of hair pulled tight behind her chiseled face. "But it don't matter. Georgie and I are survivors. We've learned not to wait to be told twice to keep movin' on."

The two started walking north, receding into the ghastly stillness that surrounded the Wooden Boys' warpath like an exhale into a cold winter's night.

Chapter Forty-One

The shades had taken up defensive positions at Ninth and Leonidas, one block south of where the theater languished on Main. The advance of the Wooden Boys halted at Narcissus, and the intervening blocks were filled with intermittent, prayerful volleys fired over parked cars and around steel letterboxes by the combatants' quivering hands. Both sides fought the way warriors have always fought—as terrified men hoping a raucous display of aggression would cow their adversary into a terrified retreat. Failing that, there was always the possibility they would be willing to crouch behind cover longer than the enemy. It would have been comical if there weren't perforated bodies lying on the pavement, blood spilling down storm drains and pooling in potholes.

Behind our front lines, the reserves busied themselves by looting the unfortunate businesses that lined the street. The vintage clothing boutique, the charity shop, the long-defunct stationary store—like a row of bodies on the cooling board, each received the same final once-over. Incised with a brick, their viscera exhumed, their looted corpse doused in petrol, their bones burned to ash. Only the mortuary was left untouched.

I scanned the scene from a safe distance, peeking around the corner of a boarded-up brownstone and snapping my head back at every rifle burst. I thought I would see Hawke or Echo directing the offensive from the rear, but in the umbral darkness below the smoke-filled sky, I saw nothing but shadows darting in and out of the firelight. The most direct route to the theater was through the contested intersections, but I knew better than to rush into the crack of errant lead. Instead, I bolted across the line of fire to the far side of the street where I hopped fences and slinked through dirt yards speckled with crabgrass until I reached the Orpheum's service entrance in the rear.

Before I can grab the handle, the door flies open and a man with a thin, hooked mustache darts past. His swollen pupils consider me, but only for a second. His head swings wildly from side to side, east to west, up and down the alleyway, looking for an escape. In his disorientation, he runs toward the battle until the street ahead erupts with the explosion of three rapidly fired shots that flood the narrow passage like a tsunami. He slides to a stop and falls to his knees, grabbing his ears.

But there's no time to cower. He is back up and running toward the exit again, an exit that now spills forth with people. Women shriek and men groan as they compress through that narrow outlet and are sprayed into the night by the pressure of the fleeing mob.

"Go right! Go right!" the mustachioed man yells as he barrels past the others, leading the stampede that will spirit them behind the crumbling façades of Main Street, to One Grace Presbyterian with its green astroturf stairs, to the sweeping bend of the elevated interstate, to the farms, to the fields, to the docile river of spilled black ink, to the everything of the nothingness that lies beyond. Only then do I think to see. A flash of silken hair, the brilliant white of searching eyes, the glint of an antique watch on a slender wrist. I call to her, but no one stops, no one turns, no one comes back to me.

It wasn't her. I was sure of it. She wasn't one to flee. She was still inside, center stage with a tommy gun in her hand, blasting everyone and everything that dared come through the front door. She was piling up the bodies of my so-called friends, cutting down followers left and right, soaking the ragged carpet of the Orpheum's aisles in Isidoran blood, and I loved her for it. I would go to her, and she would take my hand and with a single radiant smile she would absolve me of my sins, and we would walk together out of that temple of farce, past the draining corpses of my self-centered conceit, out into a future that was unknown, unpredictable, unseen.

The backstage looked like the general's square, littered with possessions dispossessed, belongings that no longer were. The figments that had been sheltering there were nowhere to be seen. Perhaps they had all just run past me. Perhaps there had once been more. The air was thick with an acridity that felt like needles digging into my molars, and as soon as I stepped through the threshold, my eyes began to burn and weep. I blinked to clear them, and the world shifted into the stop-motion staccato of an early camera's diminished shutter speed. I saw a white screen strung across the stage, then the muted glow of a flame behind. Then a line of fire splattered upwards like the wet thrust of a painter's brush, then a flash of light as the curtain combusted all at once. I raised my hand to shield my eyes. The men revealed to me on the other side saw a salute.

"The Omicron!" one of them gasped.

Rifles fell to the stage floor, and hands snapped to cover eyes, eyes swollen red, blinking rapidly above neckerchiefs tied like respirators. They stood there, all but one, in perfect stillness, statuesque in adoration of their leader's miraculous apparition despite the flames that licked the frescoed walls and lapped at the rows of upholstered seats.

"You!" Hawke squealed as he mounted the stairs at the far end of the stage.

I walked forward and grabbed a rifle dropped at the feet of a blinded

Wooden Boy. "Where is she?"

He chuckled. "After all you've seen, *that's* what you ask me?"

"Where is she?" I raised the gun and centered the sights on Hawke's cold, beating heart.

He continued approaching me. "Fire, and you'll never know."

"Fire, and I can keep looking on my own. Where is she, Hawke?"

"She's in your blood, friend. Like a virus running circles around your body, piercing your heart with each revolution. You are infected by her. You're terminal. A tiny wisp of nothingness threatens to take you down and all of Isidora with you. Thankfully, there's a cure. I'm the disgusting leech that's gonna suck her out and save Isidora from your blind incompetence."

I squeezed and was surprised to find the distance between menace and machination, between posturing and projectile, far shorter than I had imagined. The rifle recoiled into my shoulder, spinning me sideways. The bullet slammed into his. Actions opposite if not equal. At the same time, there was a crash outside the hall, and smoke and soot and ash billowed into the room like the venting plumes of a rocket at takeoff. The fire in the lobby had burned through the supports, and a section of the upper floor had collapsed. Some of the Wooden Boys ducked or turned to shield themselves from the debris. But then they stood again, saluted again, Vesuvian men content to be buried in the line of duty, their Omicron watching with pride.

I blinked, trying to regain my vision. Hawke was nowhere to be found, but if he tried to escape into the wings, he'd find the rear door his only exit. I circled backstage to intercept him, the rifle locked into my throbbing shoulder.

Thud. The claws of a hammer half-buried in the stage floor. *Slap.* And the skittering of a screwdriver as it slid to my feet. I looked up to see the shadow of a man lying flat on the catwalk. I bolted for the wings and found iron rungs welded to the stone outer wall. And I climbed.

The catwalk was a mere two or maybe three, stories above the stage, but when I reached the platform, I found him prostrate on the grate, incapacitated by dizzying vertigo. He moaned like cornered prey, either from the pulsing of his fresh wound or the twisting of his elevated intestines. Smoke clouded around the hanging stage lights, and I crouched to suck at the air beneath.

"I always knew heights would kill me." He rolled onto his belly as if he might brave another few feet of elevation to rise to his knees, but instead he curled back into a ball.

I lowered the gun and sat a few feet away, dangling my feet off the platform's edge. "I've always felt free in the open air."

"Free to plummet," he said, coughing.

"Such is freedom." I considered the rifle in my hands, then reached out and let it go. It disappeared into the darkness below me. "It didn't have to be this way, Hawke."

"Echo's dead." It was the thought that had been beating against the cage of his skull since first conceived, frantically looking for an escape. "It was the first shot they took. Must have burst his heart because the kid fell like a rock. Not sure they were even aiming. No one moved for what felt like an eternity."

I knew I was supposed to say something, but no words came. The heat of the fire consuming the hall blew up at us with each row of seats combusted. My pores began to let.

"I never saw her," Hawke finally said. "If she was there or here . . ." The smoke was thickening and he fell into a coughing fit.

"And if you had?"

His mind fled from him, back to that dark alcove where he dragged the body, where he held the man, sheltered from the eruption of bullets that followed. There was hardly any blood, no engine left running to pump it out of him. Echo was left warm, whole, complete—the absence mistakable, ineffable, inexplicable. "I would have slit her throat."

Swollen and undercut, the building began to groan. At the theater's apex, the dusty velvet rope lashed to a ring at the center of a gilded circle melted, and a chandelier, its thousands of shards of glass held in perfect unison, came crashing down into the orchestra pit.

"It's time to go."

Hawke began crawling toward me. "Gladly"

I rose and turned my back on him, scurrying down the catwalk to grab the iron rungs. Below, the inferno consumed the stage, the long black curtains dividing the wings billowing in flame like the cloaks of apocalyptic horsemen. I looked up and saw the ladder rise to a porthole on the roof.

His eyes were blurry, and he was losing blood. There was, of course, the vertigo. And the air was a smoky soup, boiling from the heat down below. In any case, it was enough. Enough to divert the snub-nosed barrel or to conceal my bobbing head from his grasping eyes. The bullet buried itself inches above me, dropping down the faintest shower of powder-white cement.

I should have fallen down and risked immolation in the fire below. Or scampered up to the hatch, hoping he couldn't track me. But I did neither. I turned to look at him, still flat on his belly in the middle of the catwalk, the revolver extended in the space between us like a poisoned olive branch. The next shot would surely hit me between the eyes.

But it never came. Before he could cock the hammer and spin the cylinder to the awaiting round, the catwalk's suspension gave way. The iron accelerated earthward, leaving him there in the open air. I turned away, unable to watch him fall. And so, he didn't. He just hung there like a bird on an updraft, relieved of the duty to act, absolved of the burden of sin. Light, tranquil, free.

****

The falling metal cracked the stage and sent up a wave of smoke and soot. I held my breath and climbed. At first the latch refused to open, and I thought I was sealed in the inferno. But then it moved, and a rush of hot air vaulted me onto the roof. I sprinted along the bowed surface and leapt across the channel to the building beyond. And I kept running—from rooftop to rooftop, past old stick antennas and shut-in chimney tops, over air shafts and alleyways, through to the end of the block. And there I thundered down a fire escape, leaping from landing to landing until I was back on solid ground.

The Orpheum collapsed an instant later with the cracking gasp of a shipwreck. I turned to see a plume of smoke and dust rise up and blot out the fire-filled sky. Shortly after, flashing blue and red lights crept up from the south. They moved without haste, allowing plenty of time for retreat, and soon lines of Wooden Boys trailed past me in exhausted victory. I didn't follow them. There was nowhere left to go.

I don't think Hawke killed her, but even without confirmation I knew, as I stood at the edge of town watching the Shambles burn, I would never see her again. I learned at an early age the nature of finality, and the hole inside me was permanent. She was gone. Squire was gone. Regina was gone. Hawke was dead. With no hope for the future, the past came roaring back, and I was shivering again on the floor of the Ark, my friends piled around me as we drifted off to dreams of Isidoran glory. I was laughing over the mountain of Thai food that burdened Squire's kitchen table as the Mouth pantomimed his latest unreasonable indignation. I was in that capital basement club double-fisting dirty martinis waiting for the dark-haired woman on the dance floor to catch my eye and come claim her drink. I was standing near a stage in a green polyester gown and a stupid cardboard hat, dumbfounded by my father who had walked up to me and rubbed his chin, and without a word, put his arms around me in a squeezing embrace. I was standing graveside, looking down, my eyes penetrating the slick alabaster lid and upholstered interior to recall my mother's face, her skin—too young for wrinkles—painted in the pastel hues of resurrection, wondering if I should have had the courage to touch her hand one last time.

Maybe others can bear the weight of all that past—the days, weeks, months, years layered one atop the other, never departing, never to return. It's a universal phenomenon, after all, as natural as breathing. But I'm not cut out to manage it on my own. So of course I ran. There was nothing left to do but run. The ground flew past my churning feet. The stars looked down in apathy.

The Mouth was waiting at the entrance to Isidora, receiving each Wooden Boy with cynical glee. And I knew just what I would say to him. I would tell him it was time to leave. I would tell him he needed to take me back.

But where is back? he would playfully inquire.

Home, I would say. *I want to go home. But how can I when you robbed me of the past and immolated my future; when all I have left is an unending Isidoran present?*

And he would say it was only ever this way, and I would know he was right—not because Isidora is true, but because it is the most beautiful lie.

Epilogue

"I said, 'you're scaring the cattle.'"

Squire wiped the tears from his cheeks and looked up bleary-eyed at the voice coming from the other side of the fence.

"Not that they couldn't use a little excitement from time to time."

A brocaded leather boot, made supple with age and sunshine and a thin layer of mink oil, rested on the bottom slat of the wooden fence beneath the black walnut.

"You're not trying to *be* a cow, are you, son?"

Squire suddenly became aware of himself, planted on all fours in the middle of the pasture, mud up to his wrists.

"'Cause them here are for breeding, if you get my drift."

"I'm lost," Squire cried. "I don't know where to go."

The man swung a toothpick from one side of his mouth to the other and considered the predicament. "Well, I imagine we can do better than this."

Squire stood and shook the mud from his hands, then lowered his head to his chest.

"You gotta name, son?"

"James, sir."

The man nodded. "Well, James. What are we to do?" A warm wind blew through the valley below, each gust a finger that stroked the wild grasses and tussled the green grains just sprouting above the soil. "Ma ain't gonna let you anywhere near her table looking—and I should say, smelling—like that. There's a hose 'round the barn and some spare overalls just inside the door. Wash on up, then come 'round the house for dinner. Don't bother ringing; just come on in. We'll hold the prayer till you're set."

"Sir?" Squire puffed up his chest, then let out a long sigh. "You don't need a spare set of hands around here, do you?"

The man stroked his whiskers, three days unshaven. "You know James, I reckon I do."

* * *

Acknowledgments

Writing is a solitary business, but I didn't have to undertake this project alone. My mother supported this book from the very beginning as my first and most wonderfully biased reader. Luke and Florence, gave me encouragement and insight that helped steer my writing in the right direction. Jodi, Dan, and Dustin saw promise in early drafts and gave of themselves to help me push forward. And Kevin Miller provided superb editing support that gave this work the final adjustments it needed. I also have my enormously talented sister, Addi, to thank for the beautiful cover.

I am eternally grateful to my wife, Jane, and daughter, Ines, who fill my life with love and joy.

www.ingramcontent.com/pod-product-compliance
Lightning Source LLC
Chambersburg PA
CBHW030227120726
47903CB00005B/1391